DANCE OF EAGLES

by

J.S. Holloway

DANCE OF EAGLES

Copyright © 2012 by J.S. Holloway
Cover illustration © 2012 by Fairytale Backgrounds

The right of J.S. Holloway to be identified as the author of this work has been asserted by her in accordance with the Copyright, Designs and Patents Act 1988.

This work of fiction was inspired by actual events, but is otherwise a product of the author's imagination. Real references and incidents are made to certain characters and events and places, but names have been changed to protect the guilty and the innocent alike. The figure of Joshua Nkomo should be easily recognised; however, the events told in the narrative are purely fictional and not based on any fact whatsoever.

All Rights reserved. No part of this publication may be reproduced, stored in a retrieval system, or transmitted, in any form or by any means without the prior written consent of the author, nor be otherwise circulated in any form of binding or cover other than that in which it is published and without a similar condition being imposed on the subsequent purchaser.

ISBN: 978-1-907984-05-1

Third Edition September 2012
Published by Sunpenny Publishing
www.sunpenny.com (the Sunpenny Publishing Group)

MORE BOOKS FROM SUNPENNY LIMITED:

The Mountains Between, by Julie McGowan (Sunpenny)
Just One More Summer, by Julie McGowan (Sunpenny)
Going Astray, by Christine Moore (Sunpenny)
My Sea Is Wide, by Rowland Evans (Sunpenny)
Far Out, by Corinna Weyreter (Boathooks Books)
A Flight Delayed, by K.C. Lemmer (Rose & Crown Books)
Blue Freedom, by Sandra Peut (Rose & Crown Books)
Embracing Change, by Debbie Roome (Rose & Crown Books)
A Little Book Of Pleasures, by William Wood (Sunpenny)
If Horses Were Wishes, by Elizabeth Sellers (Sunberry Books)
The Skipper's Child, by Valerie Poore (Sunberry Books)
Watery Ways, by Valerie Poore (Boathooks Books)

To YL.
Full circle.

Honours

Rhodesians never die. *Hamba gahle.*

My Thanks

... to the men and women of the Selous Scouts, especially Lieutenant Colonel Ron Reid-Daly (R.I.P.), Chris and Mike, who patiently answered my questions and gave me information and insights that vastly enhanced this book.

... to the DCs, ADCs, DAs and other IntAff staff, the policemen and the warriors and the friends who all contributed to my training and experiences during the Rhodesian War – in weapons, mechanics, book keeping, issuing of gun licences, and other such niceties; in cattle sales, keeps, local customs, and the difficult balance of relationships with enemies and friends; and of course in duck shoots and in hard drinking (I apologise for my failure in both of these).

... to those who entered my life briefly, shared a smile or two, and were later killed in the conflict. Not forgotten.

... and of course to my family, who continue to love and uphold me in spite of myself; to all my dearest friends, who support me with astonishing loyalty; and to Aslan, who believes in me.

PRAISE FOR "DANCE OF EAGLES"

Reminds me of some of the great works of Wilbur Smith. The author interweaves multiple, strong, leading characters and two completely different time frames masterfully. Ranks with some of the best I have reviewed. Romance, adventure, suspense, ancient tribal history and modern day action – this book has it all!
– Lillian Brummet, www.bookideas.com

A powerful, fascinating read. The narrative is fast-paced and crisply told. The author writes with clarity and style. Above all, her novel melds many universal themes – love, hatred, religion, fear and rebellion – into one insightful, compulsive narrative.
– BookWire, www.bookwire.com

I really loved this book! It should be a movie! Education for the Nation! Very well written and one cannot put it down.
– Christine Behrmann, artist

The author pulls no punches. The characters are finely drawn and the story becomes compulsive reading. Great insight into the hearts of people on all sides of the Rhodesian war.
– Lucy McCarraher, author: *Mr Mikey's Ladies, Blood & Water, Kindred Spirits, The Book of Balanced Living*

The author has a wonderful way of keeping my interest and I love reading about the woes of countries far away. A great read and a must buy for anyone looking for a wonderful story and intriguing plot!
– J.D. Tynan, author *Jill 9, Who Killed Walter Dobbs?, Charlie Ford Meets the Mole, Figuring It Out With Grace*

Held my interest right through to the last page, twisting and turning through the plot, bringing the far-away characters and scenery straight into my London pad. A fantastic read and insight into an ancient people and a war-torn country.
– 'A book devourer', independent review online

Preface

Robert Mugabe is currently, in 2012, head of the state of Zimbabwe, formerly known as Rhodesia, formerly the British colony of Southern Rhodesia. Mugabe is perhaps a culmination of our worst fears realised: a despot without ethics or conscience.

Those of us who proudly call/ed ourselves Rhodesians had a variety of reasons for fighting in the Bush War against terrorist insurgents, but most of us were united in an effort to prevent the senseless and irresponsible handing over of power to an **as yet untrained** government of indigenous peoples, to whom democracy was a completely inconceivable concept after centuries of deeply ingrained traditions of their own. And they indeed returned to what they knew best – an autocracy. A "strong man".

Yet with sublime evidence of a complete lack of understanding of the realities, and a desire to assuage their own guilt, the governments of Britain, America and other Western nations scurried to destroy the white-led Rhodesian government. They deceived their people, lied to their voters, misrepresented and twisted the facts to make them fit their own needs. They also lied to the Rhodesian people, went back on their word, and when they had wrought their evil, they abandoned the once-British people planted in that country to the hands of the Zimbabwean rulers.

The result is now plain to see: a nation governed by the madman Mugabe, supported by more madmen; wholesale genocide of their own people; the destruction of what was known as the "Breadbasket of Africa" (as built up by the Rhodesians, white and black together), and of the farmers who sustained that breadbasket; and a catalogue of other atrocities and failures. Farm murders, purges, the handing over of huge tracts of agricultural land to people with no idea how, or the motivation, to continue to produce its abundance ... criminal negligence combined with criminal intent and resulting in a country that is now literally starving to death.

Except in the Mugabe palaces, that is.

This is not a rant - simply a stating of the facts. If there is a redeeming feature, other than the incredible resilience of the ordinary peoples of Rhodesia and Zimbabwe, I do not know of it.

Sadly, Zimbabwe until recently contained nothing of interest to the governments of the West by way of resources such as oil or minerals or gemstones in abundance (though recent diamond discoveries have the Chinese quietly obtaining possession), and so she continues to be shamefully abandoned by those who spawned her.

Chapter 1

She knew that she was dying; she felt it in her bones, in her bowels, in the blood clotting on her chest, drying dark brown on the dry white sand. The pain of the slashes was different to that of the brutalisation. Her mind tried to analyse the two; to identify the different miseries, separate and give them distinction; but the effort hurt. If she opened her eyes she could see, through a haze, daylight – a backboard to the root-like branches high above, dead blackened bones against grey African skies. Enclosed in this cavern, the hollow centre of an ancient baobab tree that had wrapped its roots and branches close around the huge Matopos rocks, she was completely alone.

Rhodesia, 1975

Beneath the spreading thorn trees the water hit the bottom of the pail with a sound like distant rifle fire, the fat droplets colliding, whirling, glistening, jostling, jetting from the tap like the silvery falls of the Phumisela river in full spate. When the bucket was almost full the youth put it aside and thrust his hands instead into the crystal burst, splashing the fine layer of dust from his face, arms, legs, naked feet.

Soon, the rains would come.

The old spigot squealed in protest as he turned it off, twisting hard against its persistent leak. He stood up and looked back toward the mission buildings, the once-white paint peeling now.

He smiled suddenly. Little Chela was climbing out of

her window again before the rising bell was rung, to greet the sun in her own way.

The tiny bronze-black girl, not yet three feet tall, cautiously swung her leg over the crumbling sill and hung there for a precarious breath. The other leg followed, and she dropped to the hard, dry ground where she crouched for a moment, listening.

She turned then, and her face lit up as she saw Mandhla. Silently, duiker-like, she ran to him.

He put the pail down and swung her high, both of them whisper-laughing secretly. When her feet touched the dry grass again she scampered off into the bush. He watched her a moment, beaming his pleasure, then lifted his load again and moved towards the cook-house.

He stopped at the door and stood watching for a moment, his chest swelling. Inside, Nada was preparing the porridge for breakfast, and the yellow light of the sun that fingered its way through the high windows found her thick, glossy hair and sprinkled the tight curls with diamond-dust. She was tall for a girl of sixteen, and well-built, strong and graceful. Her hips were wide and her bottom swelled under the skirt she wore, and as she poured the mealie powder into the huge pot her muscles rippled under the purple-black velvet of her skin.

She pivoted and saw him standing there, his shadow long on the tiled floor. Immediately her curling lashes swept down over her deer-eyes as they dropped from his in respect, and her cheeks glowed red under the ebony. He moved inside and heaved the bucket onto the table for her; it was not a man's job to fetch water, but for Nada ... besides, there would be time enough for her to assume wifely chores once they were married.

The date was already set. The betrothal was itself a year old, and in another year, at the first full moon of the spring season, the mission children would kill a calf for the wedding feast. Mandhla's heart still tumbled under his ribs when he thought of it, and quickly, to hide his unmanly emotion, he poured the water into the porridge and went to replenish the bucket.

He was scrubbing the kitchen floor when John Elliott walked in, his wife following close behind.

"Mandhla, do you know where Chela is?" asked Ruth Elliott. "She's gone again!"

He dipped his dark head to them. "She went to watch the birds, Mma, by the stream. She will come soon, she is fine."

She laughed and shook her head despairingly. "No-one will ever tame that wild little spirit!"

John smiled. "Time enough when winter comes; you know how she hates the cold – Mandhla, will you please help me prepare the school books when you're finished?"

Mandhla lit up, pleased at the new responsibilities he was being assigned. He didn't look at Nada to see whether she had noticed – he knew she would have. And he had already told her of the Elliotts' plans to train him as a teacher here at the mission.

"*Ehh, Baba.* Of course, Mr. Elliott."

The missionary went out. Mandhla watched him speculatively for a moment, then turned to the white woman who had brought him up for fifteen of the eighteen years of his life. "Baba is worried." He said it flatly, a statement of fact.

She sighed. "Yes, we are worried. Another of our sponsors has left the country. It will be even more difficult – "

"We have always managed before. Our God provides, always."

The missionary's wife looked seriously, assessingly, at him. "You're absolutely right, Mandhla. Your faith is strong. We must pray about it."

She walked out, and Mandhla returned to scrubbing the floor.

At breakfast, Chela was still not back. Counting the thirty-three dark heads, Mandhla shook his head and frowned. He clicked his tongue impatiently. She knew she shouldn't be this late; she'd been told off for it only three weeks ago. Exasperated, he bent back to his plate.

She came in the middle of the first lesson. Ruth Elliott was teaching the younger pupils to read – Dick was giving Spot a new ball. The little ones were more concerned with the bright red ball in their books than with the machinations of the crawling black letters, but the bigger ones were repeating the sentences in careful unison.

The door creaked open. Mrs. Elliott hesitated, and cast a severe glance toward the round black eyes that stared warily at her. Then, round the edge of the cracked wood, a fat fist appeared, clutching a bunch of wild orange flowers.

The blooms were thrust toward the teacher apologetically. About to speak, Ruth thought better of it, afraid she may laugh. Instead she kept her face stern and gestured for Chela to sit.

The child, thrilled with her easy escape, scuttled to her place and sat, avidly joining in with the older ones as they chanted. Ruth had to turn to look at the blackboard, hoping Chela hadn't seen her shoulders shaking.

Mandhla was angry with her. "Little sister," he berated her in their native tongue, "Beware! The crocodiles are moving closer as their water dries up in the rivers."

The little girl trembled obediently. The young man, her very own personal god, straightened, glared at her, and went to help Mr. Elliott in the vegetable patch. The chastised child stood for a moment, unsure; then a butterfly bobbed past and her face shone again, her friend's disapproval forgotten.

Five of the older girls, under Ruth's supervision, prepared the supper. Today was special; it was the birthday of Mr. Elliott. They plucked the chickens and peeled the potatoes excitedly, chattering in anticipation of the feast they would have.

Earlier in the afternoon they had been taught to bake – little cakes, the size of small buns, yellow and crumbly and moist. No icing – but then, most of them had never tasted icing anyway, and the cakes in themselves were a rare enough treat. So were the potatoes; sadza, the thick porridge made from mealie-meal and used for any or all meals, was by far the cheapest staple starch food. And the chickens had been fattening for the last three months. Amidst the laughter and babbling the feathers flew, white and brown and grey and speckled.

The men were there almost before Mandhla and John realised it. One moment they were digging a new patch for cabbages, the next the strong smell of unwashed bodies was before them. The heavy rifles were pointed at their stomachs. Slowly the missionary and his pupil straightened up, fear knotting in their guts.

The leader spoke in Ndebele, Mandhla's language. "This is Elliott's Mission. You – " he gestured with his rifle, "you are Elliott."

The missionary nodded carefully, hands raised, wordless. He knew immediately that they must be ZIPRA, the Zimbabwe People's Revolutionary Army; this was their patch. The ever-present fear had finally become reality.

The leader spat in the general direction of the white man's feet, then turned his eyes on the youth. "And you?"

Mandhla could hardly speak. He felt himself sweating, but with a new kind of sweat; not that of the work he had been doing. "I am Mandhla Ndhlovu."

The big man laughed, pleased. "Mandhla – the Powerful One. That is good; you will need much power, very soon."

Mandhla moved to speak, but thought better of it. The man gestured again with the weapon he held for them to lead the group to the main buildings. With Mandhla at the end of his Russian-made AK rifle, the leader spoke again to John Elliott.

"You! Assemble all the people here. Now!"

Dutifully, they assembled. The littlest ones were curious at this change in their routine, and stared at the strange men with their funny-looking sticks. The older ones trembled, and some of the girls cried, which frightened the toddlers. Nada pulled them against her, hiding their faces in her dress to quiet them. She stared fixedly, wide-eyed, at Mandhla, as if by seeing only him the rest would all disappear.

John and Ruth Elliott stood with Mandhla, their heads high, facing the intruders, whose cold eyes roved continually over the children, calculating, assessing, deciding.

Suddenly the leader's arm shot into the air, fist to the sky, and immediately his other three men, who had still not spoken yet, followed suit. "Amaaaaaaaandhla!"

The sudden black power salute startled two of the toddlers into crying, and Nada, holding them, shushing them, began to shake.

"Freedom!" The men raised their heavy weapons above their heads with both hands and cheered, and the little ones cried more loudly.

The leader finally addressed the huddled group, in Sindebele. "We are ZIPRA. We come to lead you to freedom, to where there will be no more oppression by these – " he spat again, "Boers!"

The older children and teens glanced uneasily at each other and shuffled their feet, avoiding the eyes of their white 'parents'.

"Who among you is the eldest?" His glance went to Mandhla. "You?" He motioned for the boy to step forward. "You will come with us. You, you, you," he said, indicating the older, fitter-looking children, until twenty had been selected. They were moved into a group, where they clustered together, afraid. The youngest was twelve-year-old Mali, a mischievous imp of a child who was forever playing tricks on the missionaries.

The remaining fifteen children, their ages ranging from two to ten, including little Chela, were lined up against the dirty white wall of the mission station. The ZIPRA leader surveyed them critically, looking particularly at ten-year-old Benjamin. The child's small eyes flamed; he was fascinated by the strangely-garbed men before him, their olive-green uniforms filthy and worn.

"You!" Benjamin leapt to attention, smiling brilliantly. "Who are we?"

"The men who will give us our freedom from the white rule – who will give us our country back!" The answer was prompt and firm, and Mandhla looked in astonishment at the little boy. The ZIPRA soldiers laughed delightedly. One of them spoke.

"Let him come. He will be entertaining on the journey."

The commander grunted, still grinning. Abruptly his face changed and he spoke harshly. "He will hinder our walk. He is too small. Kill them."

Startled, Mandhla stepped forward involuntarily as Chela cried out in fright. The leader turned and looked at him coldly, then swung back to Chela. He gestured for her to step forward, then for Mandhla to come forward, too.

Terrified, shivering, Chela had to be dragged from the ranks of her peers by one of the terrorists. The commander stared deep into Mandhla's horrified eyes. Then he handed him his own rifle. He pointed at the child who was still holding Mandhla mesmerized.

"You! Kill her." The other rifles were turned threateningly on Mandhla. He hesitated, his bowels liquid, then thrust the weapon back at the officer.

"Aiieewah! No!"

The man calmly pointed at Ruth Elliott. Grinning, one of his followers pulled her forward and pushed her into a kneeling position. When her husband tried to intervene he was roughly smashed in the chest with the butt of an AK. Gasping, he fell to the ground, his cheek grazing on the hard dirt. The leader turned back to Mandhla and again gave him the rifle.

"The child – or the woman, and then the man, and then all of them."

Mandhla felt the sweat running in rivers down his body; he was wet with sweat, and he smelt his own fear. He looked at Nada; her eyes were huger and blacker than he had ever seen them, and her head moved from side to side, as if to deny to herself what was happening. He looked at the Elliots, parents to him for almost as long as he could remember; their faces white, terrified, yet a message there in John Elliot's defiant eyes, a slight shake of the head, *No!*

The youth looked back at Chela's eyes – pools of fear.

Chela ... or all of them.

Chela, then. As if hypnotised, dreamily, slowly, he pointed the rifle at the sobbing child.

Then he realised he didn't know what to do with the it; it was all he could do to hold the heavy gun level. He looked helplessly at the weapon, and the commander indicated the trigger, placing his finger on it.

Mandhla looked at the tiny, terrorised girl. Her eyes stared at him, not believing, not understanding.

As he pulled the trigger he wasn't sure which of them screamed; or perhaps it was all of them at once.

The rifle kicked him into the dirt. The unexpected power

behind the shot had surprised him; the men laughed uproariously, as he sprawled in the dust. Shaking, he picked himself up and saw what had once been Chela; little Chela who had gone to greet the sun each day, and to watch the birds.

The other children were weeping, looking away, some screaming, some sobbing, some wailing, but Nada was still staring at him. Her skin was grey, the colour of the putty he had used to replace the dormitory window last week, her eyes told him she no longer knew who he was.

Ruth Elliott keened a prayer; her husband tried to stand and was knocked to the ground again, stunned. The officer, grinning still, gestured at the guerilla with the woman at his feet. As Mandhla watched, a burst of automatic fire ripped her apart.

When they were all dead except for the selected group, the march began.

The fly rested its shiny blue-green bottom and began to salivate onto the blood, starting the digestive process before the food entered its stomach. The black bristles on its legs scraped on the dried brown clots as it moved lazily forward, sucking and spitting and sucking, over the ragged skin and the dull white bone protruding from it.

Peter Kennedy watched the fly dispassionately for a moment, listening to the newest of his men retch in the bush behind them. How long, he wondered, how long since he had done that?

His gaze rose to the dirty white walls, caked with red-brown dust and spattered with blood. Elliott's Mission. He looked down again at the fat, glistening fly. Elliott's wife. His eyes travelled further. Elliott. And fifteen black kids, none of them yet in their teens.

The same pattern as all the other mission attacks. A small group of buildings surrounded by bush, at the end of a very long dirt road and twenty miles from the nearest outpost. Close enough to the Rhodesian border for a quick strike-and-retreat; smash-and-grab in human trade – and lives. Smashed lives; smashed bodies, like those scattered around him now; black children, black bodies, black killers. Their own people. Maybe even their own clan, their own kin. But the blood ran the same deep red, from the Elliotts and their young charges alike. Maybe the terrorists were the ones who were right; maybe skin colour, tribe, affinity, didn't matter in a killing spree; all that mattered was the killing itself.

He shook himself. "All right boys, we're here to track. Let's track. Wright, you lead."

He looked at the white face of the latest recruit; the boy was shaking but trying bravely to ignore it. He was not, Peter noted wryly, looking at the bodies.

"Beridges, follow Wright. If you don't agree with him, speak. Let's get this right."

Beridges nodded miserably and took his place behind Wright. He knew his commander was trying to make up for the shame, and briefly wondered why. The man was a paradox; harsh and pushing his men to their limits the one moment, compassionate the next. He shook his head slightly, tasting the acrid vomit in the corners under his tongue, and spat into the bush.

The other six men fell into formation and the tracking began. It wasn't too difficult; twenty-four people moving fast hardly merited the skills of a tracking force such as the Sparrowhawks, but the Elliotts had been friends of someone with a lot of influence – someone who had been inflamed enough to demand that the best unit available be put on the job, and influential enough to get it.

Now and then Wright or Beridges (good lad that, in spite of his inexperience) warned of mines that had been placed to deter follow-up operations. Systematically they worked their way through, but Peter was frustrated. He knew that they were not keeping pace with the fleeing children and their captors.

Strangely, although the terrorists were taking the time to lay anti-personnel mines (and a few Claymores for good measure), they were not taking the time to attempt to cover either their tracks or their destination – the Botswana border. The children would have to rest and that would hinder them, but Peter assumed that those were the periods when the laying of the explosives took place.

He straightened suddenly and called his men's attention to himself. They bunched and he spoke quietly to them.

"We're cutting a right angle that way," pointing, "and when we're far enough over, we're going to move in the direction they've been holding. Wright, take the left flank with Grant; that's the side we'll keep them on. And watch out for ... well, everything," he concluded lamely, knowing that Wright and Grant were the best men he had and that they knew precisely what to watch out for.

They began to move silently to their right, and their pace quickened. When they were close to the border, Peter knew they must have made better progress than the terrorist force with their burden of children. He had taken a risk but he hoped the gamble had paid off. They began to move left again.

Even with the good time they had made, they did not have time to set up the ambush before the group was in their midst. Confused, both sides opened fire at first sight, but Peter's keenly trained men immediately disciplined their shock. Dropping onto their stomachs, they tried to sort out how many there were, but it was hard in the thick bush. The children were screaming and although they, too, had lain down, it was difficult to assess where each was, and which movement was that of the enemy and which that of a captive.

After a minute of panicky firing, mostly AKs, both sides stopped and there was an uncanny silence. The children had quietened, but Peter could smell their fear and feel their tension. He waited, and his men waited.

A head lifted slowly from behind a bush. It was the boy Peter had noticed first; the boy who had pushed the children nearest to him to the ground when the shooting had started. Probably the oldest there, he decided. He wondered what side the boy was on, whether he was with the terrorists willingly, or a reluctant prisoner.

Then the strain snapped something in one of the children, a girl of about seventeen. She leapt up, wailing in Ndebele.

Instantly the firing began again. Peter was never sure who fired first, but he did know that the girl was killed by bullets from one of his own men. At a guess, young Beridges.

He was surprised at the tenacity of the terrorists; usually they avoided such confrontations with security forces, breaking ranks and running, each man for himself. The fact that these men were sticking to their guns, as it were – he allowed himself a humourless smile – intrigued him.

And then he found out why. From nowhere – no, from behind the Sparrowhawks, from the Botswana direction – a new attack was launched, and suddenly the trackers were caught between two groups of ZIPRA forces. As they had been trained, half his men turned to face the new onslaught while the other half remained in their positions, but Peter realised it was hopeless.

He had to make a fast decision. His highly-trained men were, when it came down to it, more important than the children; to sacrifice a vital stick of fighting men uselessly was stupid and, at this stage of the war (in a sickeningly cold but necessary calculation), uneconomical. He and his men were necessary to the rest of Rhodesia.

He signalled them to pull out.

Beridges was missing. Peter hoped he was dead and not injured, for his own sake. Bitterly he berated himself for not protecting their rear. They all did; yet they also knew that their situation had been one in a million, unprecedented to their knowledge. An uncanny coincidence.

There is no room in war for error. Beridges had paid for his commander's mistake. Peter Kennedy filed the knowledge in his private file, the one at the very back of the cabinet in his mind. And then he set about getting his men back to base, from where he would order a retrieval of Beridge's body.

He really should think about taking a holiday.

Chapter 2

She wondered why she was still conscious, her mind still wandering, still fighting against the pain, the haze. The ancient amulet was like a vice on her arm, coiling cold above her elbow, the serpent's head nestling flat against her flesh, blood spatter blinding one eye. Words, a tune: "... these are the times when I know how alone one can be, and I yearn to go once again, back to my home down in ..." She could hear her father's voice, singing the Belafonte ballad, but she couldn't remember where home was.

Tsimbaboue, 1352

The plump, dusty fingers reached out carefully and lifted the horny black beetle from the ball it was rolling. The dung was tight-packed and fibrous, a dry bunch three times the size of the persistent insect; the child set him down a foot away from his prize and watched him hunt frantically for a moment before he latched his clawed feet into the yellow manure again, pushing and clinging, flipping over as the ball rolled, now under it, now over it, in constant motion.

The child laughed with delight, her milky teeth glistening wetly. "Now you may go, Beetle, and take your food to your wife who will scold you if you're too late. You must hurry!"

She laughed again as the beetle rolled the ball against a rock, re-orientated himself, and began his homeward battle once more.

"Xalise! I've been looking for you. Help me to fetch water – we're late!"

The child looked up at her elder sister, then down at the pan in the girl's hand. She pointed to the beetle. "He'll be late too, and his wife will scold him."

"Not as much as the Priest will scold me if I'm late! Come, Xalise, you know that today's not like other days."

Obedient, the child stood and took the proffered container. "Tcana, what will they do to you ... up there?" Fearfully she looked towards the Hill, and quickly away again.

"I don't know, little sister. That's why I'm going there – to find out." Tcana turned and led the way swiftly down the path to the spring, where the water welled up clear and cold from inside the ground.

Xalise followed more slowly. She was afraid for her sister – and for herself; in eight years she, too, must go up the Hill.

She washed carefully, meticulously. Her mother helped; she was the only one permitted to do so, and it was the last assistance she would ever give her daughter with her toilet. Knowing this, Lila was slow, and Tcana became impatient.

"Mai, I'm late already. We must hurry!"

Her mother moved more quickly, drying Tcana with soft suede, and rubbing the calf-fat in gently to make the purple-black skin smooth and shiny. She understood her daughter, and knew she was afraid. When Tcana feared, she became impatient to find out what it was that frightened her, to face up to it, conquer it.

"There." Lila straightened and stood back.

Tcana's body gleamed in the last rays of the sun that filtered through the rough cloth at the windows; even her eyebrows were plastered flat against her forehead, like spiders in the rain.

The mother looked longingly at her child. She recognised suddenly that her daughter was beautiful – when had she become so? The tiny, chubby, dirty-faced, laughing urchin – when had she become a graceful buck?

Lila sighed, deftly slipping the white cotton robe over Tcana's head and adjusting it to fall easily to the floor; in places it clung damply to the calf-fat. Cloth was expensive; the weaving looms were big and ungainly, the weaving itself tedious and time-consuming. Thus, woven cotton was prized in a fashion not unlike cattle. This traditional initiation gown was planned for from the moment a girl was born.

She lifted the hood over Tcana's head and hesitated. Their eyes met, Tcana's apprehensive and excited, her mother's pained. She dropped her fingers to touch the girl's cheek, stroking the line of the dove's eyes, and deliberately smiled to ease the worry lines on her forehead.

"Remember, you must not speak, nor cry out, whatever happens. Whatever happens. Speak only when spoken to, until your hood is removed."

Tcana nodded seriously. They had gone over this a thousand times – ten thousand. It was all her mother was permitted to tell her, and it was not enough, but Tcana knew it had to suffice. And it was this inadequacy that made Lila repeat the warning so often; there was nothing else she could say.

They both looked toward the Hill as the wailing began suddenly. It was the first wail, a high-pitched, thin, keening note, and as it died away the mother quickly slid the hood over her daughter's head. They turned and walked to the other room, where Tcana's father was waiting.

Roro looked through her, and not at her, but Tcana knew he saw her – or saw the white shape she had become. *He's already put me from his mind,* she thought. All that showed were her hands, her bare feet, and her eyes through the slits in the hood.

She kept her face averted as he recited to Muali, the creator:

> *Muali, great king, here is my seed.*
> *Muali, here is your seed.*
> *Take our seed and make it anew.*
> *Take your seed.*

Then he turned his back on her, and Tcana walked to the doorway of the hut. She looked briefly at Xalise, huddled in a corner, frightened, weeping; at her mother, anxious, fretful, loving. She smiled at them, to encourage them, but they could not see through the hood. She looked outside again. The sun was almost gone and the only figures she saw were white shapes. No other was allowed in the streets now, until dawn. She saw a ghost pass quickly towards the meeting-place and wondered briefly if it could be Niswe, her friend since babyhood.

The wail came again, a mournful echo across the valley. Tcana softly touched the red clay wall of the hut, wistful. She would never live here again. When she came back, her father would have built a smaller one, beside his own, for her to possess until she married.

Breathing deeply, she stepped out into the gathering dusk. As she did so, she heard her mother begin to weep for the loss of her child.

There must have been at least a hundred at the meeting place, standing still and silent, waiting. Tcana joined them, eyes cast down; they must not recognise each other. It was only a few minutes before the third wail was heard, and as it died away a Priest appeared in their midst. Tcana didn't see where he came from and none of them had heard him approach, but though some jumped, none cried out. He looked them over carefully, then turned, heading toward the Hill. In silence, the white-robed girls followed him, falling into single-file.

When they reached the steps that led to the top of the bouldered cliff, the Priest turned and surveyed them, as if assessing them. Which was ridiculous, thought Tcana, since he couldn't tell who was who. Could he? Hurriedly, she lowered her eyes again as his glance fell on her; she felt him look long and hard before he turned again to lead them into the passageway and up the stone steps. Here there was only room for them to walk one after the other; perhaps, had they met someone coming down, if they had flattened themselves against the rocky walls, they may have been able to pass. The way was steep, and before long Tcana could hear other girls breathing heavily – especially the heavy one labouring in front of her. Oddly, the climb didn't bother Tcana. The excitement was too great.

They were there, suddenly. They poured into an open space beneath the great walls that hid the Hill from sight of those in the Valley. Looking around as they assembled, Tcana saw twelve or fourteen dwellings built in the arena. At the doorway of each stood a Priest. They were all dressed alike, in long white robes that left one shoulder bare and fell to the ground, held in place by a wide leather belt at the waist. The robes were split up either side to mid-thigh, and the Priests wore leather thongs around each ankle, symbolically joined by a long chain fashioned from more leather, to signify their servitude to Muali. At their throats were copper necklets, from which hung tiny soapstone representations of Muali – the eagle, squatting, watchful.

Tcana suddenly realised that she was staring, and that they were staring back. Uncomfortably, she looked down at her feet.

When no more came from the narrow passageway, they moved on again, but this time the other Priests fell in behind the initiates. Although some of the girls were panting heavily, none spoke. Tcana silently congratulated them.

The procession wound its way between boulders and passages until, abruptly, it stopped in another open area. Here there were no dwellings, but an abundance of monoliths – pillars of stone that rose vertically from stone platforms, some topped with Muali's squatting form, others with patterns carved into the grey rock.

The girls gazed around them, awestruck, and for a few minutes nothing happened. Then suddenly there was movement at the top of the protruding rock that stood out above them, forming a balcony. Another Priest stood there – Tcana knew he was a Priest, because he was dressed like the others, but this man wore a mask fashioned in imitation of Muali, moulded from thick calf-skin and decorated with the green soapstone used for so many of Muali's images. He carried a long, carved stick, headed again with the eagle.

He raised the stick against the thickening light and spoke, his voice muffled by the mask, and the sound quivered in Tcana's spine.

"It is your time. Thus far, it is good. But we are a strong people, amaTsimbaboue, the People of the House of God. If any one of you weakens, you will no longer bear that honour and your death rites will be performed without hesitation. You will ask no questions. You will speak only when given permission. You will make no sound, lest your weakness betray you. Muali sees and hears all.

"You will remain here for two weeks, and at the end you will leave us, no longer children, but women of Tsimbaboue. Be worthy of yourselves. Be worthy of your mothers and your fathers. Be silent, be respectful, be dignified. You are in Tsimbaboue – the House of God."

The High Priest was gone as quickly as he had appeared. The girls were led away to their sleeping quarters.

The shuttered, blind rocks stood sentinel in the purple-black night, guarding the plains below. Now and then the cool breeze shifted the grasses that stretched and stretched away from the feet of the kopjies. Somewhere an owl slid through the darkness and a mouse cried out in fear, its life cut suddenly short.

On her hard mud bed, Tcana heard.

For three days they ate nothing, meditating, drinking water three times daily. No-one spoke to them and they spoke to no-one. They only saw the Priests who brought the water to their chamber, and were only allowed out to relieve themselves – and even then, they were accompanied by a Priest.

It really wasn't that bad, reflected Tcana. Not after the fear.

Then, just as they had begun to relax in their fast, they were fetched. It was before dawn, and the grey morning chill clung to them; they were taken to a washing area and told to cleanse themselves. The Priests turned their backs, but did not leave them. Afterwards they were led to a great room draped with cloths that had chevron patterns at the hems, and made to sit in two long lines along the walls, facing each other. Here, too, were the eagles, carved into the dagga clay or sitting regally on poles or altars.

The High Priest was waiting for them, and with him another man. This one wore a dark red robe, patterned with brown at the hem, and carried sharp blades in his hands. The High Priest sat on the mud throne at the top of the long room, watching as the red-robed man walked silently between the two lines of initiates.

He moved slowly, staring hard at each girl as though he could see through the cotton hoods that covered their heads. Though her eyes were cast down, Tcana felt him examine her and pass on. He went to the end of the room and then came back again to the top, where he stood and looked them over imperiously. Tcana shivered under his gaze, apprehensive. He nodded, and two Priests lifted the two girls at the head of the lines, gripping their elbows roughly and making them stand. Tcana, twenty-first in line, trembled for them.

They disappeared through a door Tcana had not noticed before, and after a few moments a scream split the hush in the room. The girls jumped, and one cried out. Instantly she was pulled from the ranks and taken away. Tcana bit her lip, and waited.

Several others screamed before it was Tcana's turn. With the girl opposite her, she walked into the anteroom, praying earnestly to Muali that she would make no sound. The room smelt faintly of something ... iron? She was made to lie on a raised mud couch. The lighting was dim, but when she felt the wetness beneath her bottom she instinctively knew it was blood.

Her robe was pulled roughly up to her waist and her legs spread-eagled; the Priests chanted in low voices, praying, and she heard Muali's name over and over, inside her head and out. They held her, one at her knees, the other at her shoulders. She saw the stranger in the red robe bend over her, and suddenly knew why he did not wear white. Hands pressed deeply into her thighs, creating a dulling pain, so that when the blade first touched her she hardly realised it. Then she almost screamed, and thought she would faint. But the knife was sharp, and the small foreskin at her clitoris came away easily.

Just when she thought she could bear it no longer, a cool balm was applied and the pain went, almost immediately. Her head swam as she was helped to stand, and a padding of cloth was tied around her waist and looped between her legs, spread liberally with the balm. She could not see, though her eyes were open; she felt a mug pushed against her ravaged lips and teeth, and she drank deeply.

The liquid was warm and sickly sweet, honey with spices and ... something else. She knew she was being led away; knew her legs were walking; she felt nothing but a cushion of feathers all around her. Muali's feathers, she thought, and almost giggled at her irreverence – but remembered in time.

I did not scream. Thank you, Muali.

Her dreams were restless, and seemed to go on forever. She saw the Priests, and the One in Red, and the High Priest wearing Muali's mask; their faces came and went, purple and fuzzy, and sometimes there was music. Sometimes she dreamed of the screams from the anteroom, and she dreamed of girls she had grown with and played with and learned with, but they were in a place she could not reach; she could not touch them ... somehow, she did not dream of Niswe, and vaguely tried to, but nothing came except the High Priest and the One in Red. And she dreamed often of the sweet drink she had taken before she slept, the haunting taste of something that eluded her ... over and over she dreamed of the drink.

When she awoke it was dawn again. She sat up groggily, her head thick, her teeth and tongue furry. She was on her mud couch in the sleeping chamber. The padding between her legs was clean – the Priests must have changed the dressing while she slept. Looking around at the other beds, she realised that a third of their number was no longer there. She remembered the screams, and shrunk inside her belly.

She was the only one awake, and as she sat up a Priest moved swiftly toward her between the other beds. He knelt beside her and in the morning light she thought she saw, briefly, a kind of pity in his eyes. Then it was gone, and he pushed aside the cloth of the hood and held a mug of clear water to her lips. She drank and drank – how thirsty she was! How her head ached!

She smiled gratefully to him when she had finished, then remembered the hood. She inclined her head instead, lowering her eyes, and he moved away. Suddenly she felt the urge to relieve herself, painful in her belly and loins. She rose quietly and went to the doorway, linking her fingers and touching her forehead to the Priest there. He nodded, and followed her to the toilet area, where he turned his back.

She tugged tentatively at the dressing, but it came away easily and the pain was only a sharp sting which increased with the stream she released. It was bearable. Anything, after all, was bearable.

They assembled again in front of the balcony and the High Priest. He looked them over, and for the first time his voice was gentle. It made Tcana want to cry, and she didn't understand.

"Children of Tsimbaboue, Muali greets you. He welcomes you as women, to be wives and mothers. You have done well. Truly, you are worthy to be called amaTsimbaboue."

The Priests came forward, kneeling at the feet of the girls to remove the ankle bracelets they had worn since birth, each new harvest having two more iron beads added. Twenty six now; thirteen years.

The last two beads were very different to the others. They had been bought by her father from the pale Traders who had come from the north one year past, and had a decoration on them that was strange and had filled Tcana with their strangeness – each bead carried the simple outline of a fish, crossed at its tail. Seeing his daughter drawn to the design, her father had indulged her, and these had become the mark of her thirteenth year.

Now Tcana felt her ankle beads drop away and for a moment wanted to cry out, to beg the Priest to leave them on.

"Women of Tsimbaboue, I salute you. Mothers of the amaTsimbaboue, I greet you."

To Tcana's astonishment, the High Priest went down onto both his knees, crouching, his forehead touching the rock face of the balcony. Instantly, the other Priests around them dropped too, and took up the High Priest's greeting.

Nervously the girls flicked glances at each other, embarrassed.

When the Priests stood once more, the High Priest raised his hands to his mask and lifted the calf-skin from his face. "Know one another," he commanded. And the Priests reached out to help the girls remove their hoods.

As the fresh morning air touched her cheeks, Tcana breathed deeply, thankfully. The initiates were looking desperately at each other, searching for friends; Tcana hunted, too, and at the same moment they saw each other.

"Niswe!"

"Tcana!"

The girls gripped each other's hands, laughing, and there was an air of festivity. The Priests smiled, too, but here and there some girls tried to hide their dismay that a friend was no longer there. Those who had broken tabu no longer had names; they could never be mentioned again, or acknowledged, either by friends or family. They had never been a part of the amaTsimbaboue; they had never lived.

The High Priest spoke again and the girls fell silent. "Go back to your families, to your new huts. Your two weeks here were well served."

Astounded, the girls looked at each other. Tcana mentally calculated and decided that at the most they had only been there five days – three of fasting, one of drugged unconsciousness, and this one. Then she realised that they could never have healed so well in such a short time. She remembered the dreams, the drinks ... they had been drugged for over a week while their bodies adjusted and repaired; it also accounted for the weakness she had felt on standing.

Silently, the young women, unmasked, with naked ankles and stripped womanhood, made their own way back down the narrow steps. They had brought nothing with them, and were leaving with less.

Chapter 3

Zambia, 1975

The heat was almost unbearable. They had been marching for – how long? Mandhla had lost count of the days. Their feet were blistered and bloody, their bodies scratched by the thorn bushes that reached out for them as they passed. They were quiet now, all of them, too exhausted to speak, too horrified, too shocked to know what to say. Now and then the ZIPRA men shoved them or swore at them when they lagged.

He had heard them speak among themselves; they were making slow progress – too slow. The younger children were holding them back. Already their numbers had decreased – Nada, laughing, joyful Nada, killed by the security forces! Mandhla felt the now-familiar purple rage split his head as he thought about it. They had killed his Nada! The beautiful child-woman who would have married him, borne his children ... Nada, without whom it was impossible to envisage life ... they who were supposedly there to save them!

He knew he would never outlive the hatred, nor forget the face of the commanding officer.

But then, too, Mali, in her first monthly bleeding, had been shot by their captors where she lay, too weary to go on. And all of them at the mission ... who next? He was confused ...

Mandhla looked at the other children. They had avoided him for the first few days, unable to meet his eyes, the memory of what he had done to Chela still fresh in their minds. But as they walked, Mandhla, always their comforter and protector, had been the only one they could turn to. Gradually they had begun to look to him again, their eyes pleading. And he had encouraged them when they faltered, pushing them on, afraid for them. Mali's death had convinced him that they could not, must not, dally.

The men called a halt and the children sank to the ground where they stood. Water was handed around – a few sips for each, no more. "You are children of ZIPRA now – you must learn to live harshly!"

Dully the children of ZIPRA drank their brief portions. One or two of them lay down; they were immediately prodded with the barrels of the terrorist weapons. "Get up – there is much walking to be done still. If we stay here the Skuzapo will get us!"

It was the daily reminder of their danger. Mandhla wondered who the Skuzapo were. Sheltered by the missionaries, the children had heard little of the war around them, the fight for their country; even if they had, through normal channels it was doubtful they would have found out about the Skuzapo. But they remembered Nada, and the men who should have helped them and instead had run away ...

Meanwhile, to keep their own spirits up, the leader of the freedom fighters shouted his morale-boosting phrases. "Forward the war! Forward ZIPRA! Kill the white pigs!"

His men cheered with him; the children, bemused, looked at Mandhla for guidance. Fearful, he shouted the slogans, and they copied him obediently. The commander and his men laughed, satisfied.

"We will soon be there," he told them in a moment of compassion. "Tomorrow morning we cross the Zambezi River; by afternoon we will be in camp and you will eat and drink well, and sleep."

The children murmured eagerly. Mandhla kept his silence.

Encouraged by the prospect of a camp, they reached the river fifty kilometres upstream from the Victoria Falls at three-thirty in the morning, at a narrow point between two kopjies where the river was only two hundred metres wide. Several tribesmen were awaiting them – amaZambezi, the Batonka – and Mandhla shuddered at the sight of the gaps where their front teeth should be. These were the people of the Zambezi, hated and shunned; they had begun to knock out their own front teeth in the days of the slave traders to make them unattractive propositions for those Arab merchants, and the custom had continued, becoming a sign of beauty among them. They lived mainly off fish, not man enough to hunt. Even the Mashona – the Eaters of Dirt – despised them.

The Batonka men had boats ready, enough to ferry them all across the river silently and under cover of darkness, and within the hour they were marching again. "We must get away from the border. The security forces patrol all the time."

Mandhla at first hadn't understood why they had remained in Rhodesia, until the leader explained: "We didn't. We crossed into Botswana to make them think we had left the country; but that way around would have been too long, so we came back into Zimbabwe further north. Thus we only walked two-thirds of the distance we would otherwise have had to."

It made sense, he decided. Mandhla had noticed that the commander had a habit of referring to Rhodesia as Zimbabwe; he did not question it – the term was often used to denote the country surrounding the ruins of the immense stone city that had once thrived ... He was still surprised that the soldiers had not caught up with them again; they must have been leaving a very obvious trail.

"Perhaps they didn't try," said the suddenly-friendly commander. "After all, you are black – why should they care what happens to you?"

The camp was enormous, far bigger than Mandhla had expected. They were welcomed by women, another surprise. Food was prepared and they ate, and then slept ... and slept ...

They awoke when the camp began to rise at daybreak. They were fed again, and even given chocolate by the suddenly friendly freedom-fighters. As they sat around the fires Mandhla carefully noted everything around him.

There were thirty-two barracks in all, lined on either side of the central parade ground. To one side of that was a football field, with basketball and volleyball pitches beside it. Behind those were vegetable gardens, backed by a river; in fact, the camp was in the fork of a river, presumably one that drained into the Zambezi. *Bad positioning,* was his first thought. *Two sides of the triangle bounded by water – no escape route.*

There were pig sties behind one of the barracks, and further over were smaller residences – for the officers, he presumed. There were also several buildings he could not identify, but assumed they were store rooms and arms housing. The atmosphere was leisurely and unhurried, and no-one ordered the children to do anything, though Mandhla noticed that there were constantly women in attendance.

At eight o'clock muster was called, and the men ambled to the parade ground and stood in rough formation. The children watched with interest. Then, to their amazement, two white men in uniform stepped to the front of the assembly. Immediately, the men stood to attention.

After a brief lecture in a language Mandhla had never heard, and which was translated into Ndebele, the parade broke and the men went to predetermined positions. Some took over guard duty (at the gate were four sentries), others went to train, still others to play football. Some played volleyball.

The commander in charge of their abduction came then, and took the children to one of the better official-looking buildings, where they were given instructions. The girls were to commence duties with the women immediately; they would be shown how to provide for the three thousand men at the camp – and it was apparent that this didn't just mean food. The girls were led away by one of the women who had kept watch over them earlier. To the boys who remained, the commander began to explain the Cause, and exactly who the enemy were.

"The Skuzapo are white pigs who have persuaded black traitors to join them. They hunt us down, with treachery and deceit and lies and cowardice, and then call in the airplanes to kill us. They even deceive their own people, their own army, their own leaders! They say they are trackers, but in reality they are murderers and cheats, who dress in our uniforms and speak our language until we trust them and they find out more. Then they destroy those foolish enough to have believed them! Trust no-one but those you personally know – no-one!"

The brainwashing that followed was unsubtle, and Mandhla remained aloof. His confusion was still with him; the men whom he had always been taught were his protectors had first shot Nada and then had run away, leaving them to their captors. When the body of a young white soldier had been dragged into the clearing and laid next to Nada's broken black one, the purple rage had started and he had wanted to spit on the white skin – truly white in death – for its cowardice and brutality.

And then he had remembered the Elliotts, and the mission, and the fifteen dead children ... As much as he tried to justify that, he couldn't. So he tried to justify Nada's death, and the desertion by the white soldiers ... and found he couldn't do that, either. He shook his head to clear the mist and the ache. Neither went. So he shouted with the others, the slogans and names, and the curses on the white Rhodesians, but his heart remained somewhere terribly cold, a frozen rock in his chest, and his eyes stared blankly at nothing at all.

When the session was over he was called to one side by the instructor. "You are not with us Mandhla. Do you not approve?"

Mandhla felt, in some remote place in his gut, a stirring of fear, but he dismissed it. "I shouted with the rest," he replied sullenly.

To his immense surprise the instructor laughed, and with him his comrades. "Good, Mandhla, good. You are a strong man, and when you finally realise what is best and what your ideals are, you will never fail them. Keep shouting, Mandhla Ndhlovu; one day you will mean what you shout, and when that day comes you will be invincible!"

They laughed again and left him staring after them. He sank to his haunches in the sweltering sun and hugged himself, shivering, trying urgently to warm the icy waste inside.

He asked about the dangerous location of the camp soon after the training started. The officers, white foreigners, had been watching him; they saw his agility and intelligence, and watched some more. But when he mentioned the position of the camp, in the fork of the river, to his Ndebele instructors, they laughed.

"We are in Zambia – twenty kilometres from the border with Zimbabwe, and protected by the fact that their government does not want outright war with Zambia. Why worry about the rivers? They give us fish, and water, and relief from the heat."

Still, it showed the boy was thinking. He had finally, suddenly, been surprisingly open to the propaganda syllabus. At first resentful and distrustful, he had demanded to know why the missionaries and the other children had had to die.

"They were brainwashing you," the commander countered cleverly. "They treated you well so that they could use you later against your own people. They were really agents of the government; they fooled you!" And he laughed again, side-stepping the issue of the dead children.

No-one likes the idea of being made a fool of. Gradually Mandhla began to eat, sleep and breathe ZIPRA, and obediently his trusting peers followed his lead.

He became dissatisfied with the very basic training the men were being given. He wanted to know more than he and the group of fifty he was being prepared with were being told. But the others were happy enough on a diet of fish and sadza and ZIPRA slogans, with occasional promises of what was to come thrown in, and Mandhla only asked his questions when he could be alone with his Commander.

It wasn't long before he was called before the white instructors – Russians, as he had since discovered.

"You've been chosen," they said, "to be a Section Commander."

He was shocked. "But I have only been training a short while! I – "

"Your further instruction will be seen to," they told him. "But not here. You will be transferred to another camp.

Congratulations."

The children hardly bothered when he said goodbye. Their conversion to ZIPRA was complete.

The training at the new camp was more rigorous, and there were fewer pupils there. Altogether, one hundred prospective Section Commanders, and three instructors, two of whom were Russian. At the previous camp there were those in training, and those waiting to be deployed inside Zimbabwe; here there were only trainees. And of course the inevitable women, to feed them and see to their sexual needs. Mandhla shied away from this, Nada still fresh in his mind; the Russians watched, and said nothing.

And then there was the visit of the dignitaries. Among them stood, sweating in the hot sun, an over-fat man who looked vaguely familiar to Mandhla.

The new Section Commanders paraded for them and afterwards, when he inspected the ranks as they stood in their neat rows, the Russian said something to him and they stopped in front of Mandhla. The broad lips spread into a smile and a certain interest lit the pig-eyes.

Mandhla straightened further, sensing an importance he did not quite understand. A podgy black hand was laid on his shoulder. "The war will be won by men such as you, Mandhla Ndhlovu." Then he passed on.

Mandhla threw himself into the training with an enthusiasm unrivalled by that of his comrades. The instructors noted it. At the end of the period his marks were well above average, and he was given men to command at last. Twenty men.

Together they moved to a camp closer to the Zambezi River, above the Victoria Falls, to await orders for deployment. They set up grass bivouacs to shelter under, carefully trying to hide them beneath trees from prying eyes that might fly past overhead.

Mandhla put them through their paces over and over again, watching critically. Dissatisfied with their performance, he insisted they train further while they waited. That was unheard of; they had done their training, and some had even been involved in contacts in Zimbabwe already! But Mandhla was adamant. Carefully, he nursed them through a demanding programme of his own design, one which he felt was more appropriate to what he knew they would face in Zimbabwe.

When his men had been training hard under his own supervision for several weeks, he was almost satisfied with them; certainly he knew they were better than the men attached to other commanders. He had visited other camps, and watched their cadres; they were sloppy.

The orders, when they finally came, were clear. To infiltrate into Zimbabwe and subvert the local population between Plumtree and West Nicholson, south of Bulawayo.

Their training had been very detailed concerning the subversion of locals. Although the orders did not directly say so, Mandhla was fully aware that if he could also cause discomfort to either the security forces or the white farmers, that would not be without merit.

They moved down through Botswana, staying well inside that country, until they were on the banks of the Shagne River. Then they turned east-southeast and made their way obliquely to the border, crossing at night just south of Ramaquabane.

Mandhla felt keenly the honour of their deployment. They were the first to work this area; the others had all stayed well north of Bulawayo and Plumtree, or in the south near Tuli. What they said and did in the next few weeks would sway the local black populace one way or the other – towards ZIPRA, or towards the Rhodesians. If it were the latter, it could spell death for himself and his men through someone reporting their presence to the police.

But although they were the first in the area, they soon discovered that they had been eagerly awaited by the natives, who had been assured by word of mouth that ZIPRA were the ones who would set them free. On closer examination Mandhla found that they weren't exactly sure what this freedom would mean – so he happily explained.

"When we have driven the white man from the land, all he has will be ours! His farms, his cattle, his cars, his houses – everything. There will be no more forcing you to dip your cattle – an expensive and long-winded problem for you, driving your beasts to the nearest dip-station, while they lose weight and get sick on the way!" (Cheers.)

"You will no longer be forced to plough your furrows around the hills, which is time-consuming and a nuisance; why shouldn't you make the trenches run whichever way is easiest for you?" (More cheers.)

"And the white man will no longer take your money for taxes. Your money, and his, will be your own!" (Loudest cheers yet.)

"You will live in brick houses, instead of the poor huts you have now. You will drive his cars, instead of walking. You will be free!" (Roars and ZIPRA slogans.)

Oh yes, they knew how to subvert the local population. Until suddenly, before him stood an old village headman, his head held proudly in spite of the jeers from the crowd.

"He is a sellout!" yelled his accusers. "He wants to report you to the police!" The angry crowd roared. "He must die!" They knew that in other areas this was the done thing. Traitors died; they had done so throughout the ages and there was no reason why they shouldn't now. It was only the white man and his stupid customs that put a traitor behind bars, where they had to feed and clothe him.

Mandhla hesitated. Chela flashed into his mind. The crowd hushed suddenly, eyeing him suspiciously; his men looked at him uncertainly. The old headman stared back at him, his head held high.

"Well, old man, what do you say?" asked Mandhla, thinking desperately.

"I am loyal to my country. I do not believe that by killing, you will bring us freedom. If I have a brick house, my wives will complain that they cannot keep such a big place clean. If I have a car, I will have to learn to drive, and will likely crash it and injure myself. If I have so many cattle, I will have to employ people to look after them, and then they will not be free. My skin is black; I am of the African bush. Here is my freedom!" He kicked the sand with his toes.

"Will you report us to the security forces?" asked Mandhla, sensing the crowd's impatience.

"If they ask me, I will tell them."

Mandhla admired the old man's courage, but his own men were beginning to look expectantly at him. The headman had signed his own death warrant, and they all knew it. The crowd began to mutter, and the mutter swelled. The faces before him were ugly.

"Let us kill him for you!" demanded one of the crowd, and his suggestion was immediately backed by others. To quiet them, Mandhla raised his AK rifle and fired into the air. Instantly there was silence. He glowered at them, and their eyes dropped away from his.

He looked into the old man's aging eyes, but nothing of Chela's pleading and fear was there. His training came to the fore; he was a Section Commander and he was not going to fluff this. He gestured to his men and they pushed the frail body against a tree; to the last, his eyes stared openly at his executioner.

When it was done the crowd screamed with bloodlust and demanded parts of the body for their muti. Knowing his path was now trodden, Mandhla stood aside for them to hack what they needed from the small, wrinkled heap at the foot of the bloody tree.

After the first, the disciplinary killings came easier. Some writhed in fear, and urinated, and wept. Some, like the headman, took their deaths in their stride – usually the older ones. But when one killing had been taken care of, there was no further trouble with any of the rest of the village.

Chapter 4

Her fingers touched the big bead at her throat, and she felt strangely comforted. Why was she here? Her mind had gone blank, suddenly, completely, and with it the pain had receded. She struggled against the black void, struggled to regain something she knew.
" ... to the dock, and paint the Bally Mena black. Yes, bring the Bally Mena to the dock, and..." There it was. It was all there, all back ...
She longed for it to be finished.

Rhodesia, 1975

The white lights were hot, searing, and made harsh pools on the floor. She looked up into them and screwed her eyes tightly against the blaze, trying to escape the heat, her body wet with perspiration that ran down her sides under the cotton blouse she wore. For a moment she swayed, dizzy; then they were turned off and the darkness and relative coolth swept over her.

"You okay?" Tony, her cameraman. Always concerned for her.

"Fine. January's just too damned hot for this kind of work." She moved towards the studio door.

"You were great tonight," he told her, his voice pleading with her to stay for a moment.

She half turned. "Thanks." Her cool smile moved her wide mouth, and she pulled the heavy sound-proof door open in a smooth movement that experience had taught her. "Don't be late tomorrow – we must leave at eight."

Outside wasn't much better. The stars were huge, bright and close, and even the moon seemed to give off warmth. Her feet crunched lightly across the gravel to the tiny powder-blue Fiat 500 that stood beneath the old oak tree and she paused before unlocking the door, letting her palms rest on the wet metal.

It must have rained while they were filming.

The last of the houses disappeared as the tar road narrowed to a single strip and Bulawayo fell away. The dirt road after that shook and rattled the old Fiat and Tony cuddled his camera protectively on his lap as she drove. There was no breeze to stir the dry grasses or rub the leaves of the thorn trees; the red dust layered the bushes and trees that lined the road. The heat draped heavily over the Rhodesian bundu and the skies were azure and uncompromising. Her hair stuck in strands to her forehead; wet patches stained his armpits and back. She shifted uneasily in the driver's seat, her bottom sticking to the plastic.

They drove in past the black police housing, then through another safety fence past a tiny one-roomed post-office on the left. A dusty blue VW Beetle stood outside in the parking area, which stretched along to the District Commissioner's Offices and was randomly spotted with a red Mini and two Landrovers – one, she noted, with police markings on the door.

It was her eye for detail that made her the best presenter-reporter Overseas American Satellite Television – or OAST – had.

The office boma stood beneath spreading trees, the white buildings grouped around a lush green lawn that was carefully clipped. Crimson cannas leaned against the verandah walls, setting off the red-tiled roof; gay flower beds bordered the several buildings and the orange brick paths between them, presenting a vivid scene in the surrounding dryness. The four buildings were slung in a rough square, dominated by the main office line but all facing inward to a small paved section in the centre where the flagpole stood, the green and white folds hanging limply from the top.

She climbed stiffly out of the little car, looking around

her, drinking in the splashed colours for a brief moment. Then she led Tony inside.

They were expected, of course. The District Commissioner grinned boyishly at them from under horn-rimmed spectacles and shook their hands; behind him two men stood up from the red-seated chairs they had occupied, to be introduced. The Member in Charge of Police here in Ntubu, Jack Greene – he was leaving for another posting in a few days, he explained – and the DC's brother, an army officer – she didn't catch the rank or name, perhaps because she had been for a moment put off-balance by his eyes.

She smiled dutifully and accepted the offer of tea.

While the DC described the Ntubu area to her, and the basic plans they had made for her stay, the men watched her surreptitiously over their teacups, a little intrigued by this contact with a well-known television personality.

The girl was undeniably a looker – even more so off-screen than on. Her clothes were simple and soft – dark slacks and a too-big man's shirt which made her seem cool and somehow enhanced her femininity. The only jewellery she wore was a small chain at her neck. No make-up. Her face was pale under a peachy tan – tired – making the huge, slanting green eyes more noticeable above the bridge of her strong nose. High cheek-bones slanted backwards into heavy honey-blonde hair, interwoven with darker and lighter strands, which shone down nearly to her waist in a French braid from the nape of her long neck.

She looked ridiculously young, thought the DC's brother, to be traipsing about the Rhodesian bush in the middle of a war, relaying information to the world. He noted the mobile lips, the generous mouth, the curve of the neck into the deep dents above the shoulder bones ...

The aquamarine eyes met his suddenly and he realised he'd been staring. He was startled by an expression in them he couldn't define. It was gone an instant later, quickly replaced by grey-green ice. He stared back at her for a moment, then deliberately turned to survey her companion.

The cameraman was definitely the background of the

operation – and he didn't seem to mind. Sandy reddish hair, freckles, fairly short – and doubtless in love with the girl. He allowed himself a cynical twitch at the corner of his mouth, then looked out of the window.

She didn't like being dismissed. She put her teacup down and stood, thanking the DC but suggesting he show them to their quarters. As she turned to leave she took Jack Greene's hand and shook it, then swung towards the brother.

"I'm sorry," she said coolly. "I don't remember your name."

"Kennedy," he replied. "Peter Kennedy."

"Ah, yes. Mr. Kennedy. Goodbye." She smiled distantly and turned her back.

Ouch, he thought. *Touch not the cat.*

They had arranged for Tony to sleep in the men's mess, and for her to sleep in the Female Cadets' mess, presently unoccupied but next door to Mark Kennedy's home. The house was old, but it had a good atmosphere. And, she reasoned, it was only for two or three weeks. Until they had a programme in the can.

She had had to go through various government channels – the red tape, the bureaucratic nonsense that is always implied in such matters – for permission to go through a crash Cadet training course (filmed, of course, by Tony) on a typical, small bush station. The request was highly irregular; there was the Secrets Act to consider ... was she certain no security information would be divulged? And of course Internal Affairs would have to OK the material before it left the country ... and remove anything they didn't like.

In the end, Rebecca Rawlings was sure, only her name – with perhaps some help from face and figure – had secured the necessary authorization.

The bush stations were areas run by Internal Affairs and the Police to administrate Tribal Trust Lands and at the same time keep tabs on infiltrating terrorists. Not, she had been assured by the Provincial Commissioner for Matabeleland, that there were any of those here. Ntubu was a quiet area – untouched by guerilla boots. So far.

Which was why the PC had chosen this site for her shoot. "After all, no-one would be amused if we had a famous TV personality shot at, would they? Ha ha!"

She reflected that he had found his comment funnier than she had.

The Assistant District Commissioner, who would be putting her through the course, was still on leave for a few days, which suited Rebecca fine. It gave her time to get to know Ntubu better.

The heat was constant, a heavy cloak, and on the second day she told Tony to "go soak up the atmosphere" and escaped to the club swimming pool. The clubhouse loomed large behind the pool, a sprawling whitewashed edifice with a high thatched roof. She laid her towel on the grass at the edge of the rather murky water, looked around to confirm her aloneness, then dived in.

She swam several lengths to let the cool seep through her body, revelling in the smooth rush of the water against her skin and the freedom of movement the medium afforded; she twisted and somersaulted, stretching and flexing her muscles luxuriously, and then floated on the surface, looking up into the deep sapphire of the sky.

Sated at last, she turned a final somersault and then pulled herself up the steel ladder. She dabbed her face dry, breathing into the towel and feeling the glow on her skin. Drawing the cloth down she opened her eyes – and looked directly into a pair of arctic blue ones.

He was leaning casually against the pump house door, watching as she held the towel against her wet body. Her long hair lay wet and thick between her shoulder blades, still in the braid that held it back each day. He approved of the way she moved with the grace of a model, conveying an unconscious sensuality in the tiny waist, the flat stomach and strong hips and thighs, the jutting breasts.

Her dark-lashed eyes were wide and flashed briefly with the same look he had noticed the previous morning. It irritated him that he couldn't identify it.

He spoke to break the silence. "You looked as though you were making love to the water. Ardent. A water-nymph indulging her passion."

"Did you want something?" she asked coldly.

"Are you offering?"

It was slightly contemptuous and she flinched minutely. "Excuse me." She turned to leave.

"Miss Rawlings – if you're at the club tonight, I'll buy you a drink."

"I don't drink. But thank you all the same." She wondered why she detested this man so much – and why he was so disdainful of her. She must remember to ask Tony what he thought of the tall Rhodesian. She swung away and he watched her bare back as she went.

Mark Kennedy and his wife stopped off for her on their way to the club that evening. "After all," he said heartily, "you're here to present a holistic picture of bush life, and you can't do that without a visit to the pub!" Briefly, she wondered whether his brother had put him up to it.

Tony was there already, his camera on the bar next to him. Rebecca wondered whether he slept with it – before she was distracted again by the ice-blue eyes that watched them enter.

They sat with him, of course. "My brother's here on leave," Mark told her. "Army's pushing him too hard – eh, Peter?" The DC laughed heartily; perhaps too heartily. A tiny frown flitted across Peter Kennedy's face and was gone. Rebecca's reporting instincts were aroused immediately.

"What unit did you say you were in?" she asked him casually.

"I didn't." He turned away abruptly and ordered another drink for himself, and another for her without checking.

She stood up, annoyed for the first time in her career at the rebuff, and at the unrequested order. "I'm real tired," she said to the DC by way of explanation. "Goodnight." She moved towards the door.

He was beside her almost immediately. "I'll walk you home." It was a statement, not an offer. Without waiting for a reply he steered her through the door, ignoring her cool reception as they stepped out into the night.

The sand on the road was soft and Rebecca took off her shoes, digging her toes into the cool dirt. The night air was pure and in the distance they heard the faint sound of thunder. The stars were only visible now and then through the shifting cloud overhead and the breeze pushed the cotton skirt close against her bare legs. The crickets trilled an endless night song and the leaves and grasses twisted restlessly, impatient for the rain.

"I didn't need an escort," she remarked into his silence.

"I don't know what you've been told, Miss Rawlings, but this country is at war. Ntubu has escaped the brunt thus far – that's no guarantee that it will continue to do so. I thought that was why you were here."

She smarted, feeling the rebuke. On the doorstep of the old house she bid him goodnight, unwilling to thank him for his courtesy. She made herself a mug of cocoa from the stocked pantry and went to bed, to restless dreams.

The rain came that night. She woke to the sound of it drumming on the roof, and the scent of wet earth outside. She flung up the window and leaned out into the dark, holding out her arms to feel the heavy drops on her bare skin. On impulse, pulling on a cotton gown, she ran out into the night and stood in the wet grass. She threw her arms up and lifted her face into the downpour, whirling into a dance on the newly-cut lawn, her loose hair rippling in the wind. Her open mouth caught the drops as they fell and she laughed and spluttered. The sodden gown clung to her wet body and she might as well have been without it.

She sank at last into a heap on the grass, panting, and immediately saw a shadow beneath a tree at the bottom of the garden detach itself and glide through the gate to disappear. She sat, motionless, for a full minute before she breathed again. Suddenly realising how cold she was, she crept back into the house.

In the light of day her fears seemed ridiculous, but she knew she had to tell somebody. She approached Mark.

"Shouldn't think it was anything at all," he reassured her mildly. "We aren't a hot area, you know, and I doubt a terr could have got inside the perimeter without someone knowing about it."

She was suddenly aware of Peter Kennedy standing

at the door of the office, watching them coolly. "No," she agreed hurriedly, "you're probably right. My imagination, I suppose ... the rain ... Thank you." She tried to leave but Peter was in the doorway.

"What were you doing out in the rain, anyway?" he asked, almost disinterestedly.

"I wasn't in the rain. I was on the porch," she lied. Gathering herself, she moved past him. He stood aside then, the corner of his mouth lifted in a sardonic twist she was coming to recognise.

It began to rain almost every afternoon, from lunch-time until late evening and often during the night, too. The rains cooled the air only very slightly, and damped down the dust somewhat, but the side effects were that the roads were turned into mud and filming time was limited. Rebecca avoided the club in the evenings, saying she was researching the programme. Tony shrugged, and played squash with her during the rainy afternoons to pass the time.

Alan, the Assistant District Commissioner, returned from leave, and her training began. He was a big man, a mountain, with reddish-blonde hair that grew in profusion over his arms but with less enthusiasm on the top of his head, and a smile that made you feel you'd known him all your life. Tony filmed while Rebecca learned to inspect the parade of black District Assistants every morning; after inspection the flag was raised, all the DAs standing stiffly to attention, and then they were dismissed. There was no real purpose in the exercise as far as Rebecca could see, but they seemed to enjoy the showiness of it, and it was a tradition. In the evening they lined up again, prompt and poker-faced, for the lowering of the flag.

The DAs were an essential part of the District work, Alan explained. They did a great variety of tasks, from keeping the births and deaths records as straight as was possible under the circumstances, to accompanying Cadets out on "platform duty" to gather information from the local villagers and to hand out advice to them. No-one could explain to her why this was called "platform"; it just was.

But most importantly, the DAs were a vital link with

the goings-on in the district. Things the DC would never have heard or been told without them came to his notice; some of them (this information strictly not for use in her programme) were Ground Cover men – GC – who were, in effect, "spies" among the local population. If anything serious came up, word got back through these men, whose presence was never announced and who never reported in uniform. The GC force were faceless, nameless men who rendered an invaluable service to the government and their people, and without whom a great many more lives would have been lost in the war.

Rebecca wasn't sure she approved of this "spy" system, but she was professional enough not to say so.

Alan taught her about the Sindebele people in the district – their ways, their customs, likes and dislikes. He primed her in the way to behave when amongst the locals, the proper terms of respect (which her American tongue had some difficulty with), the motions to be gone through. She followed him as he walked and talked, absorbed, scarcely aware of Tony and his camera.

"Remember," Alan warned her, "that they have their pride. Respect their ways and they'll respect yours. And try to understand them. Their beliefs are different from ours. What upsets or motivates them might mean nothing to us, and things we consider important are often trivial to them.

"For the most part their customs have been incorporated into our laws, except for the crueller ones. The sticky bits come when witchcraft is involved – especially trial by ordeal. Our laws are strictly against it, but to the black man it's the ultimate courtroom. It's usually used to prove or disprove a witch or a thief, or liar – often with poison. The accused drinks a concoction the witchdoctor dreams up, and depending on his luck with respect to the poison content, either lives or dies. If he lives he's considered innocent – if he dies, guilty.

"There are other ways. Pulling a stone out of boiling water without getting burnt, or licking a red-hot adze or hoe. Amazingly, sometimes they do come away unhurt, which we can't explain but they feel they can. So don't ridicule their witchcraft stories and ideas – a lot happens that we find hard to credit.

"Their manners are important, too. If a native doesn't get up when you walk into a room, that's because his mark of respect is to squat in front of a superior. When he walks into a room and promptly sits, it's for the same reason.

"If you have to hand something to a black man, use your right hand – that's the one that's used for clean tasks. The left is for dirty tasks, so don't insult him by giving him anything with that hand, or receiving with it. And when he holds out both his hands to take an object, he's showing that he considers it so big and generous a gift that he needs both hands to hold it. Don't accept anything from him with only one hand – it belittles what he's giving.

"Don't expect a straight answer. He'll tell you what he thinks you want to know, because it's extremely bad manners to disappoint someone unnecessarily. He'll exaggerate a calamity so that you're relieved when you find it's not that bad; he'll understate distance and time so that you're not downhearted at the prospect.

"The black man walks ahead of his woman, with her carrying the loads, so that if danger strikes he is ready to protect her without having to dump what he's carrying first. We probably did it the same way, once, before 'civilisation'. You'd also insult him if you entered a room first, assuming responsibility for lurking dangers when he should be protecting you."

And so on. For Rebecca, born in a tiny fishing village on the north coast of California, arriving in Africa for the first time three weeks previously, this was a whole new lifestyle, and as always when becoming involved in a production, she threw herself into it with abandon.

They went out with Alan to a meeting with a local chieftain. The Landrover bumped over the dusty tracks for an hour before they stopped in front of a small clutch of mud huts. An old patriarch, with a retinue of three only slightly younger men, came out to meet them, clapping his palms together and bowing his head in greeting. He wore a colourful skullcap, and apart from a fascination with her long hair ("like the wax of bees, with honey inside," he commented later to Alan) ignored Rebecca completely.

He would not allow the meeting to be filmed; he had a suspicion of technology, but since Alan had warned her –

"He may be afraid that the camera will swallow up part of his soul" – she was ready for this, and she and Tony spent the time shooting the surroundings and talking to the young children who came to stare and point at her plaited hair. On impulse, she loosened it to fly free for them, and the children gasped and shrieked with delight; when she braided it again her own fingers were helped by myriad others, and she knew the result was anything but neat. She didn't mind one bit.

On the way home, they stopped at a small shop to buy cold-drinks, and Rebecca was amazed at the conglomeration of wares that had been squeezed into the tiny room. The predominant smell was of sweets – mints and candy peaches and suckers and bullseyes; black balls and liquorice and the soft, brightly-coloured squares that the children loved. An ancient refrigerator rattled in a corner, but the drinks were icy cold from it, and while Alan paid Tony took shots of razorblades, aspirins, hairpins, combs, plastic jewellery, hats, shoes, materials, kitchen cloths, soaps, washing powder, sugar, flour, mealie-meal, salt, cheap toys and a host of other things that crammed the shelves, piled heedlessly next to and on top of each other on the wooden planks and concrete floor. Small black children with naked torsos and rags tied round their waists like belts smiled eagerly at them, holding out pudgy hands; Rebecca gave them sweets and reflected that all the children she had seen so far were the same – the same slightly bloated tummies, the same wide white smiles, the same flies.

That weekend she accepted a lift from one of the Administration women, Patsy, into Salisbury. She had acquaintances there, and for some reason she wanted to get away, although she hadn't seen Peter Kennedy all week. Vaguely, she wondered whether he was avoiding her, too.

The affectionate taunts before they left, and the warnings about her safety in Patsy's car with Patsy at the wheel, she found were unjustified – Patsy drove fast, but well. The weekend refreshed her, yet she had a nagging desire to be back in the bush, back on the job.

On the way back Rebecca slept most of the way, until

they hit the dirt road after QueQue. The jolting woke her and she sat up, pushing truant strands of hair back from her face.

"Didn't think you'd ever come back to life," retorted Patsy. "Heavy night, huh?"

"Kind of." It was easier than a denial.

Patsy was about to speak further when an African man walked out of the bush onto the side of the road and stood there, watching their approach. Patsy stiffened and pulled her small pistol from its holster. "Get the rifle," she said tersely, and Rebecca, slightly bemused, pulled the FN over from the back seat and released the safety catch as Alan had taught her.

The man was waving a piece of white cloth at them, trying to slow them down. As Rebecca opened her mouth to comment that he looked harmless enough, Patsy put her foot down on the accelerator. Suddenly there were three other men with him. Rebecca recognised the banana magazines on the weapons; AK-47s. She heard their rapid-fire rake the air, realised they were trying to kill her, was outraged, and suddenly fighting for her life. She pointed the FN out of the window and held the rapid-fire trigger down, feeling the recoil batter her. Patsy's foot was on the throttle-pedal and she was whooping excitedly, firing her pistol randomly at the group. Then she dropped the pistol and, cursing, drove the car directly at the men, at top speed.

Rebecca wasn't sure, in the confusion of her first fire-fight, exactly where her own bullets went, or where those from the AKs went. She seemed to be firing forever, her eyes screwed tightly shut; the noise was all around them – the shots, Patsy's whooping, the car engine racing, the men shouting ... and over everything, the fear – and the anger.

She didn't know exactly when it stopped. Her ears were ringing, her eyes watering, her gut clenching; but suddenly she realised that the FN wasn't responding any longer, and she was drenched with sweat. Her blouse was sopping wet, warm and sticky, and the rifle was out of ammunition.

Patsy was shrieking and laughing hysterically. "We showed 'em, girl! Who says I can't drive? We showed 'em!"

She turned, her face alight with pride and flushed with success. She stared at Rebecca for a moment. The smile faded and she turned back to the road, pressing her foot to the floor once more.

Puzzled, Rebecca looked down. Her clothes were covered in blood.

It turned out to be only a graze, but it hurt like hell once she knew it was there. The bullet had scraped the skin away below her right breast and ploughed a shallow furrow into the flesh. Mark's secretary, an ex-nursing sister, dabbed and cleaned and dabbed and dried and dabbed and bandaged, and told her she'd be stiff for a few days but that was all.

Peter Kennedy was waiting when she was dressed again. He paced the small office restlessly, seeming too large for the space available. He avoided eye contact, asking short and to-the-point questions in a terse voice, debriefing her military-fashion. He seemed a different person, a stranger, and Rebecca was startled at his hard tack. The questions in her own mind rose again, and when he abruptly dismissed her the anger in his eyes and body language made her almost believe he blamed her personally for the attack. She knew he didn't think a war zone was the place for journalism; he'd already made that loudly clear.

Tony fumed that he hadn't been there to film it all, having to content himself with footage of Rebecca's bandaged midriff and Patsy's pitted car, and the blood on the seat. They both knew that the attack on Rebecca would make for brilliant material, and Tony at once set off for Bulawayo to send off the footage to America.

Patsy was vain about the bullet-holes in her car, the torn seats into which some of Rebecca's blood had seeped. She swore at the loss of her pistol, but bathed in the admiration of Ntubu and generally turned the whole event into a personal victory – which, undoubtedly, it was. Ntubu was shaken and proud, and within two days they had word that one body had been recovered and that the three terrorists remaining alive had been caught by a special-ops tracker unit.

And Peter was somehow no longer in Ntubu.

Chapter 5

The rotten leather bag lay on the sand floor of the tree-cave, close to her head. She could see the holes where the skin had worn through. Beside it lay the bird, carved in dark green stone, almost charcoal in the light filtering through the branches above. It was small, perhaps two inches tall, yet the delicate pattern carved into the plinth on which the bird sat was detailed and distinct.
She forced her eyes to focus on the pattern.

Tsimbaboue

Xalise bounced impatiently from foot to foot. They could hear the thin, quavering voice singing across the valley, that had wailed as the girls had gone to the Hill. The families of the girls had gathered where the steps ended; they were waiting, in the silence of tabu. There was a restless movement of anticipation as the ghostly singing died away and footsteps could be heard on the rocky passageway. In silence, one by one, the daughters came from the Hill.

Eagerly, as each girl emerged, the people looked for their own, their eyes fastening on a beloved face. Some did not find whom they were seeking, and their smiles became fixed, as stone, as the last of the girls emerged from the rock face. They did not dare to ask, or call out, or ever mention their daughters again.

Tcana was there, she was there! Xalise danced in her heart, and felt her mother's fingertips tighten on her own short, fat ones, until the pain was almost unbearable. But she knew that her mother had also seen Tcana, and so she didn't mind; she sneaked a look up at her father – up, so far up! – and recognised the embarrassed joy and pride in his eyes, too.

The families pulled back, still in silence, as the girls lined up in a long thread at the bottom of the Hill, facing the people. The royal gong sounded suddenly, padded skins against a sheet of copper, hollow and full over the valley. The new women began to sing, softly at first, and then their voices rose together, soaring with Muali. Xalise shivered with ecstasy, that her sister could sing like that! One day, she would sing that way. One day, she too would return from the Hill, and sing.

When the song was gone, the people hardly noticed. The girls stood silent for a moment, looking upward, up to Muali. And then, slowly, they moved forward, with the dignity befitting a maiden who has come to womanhood.

As Tcana moved away from the Hill, a stone landed at her feet. Her heart leaped. Her first stone! True, not a large one, and ordinary granite, but her first stone! And before she had even changed from her girlhood robe! She looked up to see who had cast it, and her eyes met those of Ncube, the older brother of Niswe. He had done his Bush, his own initiation, three years previously; the boys went to the Bush only when they were sixteen. A man – a true man, casting his stone at her feet!

Tcana lowered her eyes and passed on, avoiding the disappointment in Ncube's face. But the stone had not gone unnoticed. She was the first of the initiates to be courted, to have a man's "heart" thrown at her feet; it was an honour she would not forget.

Niswe jostled against her side as the girls formed a parade, two or three abreast, and descended into the village to pay homage to the King.

"Tcana – why didn't you pick up Ncube's stone?" Her friend was excited and anxious. "I knew he would throw it for you, but I thought…"

"It's too soon, Niswe. And anyway – " the girl was a woman suddenly – "why should I pick up the first?"

Niswe giggled wildly with her; they were delirious, they were happy, alive – they were women. They could choose to accept a man's stone, and thereby his marriage offer, or they could not, whichever suited them. It was the one concession that the women had, their one choice – the man they would or would not marry. After all, if a woman is miserable, who in her home – or those nearby, for that matter – can be happy?

They danced to the massing ground below the magnificent home of the King, which lay on the Small Hill, and there they broke into song again. The King brought his huge bulk, shiny with calf-fat and decorated with his traditional cotton cloak thrown over his shoulders, bull-hides at his loins, a head dress of silver-grey monkey furs standing out around his massive skull, to the entrance in the great stone walling that surrounded his compound, and watched, waving and smiling. His courtiers and family enclosed him, each dressed in expensive foreign silks that had been traded for at some cost; the King traditionally wore only the cotton his people had made for him, to show his unity with them.

When the song was ended the silence fell again, and two-abreast the new women filed upward, upward again, through the gate that they may enter only on this one occasion – inside the stone walls of the King's Royal Kraal. Reverent now, they marched slowly behind their regent as he led them to the Life Fire of the amaTsimbaboue, enclosed in a conical tower that resembled a grain store.

Tcana was awed, not by the flame itself, but by the very wonder of a fire that was kept burning – had burned for as long as even the oldest in the city could remember – to signify the life of the amaTsimbaboue. When this flame was doused, the city would die. It was a simple fact, and one that they all accepted. The Life Fire was kept in the King's Kraal and tended there by servants whose only task in life was this one, to ensure the longevity of the stone-walled city of the House of God.

Tcana breathed deep, deeper than she had ever breathed, and passed on, back toward the gates, out of the entranceway, past the wondrous copper gong, and into the people below.

As she entered for the first time her own hut that her father had built for her next to theirs, Tcana paused to adjust to the dim light. On the bedding was a white square of linen, and on the linen lay a necklet.

Tcana gasped. She picked it up and fingered the leather thong, the calf-skin beads between those of polished wood and stone, but her eyes were drawn to the centre-piece – a large ovulate bead made of smoky blue glass, and decorated with the cross-tailed fish.

Tcana knew it had been wildly expensive; the Traders had had several, and she had been awed by this novelty, a material she had never seen before. The fish design had an oddly magnetic effect on her, and she had gone back each day of the seven that the Traders had remained with them, just to stare at those glass baubles. To have bought one back then, to have spent so much, and to have kept it for this one special occasion, for this gift to welcome his daughter back from the Hill – Tcana's throat closed and her eyes filled. He had known she would return. He had had faith in her.

Her fingertips ran gently over the dents cut into the glass, following the shape of the fish from its rounded nose to the cross at the rear, where the lines flared into the tail. That strange sensation of comfort was there again, and the sense of loss she had felt for the ankle beads was replaced with a curious relief.

Clean and fresh again, washed by her own hands and dressed in her new orange-gold robe (another item her father had only been able to afford because of his position of wealth as a cattle-owner), Tcana tentatively rubbed coloured clay onto her cheeks. She had never worn make-up before and was unsure of herself, her fingers inept.

Then Niswe appeared in the doorway, already completed, in her own new woman's robe, her face daubed beautifully in yellow and ochre. "Let me. I've helped my mother before." She knelt next to Tcana and applied the clay while she spoke, almost nonchalantly. "They're breaking down the huts. I saw four being destroyed, just on my way here."

Tcana was silent for a moment. "They should not have built huts when they had no daughters to dwell in them," she said.

The women had not been idle while their daughters were on the Hill. The feast was huge, and full of delicacies with which to welcome the new women of amaTsimbaboue. Everyone was there, the King and his families seated at the head of the gathering. One thousand people, Tcana marvelled. One thousand people at my womanhood feast!

The beer flowed freely. At first, to Tcana's tongue, it tasted bitter-sweet and sickly, but she got used to the flavour and drank more. The new women were offered the best of everything – the brains of young goats, tongues of calves, eyeballs of oxen.

The animals were roasting over huge fires, a little way away, and meat was brought to Tcana by Xalise, proud and shiny and happy. There were sweet potatoes baked in the coals of the fires, and pumpkins roasted black, and even tiny dried fish, salty and delicious, their shrivelled orange eyes staring blankly.

And afterwards there were the sweets – honeyed seeds rolled into balls; sweetened mealie porridge cooked with shaken eggs and honey; bananas grilled over the fire until their skins were nearly black, with fresh cream from the cows and honeycombs still with the young bees inside the wax.

Sixty-nine girls had returned from the Hill, but of them all, this was Tcana's night. A woman now, her unusual beauty could be acknowledged – and was. Men vied to dance for her; Ncube was first there. Since he had cast the first stone, no-one denied his right.

In the whipping light of the fires he pranced and flung and leaped; his skin shone ebony and bronze and purple and gold as his heels pounded the ground into dust for her, and the sweat poured from him. The drums beat faster and faster, a heady rhythm, and the reed pipes quavered behind them. Tcana watched in fascination as Ncube's own initiation skin, the lion he had slain, fluttered and flapped with his body. Occasionally she caught a glimpse of the long, torn scars on his upper arm, where the great beast had ripped at him before he had killed it with a thrust to the heart of his hunting spear. Her own heart beat more quickly with the tempo from the drums, and the people chanted and clapped encouragement, shouting with glee.

The drums rose to a crescendo, crashing into one long roll, and Ncube threw himself high, high into the night air, his legs kicking wildly, his knees touching his chin, then his heels knocking his back, and when he came down his eyes, proud and haughty, locked with Tcana's, and she was spell-bound for a moment. Then the drums started again, and a stone was cast at her feet – this time, the stone was not granite but a lump of pure iron, and the thrower was the son of one of the rich trading merchants who dealt, distantly, with the people from the East Coast, exchanging gold and ivory for silky cloths and baubles, and salt, and other things. He was tall and not unattractive, but his dance lacked the fire that Ncube's had, and he had no lion's mark on his body. The iron ingot remained at her feet.

There were, indeed, dances and stones for other girls, but none so earnest, nor so many, as for Tcana. And then it was the initiates' turn, and the new young women, in their new women's finery, slowly moved to the centre of the gathering, where they formed a square, facing out to the guests.

The music was soft, lilting, telling of childhood grown to the magic of womanhood. A pipe's notes floated bewitchingly through the still air, and the drummers caressed the tight zebra skins, stroking them lovingly. Tcana began to sway with the other girls and gently a hum rose from them. Their arms were linked, and they stepped slowly sideways, a moving chain. Tcana let her hips slide separate from her torso to undulate with the flute and the girls gradually passed on, watching the faces of their audience, smiling demurely, eyes avoiding direct contact with the men's.

The music beat faster and the maidens moved with it, surging restlessly inward to touch backs, and outward to stretch their arms to the limits, and in again, and they were singing now:

> Look at the maidens of Muali,
> We dance for Muali,
> For he has made us women,
> And his women must dance.
> Watch the women of Tsimbaboue,
> See us dance for the amaTsimbaboue
> For we are your women,
> And your women must dance.

They were clapping, their heels stamping the earth, their lithe bodies wriggling and curving. Tcana looked up from her dusty feet, her face bright with excitement and laughter – and her eyes were trapped.

She realised that she was opposite the Royal party, and the various members of Royalty sat watching her – them. But this one – this one was watching only her.

Mesmerised, her smile faded. She had seen him before, of course, but only from a respectful distance, and one's eyes should never be raised to the level of those of one's superiors – especially those of Royalty. She had admired his thighs, strong beneath the silks or leopard skins. Now she was held by the gaze of his regal eyes.

He was Xhaitaan, one of the King's sons. The King's favourite son.

Niswe, next to her, jostled her to move on, and hastily Tcana withdrew her impertinent eyes, remembering her place. Confused, she moved on with the dancing line, trying to pick up the words of the song once more.

And then, when the girls were finished the young men of the Royal House, Tsimbabouetcang, danced for their people. They were the last to dance, of course, because that way one would remember only their glory, their dancing, as was only right. After all, who could possibly match the King's sons and nephews and cousins – in anything?

The ten young men chosen to entertain the King's people moved to the centre, and Tcana's heart jumped unsteadily when she saw that Xhaitaan was among them. Without hesitation he came to stand in front of her, only a few yards away, staring at her, and when the music began she knew he danced only for her. He danced well – he danced beyond perfection. He put even Ncube, the pride of the amaTsimbaboue, to shame, and Tcana was utterly bewitched.

Her mother saw. And she saw Xhaitaan's mother, who glared at Tcana with a hatred that Lila recognised. Protective to the last, she touched Tcana's arm to distract her.

"Beware Nada," she whispered, without looking at the Royal party.

Tcana stiffened, remembering again her lowly place, and she put her eyes to the ground and kept them there for the remainder of the dance. When the final leap had finished he stood for a moment – she felt him standing before her – but she would not, could not, look up and acknowledge him. After a moment he walked away.

The Royal dance ended the evening and, bloated with good food and beer, and an excess of merriment, the revellers moved homeward. Roro lead his daughter to her new hut, to sleep there, alone for the first time in her life.

There were many stones thrown that season, for Tcana and for others, but mostly for Tcana. She was tall and moved with the grace of a young bushbuck, and her eyes were big and liquid black in her perfectly formed face. Her nose was high, and not flat, and her black skin was tinted with coppery undertones. Her lips were full and inviting, and her glossy hair was always neatly plaited in tight patterns over her head. Her body was well rounded and undulated as she walked, holding secret promises that turned the heads of the men around her. It was fit, and right, that many of the stones thrown for her were iron nodules, some even copper – relatives of Royalty. But Tcana would not stop and pick one up. The one she wanted, she knew, would never be thrown.

The women drew water, and chattered as they washed the clothes and skins in the river, beating them against the rocks to soften and cleanse them. The river was the great leveller, for the wives and daughters of both rich and poor must nonetheless wash their bodies and clothes. Except for the Royalty, who of course had their water brought by servants, and who washed discreetly behind the walls of their stone enclosures that signified their standing in the community.

Summer was drawing to a close, and the chill was beginning to set in the dusk air, when Chisa took the stone.

Chisa was the daughter of one of the poorest families. She was a pretty enough girl, with a bright smile, impish eyes and wicked mischief inside her, and she had an eye for Ncube.

Ncube had intensified his efforts to capture Tcana's heart. He lay in wait for her whenever he was not working – he was a carver and had only a month ago been honoured by being commissioned by the High Priest to make the great stone images of Muali – and because of his new position he was permitted to cast offcuts of the soapstone which was his material.

This he did – every time he could. He knew Tcana's routine and Xalise, who adored him, told him of any other plans her elder sister was making. In return he let her watch him carve, and sometimes gave her tiny slivers of soapstone with which to decorate her mud pots. And so he collected larger pieces of the green rock, and cast them at Tcana's feet wherever she went.

It amused and flattered Tcana, of course, that he should be so persistent. She was beginning to be able to predict just when and where he would suddenly appear before her, and drop the waxy steatite at her feet. She would smile demurely at him and walk on, knowing he was watching her retreating bare back in despair.

Chisa made a friend of Tcana. She followed her and washed clothes with her. Niswe objected, and said so to Tcana, but Tcana just laughed.

"Chisa's no good, Tcana. She doesn't follow you because she likes you, but because this way she can catch a glimpse of my brother, and smile at him."

"Then why doesn't Ncube throw his stone for her? If she's so fond of him, she'll be a good wife."

"Chisa will never be a good wife. She's lazy and selfish. Besides, Ncube wants only you. When, Tcana? When will you accept him?"

Tcana pulled a face at her friend and her thumb ran over the smoky bead that was always at her throat. She stared before her, at nothing. "I don't know, Niswe. I am not ready to settle down. I have a strange restlessness in me that I don't understand. It does not yet include a man."

Niswe looked at her sceptically. "Not even a certain Royal man?"

Tcana's fingers paused on the glass fish, but only for a moment. "All right, I have two kinds of restlessness." She giggled mischievously with her friend, and picked up the water pail – Ncube had carved it specially for her, and it was decorated with the zebra of the plain in full gallop around its sides. "Come on – I am to cook for Mai and Kai today, and Xalise wants to help."

The girls pulled skins over their shoulders – the sun would go soon, and the air was no longer warm. As they set out for the river Chisa appeared, grinning impishly, and took up position behind Tcana.

"I'll draw your water for you today, Tcana. I feel strong today – today, I know, is special. Something will go well for me today – the spirits told me so."

Tcana said nothing. Chisa often spoke of the spirits, but Tcana doubted she had any real communication with her ancestors. She was not reverent enough. They stepped down the river-path together, and as they approached the bend, Tcana began to smile. She knew Ncube would be there.

Niswe stepped out springily in front; she did not approve of Chisa and had no intention of being friendly with the girl. As she rounded the bend she smiled knowingly at her brother, standing in the shadow of a tree. Tcana rounded the corner with Chisa close beside her, and Ncube stepped forward, throwing his largest yet piece of green soapstone at her feet. Again Tcana bobbed her head at him and passed on.

Chisa didn't. She hesitated only a small moment before picking up the stone, her face alight, as though it had been thrown for her. She smiled brilliantly at the astonished Ncube.

"I will be honoured, Ncube," she said.

The world stood still. Chisa had broken one of the highest rules of etiquette! It was obvious the stone had been thrown for Tcana – those around knew it. But Chisa had picked it up. There was a frozen silence as Niswe and Tcana turned to look, along with several others who were on the path. Ncube stared, his face more shocked than those of the watchers. Abruptly, Niswe stepped forward.

"My brother threw his stone for Tcana," she said, and wrenched it from Chisa's grasp – another horrifying breach of etiquette, and Chisa immediately grabbed it back.

"Indeed he did not; if he had, Tcana would have seen, and stopped. Ncube's stone is mine, as is his hearth."

People were gathering, curious, confounded, amazed. Ncube said nothing; he could not, and was afraid that if he did he would hit this she-jackal, and that was forbidden, just as it was forbidden for a man to take back his stone from a woman.

Chisa looked challengingly, triumphantly, at him and held his stone aloft for all to see.

"Ncube is mine and I am his!" she shouted gleefully, and pushing her way through the crowd ran back up the pathway to the village.

Chapter 6

Rhodesia

Peter Kennedy was furious. There had been no warning, no information that terrorists had infiltrated this far. His commanding officer was sympathetic but blunt. "No-one knew they were there, Peter."

"Why the hell not?" he demanded aggressively. "We have a unit specialising in that sort of thing – what the devil are they up to? Why did my unit have to go after them, in someone else's quarter?"

Major Briggs looked at him thoughtfully. "Something personal involved?"

"Of course it's personal – my brother's the DC in the next district along. They shot up an American reporter who was in his charge!"

"Didn't his GC report anything, either?"

"No – I thought the Selous Scouts were supposed to be handling that sort of thing. Who the hell is running that show, anyway?"

The Major coughed. "Actually, no-one right now. Or rather, no-one for the South. He was killed two weeks ago."

It brought him up short. "Sorry." He slumped into a chair. "I'm just tense about the whole thing. Too close for comfort."

Ron Briggs breathed heavily. "Actually, I have some other news for you. You're being transferred – with promotion, of course."

"Transferred?" He was shocked.

"Well – requisitioned, if you like." Briggs was uncomfortable. "To the Scouts, as a matter of fact."

The Selous Scouts. The most secretive unit in Rhodesia. Suddenly he understood, and was even mildly flattered. They were supposed to be the most important tracking force in the army, quite apart from running the main information-gathering section for the security forces.

He was formal suddenly. "No, thank you, Sir. I'm sure I'm doing as good a job here as I could be there."

The major sighed ponderously. "Sorry, Peter. They want you, and no-one else. You're to be second-in-command over all, and commander of the southern portion of the country. And a major, I believe."

It was inconceivable. "What did I do to draw their fire?"

"Dammit, you're the best man we've got," the other man snapped irritably. "D'you think I want to lose you? I have no choice!"

So it was true, then. The Scouts had priority.

Usually," explained the commander-in-chief of the Selous Scouts, "our chaps do a course before they're asked to decide whether they still want to join us or not. That way we get a better idea of whether we really want them, too. But with a senior officer such as yourself, of course, I know your talents and abilities, or I wouldn't have asked for you."

"What exactly happened to my predecessor, Sir, if I may ask?"

Silence. Then: "He got caught in a lie," replied the mild-looking man in front of him enigmatically. Then he looked directly at Peter again. "Of course, the final decision is yours – I don't want men here who are unwilling to do the job."

"This course that the men do – what is it, precisely?"

"It's similar to a training course, but unlike any other you've been on. It has to be, for the Scouts."

"Why, Sir?" he asked directly, and was surprised to see the other man grin spontaneously.

"Because, Kennedy, we do things no other tracker force does. Of course, this discussion is highly confidential."

Peter nodded automatically. It went without saying.

The two watched each other speculatively for a moment.

"Actually, Peter – may I call you Peter? – actually, we run a very highly-trained pseudo-terrorist group."

Peter was too startled to reply. It didn't matter; Perry Fox continued without hesitating. "It's our way of getting behind enemy lines, if you see what I mean. Our chaps go through a terrorist training course, and then they learn every fact about ZANLA and ZIPRA that we can get from captured and turned terrs."

"'Turned' terrs, Sir?" The phrase was new to him, though he had a feeling he knew exactly what it meant, and he didn't like it at all.

Fox smiled indulgently. "That's also top secret, Peter. Try telling your average civilian out there that one of the guys who ambushed a friend of theirs is now fighting with us and we'll have havoc on our hands. We make them an offer they can't refuse, you see. Either they join us, or they go to court and are charged with treason – and hang. It's obvious which they normally choose. Then we immediately put a gun in their hands, to show them we trust them, and we make them betray their comrades, so they know that going back wouldn't be any use. Apart from that, they're astonished to find that with us, they're properly fed and cared for – and paid for their services to boot. We give their families protection, too. Only a fanatical fool would refuse all that for a life of hell in the bush such as they have."

Peter took his point, but it was still incredible. Nonetheless, he knew he was hooked.

"This course, Sir ... I'd need to do it myself. I have to do what the men under me do."

Perry Fox sat back in his chair and smiled smugly. "I knew you would. The training camp's called Wafa Wafa Wasara Wasara ... that's Shona. The first bit means, "I am dead, I am dead." Wasara is a shout of panic and fear. You'll like it there, I think."

Peter's first impression of Inkomo Barracks, where he and the other recruits gathered to await transportation to the training camp, was one of inefficiency. They were given a one-day rat pack and told that it was for "just in case", since food supplies on the course were irregular. Then they were left to their own devices. The day passed and still no-one issued orders, or even fed them. Finally, late that afternoon several lorries pulled into the area and suddenly they were the Military again; they piled their kit – and suitcases of civilian clothing, in many cases, since Kariba was apparently near their destination – into the trucks, and began the long drive.

Just before nightfall, on a deserted stretch of road, the vehicles stopped. Peter guessed they must be near the Kariba airport. They were ordered to disembark, kit, suitcases and all, and told that just over twenty kilometres down the road was the training camp.

"And now, my friends," sang out the Training Officer, "you will please me by running all the way to the camp, carrying everything you have brought with you. If you drop anything, consider it gone forever. It will not be retrieved for you. These two gentlemen – " he indicated two grinning black officers " – will accompany you to ensure that no-one gets left behind." He climbed back into one of the waiting trucks and pulled away.

During the run for Wafa Wafa, several volunteers dropped out along the way from sheer exhaustion in the hot, humid night air. When the remainder finally reached the camp, they almost missed it. It was no more than a stretch of bush with a few grass bashas – their accommodation – and another area where the remains of three fires lay blackly in the trodden grass.

They were informed that there would be no food that night, or for the next week, except what they might "create" for themselves. Immediately several more of the recruits, who'd been expecting barracks and a meal awaiting them, refused to continue the course. Already the selection process was in action.

At dawn the following few mornings, the remaining trainees were made to go running or do physical exercises until 0700, followed by a muster and then general training – particularly in weapons. They eked out their rat packs and foraged for berries or roots, or trapped small animals in the few moments of free time they had. And then, on the third day, one of the instructors shot a baboon.

The creature was hung in a tree where everyone might see it, and in the heat of the Zambezi valley the carcass very soon began to smell. Two days later it was cut down amid a stench that was almost unbearable; it was skinned and cleaned, and well stewed, along with several other pieces of meat which had been treated similarly and which now crawled with maggots.

Starving, exhausted, despondent, not one of them turned their nose up at the meal that evening. They had been taught that botulism, the fatal food poisoning, only sets in on re-heating, and this precious lesson would serve them well in the bush. It could even save their lives.

They were issued minimal quantities of food; for the rest they survived off the bush and their own initiative, though they were not permitted to shoot game. During those weeks they were given nothing but their rifles and water bottles, and sent into the bush to learn to survive. They ate whatever they could find, including the eyeballs and raw innards of kudu, and the flesh of baboon, snakes and scorpions. Fresh red meat was preserved by smoking, so that it would last them up to three weeks.

When they could not find fresh water, they squeezed the grassy lumps from inside a buck's stomach – the greenish fluid that resulted tasted strange, but was safe to drink. A kudu's stomach, they learned, contains about three gallons of water; an elephant's, thirty. The stomach bag was also used as a water-bag. It lasted between five and eight days as such, and when they needed thread they used the membrane from a buck's stomach, which was far more durable than ordinary cotton.

They did not wash, or brush their teeth – toothpaste is a dead giveaway to the sensitive nostrils of a terrorist. They were taught to take the bush upon themselves; to become part of it – in effect, to be the bush. The pressure was never let up. Constantly they were kept in the dark, and one by one their numbers diminished as those who could not take the treatment gave up.

And then there was the march.

They were split into small groups. Peter's consisted of six men, including an instructor who was there to observe them. They were issued with packs loaded with brightly painted green rocks – thirty kilograms worth – and normal stocks of ammunition, bringing the load up to nearly forty kilograms in total. And then they began the ninety-kilometre walk, over the rugged terrain of hills and rocks, through the vicious heat of the Zambezi valley, with little water to be found and less than a day's worth of food, and tsetse flies and mosquitos to contend with. And still, some did not give up.

On the third day a vehicle arrived and relieved them of their rocks, issuing them instead with a sandbag each, after which they were made to run back to Wafa Wafa. Dazed, almost at the point of collapse, Peter found himself back in camp in just over two hours. With him were the two others in his group who had not yet thrown in the towel; both were black, one enormous. As they slowed to a halt, approaching their bashas, an instructor appeared before them to take away the sandbags.

"Well done," he said. "It's over. Welcome to the Scouts."

Another trick, thought Peter, his mind dazed with weariness. Psychologically, the training officers had used everything in the book – and a great deal not – to force the volunteers to give in, pushing and pushing them to the edge and beyond, knowing that those who stood up to them and completed the course in spite of them were the calibre of men the Selous Scouts needed.

"Leave us alone, Mampara!" moaned the smaller of the two black men with him. "We aren't giving up. Go away!"

The instructor laughed. "They all say that. No-one believes me. But it really is over. Go and rest."

Peter glared angrily at him, willing his mind not to accept the suggestion. If he did, he was lost. He swayed on his feet, and the instructor reached out a hand to support him. Sullen, Peter pulled away from him.

"I've managed without you this far. What's next?"

The man's voice was gentle suddenly. "Bed."

He didn't know how long he slept. Vaguely he dreamed, of a pair of long, aqua-green eyes that flashed with something now and then – pain? In his sleep he shook his head to dispel the images, distantly recognising annoyance at her intrusion on his privacy.

When he awoke, the huge Ndebele who had come in with him was sitting up beside him, sewing a rent in his shirt. He looked at Peter, expressionless. "I am Kuru," he said. They had not been permitted to introduce themselves this far, or to know the ranks of their colleagues.

"Peter Kennedy. What the hell's going on? Why weren't we woken for training?"

Kuru grinned widely. "For once the man was telling the truth. It is over. We rest."

Peter sat up, disbelieving. "And then?"

"Then – more training, but not physical."

Peter looked around and did a headcount of the still-sleeping men around them. Of those who had begun the selection course with them, only ten percent remained.

One of the first things Peter noted was that roughly four out of every five Scouts were black. The reason for this became clear when the "dark phase" of the training began.

They were based in a camp set out exactly like a typical terrorist training camp, and many of the instructors were "tame" – terrs who had, as Perry Fox had explained, been "turned".

And now Peter Kennedy was taught to be a ZIPRA terrorist.

The white trainees had a more difficult job than the black; they had to learn to walk and talk like the Africans (no-one who could not speak fluent Ndebele or Shona even got as far as Wafa Wafa), even to think like them. There were things they could not change, of course – the shape of their heads and bodies. But they all grew beards which, when dyed in conjunction with the blackening agents they used on their skins, broke up the European features of the face. The blacking, of course, had to cover their whole bodies, and was hell to remove; before going home the Scouts would scrub and scrub until their flesh burned, and still the creases retained the grime.

And then they went through what amounted to the training the terrorists themselves had received. Peter began to appreciate the full impact of the brainwashing the "freedom fighters" went through. He learned several words of Russian, since he was to be based in Matabeleland and would sooner or later have to pass as ZIPRA. He structured himself on Kuru, watching him constantly, copying his movements, the inflections in the way he spoke, his habits. And when he acted "white", Kuru corrected him. They understood each other, somehow.

In a quiet moment Kuru told him a brief history of his life. He had been brought up at Elliott's Mission – a co-incidence that struck Peter forcibly. Kuru and his baby brother had been taken there after their mother had died. He had left there eight years previously to take up his own plot of land, to begin his own farm and family. Four years later his wife died in childbirth, and he had left the land.

He joined the security forces, more because he was at a loss for something to do than out of loyalty to the Rhodesian government, but the army was quick to realise his potential and he was transferred to a tracking unit. The more he saw of terrorist destruction and wanton killings, the closer grew his ties to the army he came to love, and the fiercer his determination to advance in his chosen profession.

He was contacted shortly after Elliott's Mission had been hit; he had not hesitated to undergo the necessary selection course in order to join one of the most prestigious units available to him – the Selous Scouts. His younger brother had been abducted from the Mission when the Elliott's were killed. Kuru Ndhlovu was determined to find him.

Chapter 7

Zambia

The light of the small fire eddied on the ancient face above it, revealing the pale grey pigmentation where there should have been healthy black. The flat, wrinkled dugs clung to the thin ribs; the cracked lips opened to reveal black gaps and rotting teeth, and the folds in the thin cheeks deepened with the wheezy cackle that floated over the sounds of the flames.

The big man squatting opposite her shivered involuntarily. He was sweating, and the salty liquid stained his clothing with the smell of fear. His breath came shorter – there was no efficient air vent to take out the smoke from this cave. He shifted his weight to his fat buttocks, sitting in the dirt. The eyes, so big and bright – unnaturally so in the tiny squashed-leather face – watched him derisively for a moment, then while he looked away the withered hand flung a powder into the flames. Immediately they flashed upward, blue suddenly, and a sulphuric smell filled the rocks. The heavy flesh on the man shook like thick jelly and he covered his face.

"Mwari is good. Mwari is kind. Mwari is beautiful," crooned the witch. "Mwari is good. Mwari is kind. Mwari is beautiful. More beautiful than honey, more precious than gold, and swifter than the lightning." She sang on, softly, and the man was becoming hypnotised as she swayed rhythmically behind the leaping flames.

"Rhaba –" He tried to speak, but his tongue was thick, and her singing went on. As she swayed her body seemed to become thinner, longer ... the whites of her eyes became silver rims and her tongue ...

When he woke the fire was low and early grey daylight seeped from the entrance of the cave. The hag was stirring a black spider-pot that straddled its long legs over the embers and sent forth a bubbling smell of sadza, corn-porridge. As he watched she ladled some into a wooden bowl, sprinkled crumbled honey-crystals over it and offered it to him.

While he ate she spoke. "There is an enemy, and a friend. The enemy seeks to destroy your people; to lead his army against yours. He is powerful, and more clever than those that have gone before. The friend will work for you, and later for Mwari himself. He is among the ranks of your men. Find him out. Use him well."

"How shall I know this friend?" The porridge was sweet and hot, and the words mumbled.

"You know him already. He carries the names of power, and of Mwari's Rhaba. You will find him out."

"How will I know my enemy?"

"You will know him. He bears the crest of the Eagle."

The atmosphere was jubilant. Mandhla had led his remaining men back safely through the bush and into Zambia, back to the main base where they had been trained. The fools who had messed up the ambush he had deserted immediately; for all Mandhla knew, they were dead. It didn't matter. The important thing was that a hit had been made where the Rhodesians had least expected it. The Russians congratulated his genius in getting in so far without detection. QueQue was almost in the centre of Rhodesia. Of course, security would now be stepped up even more, which was unfortunate, but no doubt the Rhodesians were smarting from the insult.

It was worthy of a beer-drink. The women served food and camp-brewed beer, the way the men liked it, and in the middle of the feastings they received an unexpected visitor. The Russians greeted him warmly, and found a place for his bulk at the table, explaining the festivities to him. He was delighted, and demanded to meet the Section

Commander responsible. Mandhla stood tall before him, and he had to look up to meet the young SC's eyes.

"This is Mandhla," introduced the bearded Russian. "Our new secret weapon!" Dutifully, those around him laughed.

"Mandhla? I hope you are as powerful as your name suggests. Have you not been given a combat name yet?" The fat man spoke directly to the youth.

"A few, Sir. None have remained."

The heavy head nodded. "Then what is your clan-name?"

Mandhla hesitated. Clan-names were used even less frequently than first names, but the Russian nodded at him.

"Ndhlovu, Sir."

"Then, Mr. Ndhlovu, I am pleased to meet you." He was about to sit again, to eat more, when it struck him, and he turned back to the boy-man, his skin crawling. "Mandhla Ndhlovu?"

"Yes, Sir."

The shiny black triple-chin nodded slowly, and then dismissed him to return to the feasting.

The house in a suburb of Lusaka was big, but not a mansion. The gardens were well kept, the hedges trimmed neatly, and once inside there was no visibility to the outside and vice versa. There were no armed guards as such – no reason for them in the capital of Zambia – but inside two men were with him all of the time. They were Sindebele, as he was, but they did not speak to him except to tell him which room to enter. Here they left him.

The room was big, and inside the walls were covered in photographs and paintings of snakes – mambas, in positions of rest and defence. But the most striking ornament was a gold snake that climbed a thick staff beside the heavy oak desk. When he looked more closely he realised that the staff was carved with the desk, and in fact a part of it.

Alone for the moment, he moved from one picture to the next, examining the snakes. Beneath a particularly beautiful one was a copper plaque that bore words. It appeared to be a poem, or a song. As he bent to read it the door opened, and Mandhla snapped upright to salute.

The huge man smiled and waved his arm down. "There is no need for that here." He settled himself in the wide chair and gestured for Mandhla to sit opposite. "I have decided upon a bush name for you," he stated. "And this one will remain forever."

Mandhla's eyebrows raised slightly. It was impossible to believe he had been called to Lusaka simply to be given a nom-de-guerre. He waited, and his host sighed heavily in satisfaction.

"Yes, indeed ... You are the Mamba," he said.

Chapter 8

Time was passing. She could tell by the movement of the shadows of the baobab's branches, cast onto the white sand floor. She imagined she could see every minute, grain by grain, as the shadows silently advanced. The one she was watching finally touched the shiny black wood of the bangle, so similar to the amulet on her arm, but made for the tail to encircle the wrist and the body and flat head to rear up along the forearm. She knew, because he had forced it on over her left hand, but she had managed to drag it off again. That was when he had hit her for the first time. Now it lay a short distance from the green soapstone eagle, and the two glared balefully at each other across the gritty floor.

Rhodesia

She saw him on the lawn in front of the boma, just before work started. His age was indeterminable; he kept his eyes cast down and shuffled his feet. His clothes hung on his thin frame, torn here and there, and dusty; his face was begrimed and weary. When she greeted, him he smiled ingratiatingly at her and shuffled again.

"Missy, I come see about court. I talk to Meestah Erkhouse, yes?"

Alan ran the small courtroom and was always being asked for by plaintiffs or defendants. She smiled encouragingly at him. "I'll find him for you."

He was in his office. Rebecca delivered the message and followed him outside, but he turned to her when he had greeted the man. "Sorry Rebecca, this one's nothing newsworthy. Would you mind finding out from Aletta when exactly the cattle sales start again? Thanks."

She left them to it, Alan speaking easily in Ndebele with the diffident visitor. For some reason she felt uneasy about the incident, but shook it off. *Sometimes your newshound nose overdoes it,* she scolded herself.

Nevertheless, she wasn't surprised when Tony came to her a few minutes later, hopping with excitement. "This is it, Rebecca. Terrs – three of them – at one of the kraals nearby. Where do we go from here?"

"Exactly nowhere." Alan spoke sharply from behind them. "How did you find out?"

"Patsy was telling Aletta..." Tony trailed off at the anger in Alan's eyes.

"Why shouldn't we know?" demanded Rebecca. "That's what we're here for – to cover anything that happens."

"The more people who know, the easier for the terrs to find out they've been spotted. Walls – and trees – have ears, you know." He indicated a queue of elderly natives waiting to collect their pensions from the offices.

Rebecca lowered her voice. "Well, now that we do know – what's happening about it?"

"The police are handling it. Alone. Early tomorrow morning."

"Do I detect a note of disapproval?"

He was reluctant. "They aren't even taking our GC man with them to show them the way. The new Member in Charge's idea. I suppose he wants to prove himself in his new district. Not wise."

Rebecca looked thoughtful. "The man who came this morning...?"

"I've told you enough," he said abruptly. "Subject closed. You'll know more tomorrow." He turned on his heel and left them staring after him.

"Tony," she began. "What do you think of us trying –"

"Uh-uh, sweetie-pie. Not on your nelly. We could foul the whole thing up and be thrown out without any story at all. And we promised to obey the rules while here. It's not worth my job."

She sighed wistfully. "I guess you're right."

She wondered briefly how Peter Kennedy would have dealt with the situation. The man repelled, yet intrigued her. She wanted to know more.

She tried Mark Kennedy. Always happy to chat with her, her offered her tea which she accepted for the sake of the information. After some small talk she asked him about himself and how he had become involved in his job.

"It's an option when a man reaches call-up age. He can choose to do his service in the police or Internal Affairs if he doesn't want to go into the army. I liked it, so I stayed on."

"What about Peter? He joined the army, didn't he?"

Something closed suddenly. "Yes." It was terse and didn't invite her to go on; she couldn't resist.

"He never told me what unit he was in. What does he do?"

"He's a tracker, in a tracking outfit. That's all. He doesn't like to talk about himself, and is even less happy to talk about his job."

"Even to his brother?" she asked craftily.

"Well ... he tells me a certain amount of things, but not much. Secrets Act, and all that." He was uncomfortable with the subject.

"Okay, I won't ask any more about his job. Is he married?" The question was direct and surprised him.

"No." He grinned suddenly. "Why – are you interested?"

"No. I was merely wondering how his wife put up with his rudeness."

He was defensive. "He isn't rude. He just doesn't know what to say to women. He spends so much time in the bush that he hasn't time to learn the civilities. And to be quite honest, I think he has earned the right to behave in whatever way he pleases when relaxing."

"Absolutely! I'm sure he has," she said hastily. "Enough of your brother. Let's talk about you."

That was a subject that flowed a whole lot more easily.

The next morning they were all at the boma early. There was no work done; they sat around drinking coffee and waiting for news. Tony shuffled his camera back and forth, checking and rechecking lighting, zoom, and anything else he could fiddle with. Mark was restive, pacing the offices, his head low between bunched shoulders, boney hands gripped behind his back.

When a police Landrover finally drew up, reluctant and hesitant, everyone stood on the verandah and stamped impatiently while Carl, one of the local police, climbed out and dusted off his hat. Tony raised his camera, but something about the policeman's bearing made Rebecca stop the filming. Carl walked slowly towards the DC, eyes on the ground. The tension climbed; the news must be bad. There was silence until the policeman stopped in front of the verandah and raised his face to the man on the steps.

"Well?" asked Mark, impatient.

"Sir. I regret to inform you that our MIC screwed up. He led us to the wrong kraal."

There was a disbelieving quiet.

"The wrong kraal?" repeated Mark slowly.

"Yes Sir." His face became purple. "The people there told us which was the right one, but we got there too late. They left before dawn."

"Do I understand there was no contact?" asked Mark, the skin over his cheeks stretched taut.

"Yes, Sir, that is what I am saying." His eyes sought the ground again. "I'm sorry, Sir," he said miserably.

Japie, the gangly workshops manager and Aletta's husband, stepped forward. "Come on, man. You need a cup of coffee." He looked belligerently around him, but no-one stood in their way as they entered Aletta's office and the tea duty DA appeared magically with coffee.

"Well," said Patsy into the silence. "At least no-one was hurt."

Wryly, Rebecca had to admit she had a point.

The cattle sales were held every few months; the buyers came from Salisbury, Gwelo and Bulawayo, representatives of the abattoirs and meat-packing factories. They arrived with overnight bags and ensconced themselves in the Police Mess.

Tony and Rebecca drove with Alan. At the sales pens they were introduced to the Veterinary Officer, whose job it was to check the health of the cattle being sold and to issue papers for their movement. Rebecca liked him instinctively, although the clear blue eyes appraising her frankly put her uncomfortably in mind of another, only slightly lighter, pair. She thrust the thought from her mind.

"Do you know anything about cattle?" he wanted to know, as the camera began to roll.

"Fish, yes. Cattle, no," she laughed.

"Oh, you fish?" he asked eagerly.

"Not often. Not for a while now. You?"

Tony coughed impatiently. "Do I stop rolling, or what?"

"Sorry – digressing. Tell me about the cattle," she smiled.

"Well, come on – you can help me with the final checks before the sale starts."

She followed him as he ducked under the wooden rails of the outer pen, and watched while he checked over the last of the cattle. He turned to find her eyes on the one shirt sleeve that flapped in spite of being pinned up.

"Don't let it worry you," he said easily, waving the stump of his arm at her. "It doesn't bother me."

"What happened?"

"A bull I was working on didn't like the idea of being conned. Have you ever seen anyone gather semen for artificial insemination?" She shook her head, fascinated, and Tony caught on film the sunlight in her plait as it swayed. "We use a cow to excite the bull, and as he mounts her we waylay his penis and slip it into a long black tube. Sounds easy, but believe me, a bull is no featherweight and if he puts a hoof on your foot he's not going to remove it until he's finished. A friend of mine lost his foot that way several years ago."

Rebecca winced. "Don't the bulls realise they've been duped?"

"Funnily enough, most of them don't know the difference, but this one did. He turned on me and I didn't move quickly enough. My fault. I should have been ready for him." Ruefully he pulled his shirt up to display the enormous scars crossing his torso. "They couldn't save my arm, but they kept my insides going."

The VO taught her to grade the cattle, so that she understood the finer points of the sales; she sat with Alan while he called, and helped shove the beasts into the ring using the electric cattle-prodder, and joked with the buyers over a sandwich lunch in the sticky heat of noon. Tony remarked that they could make a whole series on Rhodesia's Internal Affairs Department with the footage he was collecting, and she began to seriously consider it.

The sales were over too quickly for her. The smell of cowhide, the dust, the movement, the lowing of the cattle, all aroused some instinctive reaction in her, a longing to revisit her uncle's ranch back in California. She wondered briefly how long it would be before she could.

Rebecca tackled Mark once more about his brother before they left Ntubu, determined to uncover the mystery, but if anything Mark was more closed off than before on the subject.

"He's a major in the army. That's all." He moved to the window of his office, looking out over the lawn. "Why's it so important?"

"It isn't. At least, I didn't think it was, until everyone started balking. Why can't you tell me what unit he's with?"

"Because I'm not sure," he finally admitted. "He was transferred recently. Hasn't told me where to. Why not speak to him?"

Rebecca shrank at the thought of questioning those cold blue eyes. "No," she said hurriedly. "You're right. It's not important."

Back in Bulawayo she spent the next two weeks at the studios editing the programme, which was being bought by the local television network as well as going overseas. When she'd finished she knew she had a hit. Her producer in America thought so, too.

"I've had a fantastic idea," he enthused across the Atlantic. "Why don't we send you out to some more of the bush stations? I mean, maybe we could make you a kind of Forces Reporter – know what I mean? Stories centered around various sections of the Security Forces!"

The idea had merit. And when she showed the programme to the top-level government executives, they thought so too. It was about time they had some truth shown in the media overseas. So far all the publicity this war was getting had been extremely one-sided. Rebecca was granted special permission to investigate wherever she wanted, providing the relevant commanding officers were amenable to the idea, and provided that all material be endorsed by the government before release.

She had her commission.

She tracked Peter Kennedy down easily enough, through a contact in the army who happened to know a Major Briggs, who had once spoken to him about the best man in his outfit – one Peter Kennedy. Rebecca called Major Briggs.

"He's not with us any longer, I'm afraid. He's been transferred," he told her.

"I heard that. Where is he now?"

"Well, he's a major with another tracking unit. The Selous Scouts. Similar to our own." The words came easily, and she was disappointed. No mystery after all, she mused. "Would you like me to contact him for you?" he offered. "Might be a bit hard from your end – he's out a lot."

"No – no thank you. I was just ... curious. Are you sure the Selous Scouts are just another tracking unit?"

"Well – they gather information as well and feed it back to everyone else. We all do, actually. Is that what you wanted to know?"

"Yes, I suppose so. Thank you for your help."

No story. Que sera, sera.

She hung up the phone, and began to wonder what other secret Peter Kennedy's life hid. Somehow, she knew there was something more that no-one was telling.

The Selous Scouts – to the terrorists the Skuzapo; literally, "excuse me here" – a term used by a thief to divert your attention while his friend slips your wallet from your pocket.

They infiltrated terrorist areas, made contact with terrorist groups, gained their confidence with bits of the latest information gleaned from captured terrorists, and then called in the Fireforces – heliborne troops called in on a position by radio to attack and destroy, while at the same time keeping the cover of the Scouts group intact with the local people so they could continue to operate there.

Peter, as second-in-command of this highly confidential group, went out rarely. He did more organising and planning than actual fighting; the terrorists in Matabeleland were still too few to warrant it. In any case, his eyes were a problem. They were too blue to pass, even at small distances, for African unless he kept them almost closed. He had a dark pair of clear contact lenses but they hurt his eyes and close up didn't look like the real thing. But when he did insist on joining a group, he always went with Kuru. They trusted each other.

They went out together for the fourth time when it was reported that a new group was on its way into Southern Matabeleland. The report, cryptically, stated that this one was different.

Peter took a stick of ten men with him, eight of them black. They moved towards Plumtree, stopping at various villages for food and to spread the rumours that they were on their way back to Zambia after a highly successful raid, during which they had attacked three farms, killing seven whites. At first they were received with suspicion by the villagers; they had been well indoctrinated against possible overtures from the Skuzapo. But gradually, as the men told their delighted tales of precisely what they had done to the bodies of the hated whites, they gained acceptance, and little by little became aware of another group in the area.

The leader of this new group was indeed "different". Code-named the Mamba, he was far more difficult to contact than was normal. Suspiciously, he sent messages back and forth between the two groups via a young girl, not more than fourteen or fifteen years old. Kuru (who had assumed leadership of Peter's group; it was safer if the whites kept quiet and stayed as inconspicuous as possible) was asked intimate political questions; relieved, he realised that the latest information he had received related to the Group Commander that the Mamba knew best. And finally, a meeting was set up.

Peter distrusted it immediately. The location was in a tight valley where they would be hemmed in and could be watched from every point; it would be tantamount to giving themselves up to the terrorists as prisoners. But he also knew that this man was somehow more important than his predecessors and that, risk or no, he must be captured – killed, if necessary. He told Kuru to agree, and informed Perry Fox at HQ of the situation.

Carrying the radios was always a problem. The terrorists did not have them, so they were a dead giveaway should they be found. But Kuru casually carried his in a paper bag, along with a couple of bottles of whisky he said he had stolen from one of the farms they had hit, and it seemed natural therefore that he would allow no-one near it.

When at last the details had been sorted out, six black Scouts moved cautiously to the meeting site, knowing there were terrorists positioned all around them, above and beneath, hidden between the rocks. Peter, Greg and Terry, the only three whites in the platoon, and two of the Ndebele, had been "ordered" to stay back to cover their rear – after all, they had every right to be as suspicious of the other group as the Mamba was of theirs.

In the centre of the tiny valley they stood and waited, knowing they were being carefully inspected. And then four terrorists, as foul-smelling as the Scouts and almost as filthy, stepped down from their hiding places. Their beards were thick, their faces greasy and dusty, hats pulled low over their foreheads. Even a mother would have had trouble recognising her own son.

The one who seemed to be the leader stepped forward, eyeing them suspiciously. "Who are you?" And the questions began again, the drilling – from both sides.

Finally, apparently satisfied, the leader's face broke into a grin and he slapped Kuru's shoulder amiably. "Tell your men to come out now," he said, and motioned to his own. Several of his group joined them, but Kuru knew there would be more. At least five more. He beckoned, and the two blacks of the unit came forward, laughing and joining with the terrorists in their humour.

"I was told there were eleven of you," queried the leader.

"There are. You will not find my other three until they wish to be found. We have an agreement – none of us puts his own life in danger if he does not trust a situation."

The leader laughed uproariously. "So much for our training, eh? Will you move to camp with us tonight?"

Kuru cackled shortly. "And lay ourselves open to attack from you? Would you do the same with us?"

"I am the Mamba. I take no man's word that he will guard my life. Go then. I wish to meet with you tomorrow, that you might give me more details of the security forces in the area. We want to move slightly north of where you have come from. I need more details about your killings, to help us avoid those places."

Kuru and two others were led to the Mamba at his camp shortly after dawn the next morning, giving them carefully sifted information that would have checked out had the terrorist leader wished to do so. Kuru was introduced to, this time, the full band of ZIPRA, two of whom looked familiar under the filth. He could not place them, and realised that he may have met them while they had lived in Rhodesia. They shared a meal cooked by a young messenger girl, and then Kuru stood.

"Now I must go. My men are impatient to get back to Kavalamanja. We've shaken the security forces, but the men are weary, and ready to see women again." He jostled the Section Commander in the ribs, chuckling knowingly. "I'm sure you understand. Although" – he eyed the girl – "I see you are not to be found wanting, yourself!"

He walked out of the camp with the laughter still ringing in his ears, and the sweat cold under his shirt.

Peter radioed the position of the camp to the waiting Fireforce, and within an hour they had hit; they counted fifteen dead, including the young girl who had served the group, and Kuru positively identified one of the bodies as the leader who had been so suspicious. The Mamba.

The map room, the centre of operations, was sweltering hot. Peter Kennedy shook droplets of water from his grimy forehead and slapped his hand impatiently on the table.

"He's still out there somewhere," he insisted.

Kuru agreed. They were certain that at least one of the Mamba's group had escaped, but with the Fireforce hit the locals in the area had withdrawn again, uncertain of the validity of Kuru's men. Nothing had leaked out about survivors.

"Why," a suspicious headman had demanded, "were your friends hit and not you? Why do they lie dead, while you still live?"

"We are a smaller group," Kuru had tried to tell him. "And more clever. We would not allow the Security Forces to know where we were."

"Perhaps. But perhaps you are not ZIPRA. Perhaps you are Skuzapo, as they warned us you might be."

It was the last to be heard. Kuru and Peter had moved out with their men towards the Botswana border, to allay suspicion, and then worked their way back to HQ.

Kuru grunted now. "If anyone is sheltering them we will not find out now. But the only one I definitely remember, whom I did not see at the body count, was an insignificant one. A youngster. He stayed in the background, and skivvied for them with the girl. They took no notice of him; he is unimportant. But here" – he stabbed with his finger at the huge map – "is a definite report. Six terrs, overstaying their welcome at this village." He looked expectantly at his officer.

Peter sighed. He hated to leave loose ends, but Kuru was right. These six were more important.

"Go for it," he told the big Ndebele.

Chapter 9

Rhodesia

He had heard the blades of the helicopters before the others had, slicing the thick air. A short distance away, he was relieving himself against the gnarled trunk of a lightning-blighted mopani tree; although he had never been through an attack before, he recognised it immediately as such. He ran, not wasting time to do up his fly.

Afterwards he remained hidden between the rocks until he was certain they were gone. It was a precaution he took wherever he camped – finding and improving a natural hiding place, one that could be passed time and time again without discovery. He cringed inside the tiny cave, pulling the prepared rocks around him and becoming a part of the landscape, listening to the search around him, the hatred in the voices of the soldiers. But they were looking for blood-spoor, for roughly torn bushes, for signs of a frenzied run for safety.

The Mamba was too smart for that.

And also too smart to go back to the villagers for help. He subdued his hunger and thirst, and began to move carefully back towards the border.

He ate while they debriefed him. "It was reported you were dead," said the big Russian.

He shook his head, his mouth full of sadza and gravy. "The comrade whom they thought to be the Mamba, the leader, the one whom they met, is dead."

The Russian raised his eyebrows. So many of these black swine were ignorant and stupid. This one was proving different. Very different. He stood up finally. "Tomorrow you will be assigned a new command. Tonight – rest."

Mandhla Ndhlovu barely looked up as the man walked away.

He looked vaguely familiar, but it was only when they were introduced that she realised why. Captain John Kennedy was related, somehow, to the DC in Ntubu. And, she admitted, reluctantly to herself, therefore also to Major Kennedy of the Selous Scouts.

"Cousin," he explained. "I know we look like brothers, but actually no closer than cousins."

Little Heather, the telex girl from the newsroom, clung to his arm possessively. Rebecca allowed herself a moment of amusement; it was a reaction she was accustomed to from women. She held out her hand to the cloudy-haired girl. "I'm sure you'll be very happy together, Heather. John looks like good husband material."

"Oh sure – when he's not flying around the countryside," Heather giggled. "And one day I'll get him to change his flying cap for one that says Married!" She swept the dark peaked cap off his head and displayed the inner band to Rebecca. Someone had written in indelible ink, where it could not be seen from the exterior, the words: "Pilots are a girl's best friend – ask John!"

The cap was replaced, with much tittering from Heather, who was promptly pulled away by a group of friends. John smiled wryly at Rebecca.

"My cousin mentioned you'd been to Ntubu. They seemed very impressed with you up there. Especially the men."

She smiled evenly into his brown eyes. "Your cousin?" she asked.

"Mark. I don't see much of Peter. Keeps to himself, mostly."

The interest quickened again. "Why?" she asked directly.

He shrugged. "His job, I suppose. He's with the top tracking unit in the country, you know. They must see some pretty rotten sights. But Mark was saying Peter'll be in town this weekend."

"Where will he stay?"

John looked at her shrewdly. "He's not into women, you know."

She froze and her eyes retreated into the cold. Her voice was icy. "I'm a news reporter, at present specifically assigned by both my producer and your government to report on your Security Forces. If your cousin is heading up an important unit of the Rhodesian defence strategy, it might be an idea to interview him, wouldn't you think?"

She turned and he watched her walk away, hips swinging unconsciously under the soft cotton skirt, tanned calves flashing.

He was out of line. This one didn't need to chase any man.

She was repainting her lounge when he found her. He watched from the doorway for a moment as she reached upward toward a corner, her breast shaping the loose peasant-blouse she wore, her long plait tumbling in a honeyed twist to below her waist, swinging with her rhythmic movements. She rubbed her nose, leaving a small smudge of paint on her cheek, and went back to stroking the brush up and down the wall.

"I hear you're looking for me," he said in his flat Anglo-Rhodesian accent.

She jumped and almost lost her balance on the ladder, turning as she did so and spraying droplets of very pale blue across her faded jeans. Her green eyes were wide and dark with fright, and she held the paintbrush like a weapon. For just an instant he recognised that same flash behind the dark lashes that had eluded him in Ntubu, and then immediately she was angry.

"How did you get in here?" she demanded.

"Front door was open. Sloppy. I could have been anyone."

"It's open for the cat." She was beginning to recover herself, but the fury was still there. "How did you find out where I lived? I've only just rented this place!"

"Perhaps I wasn't looking for you. Perhaps I simply saw an open door and decided to see what kind of fool would forget to lock herself in." He was mocking her.

"Well, you've seen her. Now you can leave."

"So my information was incorrect? You don't want to see me? No interview?"

She was nonplussed. "I – my cameraman isn't here." Damn him for catching her off balance!

"I wouldn't allow pictures anyway. Can't afford it. Besides, I shouldn't think it would be allowed. Officers heading up important units of our defence strategy should maintain a low profile, don't you think?" He had quoted her almost word for word.

"What is your cousin – a parrot? And if you don't want to be interviewed, what are you doing here?"

"I was intrigued. You know very well I wouldn't consent to an interview. So there's another reason. What is it? And incidentally, are you going to remain on that ladder for our entire conversation?"

She was tempted to be childish and say yes, but instead she began to descend the steps. "Call it curiosity. No-one seems to really know quite what you do, Major Kennedy."

"I track. That's how I found you. Good, aren't I?"

She sat on the bottom rung of the ladder. "Well, now I can rest at ease. This country is safe." She heard the sarcasm in her own voice but he didn't flinch. He gave her a mock salute.

"Pleased to have been of service, Ma'am. Call again any time you need questions answered." Casually, he turned and walked out of the door.

This time, there would be no mistakes.

He put his new command of ten men through their paces, insisting that they hone their ragged skills before he would cross into Zimbabwe with them, and only after several weeks of his own form of training would he accept the order to move out.

The Russian officers took his refusal to advance stoically. They realised that he used more than simply the hatred they had instilled into him. This man had potential beyond their dreams. And so they watched him flog his men, and waited, and when they reckoned he was almost ready, they tried again.

Their timing was accurate enough. Grudgingly, Mandhla Ndhlovu prepared his men for infiltration.

They melted into the Rhodesian bush, moving cautiously but swiftly. Within days they had regained the position he had lost on his previous mission. He passed near the spot of the attack without glancing toward it.

He avoided the villages he had visited previously, not wasting time on them – besides, he had been informed that there were now two other ZIPRA groups operating there. His task was to forge ahead. His orders were to get in close to the small towns surrounding Bulawayo, and to work on the black population around them.

He had no intention of restricting himself to his orders.

The forestry house was a ridiculously simple target. Far from any other white housing, in the middle of wooded bushveldt, the whitewashed walls and red government roof stood out starkly against the brown and beige and green of the surroundings. There was no security fencing to protect it from attack, the servants' quarters were out of sight of the main house, and the big yard was littered with hiding places – kennels, a wrecked car chassis and body, an old children's adventure tunnel made of water barrels ... They set up a rough camp two miles away, and Mandhla, not trusting his men with the task, spent most of his time near the house, watching the routines, waiting.

The family consisted of three – the parents, and a boy of about thirteen. Mandhla grunted when he saw him. A soldier, soon.

They went out for the day on Sunday, and over the week that Mandhla observed them they received no visitors. Back at camp, he stripped himself of his denims and dressed in ragged shorts and a torn T-shirt. He washed himself in the stream near the camp, and then, his mission-boy persona complete, once again approached the homestead – this time openly.

"Please, Mem, I need work," he told the woman. The man was out, presumably working himself.

She eyed him suspiciously, the curlers in her hair askew, greying tendrils escaping over her thin forehead and scrubbed red ears. "What can you do?"

He made his face light up. "Please, Mem, I can clean the garden for you! They teach me at the mission in QueQue." His arm swept the mess around them.

She shifted onto the other foot. "Where are you from?"

"Ncube's village – there." He pointed vaguely. "There is no food there, Mem. No rain – the mealies, they die ... the cows ... aishhh..." He trailed off, looking miserable, his eyes pleading.

She sighed. "Fifty cents a day, then, and I will feed you. You can sleep with the others. Philemon!" she yelled, and as a sullen black face appeared: "Take this man and show him where he can sleep."

His face brightened and he scraped and thanked her profusely as he followed the manservant away.

"Hey!" He turned back at her call. "What's your name, boy?"

"Mandhla. I am Mandhla."

It was Friday afternoon.

On Saturday he reorganised the garden. It looked neater this way – and provided better hiding places.

The man grunted when his wife told him about the new gardener. "Too damned soft," he told her. "You'll never learn. Let the damned *kaffirs* take care of themselves."

"He looks as though he can work," she threw back as they watched from the stoep, behind the fly-screens.

"For today, maybe." He turned away.

Sunday again. Again, they went out early in the morning. To visit the woman's parents, Philemon told them. They would not be back until late evening.

Philemon was remarkably cooperative, since he had been shown the camp and the weapons and informed gently by Mandhla that there were ways of repaying treachery. And anyway, these people had not treated Philemon well. Not like his previous bosses. Philemon obligingly removed his family, the only black staff on the homestead, back to his village several miles away. There was no point in having witnesses, and as always astute in character assessment, Mandhla knew that the little black servant was too fond of his fat wife and six children to betray the presence of the ZIPRA group.

That afternoon the Mamba moved his men into the spots he had so carefully worked out for them around the property. Armed and ready, they sat as he had taught them. Silent, and still as death.

The headlights shone into the driveway after seven o'clock. Mandhla chuckled to himself, shaking his head. They would never learn, these whites. Still they came home after cover of darkness.

He waited until the car had stopped under its crude shelter of poles and corrugated iron; waited while the three doors slammed shut. The woman was nagging again. The husband was drunk. The boy was quiet, leading the way to the house.

Soundlessly Mandhla stood up. His men, waiting for this, did the same. The boy was almost at the steps when Mandhla rose in front of him. The man and woman were engrossed in their argument. Before the child could catch his breath to scream, Mandhla held him against his body, facing the parents, a hand over the wet mouth.

The woman saw first, and shouted. The man stopped in his tracks, but Mandhla had rehearsed his men well. Already they surrounded the white family.

Even in his drunkenness, the man tried to protect his child. He lunged for Mandhla, snarling, and was brought down by the butt of an AK-47 crashing into his skull, splintering the white bone. The woman stood where she was for a moment, then slowly walked towards Mandhla.

Only when she was close did she recognise him, and even in the moonlight he could see the hatred in her eyes. And the realisation that they were going to die.

"He's a child. Do such great men as you become as snakes, to kill children?" Her voice was scornful, barely afraid.

He remembered Nada.

Two of the terrorists stepped forward, each grasping an arm. Mandhla pulled out his knife and as he drew it across the boy's throat, he grinned at her through the spurt of blood that spattered them both. There was a soft hiss from the torn flesh.

"I am the Mamba. We snakes will kill what we must."

She did not scream. She watched the life-blood ebb

from her son, and it was as though it drained from her too. They let go of her arms as she sank to the ground.

They castrated the man and the boy. The woman's breasts, too, would be strong medicine in the art of persuasion at the next kraal from which they needed food. And then they bayonetted all three bodies before pouring bullets into them.

He stood back, watching. He did not feel the need, as his men did, to destroy the bodies. They were dead. It was enough.

He split the group up. As soon as the Security Forces heard what had happened, they would be on the track of the terrorists, and Mandhla had no intention of losing his whole troop again. He had no qualms about referring to himself as a terrorist. The term, to him, meant freedom fighter. It was one and the same thing. The Russians had done their work well. Sticks and stones will break my bones, but words will never harm me.

He took seven of his men. The other three (whom Mandhla had already picked out as less able than the others) were given the task of misleading the Security Forces. "You know how to shake them off," Mandhla reminded them. "You are brave men, and cleverer than they. But first, leave a trail, before you deceive them and disappear. And when they are gone, we will meet again in Zambia."

They were dubious of the honour. Mandhla didn't blame them. Carefully he led his diminished group to melt once again into the bush. But first, he dropped something beside the woman's body.

The black man heard the firing through the cool night air, distant but unmistakable. He did not move from his place at the fire, and his face was still. The other men fell silent, briefly, looking uneasily at one another, and then the conversation resumed.

They were the village elders, and it fell to them to decide grounds for divorce. Such was the subject of their discussions tonight. One of the girls was pleading that her man was unable to perform satisfactorily in bed; how, she demanded, should I have children if my husband cannot do what is necessary?

She had a point. And everyone knew that if a woman did not have children, she would bear the stigma for the rest of her life and then die alone. It was for the elders to decide whether her complaint was justified. Tonight, they would observe the couple in action, and if they agreed that he did not come up to standard she would be granted her divorce.

They talked on, remembering other such cases they had had to mediate in, and eating their mealie porridge with the little dried fish that was a staple protein for them, washed down with crude beer that they were no longer legally permitted to make.

He shifted restlessly on his haunches, trying to concentrate, willing time to move faster. Finally they stood. The girl and her husband had gone to their hut. It was time. They moved toward the mud dwelling, quiet now. The headman ranged them inside the hut, against the walls, five old men to judge the performance of one young one. No – four.

The headman clucked impatiently. Ndwana was becoming unreliable. He would have to speak to him of his responsibilities as an elder.

Ndwana had drawn away from the small group as it filtered through the door of the hut, disappearing silently into the dark. At once he began to trot in the direction of the forestry homestead. It was the only white house in the area, and it was roughly from there that the shots had sounded.

Peter Kennedy cursed violently at the sound of the shrill ringing in his muzzy head. He had spent the previous evening listening in over the radio on an unsuccessful hit; the Skuzapo unit had reported the whereabouts of a terrorist stick by radio for a Fireforce, but they had been slow in coming, and when they had, they had misread the exact location. Not entirely their fault; the dam they were told about was one of two close together, and only one appeared on the maps. The wrong one.

In the swift-gathering dusk the K-cars had strafed what

they believed to be the correct area, killing no more than a bushbuck and giving the terrorists ample warning. Unable to compromise their standing with the locals, the Scouts' pseudo-terrorist group had had to run, too. They could not risk everything by going in for a kill themselves.

Peter had finally crawled into bed around two o'clock that morning. That gave him – he glanced at the luminous face of his bedside Timex – three and a half hours of sleep. He lumbered towards the persistent telephone in the hall.

He felt the familiar anger build inside him as he listened, warm and strong. "I'll send a group out immediately," he told Felix on the other end of the line. "We'll get the bastards."

"Well, actually –" his commander hesitated. "Actually, I'd rather thought you might make it over there yourself. Something odd that the police reported they'd found ... a sort of bangle. Wooden. Shape of a snake. A mamba, they think."

Chapter 10

Tsimbaboue

"You must appeal, Ncube."

They were in his bachelor's hut, in the bachelor compound; Ncube was hunched on his favourite dagga seat, and Niswe stood at the window, fingering a small carving he had made, his first, as a child. It was an ox – no, a bull. Ncube loved cattle.

"You must appeal, Ncube," she said again. "I know you can – the High Priest will hear you. He likes you, Ncube, else why did he choose you to do the carvings for the Tsimbaboue? He's your only hope."

"I cannot." His despair showed in the very way he sat. "It's not done, it's not right."

"What Chisa did is not right! It's never happened before, in anyone's memory; therefore only the King or the High Priest can absolve you of this promise."

"The High Priest only. Marriage is sacred, a matter for Muali to decide."

"If you will not ask, I will."

He stared at her, shocked. "A woman may not see the High Priest, except at her initiation and her wedding, and after death. Or if he calls her. If you try to see him, you will die!"

"Better to die than to let you marry that hyena!" She almost spat the words. "Tcana is the one for you, and no-one else!"

His shoulders sagged again. "No, Niswe. If Tcana wanted me, she would have taken my stone before now. I've thrown for her almost every day for four moons now."

"Be patient, Ncube. Tcana's still young. She hasn't taken your stone, but neither has she taken anyone else's – yet. But if you marry that witch, she might!"

He thought for a moment. "Perhaps I will try to see the High Priest."

"I'll talk to Tcana. If she says she knew the stone was for her, and she intended to pick it up…"

"Leave Tcana alone." For the first time, his tone was firm. "This is for me to handle."

Tcana had her own problems. She had seen Xhaitaan often since the dance; she had sometimes gone out of her way to be where she knew he might see her. Never had she allowed her eyes to meet his again, but knowing he was there, and looking at her, was enough.

Nada's eyes she had met – and was meeting them now, here in Lila's hut.

"Your daughter should stay this side of the village," Nada was insisting to Lila. "She is distracting, and will cause problems she has no right to cause."

Lila looked helplessly at the silent Tcana. "I cannot order my daughter where to go. She's a woman now. She answers only to her father until she marries."

Nada knew that only a man may give an order to a man. She could not approach Roro. Instead, she looked compellingly at Tcana. "My son's life is mapped out for him. Next year, my cousin's daughter will go to the Hill, and then she and Xhaitaan will marry. It is right for the blood of Royalty to mix with that of Royalty – not with that of – of – cattle herds!"

Tcana gazed back into the tiny, narrow eyes of this scheming woman, and Nada shifted uncomfortably – they all knew that marriage plans could not be made before a girl had come back from the Hill, for she did not truly exist until then. Also, Nada was only too aware that her own background was perhaps not quite as Royal as it could have been, but she was distantly connected to one of the cousins … and besides, the King had chosen her. Only as his fourth wife, yes, but her son, her Xhaitaan, was the King's favourite, and so would eventually be made King himself. Of this Nada was positive; but a commoner for a wife would spoil everything! Kisang, the son of the first wife, waited in the wings, and his mother would not hesitate to use any tool to speed his chances at the throne.

When Tcana spoke her words startled both the older women. "If your son were truly interested in me, Nada, I would have had a gold ingot at my feet before now." She stood, her back straight, as graceful and proud as ever. "I will walk where I please unless I am commanded otherwise by the King."

She left the hut, her head high, her eyes stinging, because she knew what Nada had said was true. Xhaitaan could not afford to take a commoner wife, whose father kept bulls. The best bulls, to be sure, those that were always used by others to mate on their cows because their offspring were strong and healthy and large-boned, but nevertheless – a cattle herd. To be sure, a man whose occupation of keeping cattle was higher in caste than one who kept chickens, or tilled soil – but Roro was nonetheless not a wealthy trader, and nor was he in any way Royal.

As always when she needed the peace of Muali around her, she went into the bush and climbed around to the back of the Hill. No-one ever went there but her; they were afraid of straying too close to Tsimbaboue, the Priest's nest at the top of the cliff. But here, on the other side, the ground sloped gently and she had discovered that if she followed a trail of young acacia saplings it led to a concealed spring. There, hidden from the world by thick bushes and undergrowth, a tiny well of water gushed from a small rocky cave. The water was sweet, and cool, and the whisper as it washed the stones was soothing ...

The singing of the brook hid the sound of his footsteps – if indeed he had made any sound – and when he spoke, she was off-guard.

"Are you speaking with Muali?"

She jumped, and scrambled to her feet, then remembered that she should be squatting out of respect. She dropped down onto her haunches, and stared at his feet as he lowered himself to the same position.

"I asked if you spoke with Muali?" His voice was teasing. "You are very close to his house here, behind the Hill."

She said nothing, afraid.

"Or is it that my mother disturbed you?"

Her startled eyes whipped to his and away again.

"Nada looks to what she considers is my well-being. She has forbidden me to speak with you."

Tcana looked shocked: what woman could order a man, let alone the King's son?

He laughed. "I see I have your attention. But what is more important – do you forbid me to speak with you?"

She knew he was teasing her, but she did not dare reply; he was Xhaitaan, favourite son of the King – perhaps, one day, King himself.

"Must I order you to answer me?" he mocked her. "Or are you mute, as the rocks you sit on in this secret place?"

"Lord, I –" She stopped, confused.

"I heard that you were at the centre of a controversy only yesterday," he probed. "I've seen many young men throw their stones for you – my own cousin has cast a copper ingot at your feet. You refuse them all. Why?"

She could not reply; her heart thrust into her throat and blocked her tongue. He waited a moment, then stood up.

"Perhaps one day you will pick up a stone from your feet. When you do, I hope it's the right one."

He was gone, but her heart still beat hard behind her eyes and in her mouth and against the walls of her chest, beneath the strong breasts that thrust against her calf-skin overwrap.

The High Priest granted audience to Ncube.

"I know why you've come." He spoke before Ncube had risen from his heels.

Ncube was surprised, though he knew he shouldn't be. The Priests stayed on the Hill, and the people in the Valley, yet the Priests always knew everything that went on in the village. The Oracle, of course. The all-seeing Mouthpiece of Muali.

"The girl, Tcana," the High Priest continued. "She is not for you, Ncube. She is destined for other things. Things which cannot include you. She knows this – it's why she has not taken a stone. Chisa, now – that girl wants you."

"Lord, she took my stone when I did not throw it for her. I cannot marry a woman who will do such things to get what she wants. What other tabu might she not break?" Ncube was well aware that he would be held responsible for his wife's actions.

The High Priest nodded slowly. "True. But you may not have Tcana, and who else would you have?"

"No-one, Lord, if not Tcana. I will not marry."

"Ncube, you too have your destiny, and the Mouth of Muali says you will marry. It is Muali who guides the women to retrieve the stones of the men he chooses for them. You will marry Chisa."

Ncube was horrified. "Lord, anyone else, yes – only command! But –"

"Muali has chosen Chisa. He ordered her to pick up your stone, just as he has ordered me to condone it. You will marry Chisa, Ncube. She will not be so bad – certainly never boring!" He laughed a little at his own joke, but Ncube could not speak.

If Muali had ordered it, then he knew it must happen.

When it came, she thought he was mocking her again, until she looked into his eyes and saw the doubt hidden there, the fear that she would overlook him, though his lips curled confidently and his stance was strong.

She looked back down, and at him again, and their eyes held. Slowly, she bent her knees and touched her forehead to the ground. Then, ever so carefully, she lifted the solid gold ingot from the earth at her feet.

It was heavy – almost too heavy for her to carry, and bigger than she had imagined existed. She held it with both arms, cradling it as a baby, and they walked back to the village together, back from the concealed spring on the Hill, to where the people could see, in the light of the sun's last rays, that Tcana Ndhlovu was carrying the King's son's stone.

No-one spoke to them; to address Royalty without first being addressed was pure foolishness, and Tcana, though not yet married, carried Xhaitaan's stone. Tcana, one day, may be First Queen. And so, in silence, they progressed through the awed villagers, who bent their knees and touched their foreheads to the ground as they passed. And in silence they parted at the entrance to Tcana's hut. Her eyes met his again, briefly, before she turned to go into the hut; his own were confident once more, and she was proud.

She entered the dark room and stood in the gloom for a moment, still cradling the gold ingot, as a mother cradles her child. Then she heard a noise behind her.

Xalise stood in the open doorway, but the instant her sister turned the child dropped to her knees in the Royal salute. Tcana was disturbed.

"Xalise, I am not yet married. I'm your sister. Rise."

Xalise obeyed, but it was a response to an order. "Highness, I -"

"Stop it, Xalise!" Tcana was suddenly angry, afraid. "You are my sister, and I will not have you speak this way!"

Xalise wavered, and then, to Tcana's surprise, began to cry. The tears coursed down her chubby black cheeks. "Tcana, what will you do? Mai is crying, and Kai is kicking the new fence he has built for the bulls. And they don't even know yet about Lord Xhaitaan ..."

She clung to Tcana's knees. Bewildered, the older girl bent to her. "Xalise, what are you talking about? I cannot see, it's too dark – "

At that moment Lila came in at the door, carrying a torch. The leaping flames lit the walls and made their shadows flicker eerily, and the ingot glowed rusty-red in Tcana's arms. Her mother's eyes rested on it and widened, and she stared at Tcana.

"Xhaitaan?" she whispered fearfully.

Tcana nodded and smiled nervously. There was something here she did not understand. In silence, Lila pointed her trembling finger at Tcana's bed.

There, on the black and white kaross, lay a small pile of bleached bones.

Chapter 11

Rhodesia

Peter Kennedy swore vociferously when he realised how close the murder site was to Ntubu. Within the magisterial district, in fact. He demanded of his men why they hadn't warned him of terrorists in the area; they shook their heads, as upset as he. No word had come through. It was alarming, to say the least, and usually when their sources and warning systems dried up it meant total subversion of an area. Was that the case now, in his brother's district? He sincerely hoped not.

The tracking began immediately. A rather obvious trail had been left by the three terrorists on their way out. Heading for Botswana, of course. And yet ... something worried Peter.

The wooden bracelet beside the woman's body was familiar. It was very like one he had seen before, and Kuru bore him out. The leader of the large stick of ZIPRA they had successfully wiped out, the one they called the Mamba – there had been one near his body when they found him.

That meant one of two things. Either another Section Commander had taken the name on himself, or ...

Kuru met his eyes across the boy's broken body and shook his head slowly. The terrs did not adopt each other's bush names.

He was alive, then.

Felix denied Peter permission to join the tracking team himself. He wasn't sure how well the Major was known among the ZIPRA insurgents, and it was silly to risk his men's lives by appearing where they were working, even in heavy disguise. In fact, he added, it was time Peter stopped the bush jaunts altogether. His place as Second in Command of the Selous Scouts was organising and leading the ZIPRA counter-action. He was too important to risk in the field. Peter knew he was remembering his predecessor, who was "caught in a lie" which cost him his life.

But Peter also knew that if the Mamba had tricked them into believing he was merely a lowly comrade with no standing, and if he was back, he was too wily to have left such an obvious trail for them to follow. Which meant that he had sent men off to decoy the trackers. Ergo, the Mamba had headed in another direction altogether.

Ntubu was an hour's drive away. Perhaps he should see Mark ...

Later. Right now, there was work to be done.

Mandhla was rapidly learning what he was up against. He moved swiftly south, passing just east of Nyamandhlovu. And still, they avoided contact with the local population. His men had protested at first; they had been into Zimbabwe before and were accustomed to the good food and women supplied by the villagers, rather than living wholly off the bush. But their leader was determined, and they began to understand the benefits of no-one knowing of their presence.

Especially, there were no "mujiba" – young go-betweens, to bring them messages from other groups in the area wanting to contact them – and telling other groups they were there.

This had its disadvantages, of course. There was no way of telling what the Security Forces were doing, where they were operating, what information they had, but Mandhla knew that this was their best chance of avoiding the Skuzapo. He also knew that he was disobeying direct orders, but his intention was not simply to be used as a subversive element. He knew he was meant for better things than that. He remembered the fat man in Lusaka. No, he was going to upset the Skuzapo to the point of disruption. He had a mission.

Before leaving the Zambian camp to re-enter Zimbabwe, he had received a message from the obese leader of ZIPRA. The man who had led the tracking unit that had killed Nada, and had deserted the Elliott Mission children, was the same man whose name was rapidly becoming an anathema to the terrorist forces. Peter Kennedy, in command of the sections working specifically against ZIPRA.

He also realised that whereas his decoy of three men would have fooled anyone else, it would not have fooled Major Kennedy. Things were going as planned. Kennedy knew that the Mamba was still alive.

Just south of Nyamandhlovu, at a bend in the river, Mandhla cached their weapons and uniforms. He used a hollow under the bank that one of the comrades had found when he went in to wash – probably an old crocodile lair, but definitely no longer in use – and, wrapping everything carefully in thick plastic bags, the eight men hid the evidence of their membership, retaining only the old trousers and shirts their Section Commander had insisted they carry with them.

Then they doubled back north, carrying staffs cut from the trees and singing loudly the peasant songs they vaguely remembered from before ... before ...

They told all they met that they were from the south, heading north to find cattle to buy. In the south the drought was worse than in the north, and they needed more beasts to swell their village herds. Laughingly, they spent the first night under the hospitality of a large village near Inganga, where they drank beer and sang songs and told stories of the south and the drought.

The next morning the charmed headman agreed to allow his lovely daughter to wed one of the men; as a dowry, he gave three fat cows and a young bullock. The bridegroom agreed to fetch the maiden – and the cattle – and bring the lobola, on their homeward journey, but first his group had no choice but to travel on to increase their herd.

They left behind them a satisfied headman (the daughter had been getting old; he had worried about finding her a man), a delighted bride, and stories that would be told over and over about the south.

Kuru passed by the laughing group of carefree peasants headed north almost without a second thought. At the village the headman identified the travellers satisfactorily, swearing that since he was marrying his daughter to one of them, was that not enough proof that they were known to him? And would Kuru join him in a celebratory pot of beer?

Strange. He thought he had recognised one of them, vaguely ... Kuru shook his head to dismiss the thought. He saw so many faces. This was just another familiar one. And one bearded man looked much like another.

Mandhla took his band further north, to beyond Tsholotsho, almost to Lupani. Then they struck east, to an isolated village near the Chakwane Pan, and again asked to buy some cattle.

The villagers were delighted. They had had bad luck recently, not least of which was a stick of six ZIPRA men coming through and taking with them most of the food in the village. Money would help greatly, especially since the cattle were in any case thin.

They spent three days there, laughing and talking and drinking hastily-brewed beer, with yeast added to speed the fermenting process. They told about their travels, and asked about the men of the village. None of those present had travelled further than Lupani, except three, who boasted of their experiences as far south as Tsholotsho, where they had once driven cattle for a sale.

Mandhla chose eight men of similar build to his own group. On the third day, they explained to the headman that they must pass on to buy more animals, but would be back to fetch what they wanted in two weeks.

One week later, eight men disappeared from the village.

They marched south again, forcing their captives through isolated territory, meeting no-one. At the river, just east of Nyamandhlovu, eight throats were slit, neatly and efficiently, and the bodies replaced the AK-47s, the Claymores, the anti-personnel mines and the ZIPRA uniforms in the old crocodile lair.

The men had conceived a name for their little band.

Nyoka. The Snakes. It seemed fitting; their leader was the Mamba, and they were appreciating more and more the cunning that he employed. They no longer questioned his orders, or protested at the extra drilling and training that he put them through at every opportunity. They were different, and they knew it.

And then, to their surprise, their Section Commander began to move them north again – but this time, further into the country.

"They're gone," Kuru said gloomily at the debriefing.

Peter smacked his fist into his palm. "Damn! They can't have simply disappeared – they're out there somewhere!"

"We lost what little we considered their trail at Nyamandhlovu. Perhaps we were following the wrong signs; perhaps they simply went in a different direction."

It wasn't true, and they both knew it. Kuru was too good a man to have followed a false trail, or the wrong one.

"Who is he?" Peter demanded of the empty air. "Who the hell is this Mamba?"

No-one seemed to know. And the local population, this time, were genuinely ignorant, both of the man's identity and his whereabouts. The only interesting information that had come in was the disappearance of eight men from a village in the area of the Chakwane Pan, which was much too far north to have anything to do with the Mamba. Terrorists, probably recruiting.

By now the missing men would be in Botswana at the very least, or even Zambia. The headman had not reported their absence until a week after they had gone. Certainly, nothing to do with a band of terrs who were moving south.

It was his first real failure. Wherever he had sent men into an area, they had tracked and found and usually destroyed. Or at least sent packing. He knew the Ndebele, and ZIPRA in particular, had formed a name for him. They called him the Hyena – an animal steeped in superstition. They knew him, and were afraid of him. The Bush War, in the south east and west at least, was rapidly becoming ZIPRA against Peter Kennedy.

His men, through the Special Branch section who

reported directly to him, rather than to the police as most Rhodesians thought, knew of virtually every group of terrorists that infiltrated within days of their arrival. Some, the smaller groups, had to be left alone occasionally in favour of trapping a larger stick; sometimes he lulled them into a false sense of security by leaving one of his groups with a ZIPRA stick for several days at a time. That way, they learned more.

Constantly, his information was updated by captured terrorists. Uneasy still about "turning" terrorists, Peter recognized the value of this tactic and continued with it, always with his heart in his mouth, always waiting to hear that one of those he had passed as trustworthy had turned again and killed his own men. It was a fear that was with him night and day, and the courage shown by his men's acceptance of that risk never ceased to instill admiration in him.

He and Felix were often up against the bureaucracy of the regular Army. General Walls, of course, was behind them all the way, but their methods sometimes troubled even him. Their dress, in particular, disturbed some of the upper echelons. There was good reason for the Scouts having earned the nickname "Armpits with Eyeballs". Every one of the men sported unkempt beards. They all looked bedraggled, undisciplined and inefficient, but what stood between them and the fury of the office bearers was their undeniable record. Whatever methods the Selous Scouts were employing, they worked. And so they were left alone, to a great degree.

The secrecy surrounding the unit was something that rumour was doing its level best to overcome. If anything, rumour was building them into even more than they were, if that were possible. And rumour had Peter Kennedy as the hero of the day.

Or the arch-enemy of the day, depending which side you were on.

Chapter 12

Rhodesia

It was the secrecy and rumour that were beginning, once again, to bother Rebecca. She and Tony had just completed an episode on the African Rifles, and even there the name Peter Kennedy was becoming known. She began to feel the familiar itch, the hunger to know more that had made her the best OAST had when it came to sniffing out items with news value.

And this, her nose told her once again, definitely had news value.

Her nose. She wrinkled it, thinking of her father; he had nicknamed her Sharkie, saying that she could smell blood – and stories – miles away. Which hadn't upset him overly much; from the little coastal village in California her father controlled OAST's rival network, KTV, and he was proud of her determination and ability to make it on her own – without his name to help her along. Thinking of her father made her homesick – an alien sentiment to a foreign correspondent.

She picked up the telephone.

"Hello, Dad?"

"Sharkie?" The delight resounded across the Atlantic, and she almost cried at the soft, familiar accents. "Are you coming home?"

She sighed guiltily, knowing she rarely phoned unless she was packing for a homeward trip.

"No, Dad. Just finding out how you are."

"Fine, honey, fine. You sound tired. Are you eating right?"

She giggled. "Yes, Dad. I'm eating right. How's business?"

"Wonderful. They showed your programme on the Rhodesian bush war a few days ago on STOAT." It was his tease-name for her employing company. "I was impressed. Didn't think I'd ever see my little girl handle a rifle. I presume getting yourself shot up didn't damage you too badly, since no-one called me?"

"Oh – I'm sorry Dad, I was in the bush..."

"I understand, honey." His voice was tender. "Are you okay?"

Physically, yes. Mentally? She shook herself and cleared her throat. "Fine. I'm working on a series out here ... It's going to take a while..."

"So I won't be seeing you in the near future. At least give me your telephone number, if you have one?"

She gave it to him and kissed him across the wires before they hung up. Briefly she wondered what the chances were of a flying visit home, then dismissed the idea. Too much to do here.

And besides, she was waiting to see whether her message via John Kennedy would have any effect on his elusive cousin, who was refusing to take phone calls from the press and media.

It did. The telephone rang that evening.

"Miss Rawlings? Kennedy here." The voice was brusque. "I told you I wouldn't be interviewed."

"I don't want to interview you. I want to find out, off the record if you prefer it, why yours is the only unit in the whole of Rhodesia that I can't get access to, and that even top government officials keep steering me away from. I'm hearing rumours, and sooner or later I'm going to be tempted to put them over the air."

There was a terse silence. "Is that a threat, Miss Rawlings?"

"I have no idea." She felt her hackles rise; he was getting to her again. She controlled the antagonism she felt. "Why not explain to me the intricacies of the Secrets Act, and just where you fall under it? Then I'll know exactly what I can and can't report."

Silence again. Then, "The Web. Seven o'clock. Come alone. You're buying."

The phone clicked in her ear. She replaced her receiver in its cradle and began to smile slowly.

She was careful to look business-like, putting her heavy hair into a sleek French roll. She had to dress – in Rhodesia they still did, for dinner or drinks – but she wore a simple long black skirt and a white silk blouse with long sleeves, embellished only with a diamond-and-silver necklet at her throat – a twenty-first birthday gift from her father – and matching earrings that hung slightly below her chin line. Standing in front of the mirror, she examined herself critically and felt she would pass the test.

He was late – deliberately, she thought. She looked up from her drink to find him in the doorway, watching her. She put the glass down to disguise the sudden tremble and was furious with herself at the attraction she suddenly felt for him. He moved across the room easily, unconcerned at the glances he got from both women and men, not taking his eyes from hers until he stood beside her at the bar and looked at the glass the barman placed on the counter for him. He pushed it away.

"No thank you. There are people I know here. Let's go."

He turned and moved away, without waiting for her to follow. She gritted her teeth, gathered her purse and walked after him, humiliated and angry. He strode out of the lobby to a Landrover jeep parked outside and opened the door for her. She realised that it was carefully calculated to put her in her place, and to put him at an advantage. He slammed the door behind her, climbed in without looking at her and put the jeep in gear. She stared at him, determined not to give him the upper hand.

"Find what you're looking for?" he asked sarcastically.

"Not yet. Perhaps it isn't there." Her reply came quickly and his eyebrow raised in cynical acknowledgement.

They drove in silence for three more blocks until he pulled up outside the Dug-Out, a small steak house and seafood restaurant. Wordless, she opened the door for herself and led him inside.

The restaurateur seemed to know him; they were taken

to a private room behind the main dining area, where a table was laid and candlelit in readiness. Seated, they made their menu choices and Peter Kennedy ordered wine. When the waiter left them alone, he looked directly at her.

"Perhaps, Miss Rawlings, we should begin by calling a truce. Put your hackles down."

She met his look. "Why do you dislike me so much, Major?"

"You're American, aren't you? Where do your sympathies lie in this war?"

So that was it. "I'm a reporter, Major. Unbiased and uncommenting except on what I see."

"I haven't met an unbiased reporter yet, and particularly not an American one. Who did you vote for at the last election? Or were you too young to vote?"

"You're very direct, Major. As a matter of fact I didn't vote. I didn't like any of the candidates, and I said so on my show."

The one eyebrow lifted again, sardonically. "You must be older than you look."

"I am."

The waiter brought the wine and they sat in silence while he poured. She picked up the glass and swilled the ruby liquid contemplatively. He watched her, and she sensed a change in direction in him.

"How old?" It was abrupt, as the waiter left the room.

"Twenty-four. In May this year." She was irritated, and let him know it, spooling the information like a telex. "And because you clearly *have* to know, I was born in a fishing village, San Domingo, on the coast of California. My mother died when I was fourteen, in childbirth with my younger brother, whose name is James. I also have an older brother, Kyle. My father finished bringing us up.

"My father is the chairman of KTV, our rival network, and no, that doesn't create a problem in our family. James is now ten years old, and attends a school for retarded children due to brain damage he received at birth. Kyle is a journalist with a large paper – he also travels."

She saw him blink, and one eyebrow quirked suspiciously, but she rattled on, angry.

"I attended a good college and yes, I protested with the

best of them, but in my spare time I worked my way up in OAST until I had my own television show. From there I went into reporting; I wanted to travel, and here I am. I'm five feet six, I weigh one hundred and twenty pounds, I have light brown hair, and green eyes that don't require spectacles. Oh, and a birthmark in a place you'll never get to see it."

Then she smiled with the sweetness of elderberry wine and cyanide. "Is there anything else you need to know before you'll talk to me, Major Kennedy?"

Amused, he leaned forward and picked up his glass. "Yes. I need to know where your sympathies lie in this war." He sipped the wine and watched her carefully. "You must understand, Miss Rawlings, that I don't fight by the rules."

"*That* I have come to realise." It was acid.

"I don't mean it the way you do, though you're probably right. I'm up against an insidious enemy that takes no prisoners. One word wrong and it could mean someone's death – perhaps the death of one or more of my men. Remember the slogan, 'Loose lips sink ships?' I don't suppose you do. It was used in the Second World War, but it holds true today. And that, Miss Rawlings, is why I cannot talk to you. I lose enough of my men as it is."

She was silent, running the tip of her index finger around the rim of her glass, watching the crystal flicker in the candlelight, her eyes distant as she thought about what he had said. He leaned back and watched a heavy tendril of hair come loose from the French roll and slip into the curve of her neck. The diamond at her throat gleamed as she breathed. He had the sudden, unreasoned conviction that she was still a virgin.

The food came and she began to eat, still silent. When they were almost finished he spoke again. "Why do you have long hair if you always keep it tied up?"

It was unexpected, and she started. In the half-light her eyes looked grey-black and the shadows of the long lashes lay on her cheeks.

"Why do you ask?" She was still defensive.

"Because," he said gently, "I want to know."

Her eyes met his and he caught a sadness there for a

moment. "Because my father likes it that way, and because it's good for business. People take me more seriously this way. I do occasionally have it loose on more informal shows back home." She realised she was gushing; she bit her lip.

He reached forward and touched the soft lock that had fallen into her neck. Her eyes widened and she flushed, and he saw the trapped look again for a brief second, the search for an escape before facing the danger.

"Why are you afraid of me?"

"I'm not." It was almost a whisper. She felt an unfamiliar surge of heat in the pit of her stomach and her mouth was suddenly dry. She pulled away abruptly and lifted the glass to her mouth, the rim shaking as it touched her lips.

He took his hand away, feeling the shock through his fingers. "Do you want dessert?" The voice was terse and cold again. It gave her back her own distance.

"No. Thank you."

They left the restaurant and he drove her to her flat in silence. He escorted her up the stairs to her door and she hesitated as she unlocked it.

"Coffee?"

He looked at her speculatively for a moment. "I don't think that would be wise. Do you?"

She watched him walk back down the stairs without replying.

She packed almost feverishly, with Tony protesting behind her.

"Rebecca, you can't go now! What about the episode on the Grey Scouts?"

"Go film the horses without me," she said. "I'll dub a voice over later. I'll be back in a week or so, we can carry on then."

"What about your apartment? You've only just moved in!"

"You sleep here, Tony. It'll get you out of that commune you insist on staying in, and I won't have to put Mangoi in a cattery. And it'll be a nice surprise for any visitors I might have." *One in particular,* she thought grimly.

At the airport she handed him the key to the flat. "Enjoy." She kissed his cheek. "See you in a fortnight."

And she was gone.

At home she walked the hills and beaches with James and his imaginary friend, Mr. Cowley, and rode horses on her uncle's ranch, and went out fishing with the boats, and stood in the wind and spray on the rocks, and wished she could stop remembering the touch of warm, dry fingers on her neck.

She packed her suitcase yet again.

James was bewildered and unhappy at her going. Rebecca hugged him hard. "I'm only going for a little while, darling," she tried to reassure him as his eyes filled, the stray one quivering uncontrollably.

"Going a little while," he repeated miserably.

"And then I'll come back, and I'll bring you something, I promise. A present. I'll bring you a present, all right?"

"Present." The boy nodded, only slightly mollified. "Mr. Cowley wants to come."

Mr. Cowley was James' private friend. He existed in the stunted imagination of the little boy who more than anything needed a companion who understood.

"Mr. Cowley can't come," Rebecca whispered. "But I'll bring Mr. Cowley and James a present, all right?" She kissed him and he rubbed his head against her shoulder in a familiar gesture. Then he was distracted by something and the grey-green eyes were blank again. She held him close, savouring the frail body and the too-big head that she would not see again for several weeks, and then she kissed her father.

"By the way," he added as an afterthought, "I believe Kyle will be in Southern Africa sometime soon. I'm sure he'll contact you. I gave him your number."

Her spirits lifted. It was something else to look forward to.

Chapter 13

She moved, and instantly the pain screamed at her. Breathing carefully, she willed herself beyond it. Although she had hardly changed position, she could see now the brown backpack he had been carrying, dumped unceremoniously on the ground between the gnarled roots, and the cap he had been so eager to shove triumphantly in her face, its winged badge askew.

The cold metal of the serpent coiled around her upper arm bit into her skin. She shifted slightly again to ease it, and looked into the one eye that still stared at her, unbloodied. Her head swirled; no, it was the tree ...

The bead at her throat felt warm suddenly against her skin, like the warmth of a fire on a cold winter's night. Her eyes closed and she tried to will herself to let go. Gradually, she felt the drowsiness creep in.

Tsimbaboue

The Royal House, Tsimbabouetcang, was in an uproar. Xhaitaan walked into a nest of very disturbed bees – but these bees were not making honey.

Nada met him as he entered through the Sunset gate. He saw the fury in her eyes, but stood up to her, and as was required she reluctantly bent her head before him.

"My Lord, I must speak with you." Her voice was strangled, angry.

Wordless, he went to walk past her, towards his hut, but was stopped by a small boy – his half-brother, Lengane.

"Lord Xhaitaan, the King would see you – immediately."

He had expected the summons. Turning his back on his mother, he made his way into the sacrosanct enclosure where his father's indaba-room stood, near to the Tower of Continuation that housed the Life Fire, and the platform that contained the First Queen's pots, and called out to identify himself.

The response was immediate. "Enter, Xhaitaan."

Mgane smiled to himself as his favourite son entered. This boy, one day, would be King. His qualities outstripped those of Kisang, the first-born son, considerably, and he would be good for the people. The amaTsimbaboue needed a King they could be proud of – a King who danced, who sang, who was fair and just, and who put their welfare before his own glory. Such a man was Xhaitaan – and with a face to make one want to follow him unto death.

"I am concerned," Mgane began.

"Lord," Xhaitaan forestalled him, "there is no other as worthy as Tcana of this. There is no other for me."

"I don't know her," the King said mildly. "She certainly is one to look upon more than once. But I do not know her, and she carries no Royal blood. Nor did you ask this. You are surely being impetuous, Xhaitaan."

"I am deeply ashamed if I have grieved you, Lord. I was afraid you would refuse me ... From the day of her feast, I have known. This is no impetuosity. She's right for me."

Mgane sighed. "It's not in my hands. Tcana Ndhlovu is meant for other things. I've received a message from the High Priest; we are to go to him immediately."

The King gathered his considerable bulk and left the room, and Xhaitaan, bewildered, followed him.

In the Sacred Room, the long hall liberally decorated with muali and draped with patterned cloths, the High Priest saluted the King and Prince, and they their Priest. They sat in silence for a few minutes and then, suddenly, the Oracle was among them. Xhaitaan almost jumped, and did not know from where she had come.

The woman must have been nearing the end of her power. She had not seen more than twenty-eight harvests, he was sure, but she looked much older. Her limbs were pale, withered, her teeth gappy, and when she spoke her voice was thin, thinner even than when it spoke from the Cave to echo across the Valley.

"Tcana is chosen," she said simply.

Xhaitaan's innards contracted violently within him. Tcana - the Chosen One! For Tcana to take over from this ... this hideous witch! For her one day to look this way, her skin creased and wan from denial of the sun, her voice cracked from lack of honey, her face ... her face!

"Tcana has the Vision. She sees. She speaks with Muali." The crone nodded her long chin. Fleetingly Xhaitaan had a memory of the hidden glade where Tcana went to be alone ... and he spoke, horrifying himself with his own impudence.

"Tcana is indeed chosen. By me. To be my wife."

Shocked, they stared at him, and he was defensive.

"I am the King's son, and Muali leaves a little of his own blood in his Kings does he not? Is not a King's choice therefore that of Muali, too? And so with a King's son?"

He knew he had confused them. He knew he was right. He also knew that the Mouth of Muali was Muali's Mouth, and he trembled at his daring.

He smelt a sickly-sweet smell, a burning of sweetened fat, and his head swam. When it cleared, the Oracle was gone and the High Priest stood.

"It is something for me to discuss with Muali."

Wordlessly, the King and his favourite son left the Hill.

Tcana could not sleep. She must obey the summons of the bones before sundown the following day; she must strip herself of any finery, put on her plainest skin apron, and go to the Hill. She must say farewell to her family, to Mai and Kai, and to little Xalise - to Xalise! - and then she must forget that she ever belonged to them, and they to her. Kai would break down the hut he had so carefully, hopefully, built for her, and it would be as though she had never come back from the Hill at all.

She stood at her window and watched the clouds scud across the full moon. No - not yet full. It would be full tomorrow night, when she appeared before the Oracle.

Oh, Muali, she prayed, *is this what you have been telling me? Is this why you speak to me? Am I to be your Mouth for the people? Then why, Lord Muali, why did you send Xhaitaan to me? Why did you put it in my heart to lift his stone? I cannot be a Queen, and your Priestess, too!*

She clutched at the big bead in the necklet, and felt a calm steal over her.

Before sunrise she made her way to the spring, and crept in among the branches, into the grotto. Somehow she was not surprised to find that Xhaitaan was there before her. They stared at each other for a moment, and she saluted him, and he her. And then they were no more or less than man and woman, and he held her tightly while she cried, wetting the soft fur kaross he wore to keep him warm in the chill dawn.

They stayed there until noon, and when he stirred she realised she had been asleep on his shoulder. She woke only gradually, looking at him with sleepy doe-eyes.

"We must go, or we will never hear what Muali's decision is," he whispered.

"Xhaitaan – what if it's not Muali's decision?"

He laughed at her. "Of course it will be his decision. Who else's could it be?"

Xalise was waiting, shivering in the warm sunlight, at the end of the line of baby acacias. When she saw them, she almost forgot to salute Xhaitaan.

"I knew where you were," she said, her words tumbling over one another. "But I was afraid to go there ... Tcana, Kai has been told to send you to the Hill immediately."

Her whole self plunged, deep, deep, to the bowels of the earth, it seemed. "I must go...?"

"Not to the Mouth – you are to go to see the High Priest!" Xalise bubbled with fear and excitement. For a woman to be summoned before the High Priest!

Tcana and Xhaitaan looked at each other, and then Tcana started to run. She ran faster, faster, as though Muali himself had lent his wings to carry her; she flew to the bottom of the steps she had climbed only so few moons ago, hooded and afraid.

A Priest awaited her. Silent as always, he regarded her

dishevelment disapprovingly, then turned and began the ascent. Tcana looked up into the dark passageway, breathed deeply, and once again trod the grey stone stairs.

She recognised the room immediately. The carvings of Muali were all around her, and dimly in the corner she saw the doorway to the anteroom; she looked away quickly, remembering. Torches burned in recesses in the walls, throwing Muali into shadow and light, making him move constantly. It all seemed smaller now, somehow.

The High Priest was on his throne, surrounded by his Priests, and at his feet sat - someone else. Something else, for this old witch was surely not human! Tcana's skin crawled as the old hag came towards her and reached out her arm, an arm that looked as though it had been held in water far too long, with fingers like the ends of baobab branches in winter.

"Tcana Ndhlovu, Muali has chosen you for greatness. It is in the bones."

Tcana shuddered, but said nothing. Then the High Priest spoke. "We have prayed to Muali to reveal this mystery to us. He says - " The High Priest hesitated a moment, and his voice was bemused. "He says that you know your destiny."

Tcana gasped, and the Oracle spoke again.

"Muali demands your prayers. Here. And then he requires both you and Xhaitaan at Beyond-the-Eyes."

Beyond-the-Eyes. The place of nesting, where Muali's chosen form laid his twigs, to bear his eggs. The highest rocky peak in the area - in the world, surely - where the top could not be seen clearly from the foot. Where no man - or woman - may go, unless called by Muali to be tested.

Muali's sacred mountain.

They began to walk before dawn - Tcana, the cattleherd's daughter; Xhaitaan, the King's chosen son; the High Priest, Muali's watcher; the King, Muali's ruler; and three Priests, as witnesses.

As the sun climbed in the sky the heat rose from the ground in waves, and their progress slowed, but then they could see Beyond-the-Eyes, mauve and soft in the distance, and they quickened their pace again. They reached it at dusk, and slept at its craggy toes, and when the sun came up again it picked out the shadows of two figures moving steadily up the rock face of Muali's eyrie.

Only Tcana and Xhaitaan dared mount the sacred rock; they were the only two commanded so by Muali. The others waited, and watched.

Tcana's hands were grazed and bloody; her limbs ached, and even the hard soles of her feet had been cut by the sharp granite. Her breath came in short pants now, and beside her Xhaitaan breathed only a little more evenly. The sun had made the rock hot to the touch, almost hot enough to burn their flesh, and still they moved upward, their eyes fixed on the crag above them which held Muali's nest.

Meanwhile Muali and his wife glided high above them, silent for the moment. The High Priest stared from the black shapes on the rock face, to the great circling birds, and the King's eyes likewise. The Priests chanted prayers to Muali, to guide their eyes and not let them be deceived.

And at last, Muali reacted.

Tcana and Xhaitaan, together, were fifty arm-lengths from the fledgling eagles when the larger of the two adult birds - Tcana supposed the male, since both were alike in colouring - dropped in for a closer look.

Soaring past them, the wingspan of the beautiful bird looked as wide as Xhaitaan was tall, Tcana thought in wonder. Muali was normally seen only at a distance, sitting on high rocks, or in flight high above the earth. As he flashed past she saw that his eyes were edged with yellow, and between his black wing feathers were windows of white. She felt his wind on her cheeks, and saw that Xhaitaan was as spellbound as she.

The great eagle climbed again, and so did they, moving ever closer, inch by inch, to the heap of twigs at the crest of the mountain. Tcana dared not look down, but knew that if she did, those below would appear as pebbles beside the rock that was Muali's home.

The big bird dropped again, then climbed almost vertically, and when Tcana thought he could surely go no higher he closed his wings and fell, like one of his soapstone images. Ten feet below them he broke from his dive and looped upwards again, and suddenly Tcana realised that he was dancing.

The dance went on for several minutes, the climbing and diving and looping, the rush of wings; then, abruptly, Tcana knew the dance was over, and the ceremony was about to begin.

She and Xhaitaan froze against the rock, hearts pounding, as their god swooped toward them. They were in his hands – if he struck, they would fall, and be killed on the distant rock below. If he had made a decision, he would bless them.

The enormous wings beat above Tcana's head, as though hesitating for a second; then Muali seemed to hang over Xhaitaan's shoulders, his thick, feathered talons only a span away from the finely muscled arms. He hung there for what felt to Tcana an age, and then veered away, and then was back again for a while more. Twice! Only once more, Tcana prayed; just once more, and I shall be Queen of the amaTsimbaboue, and always, Muali, always I will revere you, be your Priestess, in my heart!

The black eagle soared away again, and Tcana thought he would not come back. She and Xhaitaan stared at each other, and then, miraculously, the god returned. A third time he held his position over Xhaitaan's head, and then, triumphantly, he climbed to where his mate met him in mid-air. Tcana thought they would collide, but at the last possible moment their meeting was a harmony. They linked their powerful claws, and whirled down to those waiting below, spiralling together until it seemed they would stop only when they smacked the hard ground. But then, only feet above the head of the King, they broke free and soared upward once more.

Slowly, carefully, side by side, Tcana and Xhaitaan began their descent.

Nada swore. Not in front of the men, of course – for that she would have been severely reprimanded by her husband, the King; nor in front of the other women of Tsimbabouetcang – she would not degrade herself that way; but before her servants. Even they, used as they were to her tantrums, were shocked enough to exchange nervous glances, and cough uneasily.

When it was clear that the Oracle required Tcana, Nada had been delighted. Muali could not be refused – the peasant girl would be lost to her son forever, and he would take his rightful place on the throne without further challenges, and with her cousin's daughter at his side. Nada would be the King's mother. Kisang's mother had scowled darkly; Nada had smirked sweetly back at her.

Now, Nada scowled, and Kaka smirked. Much as the King, Mgane, loved his second son, marriage to one so unworthy as Tcana for the First Wife would surely be intolerable to the people, if not actually to the throne itself. Kisang, both women were certain, had won the sibling battle.

Kisang, too, smirked. The detested usurper of his father's love was to be ousted. Blood to blood - and Nada, as Kaka had so often pointed out, was of peasant stock herself. It was only natural that her son should return to it. Kisang grimaced as he rubbed the hot washing-stone over his heavy torso. His skin glowed from the treatment; the rough stone had been boiled in water before he used it, and the temperature almost burned him.

Still, he could understand his half-brother's attraction to this particular peasant. Certainly, she was the most beautiful woman, at present, of the amaTsimbaboue. She moved ... she moved ... Kisang growled as he thought of the way Tcana moved. Perhaps Xhaitaan knew, after all, what he was doing. A woman like that could turn the brains of any man ... even the King, perhaps ...

The thought worried him. His future lay in the King's distaste for such a marriage. If Mgane began to like the girl ... but of course, he wouldn't. Tcana may be beautiful, may be a woman to desire, but she was not Royalty, and her manners and speech would surely instantly show her up. Why, her father was a cattle herd! Kisang's smirk returned.

Besides, Xhaitaan was too mild. What the amaTsimbaboue had to understand was that an army was necessary. They had been a peaceful tribe for too long, locked away here in their stronghold, from where they farmed the land and traded occasionally with the Coastal people, and even more rarely with the Traders who came from the north. It was time an army was built again; it was well known that other tribes had them, and who was to know when the amaTsimbaboue might be attacked? Also, of course, if there were an army - under his, Kisang's, command, naturally – well, there was always the possibility of taking from others by force what would not be given willingly ... Not that that was part of the plan. *No,* Kisang thought, *we simply need a good defence mechanism. When I am King ...*

He dismissed Xhaitaan almost humourously. Xhaitaan was a fool.

Maxa, Kisang's cousin and his wife of two years, did not find either Xhaitaan or his prospective bride particularly funny. She considered the situation a dangerous one for herself and her husband. Kisang was Maxa's route to the throne. She intended to be First Wife – and as she saw it, she was Kisang's only hope of becoming King. Mgane liked her, she knew; he had encouraged the marriage, looking forward to a grandchild.

Frustrated, Maxa slapped her forehead. After two years she was still not pregnant. She was certain the fault lay with her husband, but he was equally certain it lay with her. And so she had recently slipped out unnoticed to visit a sangoma, who, it was said, could make the most barren woman have a child. The drug she gave Maxa was evil-smelling, and worse on the tongue, but Maxa was desperate. If she gave Kisang a child, he himself would despise her less, and the child would secure Maxa's own position with the King. And so she drank the dosage dutifully, morning and evening, and waited for her husband to come to her.

Kisang, however, had virtually lost interest in his wife. She did not excite him, and it was obvious to him that she was barren. Maxa knew this, and was waiting for exactly the right time to tell him of the medicine-woman's prescription.

That time would have to be soon. The peasant Tcana looked healthy enough, and if she provided a son ...

Maxa's enmity for Tcana was, if anything, greater than Nada's.

Nada's own scowl remained. Kaka had borne the King only one child – Kisang. The second wife had been barren, and the third had given Mgane only daughters – three of them. She, Nada, had provided the second son, the favourite. And also a daughter, Xita, who was a year younger than ... Nada almost spat. Xita was a year younger than Tcana.

The fifth wife, of course, had borne Lengane, the third son. But Lengane was a child still, just seven years of age, and certainly no threat to Xhaitaan. No, there was no-one to match Xhaitaan ... unless he married that slut, who had cast herself before him at every opportunity, who had chased him shamelessly, flaunting her beauty for him, swaying her hips at him, casting the light from those buck's eyes his way ... She was surely a witch, that she had so charmed Xhaitaan, and even – yes, even Muali.

A witch! The import of the word hit Nada suddenly. Tcana Ndhlovu – a witch!

The little woman, who in some strange way resembled the Oracle, sat down to think.

Chapter 14

Zambia

The Russians were beginning to worry. Perhaps they had overestimated the mission boy's talents? No-one had heard from his stick, whether they were dead or alive; other fighters were coming in and going out, and still there was no news. It was unusual, and disturbing.

The hit in the Ntubu district, further in than any of their units had ventured yet, had been a masterpiece, of course. They'd laughed long about that information when the three who had been sent by the Mamba to mislead the security forces had reached home, by the skin of their teeth. But after that, the Mamba had disappeared.

There was another possibility. "Skuzapo," suggested the big Russian who had dispatched the group. "They have him, and that is why we hear nothing."

"No," said his superior slowly. "There is the matter of the disappearance from the Chakwane Pan of those eight men. None of our groups have reported the abductions. Those men, like our Mamba, have vanished."

"His orders were to subvert the locals."

"I don't think," said the slow man again, "that the Mamba is one to stay with simple orders. I think that we will hear of him again. Soon."

Rhodesia

He was getting restless. His group, even in this short time, were softening, falling into the life here. He had to get them out. They bought basic supplies – nothing that would need cooking, or would leave signs behind. Biltong, mainly, and dried fish, and bread. And even these were luxuries for the work that was ahead.

Kennedy must be relaxing, by now. It was time for the Mamba to strike again.

Peter Kennedy was anything but relaxed. The longer there was no sign of the Mamba, the more nervous he became. He was puzzled, and Kuru knew it.

Kuru had accepted that, for the time being, there was no way of tracing his brother from Elliott's Mission. He didn't even know if he were alive or dead ... perhaps it would be better the latter. The alternative disturbed the big Ndebele. He was now fully aware of the terrorist training procedures, the brainwashing, that abductees from Rhodesia were receiving in Zambia, some even in Russia. He did not like to think of his young brother as a terrorist.

It was true that after Kuru had left Elliott's Mission, he had been back only rarely to see his sibling, and then only in the first two or three years. The last time he had visited, Mandhla had been thirteen years old. After that there had been the illness and problems at home, and then – then he had joined the army, and somehow there was no time. But they had written. Mandhla's last letter had come two weeks before the abduction of the children. It had spoken of the vegetable garden, and of Mr. Elliott's approaching birthday, and the planned celebrations. And of Nada.

Kuru shook his head to clear it. He would not give up the search for his brother. But right now there were other, more pressing, matters to take care of. Specifically, the Mamba.

Mandhla Ndhlovu's brainwashing, the experiences he had been through, and his self-imposed mission, had combined to produce one noticeable effect on him. They had given him a pride in his work. That night, when they pulled out of Bulawayo, he could not resist indulging that pride. He wrapped a parcel, weighted it with a small rock, and threw it through a window carelessly left open at the back of a police station.

The parcel was addressed to Major Peter Kennedy.

It found its way to him fairly quickly, after it had been checked by the bomb disposal team, sniffed by trained dogs, and rattled by more than one curious hand. Now, opened, it lay on the table in the central operations room of the Selous Scouts.

Felix grunted and reached out, turning the object over to examine the back of it. Kuru sniffed, watching Peter's face carefully.

"Bulawayo?" repeated Peter slowly.

"Bulawayo," reiterated his boss.

Peter straightened from the table and jiggled his shoulders to loosen the tension. "Bulawayo," he said again, musingly.

The township revealed nothing to the searchers, except that a small group of men purporting to be from the North, from a village somewhere near Lupani, had spent a few weeks doing odd jobs to earn some money, and then left – homeward, according to some who had spoken to them before they went.

On a whim, Kuru checked their names.

So we know where they were after the Ntubu hit. We know they led us one way, then doubled back to get what they wanted and to lose us, then came south once more. Where the hell are they now?"

Peter was worried. This 'Mamba' was showing an unprecedented skill in planning and carrying out his operation – whatever that might be. And, even more disturbing, he seemed to want Peter Kennedy to know it.

The telephone on his desk rang, startling him out of his contemplation.

"Peter?" Felix's voice was brisk. Something was up.

"Find something?"

"Perhaps. Inganga. Intaff reported a sighting east of there. They say eight men, travelling."

"When?"

"Their GC man said three hours ago."

Three hours! What unbelievable luck! "I'll call you," he said, and put the receiver down. Immediately, he dialled a friend who owed him. "Kenny? Peter."

"Peter!" The voice was clear across the telephone lines, warm and pleased. "We're hearing plenty about you – none of it for public release, unfortunately! Is it true?"

He laughed politely. "None of it. Listen, Kenny, this is urgent – I need the Sparrowhawks. You're closer than I am. Have Reg Wright take them into Inganga's Intaff offices immediately; there's a very hot trail from there. Eight men whom I think I may want very badly. I'll be there as soon as I can."

"You've got them. But they won't be pleased – they only got back two hours ago from a job."

"Then they should still be nice and warm."

There was a momentary silence on the other end of the line as Ken Cosby realised the importance of the request. Then, "They're on their way."

When Peter reached the Internal Affairs boma in Inganga, the burly District Commissioner told him the Sparrowhawks had left an hour and a half previously.

"The commander left a message for you, though. Said you only got them because this one's for someone special – you." An eyebrow was raised in query.

Peter grinned self-effacingly at the man who did not know who he was. "He wants my sister," he said easily, laughing.

The sighting had been a vague one; the GC man hadn't wanted to get too close because they appeared to be camped, and he didn't like to make them aware of him. With luck, they may still be there. Peter asked to see the man, but he'd already gone back to his job.

"Can't blow his cover," the DC said seriously. "You army guys just don't realise how dicey this spying business really is."

Peter smiled amiably. "I suppose we don't," he said.

There was no point in staying here. He headed for the Sparrowhawks' base in Bulawayo.

The radio was crackling when Peter walked into the room. Ken stood behind the operator, a concentrated frown creasing his forehead. He glanced briefly at Peter and grinned. "Welcome. We're waiting for contact."

They fell silent, listening to the humming airwaves.

When it came Peter almost jumped, and waited impatiently through the identification calls. He recognised Reg Wright's voice, terse and quiet. "We're about five minutes behind them, keeping distance. Made a sighting, then hung back. There are eight of them, not being as careful as they ought – but then, they have no idea we're here."

Peter reminded himself to talk to the man later about a change of unit. He was a good tracker and a steady man. He'd like the Scouts.

Ken took the microphone from the operator. "Get them, boy. Someone here wants them real bad."

There was a quiet laugh from the speaker. "You there, Peter?"

He leaned towards the mike. "Never closer. Get the bastards, Reg."

"How many would you like dead and how many alive?" Even now Wright had kept his sense of humour.

Peter grinned in response. "Keep me the commander. I'm not so worried about the rest." He paused, remembering the escape from the Fireforce hit. "On second thoughts, no, get as many alive as you can."

"You've got it. Stay tuned to this frequency for the next exciting edition! Out."

The wireless went silent. Ken looked at Peter. "Drink while we wait?"

Cosby stared over the rim of his glass at the man whose position he had inherited. "This is important to you, isn't it?"

"If it's the right lot – yes."

"What chance they are the right ones?"

Peter faced it. "Slim. But not," he added hastily, "slim enough to pass up."

They sat in silence again, each lost in his own thoughts. Peter worried and anticipated and got excited and slapped himself down, only to start worrying again. And what worried him most was that they had missed their real target. The Mamba, he was certain, would not have been so careless. Where the hell were they?

The radio came to life again nearly an hour later. "Request body carts, Sir," Wright said. No laughter now, only weariness.

"What's the count?" Cosby was brisk.

"Their side, three dead, five wounded. One of the wounded is the commander, Sir. Our side, clear except for a nicked earlobe."

"Whose?"

There was a momentary hesitation. "Mine, Sir."

They could hear the laughter of his men in the background.

They arrived at last, pulling the bodies from the back of the truck, carrying out one of the wounded, pushing the others to the ground. Reg Wright stood over them in the grey morning light, his stare demanding answers from Peter.

He couldn't give them. There were no wooden snakes, nothing to indicate that this was the Mamba. There was nothing. He kicked the wheel of the truck, still hot from its journey.

"Sorry guys. Wrong man." He turned away, bitter, then caught himself as he saw Wright watching him. "Maybe next time," he added, forcing a smile.

The wounded commander talked without much encouragement. The information was useful, but nothing startling. Peter was becoming bored with the routine questions the interrogator was asking. He interrupted abruptly. "The Mamba – who is he?"

The terrorist's eyes widened. Peter kicked his wounded shin and repeated the question. The man bent over, grimacing in pain. "I don't know, Baas! He is the Mamba. I heard of him, a little. But I don't know him. He is new. Only a year ... less, even ..."

"Where is he?"

The man almost laughed. "So you do not know, either?

Even you? It is true then. He is lost, as they have said he is."

Peter sensed he was telling the truth. Disgusted, he left the room. What kind of soldier, freedom fighter, terrorist, regular or otherwise, would let his own side think he was lost?

In the skies above Kariba, the aircraft droned lazily along its flight path, carrying holidaymakers and tourists from their vacations back to Salisbury. The pilot, John Kennedy, sat and joked with his crew, all of them relaxing now they were in the air. It was a brief flight back to their home city.

Below them, a group moving through the bush looked up.

Mandhla had moved as far north as he thought reasonable to confuse the Hyena. He and his group were travelling over fairly open ground when the sound of the aircraft came to them. Suddenly, Mandhla knew how to make an impact that would never be forgotten.

Swiftly they hauled out the missile launcher which they carried in case of an air attack. They set it up within minutes – just as the Viscount appeared in their vision. Carefully, they aimed, and Mandhla himself set the missile on its way.

He was surprised at the way the craft went down. He'd expected it to explode in mid-air; instead one wing tore away and the craft nosedived out of sight. Moments later the crash could be heard. Quickly they moved towards the site, knowing that they were taking the risk of meeting up with security forces who would certainly investigate immediately.

Pieces of the aeroplane were strewn everywhere, but what really astonished them was that some of the passengers were still living. Walking between the distorted pieces of the craft, the group rounded up the survivors – mainly women and children – who could move, grouped them, and then shot them. Mandhla, meanwhile, had found the cockpit where the copilot lay, his head shattered like an ostrich egg dropped from a great height. But the pilot was still alive, though his legs were smashed.

Mandhla stared at features that looked so familiar, so like those of his enemy, and his heart grew even harder.

John Kennedy looked back into the face of Mandhla Ndhlovu for a full minute, and then Mandhla reached out and picked up the pilot's cap that lay at his feet. Grimly unsmiling, he slowly put it onto his head, and then fired into the face of its owner.

Chapter 15

Rhodesia

Africa again. She watched the yellow and brown spreading below the 'plane as it circled to land, and smelled the peculiar dry dusty aroma of the continent that was different to anywhere else in the world as she walked across the tarmac to the Salisbury Airport transfer lounge for her connection.

In Bulawayo Tony waited, wearing the puppy-dog expression he reserved only for her. No, he hadn't heard from her brother. And no, there had been no visitors – of either gender. She told herself she shouldn't have expected any.

He told her about the shooting down of the Viscount near Kariba, and that Hilary's fiancée had been the pilot. Sickened, she tried to call Hilary, but the girl had apparently gone to her parents in Cape Town. She called Mark Kennedy and offered her condolences; to Peter Kennedy she simply sent a sympathy telegram. She didn't feel right about telephoning him, even if he were reachable.

They spent the next week with the Grey Scouts, who appreciated not only her beauty (the army men didn't see their women much, she realised with amusement) but also her horsemanship, and the mounts were quite at home with her loose cowboy-style of riding which disconcerted some of the more carefully schooled animals around the world. These horses were trained to accept any form of riding, and any type of noise around them.

They filmed some of the training techniques which were,

as Rebecca put it, "different, to say the least". The trainers explained to her that these horses carried their riders into the heat of battle in the bush war, and had to be prepared for anything and so were, very literally, "bomb-proofed" during training. She was suitably impressed.

And when she got home, there was a message at the studio from Kyle. He was here, at the Selbourne Hotel.

She phoned him. "Big brother, is it snowing in Africa?"

He laughed. "I know. It's been too long. But I'm in Bulawayo on an assignment that may last a couple of weeks. Can you see me? Come to that, can you put me up?"

"Can I ever! D'you think we'll manage without either of us having an emergency call of some sort?"

"I'll appeal to a higher authority. He'll see to it." Like the rest of the Rawlings family, Kyle had a deep faith in God. "How about meeting me tonight for dinner, and I'll come back to your place afterwards?"

"Prawns. Can you offer me prawns?"

"Whatever the little lady desires. Meet me in the Selbourne lobby. That way I won't have trouble finding your flat."

"Of course. I'd forgotten that the great world traveller hasn't a clue about maps. Seven o'clock, and you've got a date. Don't dare break it!"

He was there before she was, pacing uncomfortably around the lobby. She watched him for a moment from the doorway, almost without recognising him. He was different, somehow.

So was she, obviously. He stared at her as if she were a stranger. "Sharkie? That you?"

"None other. Do I get a kiss?"

"I don't know. Is it safe? Won't someone shoot me in a jealous rage?"

She laughed, hugging him. "Not tonight. Let's eat. I'm starved."

He looked too big for the restaurant. He didn't fit, and he felt it. It was a big adjustment from his normal way of life – camping out with refugees or war rebels or suchlike, avoiding bombs and mortar attacks, scraping a living from the land when necessary. All for the sake of a story.

They ate quietly, enjoying being together again. Now

and then he looked at her wonderingly. "You know, when I last saw you, you were just a kid. A beautiful kid, grant you, but a kid. Suddenly you're ... I don't know. All growed up."

"It happens. You've changed too, you know." She narrowed her eyes at him. "Are you eating right?" It was the family joke line, the question their father always asked, and he laughed.

"You certainly are! How many more courses do you want to go through?" He was serious again suddenly. "Shark, I know it's been two years and I should expect you to be different. But there's some-thing else ... a man?"

She returned his look calmly. "I don't have a boyfriend, if that's what you mean. How about you?"

"Me? A boyfriend?" She smacked him with her serviette and he laughed. "When would I find the time? Besides, my best girl is right here with me." He covered her hand with his and leaned forward for a kiss.

As he leaned back her eyes caught a movement at the door. She turned her head and found herself looking into arctic blue eyes that watched her sardonically. He moved towards them, tall in his uniform, and swept his beret off as he reached the table, scrunching it into a pocket.

"Miss Rawlings. I was told I would find you here."

She remained seated, though Kyle stood, and was ignored. "Kyle, this is Major Kennedy. What can I do for you, Major?"

"I have been asked by a close associate of Mr. Ian Smith to give you an interview." Business-like and cold, he obviously didn't want to obey the order.

"That's very thoughtful of the Prime Minister's associate." She wondered which one had been irritated enough by her persistence to put Peter Kennedy on the spot. "When?"

"I'm afraid this evening is the best I can give you." He glanced briefly at Kyle. "If it doesn't suit you, I can't tell you when I'll be free again. And incidentally – no cameras."

"You told me that before, Major." She thought fast. She desperately wanted the interview, but ...

She had forgotten Kyle was also in the business of getting stories. "Go ahead, hon. I can wait."

"This'll take a while. Major, would you mind if I dropped

Kyle at my flat first? He hasn't been there before."

He raised one eyebrow and looked her in the eye. "I'll follow you there and we can go in my vehicle for the interview."

He waited outside in his jeep and watched them carry Kyle's luggage inside. When she came out again, alone, he opened the door for her and slammed it harder than necessary. As he crashed the gears and pulled away she flinched at the hardness in his face.

He finally stopped at Hillcrest Dam, and in the deserted silence they walked along the paths between night-blackened waterways that lapped the edges softly. Silvery moon-pennies glittered on tiny waves. Impulsively, she stopped and took off her shoes to feel the damp grass between her toes.

He broke the silence at last. "Do you always do grass barefoot?"

"I like to. Habit, I suppose."

"Childhood?"

"Yes. And I'm supposed to be doing the interviewing, Major."

He shrugged indifferently and waited. She felt the antagonism arise again. "Why are you constantly angry with me, Major?"

"Perhaps I didn't expect to find that you're just like other women, after all." It was thrown at her like a whiplash.

She stopped walking. "What exactly does that mean?"

"It doesn't matter. Let's get this over with."

"Why did you grant me an interview?"

"I was ordered to by someone who is impressed with you and unimpressed with my outfit, or the secrecy it requires to operate fully."

"He sounds unusual. Everyone I've spoken to has been impressed by you. A living legend, is one of your tags. Of course, another is the Hyena."

He glared at her. Not many knew about the second one, and he wondered who the hell she'd actually got at. "I wish you wouldn't ask other people about me."

"When I asked you directly I couldn't get answers. Why do they romanticise you?"

"These people make mountains out of molehills."

"I was told you'd taken the best unit in Rhodesia and made it better."

"I run a tracker outfit, Miss Rawlings. The best. That's it."

"That's not what I heard."

"You shouldn't listen to rumours. I run a security operation, and because it's a security operation I can't tell you about it."

"But it's dangerous. More so than the rest of the war?"

"My men take the danger. I put them into it. Miss Rawlings, I understand that you're still very young, but there's something you have to learn. Not all the influence in Rhodesia, including that of Mr. Smith himself, will convince me to discuss with you – or with any reporter – what my men do for this country. No matter what lengths you may go to."

She was silent for a moment. "That was below the belt."

"I don't like women who manipulate men with their femininity, particularly when it puts other men in danger."

"I'm sorry. You're right." She pushed at the mud with her toes, knowing he was wrong – at least, about the manipulating. "Your men are more important than my story, and if you'd taken the time and trouble to have this conversation with me sooner we might not be here now."

He watched her bare foot play with the water, the hem of her long skirt dampening rapidly. Her hair was up again in a French roll, with the same thick tress falling loose into her neck.

"We'd better get you back to your boyfriend."

She realised suddenly that he was annoyed by Kyle. "Kyle isn't my boyfriend, he's my brother." She watched his face as she said it, and the slight reaction brought laughter bubbling to the surface. She turned her back to him and bent to the water, trailing her fingers before she stood upright again. "I'm sorry. I didn't mean to laugh at you."

"I deserved it. I should have learned by now not to jump to conclusions."

He was relieved, and moved up behind her. She felt him touch her hair, and suddenly it cascaded free as he pulled out the big comb that held it in place. Startled, she turned towards him, one hand to her hair.

He stared at her. "You should wear it down more often." He reached out slowly and touched the waterfall, bringing it forward over her shoulder.

She was mesmerised; Move! she told herself, but couldn't. He spread the mane, and his fingers touched the skin of her shoulder and lingered there. She felt his longing deep inside her own body; then he pulled his arm away and stepped back, breathing deeply.

"I appreciated the telegram about my cousin's death. It was thoughtful." She was silent, and he watched the shadow of her eyelashes on her cheeks as she looked down. "Perhaps I should return you to your brother's safe-keeping."

He turned and strode away, and she followed, her whole body in a turmoil she was beginning to recognise.

They drove back to the flat in silence. The lights were all off. Kyle must be asleep. He walked her up the stairs again and waited while she found her key and unlocked the door. She turned back to him. "Coffee?"

He smiled. "We've had this conversation before."

"This time my brother's here." It was slightly defensive.

He looked at her speculatively. "I don't think that makes it any safer. Do you?" He leaned towards her and kissed her softly on the mouth. Her belly surged and she flinched.

"Goodnight." And he was gone. Again.

As she heard the Landrover start up and drive away she could have, inexplicably, wept. She turned and went inside.

In the jeep, Peter Kennedy cursed. For the first time he resented his self-imposed rule of no complications. But in his job, he couldn't afford them, and he knew that it could endanger the woman implicated. And now, of all things, he was getting mixed up with a child! Her actual age – twenty-four, hadn't she said? – made no difference. Beneath the brisk, efficient veneer of the television personality, he knew positively now, she was untouched.

He was far from innocent himself. Women had always come easy to him, and he had treated them carelessly and accepted whatever they offered, if they appealed enough.

He had never had to worry about involvement, had always been honest with them and quick to break off a relationship if they became too serious.

He wondered why he couldn't do the same now, but he knew the answer. She was ridiculously naïve. She hadn't known what she was offering, or perhaps even that she was offering – hadn't even really known what she was wanting. She was as gauche as a young schoolgirl, almost clumsy in her desire, and Peter Kennedy didn't think she was ready to deal with that ache. Come to that, he didn't think he was, either.

And there was something else. He wasn't sure what, but she was different in other ways from most women. It was something he couldn't quite identify.

If nothing else, it was a challenge just staying away from her.

Chapter 16

Rhodesia

She was woken by the jangling of the telephone the next morning. It was Tony. "I got a call from a friend. There's been a hit in Kweri, an hour and a half south of here, and my friend says we can travel with him if we're ready in half an hour."

Kyle understood. It was work. In any case, he had his own to do.

When they reached Kweri they headed for the office boma where men were assembling with firearms ranging from pistols to FNs and shotguns. The DC, annoyed at having extra personnel thrust on him at such a time, wasn't impressed by either her beauty or her fame, or his orders to accommodate her. He explained tersely to them: "The van Buurens are what we call 'weekend farmers' – they have a smallish place and it's run during the week by their head boy. They live in Bulawayo and on weekends they travel out to check on things. It's a dangerous way to farm; you don't know what's happening on your property until you're there. Van Buuren and his ten-year-old son were found late last night by one of the farm hands, next to their jeep on one of the dirt roads on the farm. They must have stopped to help someone, or give a lift, the fools. These people who live in the towns just don't damned well understand!"

The police arrived then. The mood was ugly; when everyone was present the DC and MIC called the farmers to order.

"All right. They've had a head start and we can't expect army help for hours yet – it's up to us. We don't know how many or in what direction they're headed yet; our GC men are already out. The cattle sales start tomorrow. Bart, you'll have to run them – I know you haven't much experience but that's the best we can do." Bart was a sixty-year-old mechanic from the workshops. "Miss Rawlings, you're welcome to cover the cattle sale if you like – nothing else. We can put you up tonight in the cadet's mess. The rest of you get your instructions from Greg – he's worked it all out." He indicated the MIC.

Bart collected Rebecca and Tony at dawn in an open jeep – "All there was left," he explained – and as they drove south along the dirt road as fast as Bart dared, with Tony's camera at the ready, Rebecca sat tensely, a shotgun ready over her knees, the pistols to hand, and Bart's FN lying alongside his seat. Bart watched the road for signs of mines, but they both knew he was unlikely to see anything in this light. Rebecca comforted herself with the thought that if they did trigger one, they wouldn't have much time to know about it.

She would never be awake at this time of day again without remembering the fear that was with her on that two-hour drive into the bundu. The grey half-light was the most dangerous time of all; movement was almost impossible to detect and normally no-one in his right mind dared the roads before the sun was well up. The roar of the jeep could be heard for miles above the early morning sounds of the bush, and she knew that if they crossed the path of the fleeing terrorists they could easily become a hit-and-run casualty.

They didn't relax until they pulled into the sales area, with the cattle milling in the pens. With delight she recognised the one-armed VO from the Ntubu sales. She willingly joined him in his inspections, chatting and laughing as they left the guard-duty to Bart and some of the cowherds.

When the farmers began to arrive they bristled with weapons. The buyers had spent the night at the Police outpost less than an hour's drive away, and each brought a shotgun. When they realised Bart was running the sale they all rallied round and took over, and between them the sale moved fast.

Tony took footage of the weapons and the watchfulness, but there wasn't much else to film and he rapidly became bored. Cattle weren't his thing. When he tried to wander into the bush in the hopes of finding game for the programme he was stopped by a burly farmer.

"*Jassis, boet, is jy mal?* You mad? You don't go into the bush when terrs are running," the man said in thick Afrikaans accents.

He contented himself with shots of Rebecca prodding cattle into the arena. On getting back to Kweri they were told that the terrorists appeared to have got away, and, disappointed, they headed back to Bulawayo.

He didn't contact her that week, and the following Monday, with Kyle temporarily basing himself in Salisbury for his assignment, she and Tony travelled to Umtali and booked into the Wise Owl Hotel, which was comfortable with a good table.

They were there to report on the "keeps", or consolidated villages. These were villages enclosed in security walls for the safety of the residents. They found the Internal Affairs offices in Umtali big and gloomy, and very governmental. The DC was sticky about them going out into the bush alone.

"Umtali is a very hot area," he explained. "Our cadets and DAs go out during the week, staying at Tyrol – that's a disused farmhouse. They come in on Friday night and leave again on Monday morning, but the place is a stronghold. The army goes out every day to give extra protection while they lay out the keeps. You can travel with them. I'll arrange it."

They gave her an office to do her paperwork in, the one in which the radio and licencing files were kept, and she worked late that evening to prepare for the next day's shoot. Tony headed for the hotel bar when she said she'd catch a taxi back to the hotel.

She found herself staring into space more often than working, and got up to open a window and let fresh air into the stuffy room. At that moment the radio crackled into life. The voice was a woman's; the static only barely disguised her borderline hysteria.

"Mayday, mayday! Is anyone there? Mayday!"

Rebecca gave it twenty seconds in case anyone in a more responsible position answered, as she'd been trained to do in Ntubu. Then, when the desperate call was repeated, she lifted the handset and pressed the button.

"Mayday caller, this is Intaff offices. What's the problem, over?" She released the button.

"Thank God!" The relief in the woman's voice was palpable. "We're under attack; my husband and sons are holding them off but we need help!"

"Can you tell me where you are, over?" She wrote the position down. "All right, I've got that. Hang in there, someone's coming to you. Good luck. Out."

She picked up the telephone, her fingers shaking, and called the emergency police number that was stuck in easy view above the radio set. She gave them the air band and position, and then listened in to the radio conversation and encouragement that followed while helicopters and men were sent to the farm's aid.

"Can you handle a rifle?" the steady-voiced police operator asked the woman.

"No! My arthritis has crippled my hands; my husband said to stay out of the way." There was the sound of a mortar explosion. "Oh please, please, you have to help us!" she screamed.

"Help is on its way," the policeman replied calmly. "They'll be there in a few minutes. Do you have a watch on?"

"Yes."

"Look at the time. In another ten minutes they'll be with you. That's not so long, is it?"

"Can't they get here sooner? My sons will be killed – my husband ..."

There was silence suddenly. Rebecca prayed, willing the woman to speak.

"Mrs. Bentley? Mrs. Bentley, are you still there?" demanded the policeman.

"Oh – I'm sorry. I was just so surprised. They've stopped shooting!" Rebecca could almost touch the hope in the woman's voice. She fumed that Tony wasn't here to record all this.

"Mrs. Bentley – they haven't gone away. I repeat, they have not gone away! Tell your family to hold their positions!" His voice was urgent.

"Yes, all right. Hold on. I –"

With a frightening suddenness the noise began again. Rebecca heard the woman scream above the racket of rifle fire.

"Hugh! Hugh! Oh God –" The button on her side was released, and immediately the police operator was back on the air.

"Mrs. Bentley, what is happening? Answer me, Mrs. Bentley! What is happening?"

A man's voice came onto the radio, shocked. "My brother, Hugh. His face is gone ... his ... his head ... oh my God ..." He started to weep, and Rebecca wept with him.

"Mr. Bentley, please don't stop defending yourselves. Get back to your positions – tell your family!"

"Yes, I'll tell them ..." He stopped, still holding the button down on the handset, and clearly above the shooting Rebecca heard the sound of helicopters. The noise level increased and then the man was shouting into the set, "They're here! They're here! Oh, thank you, they're here!" He was sobbing openly. "I have to go!"

"Good luck," she heard the operator say, and then there was silence for a moment. Then he spoke again, using the Intaff call sign stuck onto the radio. She responded.

"I knew you'd be listening. Well done. Out."

Well done? she thought, tears searing her cheeks. *A man just died!*

And somehow, the three who had lived didn't make up for the one who had not.

When the armoured vehicle stopped at the hotel for them in the morning, the eight men leaned out and whistled admiringly. Their Commander helped her into the back with them, and the two in the front groaned dramatically. They were a small unit of "Dad's Army", and the youngest was forty-ish.

At Tyrol, the cadets showed them briefly around the

encampment. The whole area was sandbagged heavily, and armed DAs were on guard at various points around the perimeter. The camp bristled with weaponry of all sorts. Like a fortress, thought Rebecca, as Tony's camera whirred. They were given camouflage to wear over their own clothes, and then they all piled into two vehicles for the short journey to the keep. The army insisted she travel with them – "After all," they pointed out, "we were assigned to look after you. Can't do that if you're in another truck, now, can we?"

As they stopped at the junction with the main road, a convoy of open trucks crawled past. "Stand up, stand up!" the men urged her, pushing her to her feet. They wriggled with her until her top half was visible through the gun slot that ran along the length of the vehicle, and as the trucks passed by the Commander waved wildly to the uniformed men seated in rows in the carriers, pointing to Rebecca. Most of the soldiers rose to their feet, staring in amazement at the camouflage-clad girl, and then started whooping at her.

The Commander, with all the breath he could muster, bellowed: "Eat your hearts out, boys!" The trucks disappeared amidst uproarious laughter, and the inmates of the armoured vehicle collapsed weakly, tears streaking their faces. The hilarity had hardly dissipated by the time they rolled to a stop in the middle of the bush.

When she jumped down into the arms of one of the men (they had tossed coins for the duty), she looked around her in disbelief. "Where's the keep?" she asked.

"You're standing on it," replied Mike, the cadet in charge, and handed her an enormous steel tape measure.

The army took up defensive positions around an area of about two acres. Rebecca, the cadets and the DAs began to measure out and plan the keep.

That afternoon a GC man panted into the area. Mike okayed him for the army guards. He spoke rapidly to Mike in Shona, and disappeared again. Mike gave the DAs orders, handed Rebecca an FN and commandeered two of the army men and one of the vehicles, with Tony filming avidly. They bumped over a barely visible track to a tiny village nearby, where Mike demanded to see the headman.

The man was surprisingly young for his position – fifty-ish, Rebecca estimated. He was hesitant and obviously scared as he spoke to them. Mike started with the usual greetings and then asked pleasantly whether strangers had stayed in the area the night before.

The headman's face became instantly deadpan. "No, Baas."

"Come now, I know there were people here. I want to help you, but you must tell me about them. How long did they stay?" asked Mike persuasively.

"No Baas, you are mistaken. There was no-one here," the man insisted, his black face sweating streaks through the dust.

"Which way did they go, old man?" Mike said patiently.

"They were not here." The greying head shook decisively.

Moving with a suddenness that took them all by surprise, Mike brought the butt of his FN rifle down hard on the ground, inches away from the bare black toes. Involuntarily, Rebecca stepped backwards.

Mike's face was ugly as he repeated his question. The African shook visibly, but still admitted nothing. Mike stepped up very close to him and raised the rifle so that the tip lifted the headman's chin. The dark eyes widened and the man sweated more profusely.

"Please, Baas, please – I can tell you nothing! Leave me now, please," he begged. Rebecca turned away, feeling sick in the pit of her stomach, acid in her throat, her limbs shaking.

Suddenly, Mike shouted and the headman leapt back as though he'd been shot, cowering on his haunches and mumbling, terrified. Mike leaned closer to hear what he was saying, and then abruptly, after speaking harshly to the man, he ushered his group towards the truck and drove back to the keep.

Rebecca felt ugly and betrayed, and something hard grew in her stomach. She had a dirty slime in the back of her throat, and looked out of the window at the passing bush to avoid Mike's eyes. Like it or not, she was becoming emotionally involved in this war.

Later, in the armoured truck on the way back into Umtali, the Commander tried to explain to her. "It has to be done, Miss Rawlings. If they won't answer truthfully, then they have to be forced. That's the worst of this goddamned war – they're threatened by the terrs if they do speak out, and then they're threatened by us if they don't. And if we don't get the information from then they'll die anyway at the hands of the terrs. It's a filthy, vicious circle, and none of us like it any more than you do. But wait until you've actually seen an example of terrorist warfare, and then see if you feel quite as righteous as you do now."

The opportunity arose two days later, while they were helping with another keep in the bush. The order came over the radio from the offices, and Mike was reluctant to take her.

"It's no place for a woman," he said gruffly.

If her brother could do it, so could she. "Don't try to protect me, Mike. I'm here to do a job, just the same as you are. What's going down?"

"The terrs have made an example of an old headman up there –" he pointed into the Eastern Highlands – "and we have to check the report out. I gather the body is several days old. The people deserted the place, probably when it happened."

The truck bounced over a rough track into the mountains and eventually stopped next to a remote clutch of huts. The DAs piled out of the back, FNs at the ready, and took up protective stances around the central hut. Mike helped her out and looked at her compassionately as Tony filmed. "Ready?" he asked.

Rebecca nodded. Taking a deep breath, she ducked and followed him into the hut.

The stench hit her first, hanging heavy in the gloom, and it took her eyes a few moments to adjust. The old man lay sprawled up against the mud wall, one sightless eye staring up at the grass roof, the eyelid cut away. The other eye was missing; possibly his murderers had eaten it in superstition. Eating parts of the body, Mike expounded, was believed to offer protection from the dead one's spirit seeking revenge.

The lower half of his face was a beaten pulp, and his ears and lips had been removed. He was naked and had been castrated viciously; the members were also missing. The remains of the body showed evidence of a harsh beating, and superficial cuts made by a bayonet, before bullets had slammed into his chest to ensure death. The terrs took no chances.

Rebecca stood it for ten long seconds; then she ran outside and was sick into the dust, over and over. When she thought the lining of her stomach must come up, Mike and Tony came out to her.

"I'm all right," she insisted. Suddenly the interview of the headman two days previously had taken on new meaning. So, in fact, had the whole Rhodesian war.

Chapter 17

Zambia

In Lusaka once more, he answered the summons and was allowed in by the bodyguards. This time he was taken to a room which was done out as a shrine; black and white curtains draped the walls, and at the centre of the room a life-sized model in copper of a Mamba stood, gleaming in the dark light of the room. Before it knelt the fat man, in an attitude of prayer.

Mandhla said nothing, waiting, and eventually the man lifted his bulk and turned to face him.

"Mandhla Ndhlovu," he said musingly. "Come with me." He led Mandhla into the office they had met in previously, where he drew a deep breath. "Who told you," he demanded, "to shoot down an airplane?"

"It was necessary," replied Mandhla.

"It was not necessary!" The voice was harsh. "You overstep your authority, and you expect me to back you up!"

"No, Sir, I expect no backing up."

"I have done so already. The media from around the world have been pounding on my door; I was in England when you did this thing, and I was brought before the British Prime Minister to answer for it! When we are trying to convince the world that we are fighting for the freedom of the country, such a disgraceful occurrence as this is difficult to justify."

"I thought it was an army plane, or one carrying army personnel," he lied quickly.

"I am glad to hear it, because that is how I explained it

to them." He paced the room, considering the silent man before him. Then he stopped before the large picture of the Mamba with the copper plaque beneath. He indicated for Mandhla to join him.

"This picture," he said, "was given to me by an American Negro who believes that our fight is justified, and who has heard of my religion. I wish now to explain this religion to you, because I have been told by the Rhaba that you are the man who will combat my greatest enemy."

When he had finished the detailed history, Mandhla was awed. This was something totally against what he had been taught at the mission station, and he was unsure how to react. Deep down, something told him he was dealing with a man who saw things very differently to himself.

He leaned closer to the picture and read the words on the copper plaque beneath:

"May Muali bless your struggle against the Eagle."

"You see," said the bloated man before him, "for us, you have become the representative of Muali. Truly, you are the Mamba."

Once more travelling without the knowledge of the natives, the Nyoka re-entered Zimbabwe and moved south. East of Bulawayo they again hid their war-tools. Their best cover now was to become part of the populace.

They moved into Bulawayo, into the townships nearby, and established themselves there, using the paperwork and new identities the Mamba had chosen for them – those of the eight dead villagers. They did not make the mistake that previous comrades had. They disclosed to no-one their real identities; even the most fervent ZIPRA supporters in the township were unaware of the presence of their heroes. Mandhla felt almost secure. And very sure of himself, since discovering totally by accident that the pilot of the aircraft had been the cousin of Major Peter Kennedy.

They began to look for odd jobs.

Reg Wright passed the selection course with flying colours, as Peter had known he would. He was duly given promotion, and placed at the head of one of the units.

In the Scouts there was no colour distinction between

the men. The regiment of necessity comprised more blacks than whites, and the blacks were the forefront of the whole operation. And these African soldiers had much to recommend them. Peter had very quickly discovered that they had incredible physical endurance. Also, the African has very good night sight, giving him a sense of direction the European lacks without a compass. He has excellent powers of observation and is able to memorise what he sees.

But he also has a tendency to break down if suddenly faced with a totally unexpected situation, and finds it difficult to adjust to swiftly changing conditions. Therefore, in a surprise attack, he is liable to cut and run. This was something the leaders of each unit had to face, and deal with. Many of the men's weaknesses – such as their natural fear of heights – were dealt with during training; they were forced to climb, and to cross ropes strung between tall trees. They were made to fire their rifles over and over and over, gradually wearing the noise into them to eradicate their habit of jumping each time the weapon went off. And they were made to face situations that the whites too had difficulty adjusting to.

Thus, on the whole, the African soldiers' strengths outweighed the dangers of their giving in to natural fears, but the possibility of a break-and-run was always in the backs of the leaders' minds.

Not, Peter told Reg, that it had happened yet, just as turning a terrorist had only once been fatal to the unit he was working with. But the dangers were ever present.

Reg Wright didn't mind. Danger was his hobby.

Once again, he was gone. Vanished, without a trace. Peter Kennedy could have spat. Nightly, lying in his cold bed, he castigated himself for his inadequacies.

The Scouts' record was improving all the time. They were being used on operations within Zambia and Mozambique, strikes at the bases of the terrorist headquarters. Their standing with other regiments, and with all those in the know, was improving all the time. They were receiving accolades from all quarters – and, of course, the inevitable backbiting from the envious, especially from those whose thunder they were stealing.

Yet still the one man they wanted so badly eluded them. After the aircraft, where a wooden snake had been found beside the body of the murdered pilot – Peter's own cousin – the Mamba had done his usual disappearing trick, but had struck again three times since. All in totally unexpected quarters, and without following a straight path. And always, there were the carved serpents to remind Major Kennedy that the Mamba lived. In total, over the past few months since his first appearance near Ntubu, he had been responsible for the murder of fourteen whites. Peter wasn't sure about black deaths; he assumed they occurred, but if they did, no-one was reporting them – understandably. They had identified all the reported tribal deaths, and the groups who had committed them. No, if it weren't for the white hits and the carvings, the Selous Scouts would doubt the Mamba even existed.

Which was exactly as Mandhla wanted it. He twisted and turned, leading his Nyoka in a zig-zag route but aiming eventually for Zambia. He knew he was a thorn in the side of Peter Kennedy, and that was as it should be. But it was time he reported in, before he was cut loose by the Russian commanders.

Besides, his ammunition was finally running out. They were travelling lighter, but they had eked their supplies out. They had wasted nothing, using bayonets to do their work for them, with a few rounds of tracer ammunition to push the point home. But because they had not had to show off to villagers, or for that matter kill African tribesmen, their supplies had gone much further than expected.

Mandhla did not hold with the killing of black men – even less with that of women and children. He was here ostensibly to fight for freedom from White Rule, and to him that did not include bully-boy tactics. He recognised the necessity to kill those who were a danger to him, or those who were more useful dead, but he deplored an overkill, and the waste of black lives. He had no intention of furthering the aspirations of jealous villagers by killing whomsoever they wished to dub a "sellout". That was not his mission. And so he continued to keep his presence a well-guarded secret. No-one but the Nyoka knew where the Nyoka were.

He selected his killing sites carefully, watching the victims, picking his hiding places, choosing his escape route, planning the most efficient way to do the job. And when he struck it was swift, with immediate withdrawal. After, that is, he had left his calling card.

He whittled those whenever he rested, remembering the descriptions given to him by the fat ZIPRA leader, and the pictures in his lounge. The illiterate are gifted with a brain that retains stories and descriptions to perfection so that they are passed on from generation to generation, and the word-pictures of the armbands the high priestess had worn had not varied from one teller to the next down through the centuries.

They were not difficult for him to make. He had always been interested in carving, and the Elliotts had encouraged the art form. He was working on another right now, as they rested in the cover of the silent bush.

One more hit. It was scheduled for that evening, and Mandhla was completing the last touches on the curving snake in his hand. After this one, they were going home. He paused. Home? No. Back to base.

This would perhaps be the easiest. An elderly farming couple who had refused to leave the land they and their families had nurtured for over a hundred years. They were both short-sighted, and very much at one with their black staff; they were ready to meet death, if necessary, but didn't really believe it would come through violence. In fact, any resistance offered would probably come from the house servant. He was a big man, and he carried an old shotgun with him everywhere. He did not leave his master and mistress alone for more than a few minutes at a time. Mandhla knew that this man was too loyal to give his people away.

What he didn't know was that the manservant had his suspicions. One of the children had seen a shadow slip through the surrounding bush that morning; the man had reported it to the nearest police station by telephone. He had tried the AgricAlert radio issued to all farmers, but as usual the battery was flat. He gave himself a sharp reminder to have it seen to.

It was dark when they went in. The couple were eating their dinner, served by the big Ndebele. Silent as always, Mandhla appeared in the room before they heard him enter the house. He stood before them, his AK-47 pointed at the old man, who looked calmly back at him. Mandhla almost shivered, remembering the first disciplinary killing ... the old man who had no fear. Impatiently, he dismissed the vision.

Behind him, his seven men filed into the room, their weapons ready. The man and his wife raised their hands, staring back at the intruders. The house servant stood, his face impassive, watching only the Section Commander. Mandhla turned away, looking out of the window, and then stiffened. He thought he saw a movement, out in the driveway. He stared for a moment, then decided he must have imagined it.

As he turned back, the servant lunged for the shotgun which stood, ready, against the wall. He brought it up, but before he could aim it, the bullets from seven rifles had torn his arms from his body and bloody pieces of tissue and white bone spattered the wall behind him.

The old couple bent their heads, their eyes tightly shut, and began to pray, muttering together. Mandhla hesitated, remembering the Elliotts. Then he brought his own rifle level to his hip, pointing directly at the man.

He didn't see the headlights, since the lights in the house were still on, and he could not have heard the vehicles above the laughter of his men as they commented bawdily on their bravery, spitting in the general direction of the dead servant. But he froze for an instant, warned by some inner alarm, then leapt to switch off the lights.

His men, as he had trained them to do, dropped to the floor, finding the windows. He ordered two of them to the entrance and watched as several policemen ran across the lawn, finding cover. Mandhla's mind raced. The old people! He found his way to them in the light from the other room, pulling them to their feet and forcing them towards the door. They moved slowly, frightened now, yet still contemptuous. It angered him.

One man crept below the window level to the light switch

of the next room, and turned off the shaded bulbs. The group moved through to the front entrance of the house, where they stopped.

"Tell them we are coming out," Mandhla hissed at the old man.

The voice wavered, old and tired, but defiant. "Please don't shoot – we are coming out!"

Mandhla waited for an acknowledgement, and when none came he prodded the man with the butt of his AK. "Again!" he ordered. The man repeated his plea, and this time there was a return shout.

"Come, then!"

Slowly they moved out of the door, keeping their backs against the wall of the building. The woman almost tripped, and whimpered; the man reached out to support her. When they were all out of the house, in a close group, shielded by the old people, they moved away from the protection of the house. Mandhla whispered another order to the man.

"Please," the quavering voice called out. "Please – you must all stand up and throw your weapons onto the lawn. All of you."

Mandhla waited. Slowly, one by one, seven men stood up. He calculated, remembering what he had seen from the window. Yes, that was about right – possibly even more than he had thought. The FN rifles were hurled onto the grass in the dull moonlight.

"Let them go," said the MIC, "and we will leave you alone."

Mandhla laughed out loud. "Do you think I am a fool? They stay with us until we are safe!" His group began to move towards the two Landrovers parked a short distance away. The old man took his wife's hand and squeezed it reassuringly. He said something quietly to her in a language Mandhla did not recognize.

"Speak only in English!" he commanded. "No talking!" But he had heard the tone of the voice; the man was simply comforting the woman.

She bent suddenly. "I have a stone in my shoe." The man behind her pushed her, and she would have overbalanced had her husband not been supporting her.

"Move on!" Mandhla instructed them. The man pulled

his wife quickly and they stepped away in front of the terrorists. And then, suddenly, he shouted strongly, "*Maintenant!*"

His wife followed him. They broke away, running forward, and immediately there was a burst of fire from their side. Mandhla cursed himself for having trusted the white officer. Some of his men had remained hidden, and somehow the old man had realised it.

His own men opened fire in retaliation. The couple were still running, and two men had come to meet them, to pull them away. Mandhla ran for the bush.

He didn't look to see who was with him. He heard the noise of battle behind; in the confusion his only thought was to get away. His mission was too important to end this way. He found the place he had picked out before the attack, and within minutes of leaving the house he was better hidden than a piece of coal in a coal yard.

When they had gone, chasing the terrorists who had escaped and leaving two men with the old people waiting for the clean-up squad, Mandhla emerged, stiff and furious. Somehow, someone had slipped up. He knew it wasn't him. Probably the one called Simon – he had had to reprimand him for taking a walk on his own that morning. He must have been seen.

Mandhla dumped the weapons and uniform he had on for the attack, and worked his way in the opposite direction from that in which the trackers would expect him to go. He moved further into the country, and only when he knew he was safe did he make his way towards the border.

At the base camp, eating decent food at last, bathed, dressed, his cuts seen to by one of the women, he reported for the debriefing.

The Russians were at first annoyed with him. "You disobeyed your orders and did not report back to us. It is necessary ..."

And so on. And on. Mandhla sighed and let the words run over him, until eventually the quiet man, the big one in the corner, interrupted. "Enough," he grunted at his companions. He leaned forward, his heavy red beard brushing his arms as they lay folded on the table.

"I, at least, am impressed," he told the youngster in front of him. "You are not meant for ordinary bushwork, Mandhla Ndhlovu – the one they call the Mamba. I wish you to have extra training. There may be a certain mission for you ... later – promotion, perhaps ..."

Mandhla looked impassively at the man. "I have no wish for promotion. The work I must do, I will do as I am. I have no time to worry about fools who cannot take care of themselves, and who will lead the Skuzapo to me."

The Russian raised his sandy eyebrows. "What 'work' do you speak of, if not that of the Cause?"

"The work I wish to do will only benefit the Cause. But I must be free to do it in my own way. For now, at least."

The bearded man rubbed his earlobe thoughtfully. "But you would benefit from further training ... in Russia ..."

"No. I must remain here. Russia is too far. Later, when it is finished, maybe ..."

The officer nodded slowly. "What is the name of this 'work'? Who is he – or she?"

Mandhla looked into the man's blue eyes. He held the gaze for several seconds before the Russian began to smile, then laugh. "Indeed, Mamba, you are more than wise." He stood up. "Rest, eat, relax ... there are women here to see to your needs. In two weeks you will again leave for Zimbabwe."

Four of the Nyoka made it back, making five with Mandhla. The other three were, according to the survivors, dead.

Peter Kennedy knew otherwise. Two had been killed, one severely wounded. And in the kit that had been dumped near the farmhouse, they had found three wooden snakes.

Impatiently, he waited for the captive to come out of his coma.

Chapter 18

She knew no-one would ever find her here. She could blame herself for that. They'd tried so hard to protect her, and in the end she'd been her own executioner. No. He had been her executioner; she had merely helped, unwittingly, to make it easy for him. She should have listened. To everyone, even little James and Mr. Cowley, who had wanted her to stay home ... but especially to Peter.

Her eyes opened again and she caught a gleam on the soft green figure of the eagle. She recognised it, of course, it was so similar to the ones at the Zimbabwe Ruins. The strange squatting shape, the watchful head, the triangular marks on the base ... Her eyelids were heavy, so heavy ... she let them drop again.

Tsimbaboue

Chisa and Ncube were married after the proper time required. The wedding was plain, and depressing. The Words were spoken on the Hill, while the High Priest stood on the Balcony Rock and the couple knelt on the hard earth below him. All the Priests, as was usual, attended the Words, but no-one else - except, of course, Muali, who was there in spirit and in his images. And the High Priest wore his ceremonial calf-skin mask.

Chisa gave her answers glibly, and with a sense of triumph; Ncube gave his more thoughtfully, less enthusiastically. Then they joined the procession of their families and invited guests who waited at the foot of the Hill, and attended their wedding feast. Chisa's sister, Mina, carried the stone Ncube had thrown - it was a position of honour, and the bearer of the stone stayed with the bride throughout the ceremony, except for before the High Priest on the Hill. Indeed, the only happy ones present were Chisa's family.

Tcana had been invited, of course, but she had refused on the pretext that she had much to prepare for her own wedding. Throughout the feasting and dancing Niswe glared at their new sister-in-law, hating her for stealing Ncube, for cheating her beloved brother from a wedding with her equally beloved friend.

There was no dowry, of course - or almost none, since Chisa's family were poor. They did send two chickens which were almost ready to lay, and a young cockerel. And Ncube was required to provide lobola, the marriage payment, to Chisa's father, but since both knew the circumstances Ncube was only asked for one fat cow, in calf by Tcana's father's best bull.

Tcana found Niswe at the river.

"Niswe - why have you not come to me since Ncube's wedding?" she asked anxiously.

"I - I've been busy," explained her friend uncomfortably.

"No. It is that I am to marry Xhaitaan, and Ncube is caught by Chisa." She dropped to her haunches beside Niswe, touching the other girl's shoulder. "I wanted that no more than you did, Niswe. Ncube does not deserve Chisa, and she most certainly does not deserve him. But are we to let it come between us, when you and I have been friends for so long?"

Niswe shrugged unhappily, looking away. Tcana sighed, and used a childhood pet name for her friend.

"Please, Nisweswiswi - I need you now, more than I ever did. I am so ... afraid ..." She trailed off, feeling foolish. Slowly Niswe turned to her.

"Afraid, Tcana? Of what? You will be a Queen - or at the very least, a Consort. What do you have to be afraid of?"

"I am afraid," she whispered, touching the bead at her throat. "Muali speaks to me, and yet I do not understand him. He wants something of me, yet I cannot tell what. And so I am afraid."

"He wants you to be First Queen," Niswe reassured her. "He wants you to guide Xhaitaan when he is King."

"Yes." She stared into the sky for a moment. "Niswe, do you remember when the Traders came from the north?"

"How could I not?"

Tcana turned to face her. "Do you remember the tall one, who sold these beads?"

Niswe reached out to Tcana's necklet. "Of course. He was ... so different."

Tcana nodded earnestly. "He talked of a man who was God."

Her friend's eyes went misty. "A man who died for the love of his friends. I remember. I remember it all."

They looked deep at each other. "So do I. All of it. Do you think it was true?"

Niswe's eyes broke away first. "I don't know."

"Do you want to know?"

Again their eyes met, and lingered. "I don't know."

They stared at each other many moments more. Then Tcana gave her a watery smile. "Niswe, will you carry my stone for me?"

Niswe drew a sharp breath. "Tcana, I cannot! To be Marriage Maid to a future Queen - it will not be allowed. Your Maid will have to be Royal - Xhaitaan's sister, or a cousin."

"No." Tcana was firm. "I want you, Niswe. I want you to carry my stone, and I want you to visit with me, the way we always have."

Niswe shook her head. "Tcana, that cannot happen. You will live in Tsimbabouetcang, and the only peasants you see will be from a distance, or your servants. You know that once you're married I'll be forbidden to treat you as a friend."

Tcana, too, shook her head, but vigorously. "Niswe, no - I will not let that happen! I -" She cut herself off as an idea came to her. Excited, she squealed: "My servants! Niswe - you will be my handmaiden! My lady's maid!"

The girls stared at each other, and suddenly they were laughing, and Niswe shoved Tcana and Tcana grabbed Niswe, and the two fell together into the clear water of the river below them.

It is indeed true, my Lord." Nada knelt humbly before Mgane in his indaba-room. "There is a peasant man who will testify – but he is afraid."

Mgane gestured to one of the guards who flanked him. "Fetch Xhaitaan."

They waited in silence. Then Xhaitaan came, frowning in puzzlement at his mother, who would not meet his eye.

"Your mother has a serious accusation about your chosen wife." Mgane stared at Xhaitaan, who returned the gaze. "Nada says she has proof Tcana is a witch."

Xhaitaan shook his head dumbly. He glanced at his mother, incredulous. "It is a lie, Lord." It was almost as serious an accusation as the first. Nada glared at him. "Not," he added hastily, "my mother's lie – but that of the proof. What proof is there? I defy it!"

"Fetch your peasant man," the King ordered Nada.

The old man had not bargained on being called a liar. The Fourth Wife had told him it would be simple – a matter of accusing the girl, relating an incident she would cook up for him, collecting his cow and sheep, and leaving. But now ... He sat on the other side of the fire from the girl, and the whole of the Royal House watched. In silence, they waited for the pot of water to boil.

Tcana, terrified, was nonetheless sure of herself. Muali would not allow her to be burnt; Muali knew the truth, as she did – as, indeed, Xhaitaan did. It was not the test that she was afraid of, but the force behind the test. Nada. Her future mother-in-law hated her, and if she would try to have her killed as a witch, she would try anything. This test Tcana knew she could pass. But later ...?

Kisang sat near them, watching her. He smiled again as she met his eye; earlier, he had whispered to her in passing, "I know you are no witch, little sister." He, at least, was on her side, though why she could not yet understand. Beside Kisang sat Maxa, making little effort to hide her enjoyment of the procedures. Silently, she congratulated Nada on her brilliant scheme. Unwittingly, Nada was playing into Maxa's hands.

The water began to roll gently in the wide-mouthed pot. The

King stood up heavily from his stool beside them, staring at the steam rising from the bubbling liquid. He looked at the peasant, and at Tcana, and to Xhaitaan, who sat opposite, in the ring of watchers. Xhaitaan had eyes only for Tcana, and she for him.

"Begin," ordered Mgane.

Tcana reluctantly pulled her eyes from Xhaitaan, and she and the peasant surveyed each other. Something in the old man's eyes ... she was sorry for him. Together, their hands moved forward, to hover over the boiling water.

"Begin!" said Mgane again, anxious to have this trial over. Breathing deeply, Tcana plunged her arm up to the elbow into the water. The old man only briefly touched the surface with his fingers, and screamed in agony, pulling away, his fingers already fiery under the leathery skin.

Tcana was again looking at Xhaitaan; his eyes gave her strength, and she held her arm in the seething fluid a moment longer, until Mgane cried out, "Enough!"

Tcana calmly withdrew her arm, and the Royal House gasped. The skin was unmarked. For a full minute there was silence, and then Nada leapt to her feet, screaming in fury: "She is a witch! She is not burnt!"

"Quiet, woman!" Mgane glared at her. "Tcana has taken the test of the liar, and has not been scathed. Muali stands with her!"

Instantly Nada remembered her place and flung herself forward, her head touching the ground, in submission to her King. "Lord, forgive me – the peasant swore ... I will have him killed! Forgive me – the tension – "

"Go to your house, woman, and stand not in the way of your son again. The wedding continues."

Later, Tcana felt the heat in her arm, but only as a distant warmth; her skin glowed a little, and a small blister appeared at the wrist – but so small it was hardly noticeable. Certainly, when she was dressed in the regal red silk wedding gown, cloth traded with the people from the Coast, and the serving maids adorned her with gold – neck wire, bracelets, earrings, leg bangles – it was invisible.

Her hair was combed out for her and plaited carefully in

bone patterns across her head, with the tiny white flowers that came from the frost-bush, while another girl anointed her feet and hands with calf-fat scented with flower-honey. A third meticulously drew tiny patterns on her cheeks and forehead in coloured clay, and when everything was finished the singing began from the Cave - the Mouth of Muali, announcing the wedding of the King's son in her papery voice.

It was time. Tcana stood, and once again her head was covered, but this time with finest silk, so fine she could see through it - a cascade of golden cloth that fell all around her, over her shoulders, to her elbows. The maids adjusted gold strips around the top of her head, to hold the veil in place, and she stepped out into the sunlight.

Immediately she was surrounded by hand-maidens of the Royal House, twenty of them, and as the Royal Gong throbbed slowly twenty times, they herded her protectively to the foot of the Hill.

The wavering voice of the Oracle sang on above the silence of the amaTsimbaboue as they waited for their Prince to ascend the Hill. The maids delivered Tcana to him, and, led by a Priest, together they began the climb.

Before the High Priest, they knelt under the rock balcony for the Words. *How strange*, thought Tcana, *that the ceremonial words are the same for the King's son*. Obediently, she promised to hoe her husband's crops, to tend to his food, to provide sons to herd his cattle, and daughters to draw his water, Muali willing. She promised to give him comfort when he needed it, to warm his bed - and his only, and to obey him in all things.

In turn, he promised to tend the cattle and earth well, to ensure that they multiplied and were fruitful, so that he might provide his wife with what she needed - food, clothing, bracelets, to the full extent of his riches, and later the same for his children. Tcana almost giggled at the thought of a King, or Prince for that matter, grazing cattle, or drawing water.

Then their allegiance to Muali was sworn, and to the King of the amaTsimbaboue, whoever he may be at any given time, and it was over almost before she knew it. Again they stood, and again Tcana's face was uncovered before the Priests of Muali. And when the veil was removed, she was a Princess of the amaTsimbaboue.

At the foot of the Hill the people awaited them, and when they appeared and it was seen that the veil was removed, the dancing and singing began. In procession Niswe, carrying the heavy gold ingot, followed Tcana and Xhaitaan through the village to the feast - a feast such as Tcana had never known. For two days they sang and danced and ate, and when at last the newlyweds slipped away to their new hut within the enclosure of Tsimbabouetcang, the celebrations continued without them.

Alone. Xhaitaan pulled the red silk robe softly from her body, letting the material whisper over her shining skin. She stood for him, nervous, afraid, yet strangely sure of herself and of her power over this man who knelt before her, his fingers shaking as he touched her.

It was not, of course, his first time; the servant girls of Tsimbabouetcang were not all for drawing water, and a man's needs must be satisfied - especially a Royal man's needs. But this was Tcana, the girl he loved and desired more than anything in the world; when she looked at him nothing else mattered; when she touched him, the King's Tower of Continuation could crumble, the Life Fire quench, the First Queen's Pots crack, and he would not care.

Tcana submitted - not to a King's son, but to the man she loved.

Chapter 19

Rhodesia

Finally, the man was ready to talk.

Protective, the doctors had slowly brought him round, sustaining him, knowing he must live, though not why. Peter had waited until the terrorist was judged fit enough to be moved, then had him transferred to the small hospital at the Scouts' barracks. Now he was under the care of the Skuzapo.

At first he'd been surprised. The black eyes had moved around the room, watching the white medical staff, all men, tending him. He had flinched away when they had approached with needles, his eyes widening with fear, expecting ... what? But gradually, as his health improved, he realised they were not going to kill him. Yet.

The food was good, and outside on the parade ground he heard the laughter and chatter of men. Black men. Ndebele, like him. From the snatches of conversation he sometimes overheard, he realised where he was. He wondered whether they wanted him to fight for them. After all, the Russians had told them over and over that the Rhodesians were short of men, and were less efficient than the freedom fighters. It stood to reason that they would try to steal the ZIPRA soldiers.

The thought made him proud. They had spent much money and time bringing him back to health, just so that they could ask him to fight for them! – He was obviously important.

He was indeed important. Impatiently, Peter waited for

his medical men to tell him that the man was in a good enough state of health to talk.

Unable to keep on resisting, he tried calling Rebecca, but there was no answer at her flat and the studio didn't know where she was. He turned his thoughts back to work.

When the time came at last, the terrorist was more than ready. Peter took with him Fletcha, one of the terrorists they had "turned", and who was proving to be one of the best of the Selous Scouts. Together, they entered the hospital room that still smelled of ether and medication. He addressed the man in Ndebele. Fletcha stood by his side, silent, watching.

"What is your name?" Peter asked. The black man's eyes flickered and he looked at Fletcha, who stared impassively back.

The eyes moved to Peter. "Simon." It was little more than a whisper.

Peter nodded. "Very good. We will not begin with lies. What unit were you with?"

Simon hesitated. "If you know my name, you also know my unit."

Peter grinned at him. "Excellent. Your brain is still working. We know your number, too. And that your commander was the Mamba." He watched carefully but the terrorist only shrugged painfully. "I want to know about this Mamba. What is his real name? Where is he from?" Peter pressed him.

The man shook his head, the skin dull charcoal, sweat appearing at the hairline. "You know we are not told these things, Baas."

Peter almost chuckled at the form of address. So much for the brainwashing. "I am not your Baas. I am a man, as you are. And since I am a man, I also know that men talk among themselves. What is the name of the Mamba?"

The man continued to sweat. "I do not know."

Fletcha moved forward and lifted the blanket from the cage protecting the man's broken leg. He gazed almost disinterestedly at the purplish toes, then reached out and pinched the biggest.

The terrorist whimpered. He knew that this was only the first warning. And after all, what was the Mamba to him?

"He is Mandhla Ndhlovu."

Peter felt his pulse stop for an instant. "You are lying," he said. He nodded to Fletcha, who reached for the water bag at the end of the traction pulley that held the broken leg in place.

"No! It is not a lie!"

Fletcha withdrew his hand. Peter breathed out hard. It was, after all, not an uncommon name. "Where does this Mandhla Ndhlovu come from?" He waited, his heart pounding.

"I do not remember – no, wait – a mission. They talked of a mission station ... he did not speak of himself." The dark eyes were pleading. "I tell you only what I heard from others ..."

"What mission?" Peter was vicious suddenly. "What mission – where?"

"I do not know ... I think ..." His voice was desperate as he racked his memory. "Near Plumtree ... Ellis? I think it was Ellis ... no ... something like that!" The eyes were wide and Peter could smell the fear on the man. It was the truth.

He turned abruptly. "Fletcha will speak to you now. He has a proposition for you." He closed the door softly behind him.

Kuru said nothing when he was told. He stared out of the window until Peter had finished, and then turned slowly, as if he hadn't heard. "Philemon Dube wants leave, Sir. It is due him."

Peter nodded. "He may have it." The hairs on the back of his neck prickled. "Kuru, your brother – "

"I have no brother, Sir," Kuru cut in firmly. "May I go now?"

"Of course." Peter watched the big Ndebele leave and realised how dry his mouth was. He went to the cupboard on the wall and pulled out a bottle of Scotch. Then he picked up the telephone and dialed.

No answer. Again.

The time was coming. Too many black men – Ndebele – had died because of Peter Kennedy. The Selous Scouts were undermining the morale of the freedom fighters. So many were killed through the treachery of the Skuzapo that the units were becoming afraid. Once in Zimbabwe (ZIPRA never used the country's current name, Rhodesia), they were reluctant to contact each other, yet reliant on each other for information and moral support. They did not use radios; instead they had an intricate system of letters for passing on information. But the Skuzapo had even caught onto that, and often there were false letters in the "mailboxes" to mislead the recipients and persuade them to their deaths.

Mandhla knew it was impossible for all the units to operate as he did: alone, without contact with others. The war had a method of operation, and it was for the Cause that the others were dying. But Mandhla had no intention of joining their numbers. Not, at least, until his score was settled. Then, it would not matter. Nothing would matter.

This time, he took the four men from the Nyoka with him. The smaller the group, the easier – and safer – movement would be. Besides, these men had proved that they had more in them than the others. They had made it back. And they knew his methods. He was comfortable with them.

Before they left he spoke to the big Russian with the red beard. The man had listened, smiling his slow smile, and when Mandhla had finished he had chuckled. "You still only tell half the story, Mamba. But you are wise in doing so. You shall have your identification papers."

True to his word, the papers were delivered two days before the Nyoka were ready to slip back into Zimbabwe. Mandhla Ndhlovu, ostensibly, was David Ncube, and his four men also had new identities. This time, there would be no need for justified killings.

They moved swiftly through the bundu. Mandhla watched his men carefully; their muscles were hard, their senses alert. Being back in the base camp, watching the other men work out, had made Mandhla more appreciative of his own men. Between them, they had formed a good group. One Mandhla could almost rely on.

Almost. He had no intention of trusting his life to anyone but himself.

He had chosen the man he wanted. Quietly, alone with

him, he had told him what was expected. At first, Graham's eyes had widened in disbelief and he had shaken his head in fear. But Mandhla had convinced him. Mandhla could be very persuasive. The two had gone over and over the plan, until Mandhla was certain both of his man and himself. And that only the two of them knew what was to happen.

It had not been difficult to get the information he wanted from the Russian. He had simply asked, casually, exactly where the Skuzapo were based. The Russian had looked him up and down consideringly. "They are well inside the country. Far from our lines."

"Where?"

"Why do you ask?"

"Where?"

The Russian had chuckled indulgently, and told him.

They made their way almost to Gwelo, in the heart of Rhodesia, and found themselves a farm. Patiently they waited, watching.

The man was in his late fifties, Mandhla guessed. Portly, his stomach swaying before him as he walked, his grey hair shrinking back from his forehead, his face ruddy, he laughed a good deal. His wife was perhaps the same age, maybe older. She too was stout. She wore her streaky grey-black hair in a bun at the nape of her neck.

They did not carry arms, this far into the country. They were too far from the borders, too far from any "hot spots". And when Mandhla approached the woman at the house for a job as under-houseboy, she opened the door willingly to him, eyeing his ragged clothes.

"Ye could do wi' a guid meal, to be sure," she told him. "Ye're too skinny by far. Our Solomon's getting on a wee bit, he might like some help wi' the floors and sichlike."

She fed him, and showed him a clean room in the servants' quarters where he could sleep. The bed was comfortable, the food was good, and the Nyoka were well hidden. Mandhla settled in for the time being.

There was a gun cupboard in the bedroom, and one in the study. Both wore strong padlocks across their bolts, and Mandhla was willing to bet that the keys were not easily accessible. There were four bedrooms altogether, including the main one in which the farmer and his wife slept. The smallest contained a cot and nursery furniture, but was merely a spare room, as were the other two. Solomon informed him (loftily, since he was a Shona and had little time for the Sindebele people) that the rooms were kept ready for when the couple's children visited, bringing grandchildren with them. Since they often descended upon their parents without notice, the rooms were kept ready and clean.

He emphasised the "clean", and pointed to a cobweb in the corner. Obediently, Mandhla cleaned.

After four days he removed his few belongings from the room he had been allotted and located the Nyoka.

"Tomorrow night," he told them. He didn't want to wait for the weekend, knowing there may be visitors then. His eyes met those of Graham briefly and he half-smiled at the man. His best man. Nothing must be allowed to go wrong. Nothing would go wrong.

The disappearance of the new houseboy did not unduly concern the farmer and his wife. They were used to the inconsistencies of the black people. Obviously he had not been happy here. Perhaps he and Solomon had not got on well. Solomon could be a hard task-master, and there was the tribal difference to consider. Nothing was missing, nothing had been stolen. There was no cause for upset.

The day drew on.

They made the hit at ten o'clock that night, when Mandhla knew Solomon would be in his room and out of the way. It was a silent job. This couple were popular with their workers, and Mandhla had no intention of running into resistance. They waited for the last lights in the farmhouse to go out, watching from a distance, and then they waited some more. Farmers were early bedders and heavy sleepers.

The locks were simple, and gave easily and without too much protest. In silence the five guerillas slipped into the house through the kitchen entrance and followed Mandhla into the bedroom passage. They could hear the snores from the main bedroom. Mandhla turned on the passage light.

He pushed open the bedroom door, soundlessly, and Graham moved to the woman's side of the bed while the Mamba stood over the man. At the same moment they struck, holding closed the mouths, preventing any noise while they slit the throats. The bodies heaved for a few seconds, and the bed groaned protestingly, but then they were dead.

Quickly Mandhla looked through the window towards the workers' rooms, wiping the sticky blood from his face. No lights came on. He dropped the carving beside the man's head. They moved back into the passage, still quiet, and walked towards the kitchen.

The baby's cries stopped them in their tracks. Alarmed, the four faces stared at their commander in the moonlight. Mandhla froze, listening for a response from one of the other bedrooms. It came almost immediately. A woman's voice, cursing sleepily, and the sounds of a bed creaking. A light shone suddenly from under a door, and swiftly Mandhla moved against the wall.

The door opened and as the woman stepped out into the passage he pulled her against him, one hand over her mouth. Graham ran into the bedroom but there was no-one else there. Mandhla nodded toward the other spare room and two others pushed open the door. It too was unoccupied. Just the woman, then. And the child.

She died as quickly and quietly as her parents had. The baby was still crying, and Mandhla dropped the floppy form of the mother and went to the infant. He did not turn the light on; the windows faced the servants' quarters. He bent over the cot and the crying ceased for a moment, becoming a gurgling sob. Then, when she realised the visitor was not her mother, the screams began again.

Mandhla watched the tiny red face screw up like a paper bag. He glanced out of the window; still no lights. Bending, he lifted the squawking creature and held it to his chest. The screams intensified. He glanced around. There was a bottle on the dresser, half-full. He pushed the teat into the wide mouth and the lips clamped shut. The crying stopped instantly, the eyes closed blissfully and the only sound was a soft sucking. Carefully, he put the child back into its cot on its side, still sucking at the bottle. He backed away. There was no sound, and still no lights from the rooms at the back.

He turned to leave the room and met Graham's eyes. Defiant, he stared back. "We are not here to murder babies," he said, and led them out of the house.

When they had reached the bush, creeping from shadow to shadow to avoid the moonlight, Mandhla turned. He pushed his chin out at Graham. "You. Stay and watch a while. Follow us in one hour – less if anything happens. We will wait at the Elephant Tree, two hours' walk away. I wish to see how fast the Security Forces will react to a hit so close to their belly."

Graham stared back at him, impassive. "How long will you wait?"

"Two hours. No longer."

He turned and led the others away. They did not query the instruction, though they may have had their own thoughts about it; they knew what the Mamba did was always best. For all of them.

They hid their uniforms and weapons inside the tree, having to climb high into the branches to access the aperture in the trunk. They kept only their civilian clothes and the documents bearing their new identities. They waited for two hours, then made their way towards Bulawayo, presuming their comrade captured, or dead.

Graham waited fifteen minutes more and then, carefully, he shot himself in the right calf.

Chapter 20

Rhodesia

It was typical, of course, of the profile Peter was building up of the Mamba. A man of that calibre would not stop to help a wounded comrade if it meant endangering the others – especially himself. If the fool had accidentally shot himself in the leg as he ran, he would have to face the consequences.

What didn't fit was the child. Peter shook his head irritably. Why had the baby been allowed to live? The Mamba was an enigma, far more complex than any terrorist Peter had come up against yet.

The servants had, of course, been aroused by the shot. Solomon had radioed for help (he was extremely proud of his ability to work the wireless) and the police, on finding the wooden bangle, had called in the Selous Scouts. The tracking party came up with nothing, as Peter had known they would. But he had something very worthwhile instead. A very hot informant.

The man was reluctant to talk. They traced his name through the serial number of the AK-47 he carried; it was issued to one Graham Chobe. And that much he admitted. Peter did not advocate heavy torture. He saw no benefit in breaking the spirit so that the body was useless to man or beast. Instead, he played his trump.

Simon had converted swiftly once he had been persuaded of the good sense of it by Fletcha. He also soon realised that he had been drastically under trained, and that his Russian comrades had lied to him about many,

many things. These men were well-oiled machines in comparison to the ZIPRA soldiers. It was only too plain which side he would do best to be on.

He was delighted now to find that another of the Nyoka was present at the base, and only too pleased at Major Kennedy's suggestion that he speak to the man. Enthusiastically he poured out his story to Graham, dwelling on the good pay the unit received, the protection offered to the men's families, the food, the camaraderie between the men.

Graham had himself been more than a little surprised to find Simon, whom they had thought dead, here. But it made his own task easier and, faced by the two "tame" terrorists, Fletcha and Simon, he grudgingly agreed to talk to Major Kennedy again.

Yes, he admitted, he was one of the Nyoka. So what?

"Where are the others heading?" Peter asked pleasantly, offering the man a cigarette. He took it and Peter lit it for him.

Graham sighed heavily. "Why do you ask me to betray my comrades?"

"They betrayed you when they left you to die at our hands." Peter saw the black man's eyebrows raise suddenly.

"They had no choice."

"My men do not leave each other to die. Ask Simon."

"Simon has told me that," he admitted slowly. "What will I get for being evidence for you?"

"You will get the same as Simon. You will have good pay, and protection for your family from reprisals, and more than that – you will have the pride that comes from being a Skuzapo."

Graham shook his head, chuckling. "Truly they are right to call you the Hyena. You have powerful jaws." He paused to suck blue smoke into his lungs. "The Mamba has been recalled. He wanted one more hit before he went back into Zambia."

"Which way?"

"Not the normal way. He is too clever for that."

"I know. So which way?" asked Peter again, patiently.

"By Salisbury. He thinks you will not find him there. Then he will go past Kariba."

"Where did you hide the men from the Chakwane village?"

Graham laughed shortly. "Have you still not discovered them?" He got up and limped to the map on the wall, pointing. "Here – at the curve of the river, under the bank, is an old crocodile lair." He grinned proudly. "I found it."

Peter nodded. "Well done. You're obviously a good man to have, with brains." He stood. "We'll talk again later. I must send men after the Mamba, who left you to die."

Graham Chobe watched him walk out. He rubbed his bandaged leg thoughtfully as he began to smile.

He learned quickly, and once into the training showed an eagerness that impressed the officers. He seemed to drink in all they taught him, absorbing it as blotting paper takes in water. For his part, Peter watched with interest. Simon, better trained than the average terrorist, had spoken of the extra sessions he had had to undergo under the command of the Mamba, but this man was even more finely honed. A window into Mandhla Ndhlovu.

Of course, he couldn't lead them to other terrorist groups, as most of the "tame" terrs could, since the Nyoka did not keep contact with their comrades. But when the time came to pit him against a ZIPRA unit, he came out with flying colours.

He told the target group that he was part of the Nyoka and that the Mamba was in need of help. The name of the Mamba was already almost legendary amongst the terrorists, and in their excitement at the meeting they forgot caution. Graham Chobe personally killed three of the gang, sealing the Scouts' trust.

Graham's personality endeared him to the Scouts he worked with, and he made a point of being friendly to Peter while showing a large modicum of respect for him. He made his admiration clear, and since Peter was always readily available to any of his men, Graham was a fairly frequent visitor to his office.

Kuru objected. "We don't know him yet," he told Peter. "I don't trust him."

Peter laughed. "He's a good man, Kuru. He has proved himself."

Kuru grunted. "He misled us about the Mamba's whereabouts."

Kuru never referred to his younger brother as anything but the Mamba. Peter sometimes wondered what Kuru's reaction would be were he to come face to face with his sibling in the bush. It was a potentially explosive situation, and one Peter sincerely hoped would not occur.

"You know how elusive the Mamba is, Kuru. If he thought he had left behind someone who might disclose his plans, he may have changed them."

Kuru was unconvinced. "He shows much interest in you."

"He likes me. Are you jealous?" he teased.

"I owe you my life. I do not owe you trust in a man I do not like."

They were both silent, remembering the ambush in the early days together. Kuru had been leading, but Peter had seen the dull sunlight on the barrel first. He had shouted and lunged forward, thrusting his friend to safety and sustaining a shoulder wound in the process. It hadn't been serious, healing quickly, but the white man had risked his own life for the black man, and Kuru Ndhlovu knew his obligations.

Peter laughed to break the mood. "I hope that the debt will never have to be repaid, if the only way you see is to die for me."

Kuru shook his head sadly, gazing speculatively at his commanding officer. "You have never made a mistake with a man yet, Sir. I hope that you are not making one now."

He turned on his heel and strode out, leaving Peter staring after him. He cursed, and picked up the telephone.

She answered on the third ring, breathless.

"Where have you been?" he demanded, rattled. "I've been trying to get you for weeks."

"Why, Major Kennedy – how nice to hear your pleasant voice again," she said, too sweetly.

"I'm sorry. I was worried. No-one knew where you were."

"I'm flattered, I'm sure." Then she dropped the Southern Belle act. "I wasn't aware I was under surveillance. I have work to do, Major. I've been in Kweri and Umtali, and then back in Ntubu, and now I'm home to do some editing.

You obviously haven't tried to reach me in the last three days."

"No, I suppose not. There's a lot going on here. Look, are you going to be in Bulawayo for a while?"

She was curious. "Yes. We're going to be doing some filming at local police HQ and Special Branch. Probably until after Christmas."

"I have something for you. I'll try to come in ... I'm not sure when."

"Is that 'something' information?"

"Is information the only thing you'll accept from me?"

She was annoyed again. "Do you always have to answer my questions with a question?"

"Habit. You do the same, you know. Are you going away or not?"

"I'll be here."

They met some distance from the farm that embraced Inkomo, during the recreation period after supper, when it was unlikely he would be missed.

"It goes well," he reported. "They are certainly an expert team of men. It is little wonder they have our people on the run."

Mandhla laughed silently. "Soon, it'll be the other way around. For one man, at least."

Graham bobbed his head. "He's a good man. He knows his job and he's popular. He's fair and reasonable. He treats all men alike, regardless of their skin colour. He carries a loyalty among the men that I have not seen before. They would die if he ordered them to."

Mandhla dismissed this, spitting impatiently into the grass. He hoped he hadn't misjudged Chobe. "But you're safe there? They do not suspect?"

Graham laughed. "Haii! There are so many of our people there, you would be amazed. They refer to our comrades as 'tame'. Indeed, they are little more. Although," he added thoughtfully, "if I had not been under direct orders from you, whom I know to be the Hyena's match, I, too, might have been swayed."

Mandhla sniffed irritably and rubbed his nose. "Tell me about him."

"As I've said, he has loyal men. One in particular is close to him and serves him with a determination. He's also probably the only danger to me."

Mandhla raised a brow. "Who is he?"

Graham met his eye directly, then looked away. "His name is Kuru Ndhlovu." He heard the sharp intake of breath from Mandhla, and waited for a moment. "He knows who you are, but he says he has no brother. You are simply the Mamba to him. I believe he would kill you if he had to."

"Then," said Mandhla grimly, "I would do the same. I, too, have no brother." He shifted on his haunches and went back to the subject of his interest. "Hyena."

"A silent man. He doesn't speak of himself or his cares. He thinks of his men. He has no family in this country."

"A woman, then."

"I've heard him speak to only one woman on the telephone, once – today. I was lingering beneath his office window. I don't know their relationship – it was difficult to tell. I didn't hear her name. He's going to visit her soon, though. And I think I can find out who she is."

Mandhla let out his breath. A woman.

Graham had always preferred the direct approach. He asked Major Kennedy the next day about his wife and children.

"I don't have any," the Major laughed. "Why do you ask?"

Graham pretended surprise. "A man as handsome as you, and of your years, must surely be married!"

"No."

"Then you must have many, many girlfriends. I had many girlfriends, too. I am considered handsome, in my village."

The Major wagged his head, grinning. "I hope you've settled down since you married. I certainly am no playboy. I have no girlfriends – they're too much trouble!"

Graham laughed dutifully with him.

There must be another source.

There was. She'd been watching Graham since he had arrived; certainly, he was a fine figure of a man, with a good sense of humour, and she responded well when he began to wink at her as he walked past her office.

Two days later he casually entered the office. After some joshing, they got onto the subject of the work at the barracks. The woman thought highly of Major Kennedy, and was well aware that so did Graham, and so they had a good subject of mutual interest to discuss.

"Isn't is funny," said Graham jokingly, "that such a man has no woman!"

"Oh, but he does. Well ... I don't know that she is his woman, but I do know that he tries to call her often, and when she is away he worries. I heard him say so to her." She smiled impishly. "I plugged in the wrong line by accident one day."

He grinned back playfully. "Ah, she must be very beautiful to have captured Major Kennedy's attention, do you not think?"

"She is. I've seen her on the television – she's a reporter. You must have seen her, too. She's American."

"I think I know the one you mean ... the one with black hair?"

She giggled. "No, silly! She has very long light hair, the colour of pale honey. Rebecca Rawlings."

Rebecca woke late on Christmas morning, deflated and lonely. Kyle would only be back from Salisbury the next day. She was alone for Christmas. Except for Tony, of course, who would in all probability call or come around.

She stretched and pushed Mangoi, the big silver-tipped Persian given to her by an admirer at the TV studios, off the bed. In the kitchen she poured him cream as a special treat, and made Milo for herself. Then she wandered through to the lounge and opened the parcel her father had sent – expensive French perfume from him, and a strange pair of spotted ankle socks from her younger brother. She smiled and held them against her cheek; as usual, he'd been allowed to choose her present himself.

Rebecca was tidying the flat when the flowers came, two dozen deep red roses, heavily perfumed. The card said simply, "From an admirer." She separated them and put them in vases and glasses all around the flat, and almost before she was finished the doorbell rang again.

The messenger had two bunches of flowers this time. Red carnations from Tony – at a guess, since the card said "With love, in camera!" – and three dozen white roses with fluffy baby's breath. She knew these were from her father, an annual ritual they shared.

And then, just before lunch, another messenger knocked on her door. He asked her to sign a small delivery book for the flame lilies and a wrapped gift. "I hope Missy likes the present," he said as he turned to go.

She looked at him and smiled. "Thank you."

The flame lilies were glorious in their fiery red and yellow. She put them in water and unwrapped the gift.

It was stunning. It at once fascinated and repulsed her, but it drew her strangely. The black stone was cold to her touch, and stood perhaps three inches high from the coiled body to the raised head. The eyes were tiny silver dots and the mouth that was carved into the shiny stone was open. The neck was slightly flattened, in the classic warning pose, and as she looked at it she could almost hear it hiss. It was beautiful; she couldn't wait to show her father.

She took it to the bedroom, and gave it pride of place on her bedside table. Then she began looking through the mounds of research she'd put together for the police HQ episode.

It was nearly three o'clock when the knock came. Absorbed in her work, she realised with a start that she was still in her nightshirt, barefoot, her hair in two plaits. Tony had seen her this way before; she was unconcerned and opened the door for him.

The eyebrows above the blue eyes lifted; her own eyes widened in surprise and she moved behind the door, embarrassed.

"Major Kennedy! I wasn't expecting you ..."

"So I see." He was carrying a large, flat parcel. "Perhaps I should just leave this with you ..."

"No, of course not." She recovered herself quickly and pointed to the lounge door. "You go in there and I'll be ready in a moment."

Ten minutes later she came into the lounge, refreshed, with jeans and a peasant-top on, her hair still in the two plaits, child-like. He turned back from the window, and she could swear he'd been looking out of it since he entered the room.

"I'm sorry, I was working and didn't realise it was so late."

"Do you always greet your cameraman in your nightshirt?" he asked caustically.

"Are we going to quarrel on Christmas day, Major Kennedy?"

He smiled ruefully. "My turn to apologise." He thrust the gift at her. "This was painted by one of the men in my outfit. He said to give it to someone special, but since I don't have anyone who fits that description I thought you might like it."

She bit her tongue and took the parcel from him, pulling off the brown paper it was wrapped in. The painting was breathtakingly beautiful, and she was awed. It was an osprey about to strike. It measured about four feet square, and Rebecca could almost feel the texture of the feathers and hear the scream from its open beak, yellow and curved and cruel. The orange eyes seemed to stare out at her, and there was a strange ache in her stomach when she looked into them.

He was pleased with her reaction. "The osprey is the insignia of our unit. It's on our badges in the same attitude." She remembered; she had seen it on his cap.

"It's beautiful – breathtaking!" Indeed, her chest was constricted with its loveliness. He watched her parted lips and the flush on her cheeks; she was captivated. "Help me put it up," she commanded, and led the way to her bedroom. He looked around briefly and noted the rumpled bed, still unmade, and the closed curtains. The room smelt of her perfume and he found himself breathing deeply to absorb it.

She stood on the bed and removed a seascape from the wall, handing it to him and taking the eagle to replace it. He stood back critically to be sure it was straight; then she flung wide the curtains for light and came to join him. She stared at the painting and he spoke to break her reverie.

"I like it there. It's protective, above your bed, like part of my unit here taking care of you."

She looked at him, her lips twitching. "Why, Major Kennedy! I didn't know I was that 'special' to you."

"You're laughing at me again." He turned to leave the room, but something beside her bed caught her eye and she heard his sharply indrawn breath.

"What's wrong?"

"Where did you get that?" He pointed to the jet snake on the table.

"Isn't it beautiful?" She walked back and picked it up. "Someone sent it to me for Christmas. Probably an admirer. I often get gifts from the public."

He took it away from her abruptly. "Wasn't there a note or anything? Where was the delivery boy from?"

She was piqued. "I didn't notice. What's the matter?"

He turned the creature over in his hand. It wasn't wooden, and it wasn't a bangle ... but it was obviously a cobra, a mamba. It bore a resemblance, with its open mouth and flat neck, to the bangles. He calmed himself and casually put it back on the table. "Nothing. It's rather lovely." He made himself smile. "If there's coffee, this time I'll accept."

Coincidence, he decided. It must be coincidence. I'm obsessed with snakes.

Back in the lounge he commented on the abundance of flowers.

"I always receive lots of flowers on special days. I love them; everyone close to me knows it. The white roses are from Dad back home, and the carnations are from Tony. I'm not sure who sent the red roses." She had to admit, the small flat looked and smelt like a florist shop. "The flame lilies came with the snake. An unusual choice of flower, don't you think?"

"It's the Rhodesian national flower." He went back to staring out of the window, coffee mug in hand. "How's the programme getting on? Enjoy your trips to Kweri and Umtali?"

She hesitated. "I have to admit something to you, Major. Do you remember asking where my sympathies lie in this war?"

He turned back, interested. "Of course. You claimed to be unbiased."

"I've changed my mind. What I've seen in the past few weeks ... especially in Umtali, I suppose ... well, anyway, I've thought a lot about it and you're right. I'm not unbiased. I find myself aligning with the Rhodesians."

It seemed to worry her; he wondered why. "Do you have a problem with that?"

"I guess so ... I think maybe I'm too idealistic. I want things to be just right, and if they're not, I fret. I don't think someone in my position should be prejudiced one way or the other, and now I find I am. Of course, I try not to let it come through into the program," she added hastily.

"Miss Rawlings, you're a good reporter and an excellent television presenter. You do a great job on your programmes, but maybe it's time you realised that you're human, like the rest of us."

Her voice was low. "I'm beginning to find that out." *In more ways than one,* she thought, remembering his kiss. "Don't you want to sit down?"

"Sorry." He sat. "Force of habit. When I'm thinking, I stand."

"Is something worrying you?"

"No. Yes. I should go. I have to get back to the base. There's something I have to see to." He stood up again, preoccupied.

"I know. More secrets."

She joined him at the door. There was no kiss this time as he strode to the stairs. When he was almost gone, she called after him: "I'm glad you chose me to give the eagle to, Major. Even if I'm not special."

She was laughing at him again.

Chapter 21

Rhodesia

"It was a coincidence."

"You don't believe in coincidences. And neither do I."

"No." Peter Kennedy turned back from the window to face Kuru. "That's why I'm going to put a guard on her."

Kuru nodded. "Day and night?"

"Day and night. If that bastard's planning anything, he's got another think coming."

"Who shall guard her?"

"Special Branch in Bulawayo. I spoke to them earlier, they have her covered already. They're also doing a general search of the townships again."

"He won't be there."

"I know." He slammed his fist into his palm. "How in hell did he find out about her? Not even the men here know – even you didn't, until now."

"Have you telephoned her?"

"Sometimes. But he can't be tapping the 'phone lines. That's too sophisticated, even for him."

Kuru came to stand beside him at the window, staring out over the parade ground. "Now and then," he said slowly, "Graham Chobe cannot be found for about an hour. He appears again suddenly."

"Have you questioned him?"

"Casually. He says he needs freedom now and then. I'm putting a guard on him."

The two men smiled at each other. "Day and night?"

"Day and night."

"He's worried. He has placed a guard on the woman."
"How do you know?"
"The telephone operator. A fine Ndebele maiden of many talents. She's not particularly pretty, but ... she has other points. She is highly flattered by my interest in her. And in her job, of course. She reveres Major Kennedy greatly, and also appreciates my own reverence of the man. We discuss him often, and his worries too."

Mandhla laughed. "So much for their security. Do they so trust their own people that they allow hobnobbing?"

"No. We are just ... clever about it. It adds to the excitement. I must go. I think your brother watches me. I don't like to delay too long."

"If he questions you?"

"I am a man of the bush. I do not enjoy being cooped up. They understand that, here."

Peter stood upright in front of her desk, calm and quiet. "You're being transferred, Elizabeth. They need a good switchboard operator at the Police Station in Nyamandhlovu."

Her eyes widened. She immediately understood it to be a demotion. "Sir, I always do my best for you ..."

"I know you do, Elizabeth. I appreciate your loyalty. But you are too easily distracted by the men. In particular, by a traitor who is within our ranks."

Her mouth opened slightly and she licked the thick lips. "I don't understand."

"You don't have to understand. You simply have to learn to keep your mouth shut. Pack your things. You're leaving tomorrow morning, and until then you will speak with no-one at all. No-one will know you're going. Is that understood?"

She nodded dumbly, tears welling up. Deep in her belly, she wanted to die.

They waited till he slept, then prodded him awake sharply. He roused to find himself staring at the barrels of three AK-47s. Simon was particularly sensitive; this man had failed him. Kuru was cold and impassive. Peter was controlling his anger.

"Get up, wretched snake," he ordered as the men around them began to waken. "Indeed, you are well named, for you crawl on your belly and deceive, waiting for your chance to bite the heel of the men who took care of you. Get up." He pushed him roughly with the rifle and the black man, sweating already with fear, rolled out of the narrow bed.

"Sir, I do not know ..."

"Shut up!" Peter crashed the butt of the AK into Graham's ribs and he doubled in pain. "Killer of women! You will eat dirt, like the amaShona you hate so much!"

The other soldiers in the dormitory were gathering, their anger building as they realised what was happening. They followed the prisoner to the parade ground, murmuring amongst themselves.

By the time they reached the centre of the field, the news had spread like wildfire and every man in the barracks was there, some dressed only in the underwear they slept in. Black and white alike, they were furious at the treachery in their midst, and thankful that a disaster had been averted in time.

The girl, Elizabeth, was there, defying orders, her faded mauve bathrobe folded and tied across her ample melon-bosoms. Bitter, she pushed her way to the front and there was a sudden hush as she stood over the kneeling African. The Major made no move to stop her.

She stared into Chobe's eyes and then, contemptuous, spat in his face. She watched the fat, foamy globule of spittle run from the corner of his eye, moving slowly over his sweating purple-black cheek, and then she turned and walked away.

Peter realised he had a lynch mob on his hands, eager and waiting. They began to mutter again, and some of the Ndebele began a war chant, a revenge song of hatred and despising. More joined in, the whites among them, and they began to stamp their feet on the hard night earth, keeping the rhythm like a taut-skinned drum, humming behind the words. Peter's skin prickled and he felt the hair on the back of his neck rising.

He stood to his full height and spoke above them, his arms raised. "This man is a traitor and will get what a traitor deserves. But not from us. We will not lower ourselves to creep on our own bellies with him. He will face the rope."

The men began to murmur angrily again, the mood ugly, but Kuru stepped forward and dragged the frightened terrorist to his feet, pushing him forward, thrusting him through the crowd. Reluctantly they parted, the chanting dying. Then someone – Fletcha – began the regimental song, a haunting funeral march in Sindebele, and they all took it up, swaying with the deep, hollow despair that echoed in the words of the overcoming of death, in a primeval sound so intrinsically African that nowhere else in the world would it be heard in this way.

The harmony rose to an unbelievable beauty that struck out across the flat-topped acacia trees into the darkened bush surrounding them, and even the night creatures stilled to listen as the wonder of the music rebuked the treachery of the man they pushed towards the holding rooms.

In the single jail cell in the barracks, Peter and Kuru faced the traitor.

"Why did you do this?" Peter demanded.

"There is a man now who can match you," Graham spat. "A man who can think the way you think, who will do the things you do, and turn your own plans against you. You will pay for the men you have cost ZIPRA! You will die, Major Kennedy, soon – but not before your woman has suffered."

Peter was not himself, suddenly. A red fog rushed at him, engulfing him, tingling under his skin. He felt a throbbing, a humming in his ears, and everything moved in slow motion. When his boot connected with Graham's chin he hardly felt it, and he only came back to himself when Kuru pushed him outside.

"Get the doctor!" Kuru shouted at him, and he turned and ran out his fury.

It was too late. The savage kick had shattered the terrorist's jaw and smashed his teeth, throwing him backward into the rough brick wall and crushing his skull like a half-conceived eggshell.

Mandhla heard through the surrounding populace of the untimely demise of his best man. It was another point against Kennedy, and one more thing to make him suffer for. His anger was not brought about by any special feelings he may have had for Graham Chobe. Rather, he was infuriated at the useless waste of yet another life, yet another comrade, and one he had trained himself. He remembered the nights of hard coaching, the ease with which Chobe had learnt, and he slapped his palm against the rough bark of a mopani tree in frustration. He would have to begin again.

His mind carefully went through the three remaining men of the Nyoka, and dismissed them. They were good enough for bush fighting, for murder, but that was all. Then he thought again.

David. David Khumalo. The man could track a fly across a rock. He rubbed his ear, nodding to himself. David.

The other two were becoming soft. They had jobs now, gardening for wealthy whites in Illovo. They ate well and slept well and were taken care of by the local girls, and when Mandhla had reminded them of their real objective here each looked reluctant for an instant. They were no longer primed. It was time he poured heat over their flaccidity.

And if Peter Kennedy thought the Mamba was moving towards Zambia again, he would perhaps remove the men who now watched the woman.

As usual, the hits were meticulously planned and Mandhla went over and over the details with the Nyoka. The first was a little to the north of Tsholotsho. They scouted the farm carefully, allowing nothing to fall in the way of chance, and this time they would make their full impact felt.

There were eight family members in all. The farm was well protected by security fencing, but a closer inspection indicated that it was not electrified. It gave fairly easily under the big cutters Mandhla had purloined from a nearby outhouse. The servants' quarters were some distance from the house, and hidden by trees. But Mandhla had no intention of making another silent hit. This time, his modus operandum was different.

At eleven o'clock, when all the lights were out, he cut

the telephone lines. They began the assault at two a.m., the time when a man's spirit is at its lowest ebb, with a mortar attack.

When three holes had been blown in the roof (Mandhla had trained his men carefully; unlike the usual terrorist groups, they knew where to place their shots), they went in at a run. There was no movement from the workers' rooms.

As they approached the house two FNs and a shotgun began to fire at them. They took the cover they had prearranged and returned the fire. Mandhla cursed; any delay would give them time to call the Security Forces on their AgricAlert radio system. He knew that there would be no flat batteries in this homestead.

He waved frantically to Chesa and Albert, the two men carrying the mortar, and they sent another through the window near the most persistent FN. It exploded violently and someone screamed, sobbing loudly, then quieted, and the shooting began again – one rifle less.

This time the rapid shots were more indiscriminate, and Mandhla sensed the panic in them. He smiled mirthlessly to himself and waved again; another mortar smashed into the wall near the second FN position. As it exploded Mandhla and David ran towards the shattered French windows and ducked into the lounge. While the other two kept drawing the irregular fire from the shotgun, they crept silently into the main body of the house.

In the dining room there was very little left of what had probably been the man of the house. His FN had exploded when the mortar came through the window, and his body was a tangle of bloody pulp and shattered bone. Pausing to listen, Mandhla could hear a woman's voice. She was speaking into the radio, terrified, barely able to enunciate her words. He found the room where she was – the main bedroom, he guessed – and walked in, the AK at his hip.

She was on her knees before a small table in the corner of the room. The shotgun stood against the window frame, a box of cartridges dropped and scattered on the floor beside it. He reached out and turned the light on.

She whirled to face him, still crouching on the floor. From the radio a man's voice was still gently calling her name. She dropped the microphone and whimpered, her eyes huge and dark in the parchment face. David put a few bullets into the radio and it went silent. Her eyes closed, and he shredded her body with tracer. Then he dropped the wooden snake beside her.

In the next room the old man and woman cowered beneath their beds. The woman had urinated and released her bowels in fear, and the stench filled the room, even over the smell of the mortar explosions. They died quickly, holding tightly to each other's hands.

The next bedroom contained the remains of a teenaged boy, the outer wall crumbled from the impact of the bullet and cement dust and brick sprayed across the young frame that had bled in so many places before the heart had stopped pumping.

He moved on to the last bedroom. There were three beds here, and a gaping hole in the roof told its own tale. He thought they were all dead, and turned to leave, but then there was a sound from the furthest cot.

He bent over the child, and put his filthy forefinger below her chin to turn her face. Her eyes were huge, trying to understand what was happening to her. Her legs were trapped beneath rafters that had crashed down from the ceiling; gently, Mandhla lifted what he could. Her legs had been crushed – perhaps also her spinal cord, for she was beyond pain. Her hands lay uselessly at her side and flopped nervelessly when Mandhla picked them up.

There was a bitter gall taste in his mouth. She was no more than six years old, and there was nothing left for her to live for. Hastily, he pushed the emotion aside. This was a war. These things must be done. Had she been only slightly wounded, he would have left her. As it was, he placed the barrel of the AK-47 at her temple and released the bullets into her brain. He saw the eyes glaze, and turned away. Too much time had been wasted.

Throughout the attack there had been no interference from the farm workers. Mandhla knew that, terrified, they would either have fled or would be hiding under their beds. He left them to their escape.

They moved fast, not bothering to lay mines in their wake. It would only hold them up. They took a chance and found a village they had watched before the hit. As Mandhla had suspected, there was total subversion here; the headman hid them well and lied perfectly to the soldiers when they came, sending them on a trail his own herders had made for them.

When they were safe, two of them moved north again, this time to a farmstead south of Korodziba. Here there were only four to kill, and they did it swiftly and well, leaving a carving before disappearing across the border into Botswana.

Meanwhile, Mandhla and David carefully moved south, without leaving a trail.

Peter Kennedy was fuming. The Mamba had gone again, leaving death in his trail and his carved snakes to taunt the Skuzapo. He had obviously crossed into the neighbouring country, presumably to head back to the base camp and refuel. After all the ammunition he had spent on the two hits he made, his supplies must be low.

But one thing gave Peter immense satisfaction. Although the Mamba had slipped between his fingers again (he cursed the uncertainty of the Scout who had followed Chobe to the meeting with Mandhla, listening instead of killing), Peter had struck back at him by killing a man who must have been worth something to him.

And the Mamba had responded by running.

Or ... had he?

Chapter 22

Tsimbaboue

Kisang knew that one day he would lead an army. He did not question the knowledge, he accepted it. He did not consider what people it would consist of. He realised that the amaTsimbaboue had grown soft under kings such as his father, who wanted only to trade and continue to live as they had always done.

He had seen a small *impi* once – during his Bush time, the period he had had to be alone for two weeks, living solely off the bush and what he knew of it. He had to kill one large animal and bring its skin back with him; this was his initiation skin. The creature had to be categorised as dangerous – buffalo, elephant, rhinoceros, leopard, lion. There were many in the area he had been left in, of course. Surviving them, alone, with only his knife and two spears, was part of what was expected – even of a King's firstborn son. Perhaps especially so.

He growled as he remembered his Bush time. If he hadn't climbed so high in that tree ... if the branches had given under his weight ... the buffalo would have killed him. As it was, it had paced around the bole of the tree for two days, reaching up now and then to try to lick the soles of his feet so that he would bleed to death. If the impi had not arrived when they had ...

Of course, he had paid them well for the skin. It was only fair. They had been on their way north to repay in kind an insult that their King had received from a tribe near the great Zambesi River. Dressed impressively in bold skins and feathers, they drank the blood of the buffalo to give them its strength –

cut its throat and let the warm liquid squirt directly into their mouths.

They had wanted to kill him, also, but he had persuaded them not to. After all, he did know of a smallish kraal nearby, where he had cadged beer from one of the girls ... there were cattle there, fat cattle. The impi, he quickly realised, almost worshipped cattle. And the men could use a few women each, to tide them over their journey. So an exchange was made. Kisang's life, and the buffalo skin, for directions to the kraal. They knew he would not lie – he would not have dared.

The buffalo skin was not nearly as prestigious as those of the two leopards that Xhaitaan had brought back four years later, but it was sufficient – especially when he showed them the grooves he had slashed into his arm, rubbing ashes into them to make the scars stand out, and told them the animal had attacked him. True, his father had hesitated before accepting the story, but it had been accepted by the King, and so by the people.

He had married Maxa two years ago, but as yet she had failed to produce a son for him – or, indeed, any child at all. It was obvious the sour-faced witch was barren. Of course, she'd tried to blame him, but Kisang was certain this wasn't so. A man of Kisang's stature was always able to reproduce himself! Of course, it was true that none of his concubines, the girls in the compound allotted to him, had fallen pregnant in all the years he had lain with them, but ... they were taught to avoid these things, weren't they?

Maxa was not particularly passionate in bed, anyway, and a man needs stimulation when he is expected to lie with a woman of his mother's choice. Admittedly he had looked at other women now and then, had considered marrying a second wife, but none met his requirements. It was forbidden to force oneself onto a free woman, one who was not in bondage for the purpose; Kisang, however, didn't take the rule too seriously, and found that the peasant women on the fringes would remain silent if paid well enough. Besides, how could they accuse him, a King's son, of such a thing? The idea was ludicrous.

Meanwhile, as Kaka never ceased to point out to him, the girl Tcana was rapidly becoming popular with the King. Since her marriage to Xhaitaan six months previously Mgane's attitude of wariness had changed to one of genuine liking. And Kaka had been urging Kisang to marry a new wife, to provide the King with a grandchild. The first grandchild. He had, at his mother's insistence, thrown a gold ingot quite recently – for his uncle's cousin's daughter, who was comely enough in her way and had hips like a breeding cow's. But she obviously hadn't seen it; she had walked on past, and he had decided that he wouldn't try to attract her attention again. Not after she had looked at him that way ...

Kisang's fist closed at the memory, his nails biting into his palm. Jackal! But one day she would be made to remember it. Of that he was sure.

His mind wandered back to the grandchild factor. Certainly, it did not look as though Tcana was being very successful in that respect, though it was well known that the King would have liked it. Kisang watched his sister-in-law's belly closely, and each day it seemed flatter than the last. Mgane, too, watched. Perhaps ... The handmaiden, Niswe. She was a strong girl, good natured, always laughing – and very much a woman. That one would bear children the moment a man used her. And he had seen her looking at him; as soon as he looked back she busied herself elsewhere, of course, as was fitting and proper for a servant.

And that was another point – she was a servant. True, not of the caste that were used by the men for that purpose, but nevertheless ... Kisang felt a stirring in his groin as the idea festered.

Niswe had indeed been looking at Kisang. She did not trust him; indeed, she did not trust anyone here. Except for the King, of course. But Tcana had been ill recently, and Niswe was certain it had been something in the food.

The food was prepared by servants, but the kitchens were open to any of the Royal Family, and Maxa spent much time there. It wouldn't have been difficult to arrange to have something put into Tcana's food, or drink, for that matter. The Royal men ate together, apart from the women, and Tcana, rather than sit with the women who did not like her and whom she had no affinity for, ate alone in her hut, from a tray prepared specially for her.

It bothered Niswe. But Tcana seemed happy enough - and Xhaitaan spent more time with her than was precedented for a man and wife. When he could not be with her, Tcana walked - either with Niswe, or slipping away alone. Niswe suspected that at such times she went to the other side of the Hill, to the hidden spring.

In fact, she was only half right. Tcana did still go, sometimes, to the spring, but lately she had stayed in the open more, straying further and further from the village. Xhaitaan worried about it - he wanted to send men to watch over her, but she told him that would spoil it for her. She wanted - needed - to be alone. When she walked she took off her finery and simply tied an apron skin at her loins, letting her breasts bounce free in the sunlight. From a distance she could have been any pretty young Tsimbaboue maiden. She also carried a water-pail, which helped the image she wished to create. Anonymity, she told Xhaitaan, was her protection.

Still, Niswe worried. Tcana was - different. She had a restlessness in her, a desire to wander. "I am afraid," she had said again to her friend. "Muali wants something of me, and I cannot understand what it is. I walk, in the hopes that he will tell me, but nothing comes. I pray - oh, how I pray! - but there is only silence. Not the way it used to be; not the peace and well-being he sent me when I prayed before. Just a - a waiting."

It disturbed Niswe. After all, the Oracle had claimed her at the same time Xhaitaan had - perhaps, after all, Tcana had chosen the wrong path? Though Niswe couldn't see how, when she had taken the test of Muali and Muali had obviously chosen Xhaitaan's desire over Tcana for his Mouthpiece.

So Niswe watched Tcana's food more carefully, ensuring it was safe; and she watched Nada, though the older woman seemed to have settled now she realised that Mgane liked Tcana so well; and she watched Kisang, though why, she didn't know; and especially she watched Maxa.

Mgane had indeed decided that he liked Tcana. She was truly pleasant on the eye, and in spite of her respectful manners, she managed to convey a sense of wit and humour. She made the King laugh, and he liked to laugh; and when he laughed her eyes danced, which pleased him. And his son was happy, which was even more important – a people should have a happy King. Certainly, he decided, life was going well. Nada was happier – Mgane realised she was insecure of her son's position, particularly as he was not firstborn; but as Mgane had pointed out, Muali had hovered over Xhaitaan three times, and that meant that Xhaitaan was Muali's choice, too. In Mgane's mind there was no doubt.

And Tcana, he knew, would make a good First Queen. The girl was brave, and wise beyond her years. She was peaceable, and wanted only the happiness of those around her. Between her and Xhaitaan his people would be ruled perhaps better than ever before.

Soon, now – soon would be his time. He knew that Muali called him; the pains in his left arm were more frequent recently, and the sensation of a grinding-rock pressing on his chest, forbidding his breath, was stronger. He must make his intentions public. He called his Ambassador to make the arrangements.

Nada would be pleased, he reflected.

Nada was indeed pleased. The feast went well, and with her son at the King's right hand, now finally named his successor, everything was going right at last. She sneaked a look at Kaka. Poor woman. Now that Nada's position was finalised she could afford to be generous, and Kaka had not wanted anything for Kisang that Nada had not pursued for Xhaitaan. As she caught Kaka's eye, Nada smiled condescendingly at her, but was rewarded only with hatred glowing from the fat eyes. Nada smiled again, self-satisfied. She picked a sheep's eye from the soapstone platter before her and savoured the jellied ball in her mouth.

Her eye wandered to Maxa and lingered thoughtfully. Maxa was glaring covertly at Tcana, and the intensity of the rage surprised even Nada. Suddenly, Nada realised that she would do well to look to changing her stance on Tcana. Tcana was no longer to be fought, but supported – even, Nada thought, glancing again at Maxa – even protected. And, of course, encouraged to bear a child.

The people had welcomed their King's announcement with frenzied excitement. They, too, had lived in concern over Kisang's possible ascension to the throne. Now, unless some disaster prevented it, their King-designate was affirmed. Xhaitaan, the King's favourite; Muali's favourite; the people's favourite. And so they danced, drank beer, sang, and danced again.

In the silence of the marriage hut, Tcana stared through the morning grey at the ceiling, disturbed without knowing why. Beside her Xhaitaan slept soundly, exhausted from the dancing. The delighted amaTsimbaboue had called for him over and over, until he could hardly walk; now he must sleep. Quietly, careful of disturbing him, Tcana moved out from under the kaross. She went to the door and stood for a moment, looking out over the Royal Compound. Soon the sun would appear, behind the Tower of Continuance, the conical tower that signified the King's provision for his people, and theirs for him.

It was a grain bin, of course, in design. And beside it, in its own conical enclosure, burnt the Life Fire.

A movement caught her eye and she turned her head slightly in the shadows of the doorway. It was Kisang, cautiously making his way through the slowly advancing light, to stand a little way away. He was looking at the hut Niswe shared with another handmaiden. She stiffened. She didn't trust Kisang; she had seen the way he looked at Niswe, and although Niswe was not a sleeping-girl, Tcana was uneasy. A handmaiden was, nevertheless, a servant; Kisang was still a King's son, with an unhealthy appetite for the servant-girls.

As the heavy form moved towards her friend's hut, Tcana came silently out of her doorway. Kisang was intent on his prey; he did not see his sister-in-law.

Tcana thought desperately. She was a woman, half the size of Kisang. As a woman, she had no right to interfere with him. If she woke Xhaitaan – no, she would waste too much time trying to explain the situation to her dazed husband. Her brain raced. What would be the penalty for stopping a Royal man from committing a crime? Who would be judged first, he or she?

Kisang stopped at the entrance to the hut and as he glanced furtively around him Tcana flattened herself into the shadows, thanking Muali that the sun was still not up. Kisang turned back and entered the hut.

Tcana ran. Light-footed, she heard her every step pound the earth, and prayed that he would not. As she reached the doorway she looked carefully around the wooden door, now standing open.

Kisang stood above Niswe, who had just woken to find him leaning over her. Her eyes widened in fright; she could not possibly mistake the reason for his presence there. She looked to the other girl who shared the hut with her, but the maid scurried up, grabbing her blanket, and ran out. Tcana saw the girl falter as she realised her First Princess stood there, but then she was gone. She would not dare to defy Kisang.

Tcana's heart beat fast. Without further thought, she entered the hut.

"Niswe, I – oh, Lord Kisang." She feigned surprise, and touched her forehead in salute. "Did you need Niswe for something? I want her to help me wash and dress."

The big man whirled his bulk around, furious, but had no answer. Niswe scrambled to her feet, her face grey in the first fingers of the sun that crept their way into the hut.

"I am sure that one of the other servants can get you what you want," continued Tcana sweetly. "If you like, I will call your own servant girl."

Kisang stared at her, and the malice in his eyes frightened her. Then he was gone.

They walked together, behind the Hill and further. "I'm afraid for you, Niswe. I think that you had better go home to the village."

"I'm afraid for you, Tcana. I will not leave you in that nest of crocodiles. Kisang wants you as much as he does me – he wants every woman he may not have. But more than that, he wants the throne, and you and Xhaitaan are in the way. I – " She stopped in mid-sentence, seeing the look on her friend's face.

Tcana had halted abruptly. The strangeness was there again, but stronger this time. Her head swam and the urge to run was almost over-powering. The inside of her skull held only one thought that whirled and danced. Muali. Perhaps this time ...

"I - I must go," she said, her tongue thickening. "Leave me, Niswe."

Niswe was concerned, but Tcana had told her of these times. She touched her friend's shoulder before she went. "Muali defend you."

Tcana stumbled on, faster and faster in the early morning sun. Her shadow was long in the grass behind her, and her feet were washed in the dew that had not yet dried. If her toes struck stones, she did not feel it; her eyes hardly saw what she passed. She ran on and on, until her breath was big in her chest and her throat would not open; she fell, pulling for air.

She didn't know how long she lay there, but when she awoke the thickness was gone. The sun was high and hot, but she was in the shade of a huge baobab tree - a sacred baobab, that Muali put there for travellers who thirsted, or who needed comfort or rescue. She sat up, and there was a humming in the warm air. Never had she felt her head so clear, never had she seen so far, or breathed so sweet. She stood, and the humming turned to a singing that she could not place; when she walked the ground was like a soft kaross under her feet. She felt she could fly; she felt there were feathers around her, that she had wings.

There was a whirlpool in the air and a cold wind; her mind swam away from her and suddenly she was above the big tree and the sun was closer, and she was looking down on a girl standing below the baobab. The girl had a high nose and darkly bronzed skin, and ...

She spread her black wings, letting the white windows show through, and soared above the tree, higher and higher and higher, gliding, looping, dropping, soaring again, until the tree was little more than a pinprick below her; she rode the winds and they ruffled her feathers, and the glory of flight was the most wonderful thing she had ever experienced.

She dropped lower again and saw it suddenly. The long, lithe, dark shape moved lazily through the grass toward the girl below, and, positioning herself, she instantly clipped her wings to her sides and let herself drop, down, down, faster and faster. The wind held her up but still she fell, until she was on top of the snake and her strong claws reached out to clutch the body, which unexpectedly wasn't there.

A split second before impact she spread her wings and lifted herself again, but not very high; she hovered over her prey, watching as it raised its head higher off the red ground, flattening its neck, and stared at her from silver-lined eyes. They hung there for a moment, scrutinizing, each trying to force the other to give, and Tcana felt the hypnosis of the Mamba.

She felt inexplicably, irresistibly drawn, and afraid, but knowing she must go on ... Closer and closer she hovered, unable to stop herself, and then the serpent struck.

She was floating, back, back into the body of the maid who stood watching; she felt each part of her fit back into place - her toes, her legs, her fingers, her arms, her body, until finally she saw through her own eyes again.

The Mamba was swallowing the Eagle.

Chapter 23

There was a buzzing, growing gradually, inside her skull, gentle but rising. The dizziness was greater, and she felt nauseous. Strangely, the taste of honey, vague but familiar, lay on her tongue. A sound; something moved outside; a flitting across the sand floor. A wild spasm of fear wracked her muscles. Pain crashed through her, but the fear was greater – until she heard the call of an eagle, and realised its shape in the branching shadows across the sand.

No one must find her. They mustn't find her.

Oh God, please don't let him find me ...

The heat from the dark bead at her throat rose and grew, until at last it was all she could feel.

Rhodesia

Her voice was acid across the telephone line. "Major Kennedy, take your men off my tail immediately."

"Miss Rawlings, is that you?" he drawled back.

"Are there many other women are under your surveillance?"

He hesitated. "It's necessary. How did you find out?" He knew the SB men were too clever to have been spotted.

"Major, I have spent the past several weeks in police HQ in Bulawayo. They treat me like an old friend."

He cursed inwardly; loose lips ... "Miss Rawlings, I'm not happy about your safety at present."

"My safety is all of my concern and none of yours. There is no earthly reason why anyone would be gunning for me! I'm beginning to think you're perverted, Major. You have a very strange way with women and it isn't in the least endearing. Plus, if you don't get your men off my back, I'll complain to Mr. Smith's colleague."

It hit home. "It's your skin," he said coldly, and hung up.

After all, he thought, the man was moving back into Zambia. Perhaps he could remove the guard – for the time being.

He picked up the telephone.

She found the note when she got back from the studios that evening. Kyle was now somewhere in South Africa, but he promised to come back to Rhodesia in a few weeks' time to say goodbye properly. She smiled cheerlessly; she would miss him.

She let Mangoi out of the back door while she made herself a mug of Milo. He miaowed to come back in before she had finished with her drink; distracted, she opened the door for him and poured the hot milk onto the chocolate powder. A moment later she followed the big cat through to the bedroom, where he always slept on the bed with her.

She woke when Mangoi sat up. She knew there was someone in the room with them, not so much because she heard him but because she sensed him. Her door squeaked slightly and she sat up, the bed whispering in the dark. There was a startled breath and footsteps in the passage. Rebecca jumped out of bed and ran after them, but when she reached the end of the hall there was no-one there. Disturbed, she turned on all the lights, checking windows and doors.

The back door was slightly open, and she realised she'd forgotten to lock it after Mangoi came back in. The only thing that was missing was her brown leather handbag, from the small table beside her bed, a foot away from her head. Annoyed, she slipped on some jeans and telephoned the police.

They were there in ten minutes, with two dogs and their handlers. Mangoi arched at the German Shepherds from his perch on the armoire, but they had more important things on their minds. While they sniffed around and then disappeared down the road, their handlers behind them, Rebecca explained what had happened to the detective who had come with them.

"I doubt we'll get him," he said when she'd finished. "There's a pretty clever cat-burglar around at the moment. It's probably the same man. But don't worry. He hasn't hurt anyone yet."

Small consolation, she thought as she went back to bed and tried to sleep.

The handbag was returned two days later by a man who worked for the electricity board. He'd found it in a hedge, two blocks from her flat, and checked inside, finding her name on her OAST identity card. He brought it to the studio where she was editing footage.

The money, to the cent, was still in the purse, and nothing else was missing. But there was something extra. She unwrapped the brown paper and removed the tissue paper, then stood the object on the table in front of her, staring at it. Something rang in her brain; remembering his reaction to the jet snake, she reached for the telephone and dialled.

"Major Kennedy? Rebecca Rawlings. Something peculiar has happened. My handbag was stolen a few nights ago, and it was brought back today. Nothing was missing, but the burglar left me a gift."

"What?" he asked sharply.

"It's a carving. A sort of arm bracelet, I think. A snake."

He was there an hour later, imposing in his uniform with the brown beret and the badge of an osprey about to strike its prey, the wings outstretched, the claws reaching, just as it was in the painting. Hilary and the receptionist gaped at him while he waited for Rebecca in the lobby, and at his black companion, huge and intimidating, the muscle in his right cheek gripping and loosing rhythmically as he stared indifferently at the Constable print on the wall.

In the editing room he turned the wooden bangle over in his hands, inspecting the carving, then passed it to Kuru, who checked it briefly and handed it back with a nod.

"Are you still without transport of your own?" he wanted to know. She nodded, bewildered by the question. The little old Fiat had died two weeks ago. She didn't ask how he knew. "Get some. I don't like you on public transport, it's too vulnerable. And I'm putting my men back on guard."

She shook her head emphatically at him. "Not until I know what this is all about."

He sighed and leaned back against the editing console, his hands gripping the edge. "Someone has it in for me. I think he blames me for something that happened once; he doesn't understand the circumstances."

"What?" She was unrelenting.

Kuru moved to the door of the room, legs astride, arms folded, glaring out at the passersby in the passage. How dramatic, she thought, without taking her eyes from the Major.

He sighed. "This is my business, okay? I'm sorry that he's picked on you to threaten me through, but he has, and I have to take care of it. I don't know that he'll actually hurt you, but I want to be sure he doesn't."

"I'm not afraid."

"I know you aren't. But I am." His voice was brusque. "If anything happened to you because of a mistake I made, I would never live that down. Do you see?"

She nodded slowly. "Why has he chosen me?"

"I'm not sure. Perhaps because you're the only person I've had contact with recently, outside work."

She sighed, biting her lip. "All right. But my life is my own. Your men are not to interfere unless I'm in danger – real danger – okay?"

"Okay. No reports, no interference. I have to go." He picked up the snake carving from the console and tucked it into one of his pockets. "Be careful. And if you're worried about anything at all, call me. "Oh …" He turned back, looking directly into her eyes – "and please keep your doors locked from now on."

It hit home.

He went, with Kuru striding purposefully behind him. Hilary poked her head in immediately. "So that's the famous Major Peter Kennedy! He certainly caused a stir in the offices." She looked closely at Rebecca. "Everything all right?"

"Fine, thank you," she said clearly, and went back to her work.

She fell in love with it the moment she saw it. It was a black five-year-old model 500cc Honda, with an ostentatious white eagle in flight blow-painted onto the side of the tank. It reminded her of the beret badge.

Tony was doubtful. "It needs a good service. Maybe more."

"You can help me with that, can't you?"

"Yes, but –"

"Then I want it." The excitement in her eyes was patent. He gave in and the money exchanged hands.

They worked on the 'bike for three days, and when they had finished it looked almost new. The eagle gleamed in the sunlight as Rebecca inspected it. "Osprey" she announced. "That's his name. Osprey."

"Vehicles are shes!" Tony protested.

"Not mine. He's a he. Osprey."

"And that painting isn't an osprey, it's the American bald eagle," he grumbled.

"I know," she dimpled at him, and he growled back.

Tony was stern with her. "When you go out on that road, remember every other vehicle there is out to kill you. It's the only way to stay alive." He reminded her of emergency procedures and repeated over and over that everyone on the road was out to kill her, until she finally stopped him with a finger on his lips.

"Enough. I am now aware that I'm the moving target of every idiot who sees or hears me pass by. Tony, you know I ride 'bikes back home. Kyle taught me years ago. I know what this is all about. Let me go – I want to ride."

She moved slowly out until she reached the wide tarred road that ribboned out past Riverclub, and then opened her throttle and relaxed in the familiar thrust of the powerful engine. She exulted in the wind in her face and her hair tumbling out from beneath the helmet and whipping out of its braid behind her. Carefully she experimented with the feel of the 'bike, its balance, until she was satisfied, and then she headed back to the flat where Tony waited.

She pulled the 'bike up sharply in front of him, took her helmet off and shook her plait out, her face alight with the joy of riding again.

"Wait till Kyle sees this!" she exclaimed, delighted.

He groaned and covered his eyes with his fingers. He had a feeling Kyle would blame him. But more to the point, so would Major Kennedy.

She became more and more involved in the abandoned freedom of riding on the open roads, and often went out alone, venturing further and further afield in the hours she wasn't working. Tony didn't like it, but she ignored his objections.

Peter Kennedy liked it even less. "I meant for you to get a car," he pointed out over the telephone, "not a weapon to kill yourself with!"

"Don't be stuffy. And I thought you promised your men wouldn't report back to you?"

"This wasn't a report, it was disbelief. In Rhodesia, women don't ride 'bikes. Scooters, maybe, but not 'bikes."

"In America, women do what they want!" she retorted, and hung up. She knew that his protest was partly because she was managing more and more often to shake the tail he had put on her.

Kyle arrived back on Thursday. "For one week's leave, little sister. Then I have to go down to Cape Town."

"Whatever I can get. In fact, I'll tell Tony we're on leave, too!"

"Ah, the freedom of running your own programme schedule," he commented, and kissed her forehead.

And he loved the 'bike.

The phone rang on Friday morning.

"Miss Rawlings." He was stiff and formal. For a moment she thought she had done something wrong again. "I wondered whether you would care to take a look at the bush itself, first-hand, and perhaps some of Rhodesia's history at the same time?"

"That depends." She was guarded. "Where would it fit into my programme?"

"That's up to you. But if you and your brother are interested, I'm spending this weekend at a cottage in the bush. I have to warn you that it's perhaps a little rough and ready – but it's safe," he added quickly.

She noted that he knew Kyle was back. "I'm sure my brother would love to – I don't think I can make it, though," she said mischievously.

He was silent for a moment. "You're teasing me again."

"Yes, I am." She laughed aloud. "I'd be delighted, Major Kennedy. And I'm sure my brother would, too. We don't mind rough and ready."

"I'll pick you up at fourteen hundred."

Kyle came in as she was packing food to take. When she told him he gave her a waggish wink. "Something tells me," he said with a twinkle, "that you do have a man in your life."

"It's just an extension of the interview, Big Brother. And even if it wasn't – would it upset you?"

He considered this. "I don't really know. The only time I met him he seemed pretty uptight to me. Do you really want a chaperone?" he teased.

"Yes! So does he, apparently. And bring your photographic equipment, because I have a feeling we're going to be doing more than sitting around eating, and Tony wasn't invited so maybe I can use some of your stills. Just watch where you point your lens – Major Kennedy is extremely camera-shy."

He collected them promptly at two. He was dressed casually in jeans and a loose shirt with short sleeves that revealed muscular, tanned arms. In the sunlight his hair had a chestnut burnish, and she suspected that it would have been darker had he spent less time in the sun. He brought, once again, the open Landrover jeep. He hesitated when he saw Kyle's camera and paraphernalia, but said nothing. She noted the FN and shotgun in leather sheaths on the doors; a powerful-looking handgun in the open glove-compartment.

"I thought you said where we're going is safe?" she queried.

"It is, but we have to travel to get there. Can you use one of these?"

"You have a short memory," she retorted, remembering the attack on the QueQue road. The scar still stung sometimes.

They arrived two hours before dusk. The cottage was in the rolling hills near Fort Victoria, overlooking a rocky, fast-moving river. Rough and ready, she commented to herself, was right. There were two bedrooms with the doors opposite each other, across a porch with a sink along the back wall and an eating table in the centre – open at the front to the wilderness.

The toilet was a longdrop some distance from the cottage; when he saw the look on her face, Peter said curtly that it was that or nothing. Attached to the back of the cottage was a zinc shed which contained an old rust-patched, lion-footed bath, and a water tank above a fireplace for heating. There was a wind-driven borehole at the top of the hill which pumped water down to the cottage.

Peter pulled the fishing rods off the side of the jeep and handed one to each of his guests. "I hope you fish," he said. "Dinner depends on it."

They did. Rebecca had never been permitted squeamishness back home; Kyle had seen to that. Three years older than she was, and unimpressed at being presented with a baby sister rather than a brother, he had considered it his duty to treat her in the same way he would a boy. She could not only ride big motorcycles; she could also string worms with the best of them.

Kyle didn't stay interested for long; he wanted photographs, and disappeared into the bush in search of subjects, taking the handgun with him. Rebecca shifted position and stretched her bare legs out in front of her, leaning back against a tree trunk in the late sunlight. She put her face up into the breeze and breathed, her eyes closed as she savoured the scent of the bush.

Peter, standing, watched the curve of her neck and chin reaching upward, and followed it down to the strong swell of her breasts under the tee shirt. His eyes travelled down the flat stomach, the strong thighs and well-shaped calves that glowed peach in the thickening light, and stopped at the naked crossed ankles and the feet enclosed in canvas takkies. He turned away and spoke abruptly. "You shouldn't wear shorts in the bush."

She opened her long eyes and watched his back speculatively as he played the line. She got up and went to stand beside him, picking up her rod as she did so. "Does it bother you?"

"What?"

"My shorts."

"It'll bother you later tonight when you discover how many insects have bitten you."

"Are you always so practical, Major Kennedy?"

"Most of the time. Sometimes –" he looked into her wide eyes – "sometimes I get very impractical."

He got a bite then and landed a fair-sized fish. "We need two more," he commented, and concentrated.

She caught them both, and in the last rays of the sun they gutted and cleaned them, and then went back to the water to wash off the blood. She stepped into the moving flow and bent to wash her legs, her plait falling forward and dipping into the river. He caught it back for her, and took out the band that held it, digging his fingers into the thick braid to free the hair. She stood with her back to him until he reached the root at last and shook it out, then turned to face him and shook her head vigorously to loosen the tresses. They fell in a cloud around her shoulders. She raised an eyebrow questioningly at him.

"I like it loose," he said, and walked away.

Kyle reappeared moments later; he made no comment about her liberated hair, and the men built a bonfire in the sand beside the river. Rebecca wrapped potatoes in foil, and buttered bread rolls, and tossed the salad. The potatoes were pushed into the bottom of the fire, and they talked about Kyle's experiences in Asia and North Africa and Australia, the wars and the peaces, and Rebecca listened, and learned more about her brother than she ever had before. She realised that a bond was forming between the two men; they were similar in so many ways – little time for anything but the job in hand. And neither, she noted, was involved with a woman.

They fried the fish in butter over the embers of the fire, and she thought she had never eaten food that tasted quite like this. Somehow, Kyle had gotten onto the subject of his faith, and Peter was listening intently. Through Kyle, he was beginning to understand Rebecca better. When Kyle made a statement of his faith, Peter Kennedy realised it went for his sister too.

It confirmed what he had suspected for some time. Untouched, she wore an intangible sense of purity like a mantle, of which she was wholly unaware.

Rebecca had been given one of the bedrooms, Kyle the other. Peter insisted that here, he always slept outside under the stars and wouldn't want it any other way. Kyle left them soon after supper as they sat around the still-glowing embers. "I want to be up early to take photographs," he said.

Rebecca stretched. "I think I smell rain on the wind."

Peter sniffed, testing the air. "Are you considering dancing in it?"

She stiffened. "It was you!"

"Me what?" he asked innocently.

She looked at him, considering. "You're a strange man, Major Kennedy."

"I haven't been caught dancing in the rain yet." She heard laughter in his voice.

"You let me think it was a terrorist."

"Would you rather have known it was me?"

She thought about it. "No. What were you doing there?"

"Walking. I like the rain, too. And I was fascinated by your reaction to it. I thought for a moment you were a water sprite, or a magical nymph from *A Midsummer Night's Dream*."

"I didn't take you for the literary type."

"Surprised?"

"Yes. But Shakespeare could be a bit bawdy. I prefer the purist poets, myself."

"Ah. You mean, like:

> *Woman! Experience might have told me*
> *All must love thee who behold thee:*
> *Surely experience might have taught*
> *Thy firmest promises are nought;*
> *But, placed in all thy charms before me,*
> *All I forget, but to adore thee.*
> *Oh memory! thou choicest blessing*
> *When join'd with hope, when still possessing;*
> *But how much cursed by every lover*
> *When hope is fled and passion's over.*"

She laughed. "That sounds rather bitter. Do you share Lord Byron's rather suspect opinion?"

"Perhaps."

She was quiet for a moment. "How old are you?" she asked then.

"Is it important?"

"Perhaps," she imitated.

"I'm thirty-two."

"Family?"

"Dead. Terr attack. I was with the army, Mark with Intaff."

She was silent for several moments. "I'm sorry." She played with the embers of the fire. "I guess I should go in. I'm pretty bushed. I hope for your sake it doesn't rain tonight."

"If it does I'll move my stretcher onto the porch." He stood and helped her carry the plates to the sink. "Leave them for the morning. There'll be plenty time then."

She stopped at her door. "Well then. Good night." He caught her arm as she stepped away. Deliberately he leaned forward and kissed her mouth, almost passionlessly, and she felt the jolt in her loins. He drew away, but as her body followed his, he hesitated only fractionally before putting his arms around her and pulling her closer. She slipped her own arms around him and buried her face in his chest, breathing him in.

They stood that way a full minute and she felt the tension in him; it frightened and excited her and she didn't dare move until he straightened up and took her face in his hands. He carefully kissed her forehead, as a brother kisses a sister.

"Goodnight, Becky." It was a hoarse whisper, and then he moved away to the fire to set up his camp bed.

Becky. She had never allowed anyone to call her that; yet somehow from him it was all right. She watched him for a while from her window, and when she finally went to bed herself she knew he wasn't sleeping, either.

Kyle was awake before either of them, gone with his camera when Rebecca emerged, dressed but sleepy-eyed, from her room. Edging past Peter's camp bed and still figure in the sleeping bag, she moved to the river and sat on a rock, watching the white foam as she brushed out the knots in her hair. It settled like a cloud around her shoulders and flicked the red earth with its length.

The sound of the water covered his approach. "Good morning."

"Hi. How'd you sleep?"

"Let's just say I'm usually up long before this." He squinted into the sun and then watched the brush stroking her hair. "Here. Let me." He took the brush and squatted on his haunches beside her. Starting at the bottom, as he had seen her do, he began to disentangle the mass. "I'm beginning to see why you keep it tied up," he commented after a moment.

"That was too good to miss," a voice behind them called. Kyle came across the rocks, waving his camera. "Don't worry, Major – not for anything but the private albums."

Rebecca saw Peter's embarrassment and took the brush from him, standing up. "Isn't it breakfast time? I'm starved!"

Kyle shook his head despairingly at her. "Don't you ever stop eating? I warn you, Peter, she has a massive appetite."

Peter smiled down at her. "I think I can handle that," he said, and she wasn't sure that he was referring to food. It was her turn to be flustered.

The Zimbabwe Ruins – with the largest ancient stone structure south of the Sahara, and spreading over a total area of two hundred square miles, with the centre of the city right where they stood now – absolutely captivated Rebecca.

The vast 'keep' of outer dry-stone walling – the Great Enclosure with its conical tower; the tall narrow passageways that wound their way over a large area of the hilly ground; the mountain fortress of the Acropolis high above, overseeing and overshadowing – all built in intricate dry-stone walling several metres thick and up to ten metres high, and using the enormous natural boulders as part of their architecture. All around, Peter explained, would have been thousands of families living in dwellings of mud and thatch, farming and tooling and weaving and trading, and going about their day to day lives. An entire civilisation who one day just ... disappeared.

Rebecca wandered through the passages, her palms trailing on the cool shadowed stone; she studied the distinctive chevron patterns in the rocks, strangely drawn by them, and felt an energy move through her fingertips as they played across the granite. Her feet climbed the well-worn paths and stone steps through the winding, almost claustrophic passages, all the way up to the big, open area within the Acropolis, built on an immense dome of granite.

She had visited other ruins, of course, but these were different than anything she had seen; she felt an affinity here, as though she'd known it, once ... long ago ...

She shook off the fanciful notions, but they made her wonder about the people who built this place, who'd lived here, cried and laughed, birthed and died here ... where had they gone? Why had it all ended? Had this all really been part of the stomping ground of the fabled Queen of Sheba? Could it really have been the location of King Solomon's Mines?

Peter was far more down to earth. "No-one really knows who exactly built it all, or who lived here. The archaeologists reckon the ruins were built around the 13th Century, though there were people on the site from about the 4th Century, right up through the Iron Age. They traded with Arab and Chinese merchants, because odd bits of imported pottery and jewellery were found, but they seem to have been largely self-sufficient, in which case there's no apparent reason for their leaving."

"You mean – *no-one* knows?" She was astonished.

He shook his head. "Not even the natives of the area, though the maShona claim to be their descendants. The Ndebele disagree, of course, and there are all sorts of theories about Phoenicians and various others ... I'm inclined to believe it was a native black civilisation, though. I'm told there are still today the remnants of a religion that may have stemmed from this city. It seems unlikely to me, because the obvious worship-symbol here is the eagle, and the other religion is snake-orientated. The huge stone statues of eagles, and all the soapstone statuettes, have all been removed now, to museums and the like, and they've never found anything here relating to snakes."

As he said it, something whispered in his brain, but he discarded it, annoyed with himself. He was getting as fanciful as she was!

Rebecca was fascinated; she felt a closeness to the tumbled stones that was hardly warranted, she told herself. There was, she knew, an incurable romantic deep within the hard-nosed journalist she believed herself to be. Still, there was something ... She rubbed the gooseflesh on her arms, shook it off, and laughed at herself. Stupid!

Kyle bought her a small soapstone eagle from the gift shop, in the tradition of the Great Zimbabwe eagles, crudely carved yet beautiful in its simplicity. "For your flat," he said.

Back at the cottage they settled next to the water again with fishing rods. Unexpectedly, Peter sat down behind her, his knees drawn up on either side enclosing her body, and wrapped his arms around her waist, his chin on her head. She felt somehow secure with the warmth of his body against her back; she felt the fire rise in her belly and she had to force herself to concentrate. Kyle fished harder and said nothing.

The afternoon sun had a soporific effect on them. Peter spread her hair in a curtain and leaned his cheek against it, rubbing into the softness and breathing her perfume. Content, she watched a score of tiny black ants moving a dead grasshopper towards their home, and marvelled at their strength. A kingfisher sat in the branches of a nearby thorn tree, watching the water and occasionally making a dive for food. The quiet hum of the bush was all around them, and she relaxed into him.

They caught nothing, but it didn't matter. Instead they cooked steaks over the fire, taking turns to hold the grid over the flames – Peter insisted the resulting flavour was far better than resting it on bricks above the coals after the flames had died. He was right. They ate slowly, lavishing butter onto baked potatoes and savouring the fire's touch on the meat. Kyle kept rebuilding the blaze and they sat in magical silence around it, watching the orange phosphorescence and the shooting sparks. They drank wine with the food, and by the time the flickers were dying down for the last time Rebecca felt a little heady.

Earlier they had started a fire under the water tank, and finally she headed for the bathroom with a torch for light. The water was rusty red and when she'd finished she wasn't sure how much cleaner she was, but at least she felt refreshed.

"Your turn," she called to Kyle, stepping out in a bathrobe. Her hair was damp and small curls stuck to her forehead and cheeks; Kyle disappeared towards the bathroom and Peter stopped her at her door, pushing the tendrils away from her face.

"I guess it's goodnight again," she said in a low voice, holding the terry towelling closed.

He played with her ear for a moment. "Is that a problem for you?"

She breathed deeply. "It's getting to be one," she replied honestly.

He bent suddenly and put his lips against her neck, below her right ear. He felt her gasp and move against him, and he pulled her closer. His breath was hot on her ear and she could have cried with the longing she felt. "In that case," he said quietly, "it's just as well Kyle's here to protect us both."

He left her again and she closed the door, trying to control the vulcan inside.

They left after breakfast the next morning, and she sensed Peter's need to get back to work now that their time was over.

At the flat she couldn't settle, fiddling in the kitchen and pacing the lounge while Kyle read quietly. Finally he put his book down.

"Would you like to attend a church service?" he suggested. "There must be an evening one some-where."

She considered it, then dismissed it, feeling guilty. "No."

Kyle looked at her thoughtfully. "You're suffering, huh?"

She plumped down beside him on the sofa. "Kyle, how do you manage? You're not married, but you must have had relationships with women. Have you ever slept with anyone?"

She knew the answer as she asked. "No." It was gentle.

"Oh, don't think I haven't wanted to! But I haven't met a woman I could marry who would understand my kind of job, and I don't think I could give up what I do. And you know I couldn't give up on God. So I do the next best thing. I don't mix with women socially. That way the temptation is avoided."

"And that way, you'll never know whether you've met the right woman or not!" she retorted.

"That's true. But I guess once I get a bit older, this job'll wear itself out of my system and I'll settle down. I'm just not quite ready yet. I'll know when I am. Just as you, young lady, will know when *you're* good and ready."

"What do you think of him?" she asked, a little wistfully.

"I like him. But I'm glad I went along to chaperone. You didn't look much like you were in control of the situation."

"No," she said unhappily. "But don't worry. He was."

Chapter 24

Rhodesia

Kyle left two days later to go to Malawi, and she missed him even more than she'd expected. She'd heard nothing from Peter, but she wasn't surprised. She had a feeling he thought distance was the better part of valour. Which, on reflection, it probably was.

When the phone rang that evening, it was Tony. "Alan's invited us to spend a few days with him at Inganga." Alan was the ADC from Ntubu who had put Rebecca through the cadet course; he'd apparently recently been transferred to Inganga, an hour and a half north of Bulawayo.

She telephoned Peter. "Your bully-boys can take a rest," she informed him. "I'm going to spend a few days with the ADC at Inganga."

"Well, I admit nothing's likely to happen to you there. They're pretty well on the ball, and close to Bulawayo. The terrs haven't hit a station yet, but keep an eye open all the same."

"Stop faffing."

He knew she'd be safe at Inganga. Nevertheless ... he had lifted his guard once before and she had been presented with a mamba in her handbag.

Uneasily, he tried to shrug it off. Those men could be made good use of while she was away.

The peace at Inganga was as soothing as a warm mineral spring, and the small bedroom off the verandah was almost like coming home. Zulu, the cook who had moved from Ntubu with Alan, built a fire under the water-tank for her bath while Rebecca, Tony and Alan had tea on the front lawn.

"Did you hear about Don?"

"The Vet with one arm? What about him?"

"Killed. Ambushed on an early call."

She felt an unutterable sadness for the man she had thought of as a friend. Then Zulu appeared at her side, his strange grey-blue eyes shining in the wrinkled black face.

"Missy's bath, it is ready."

From the bathroom she could hear the braying of love-sick donkeys in the open bush around the house – a harsher, more strident shout than the usual hee-haw, and occasionally there was a stumbling crash as the roaming beasts had their way with the mares. She smiled at the noises, and let the hot water lap around her body.

Her head lay back on the hard white enamel of the bath and she began to relax.

Rebecca was woken the next morning by the sound of a Landrover bouncing down the steep driveway, and Rastus, Alan's bull-terrier-cross, whom Alan boasted had once withstood a crocodile attack, barking excitedly in the back. Tony and Alan were going duck-shooting. She had turned down the offer; she'd had enough of shooting for a while. Both kinds.

She turned over lazily and wondered how she'd slept through the din of the morning chorus outside her window – it seemed a long time since she'd experienced the bush choirs. She stretched luxuriously and climbed out of bed, pulling on a robe.

She found Zulu in the kitchen. He bobbed delightedly and pointed to the boiling kettle. She smiled back and nodded. "I make breakfast for Missy?"

"Whatever you've got, Zulu. I'm starving!"

She went out onto the front steps; the grass was dry already in the sun, but from the lowest branch of the shade tree a new spider's web shone silkily with a necklace of tiny pearls of dew, stretching to the top of a moonflower bush.

The house was on a slight hill, the last one on the outskirts of the small community, and as usual painted white and red-tiled. The garden was well kept by the prisoners who came twice a week, five or six of them, to tend it, guarded by two DAs. Not that they needed the guard; these were the least criminal of the inmates of the police cells – in for petty theft, or drunkenness. They were rarely sentenced to more than a few days' hard labour, and tidying the government gardens was the hardest labour in the district that anyone could think of.

The donkeys were beginning their serenades again, and peacocks strutted over the lawn or shrieked in the trees at their mates. A small duiker was nibbling at the fresh grass, hobbling on a plaster cast that supported its broken front leg. A trap, Alan had told her.

Liza, the mongrel bitch, was sitting at the bottom of the drive looking mournfully in the direction the Landrover had taken. Alan had left her behind to keep Rebecca company, and she didn't appreciate what she obviously considered a desertion. Rebecca called her and she looked around in surprise, then bounded up across the sloping grass, her tongue lolling in her grinning face.

"Didn't know I was still here, did you, girl?" Rebecca patted the flat yellow head and the wildly rocking rear quarters. "You'll wag it off if you're not careful," she laughed.

Zulu brought her breakfast on the verandah and she sat on the steps and looked out over the bush below. To her left were the government offices and the other housing, but to the right was only bundu, hiding the donkeys and the birds ... Alan had told her there was a small dam further round, behind the house and a little way off. After she'd eaten the enormous plateful of bacon, sausage, eggs, tomatoes and potato chips that Zulu had conjured up, she dressed and climbed through the broken hedge behind the water tank.

There is a special ancient smell to the Matabeleland bush – not quite smoky, not quite rocky, not truly dusty – somehow harsh, and fresh at the same moment. It doesn't simply enter your nostrils, but seeps through your lungs into every organ in your body, and is absorbed by the very pores in your skin, till you feel light-headed and light-limbed and somehow light-hearted. The air buoys you up; it has a substance that you can feel on your skin, and in your veins, racing with your blood. Years later it is still with you, when you bring it into your mind's eye – the brown-and-black wilderness, the grey twigs and faded grasses that prick and scratch at your ankles, the hard trees that foliate each year in a dull defiance of the dry winter, and that vastness of space and air about you that gives your hair bounce and your lips and cheeks colour. It is alive with the past smells and sounds of elephant, lion, cheetah, buck. The Matabele say it is the spirits surrounding you, speaking to you – and perhaps they are not far wrong.

Rebecca found the little body of water in an hour, with Liza sniffing and cavorting at her heels as though it were her first outing. A group of five donkeys stood in the muddy grey water, drinking. They ignored her approach until Liza rushed towards them, barking vigorously. Then they scampered away, braying as though the devil himself was after them, and Liza returned looking proud of herself to flop at Rebecca's feet.

She found a spot to sit, leaned against a tree and rested, watching the water and the ducks who gathered near the edge, observing her suspiciously and muttering among themselves at the intrusion.

She really was remarkably careless.

He watched her at the little dam, standing a good distance away and utilizing his sharp vision. Grudgingly, he admitted she did have a certain something. He'd heard the men who guarded her speak among themselves, and what they said was not for the ears of Major Kennedy. But her eyes were light-coloured, not full and dark and promising as the Ndebele women's.

No, her promise was in her body. His tongue ran over his thick dry lips as he watched her lie back in the sunlight, her torso curving across the scorched mud, her legs slightly spread. Her long hair was in two plaits beside her head, like the sweet golden koeksisters Mrs. Elliott had once made, with Nada's help ... Nada ...

The girl moved slightly; nearby a donkey brayed harshly. Mandhla thought of how she would look beneath the clothes; her skin had just enough tan to detract from the sickly white of her flesh that revolted black men so much, and her hips were broad and inviting. His tongue moved again over his parched mouth and he realised how thirsty he was. He straightened carefully, out of habit avoiding any chance of the movement being spotted, though her eyes were closed against the sun.

He could be patient.

He was uneasy here at Inganga. It was too close for comfort to civilization, yet he wanted to watch her. In so small a community there was no possibility of passing himself off as a traveller; he stayed in the bush, alone, in hiding.

Once he and David had reached Bulawayo he had taken a job there while David remained in the township. He laughed when he thought about the job. He was the gardener for the block of flats in which Miss Rebecca Rawlings lived. He had avoided her, though she never seemed to notice him anyway, but he was wary that she may recognise him as the delivery boy who had brought the jet snake to her. It was chancy, working there, but his craftiness amused him.

And the more he watched the woman, the better he felt about how he would hurt Major Kennedy. He lay awake at night, picturing her body, planning what he might do to it. It was a pleasant way of passing the dark hours when he couldn't sleep. He hadn't decided on a particular date yet, though he had planned first a surprise for Major Kennedy. A small scare. It would make Peter Kennedy even more nervous and upset, and that idea pleased Mandhla Ndhlovu.

The girl was rising now. She lifted herself gracefully, the plaits swinging around her, and the dog stood up too. She stretched, her arms behind her head, her breasts catching the light, and then she turned back to the house. He followed her, carefully, and then went back to his hiding place in the bush.

When she got back to the house, Zulu was in a panic. "Missy is back! Master tell me to look after Missy; I don't know where Missy go; Missy must tell me when she go. Master very angry if Missy lost!"

"I'm sorry, Zulu," she said contritely. "I was only at the dam. And Liza was with me; she wouldn't have gotten lost."

"Would get lost if terrorist comes," Zulu mumbled, unconvinced.

"Zulu! I thought this was a 'cold' area?"

"Is cold – until is hot!" He marched out self-righteously, leaving Rebecca to the pile of roast lamb and vegetables before her.

That afternoon she pulled a deck chair out into the middle of the big garden and sat reading in the sun. Something caught the corner of her peripheral vision, and she looked up. At first she thought she was wrong, and nearly went back to her reading; she only saw it because it moved its head.

She couldn't see its full length because she was transfixed by the round charcoal eyes, the pupils edged in silvery white. For a moment the head stayed two feet off the ground, perfectly still; then it raised higher, and the snake slid over the coarse grass towards her, the head still up. It stopped again a yard in front of her, and the head lifted even further. The black mouth opened slightly and the tongue flickered from side to side, testing her scent. Then the neck flattened in warning and the snake sounded its hollow hiss.

She registered the dark olive-brown body with its lighter, greyish-white underside; he was so close that she could see each tiny segment of his skin separately. For a few eternal seconds they stared at each other, the serpent and the girl, and suddenly Rebecca realised that she was no longer afraid. The discovery gave her a sharp pang of surprise; almost at the same moment, she thought she felt wind on her cheeks, the rush of air such as the beating of wings might make; a moment's dizziness and the strange sensation of hovering above herself, looking down ...

The snake's neck rounded and the mouth closed suddenly. The black tongue still tested the air, but the head drew slowly back; the lithe coils thrust suddenly and the snake slipped around her chair and made for the hedge.

Ten feet, she estimated. She moved suddenly, her body oddly stiff and sluggish. When she called Zulu, he fetched prisoners who were working in the next door garden and they found it again, and killed it with gusto. They measured it; it was nearly twelve feet. They cut the head off, wrapped it well in plastic and buried it to contain the venom, which would stay poisonous long after the mamba had died. They buried the body separately, some distance away; she wasn't sure why.

Afterwards, when she told them what had happened between herself and the snake, the prisoners exchanged superstitious glances, and looked sideways at her, muttering and shaking their heads, but wouldn't explain their reaction.

When they were gone, she demanded an explanation from Zulu. He looked at her and shook his head sadly, embarrassed. "Please," she urged him. "It was obviously important to them. Will you explain to me why?"

He rubbed his black eyebrows, defeated. "The Blackmouth will be back for Missy."

She rocked a little, startled. "They killed him. You saw. How can he come back?"

"Blackmouth does not die. He knew that it was not yet your time. You have yet to laugh more, to weep more, to learn more, before your spirit can be free. But when your tears have wet enough rocks, he will be back for you."

She shivered in the hot sun as she watched him walk away.

The men returned, triumphant with five ducks to their tally, at five o'clock. They ate dinner early and then moved to the verandah for coffee and Zulu left. Rebecca told them then about the snake, leaving nothing out, and then asked Alan about the black men's reactions.

"It's to do with an ancient religion. Some of them still have their superstitious beliefs, all tangled up with the modern religions."

She persisted. "Peter mentioned some sort of snake worship when we were at the Zimbabwe ruins. Is it the same thing?"

"I can only tell you what I've heard from the Africans. It's all rather fuzzy, but they insist an ancient high priestess wore a copper bangle on her arm in the shape of a mamba. She's also supposed to have carried a wooden staff with the image of the snake crawling up it. They claim a mamba ate an eagle, which was the form of worship at the time, and that the high priestess saw this and led them away from the old religion, which caused the death of the city of Zimbabwe. Some say that later she changed the god's image again, to a fish, and that the fish eagle is eternally getting its revenge by eating the fish ... but others say that's nonsense. It's all rather confused, and there's nothing to substantiate any of it. Interesting point, though – rumour has it the head of ZIPRA is involved in the mamba religion."

He saw her eyes, and dismissed it all with a shrug. "I wouldn't let it worry you; this is real life. A snake is a simply a wild creature and this one left you alone because you made no movement and it realised you weren't threatening it."

But I had it killed, nevertheless, she thought.

She was collecting the coffee cups when the dogs began to bark frantically. Instantly they all stiffened, listening. There was a sharp crack as something connected with one of the dogs' skulls, a brief cry from the animal, and then they heard Liza running to the front of the house, whimpering.

Alan moved like lightning. "Weapons!" he ordered them; from before sundown the loaded guns were put into the lounge by Zulu. She and Tony followed Alan towards that room on all fours, and he doused the lights as they went. Once there, in the dark, Alan took the FN and handed Tony and Rebecca each a shotgun; wriggling on their stomachs to stay below the level of the windows, Alan moved towards the back door while Tony covered the front. Rebecca stayed in the lounge, watching the side of the house.

Outside, everything was quiet – too quiet. Apart from Liza whimpering at the front door to be let in, there wasn't a sound. Alan whispered loudly from the hall: "Get to the 'phone and ask for the police!"

Rebecca made her way across the wooden floor to the small telephone table and lifted the receiver. Relief rushed over her when she realised it hadn't been cut off, and she spun the handle at the side.

"Police," she whispered urgently to the operator. A moment later a black constable was asking if he could help. "The ADC's house. We think we have terrs in the back garden."

"Hold on, please."

A white man came onto the line. She repeated herself to him.

"How many?" he asked briskly.

"I don't know. I think they've hurt one of the dogs; we can't hear anything happening right now."

"Wait," he said, and rang off.

Rebecca crawled to the kitchen doorway and heard Alan shuffling over the floor. "They're coming," she told him.

"There's a movement near the chicken run," he murmured.

"Are you as scared as I am?" Rebecca whispered back.

"I'll need a change of pants when they're gone."

Rebecca muffled a giggle. Terrified, she was on a nervous high. "Should I let Liza in?"

"No! We don't know how many there are, or where they are."

"Oh Lord! When are the police going to get here?"

"Give them a chance – you've only just called them!" He lifted his head slowly and peered out of the window into the darkness. "I can't see a thing."

"Maybe they've gone," she said hopefully.

Suddenly the chickens squawked indignantly and there was mayhem in the henhouse.

"Food!" said Alan. "That's what they're here for – food! I knew they had to be crazy to attack a house in a settlement. They'll take what they need and run; they know we know they're there and they'll know we've called for help ... There! There they are!"

Rebecca raised her head, frightened but curious. She saw two shadows flit, one after the other, from the chicken run to the hedge. "Two of them!"

"Three – they'll have posted one on guard. Maybe more."

"Damn it!" She was angry suddenly. "Shoot the bastards!" She pulled her shotgun up and he slapped it down.

"Are you crazy? We start shooting and God knows who'll get hurt! The army will pick up their trail; let them go."

She knew he was right, and she was shocked at her own reaction. She had been prepared to kill a man! This war, she was finding, was digging too deeply into her inner being.

A few minutes later the night sounds began again; nature was relaxing.

"They're gone." Alan stood up.

There was a stealthy bumping on the front door. They stiffened, but the bumping started again, three knocks at a time, repeated over and over.

"The police," said Alan, and walked through to the lounge. Rebecca followed, every part of her body throbbing with excess adrenalin. They let the man in.

"We can't see anyone but the others are still combing. There'll be a bunch out from Llewellyn Barracks within the hour. Everyone all right? We didn't hear any firing."

"There wasn't any. They took chickens and left." He turned suddenly, remembering Zulu, and strode out of the back door with Tony and Rebecca following him. He went directly to the cottage at the back of the property, police rising all around him, the weapons in their hands gleaming in the half-light of the moon.

"Zulu!" he called. The door opened and the old man appeared.

"I am right, Master."

One of the policemen thrust him aside roughly and entered the room, their rifles ready.

Alan turned to the MIC who had come out with them. "Tell them to treat my man with more respect. He's saved my life on more than one occasion," he said angrily.

The men reappeared and apologised to Alan. "We'll stick around until the army arrives," said the MIC.

Tony put an arm around Rebecca's shoulders and steered her towards the back door. She shivered, cold suddenly in the hot summer evening. Liza crept around the house on her belly and stopped under the hot water tank, sniffing at a heap that lay there. They changed course and walked towards the mongrel, Alan getting there first.

Rastus had been brained, probably with the heavy butt

of an AK-47. The indomitable dog had died still snarling at his master's enemies.

The army had come, been briefed and gone, and Zulu had retreated to his own room. They buried Rastus at the bottom of the garden, under the hedge.

"Must have been a weak spot on the skull," mumbled Alan miserably before he threw dirt onto the body. "How could he have lived through everything else, and not this?"

Rebecca put a hand on his arm and squeezed; he smiled half-heartedly back. They went inside and he poured himself a double brandy, and she and Tony watched over him while he drank himself unconscious, and then they carried him to bed.

Chapter 25

Tsimbaboue

Chisa held the smooth pestle between both hands. It was almost as tall as herself, thinner at the top, a thick knob at the end. Rhythmically she pounded the mealie kernels in the deep-necked wood bowl, using her thighs to lift herself back as she raised the club, then leaning forward to bring it down hard into the mortar. The dry yellow seeds crushed to a white powder as she sang with the other women, a song that helped to keep their bodies swaying in time to the thud of wood against wood.

Ncube, whittling soapstone, watched from his window. He had to admit that in some respects he had been wrong about Chisa. A gossip, yes; wicked, yes; unscrupulous, yes. But lazy - no. She cooked well for him, and ran for his every whim. She hoed their vegetables, and milked the cows, and fed the chickens, and washed the clothing, and tended to cleaning the hut.

And she had never complained that he had not consummated their marriage.

That, to Ncube, was most surprising of all. She insisted on sharing his bed, but never more. Neither of them had ever spoken about the fact that they slept back to back; that Chisa's family's expectations of children would never be fulfilled.

At least, not yet. Chisa herself was confident that her patience would win out. She knew this man; she understood his yearning for Xhaitaan's wife. It would go, and his body would take over his mind. In the meantime she knew that her willingness to work was impressing her reluctant husband.

Ncube's work had suffered. The enthusiasm was no longer in it; his images of Muali were dull, lifeless. His carving had become a job - no more, no less. Sometimes he imagined himself out looking after cattle, the cattle he loved; but his thin, long fingers would wind among themselves, and he knew that one day his art would come back.

He saw Tcana sometimes, from a distance. He knew she walked alone; when he could, he would follow her at a distance, but he realised there was more to her walks than he could understand, and he never came close, never allowed her to realise he was there. He had seen her come back earlier this afternoon from another of her rambles, but this time ... this time something was different. It worried Ncube. He could not put his finger on it. Tcana had been ... sad? Thoughtful, and sad. She had not seen where she walked, or how she walked. She had moved wistfully along the path that led to her husband's home.

Ncube put down his carving tools and closed his eyes tightly, squeezing and rolling them until they squeaked. He needed air.

He took the path she so often took, towards the back of the Hill. Never had he tried to go closer than the line of saplings; the Hill was still the Hill - Muali's home. When he reached the young trees he peeled a strip of bark off one of them, dug deeper with his knife and put the juicy young wood into his mouth, chewing, staring into the distance.

She was afraid. The message was clear, and it had been given to her. All the wondering, the fears, the worrying over what Muali had been trying to tell her ... were over. This, then, was his message. She ran her finger over the chalky image that squatted on top of the pole in the hut she shared with Xhaitaan. The eagle. Muali.

No. No longer Muali. Muali had changed his form, and she, Tcana, had been chosen to give the message to the people. She shivered, cold suddenly. How could she, a mere peasant woman, convince them to change their minds? The High Priest, the King, her husband - devout in his worship of the bird.

She jumped when Niswe touched her shoulder.

"Tcana, what is it? Your cheeks are wet; you're crying."

"It's nothing Niswe ... a - a child. I want a child for my Lord

Xhaitaan, and still I am barren. Why?"

But now she knew why. Muali's message was more important than any child she could produce. She was, indeed, still Muali's chosen Priestess.

"It will come, Tcana. Sit. I'll bring you warm honey-milk to drink." Niswe disappeared through the opening, and Tcana shivered again.

That evening she watched the white-sheeted girls wind their way to the foot of the Hill; Royalty alone was allowed this privilege. Tonight Xita went with them, and Tcana knew that Xhaitaan was anxious.

Xita was his little sister, his beloved one, who adored him and in whose eyes he could do no wrong. But she was soft, a baby still, spoilt by all around her, afraid of shadows, unable to stand pain. Although no-one had verbalised the thought, all knew she would not come back. Xhaitaan had helped build her woman-hut; he had set the decorations on the poles, the soapy statues of Muali, to watch over and guard her. He had added figurines, three of them – for her grandfather, her great-grandfather, and for her great-great-grandfather. The Spirits of her ancestors must take care of her. He was praying even now. It was all he could do.

And, thought Tcana suddenly, *also what I can do.* She padded into her hut and found her prayer-kaross, made from soft feathers gathered from under Beyond-the-Eyes; unrolling it, she knelt before the eagle perched on the pole. Reverently, she closed her eyes and called him to her mind.

He didn't come. She tried again, visualising the serpent's eyes, staring into hers, but still there was nothing. Confused, she grasped at the necklet, her fingers going unerringly to the smooth cool of the glass bead, the etched outline of the fish ... and she became calm, and tried to think. Muali. Not the eagle, for she had seen the snake swallow him. Yet the snake would not speak to her, either.

Finally, crying quietly, she moved away from the foot of the pole to the thick skins on her bed. Still she did not understand, and her weeping was for the loss of the one and the lack of the other.

The tears stopped eventually, and slowly she sat up. She set her prayer-rug again, but this time facing a different direction, and humbly she knelt to give homage to Muali, without form or face in her mind.

He was there. No image, but he was there, somehow. And when at last she rose, she knew absolutely that Xita would return from the Hill.

She told him everything. And when she had finished, she could not bring herself to look at his shocked face, his eyes wide with betrayal.

"Tcana, no! This is an evil spirit! It's not true – we've worshipped Muali as ... as he is, for longer than anyone can remember! Muali chose me! You're blaspheming – I beg you, Tcana, don't speak to anyone of this!"

She looked at him sadly, but knew what she must do. "I have to, Xhaitaan. I too was chosen, remember? By you and Muali together. I was chosen ... for this."

He stood, angry then. "And you prayed to this ... this Blackmouth ... for Xita?"

"Yes. I – I suppose it was to the Blackmouth ..." It was barely audible.

"Again!" he demanded.

"Yes! And he has promised me that she will return!" At that moment she was more sure of this than of anything.

"She will not return! Xita is unable to go through any sort of pain; if she hurts her finger, she cries and wails like a calf taken from its mother! It's cruel of you to say such a thing – Muali demands strength, not weakness. Xita will die."

"No." She touched his shoulder gently. "Muali is not what we have thought, Xhaitaan." She surprised herself, but the words were not coming from her own mind; something inside guided her tongue, and she knew she was right. "He wants an end to – to this!" She waved her arm involuntarily at the Hill. "He wants no more death; his children must return, that we can grow and prosper! And this time, all of the new women will return from the Hill. Even Xita. I, Tcana, I promise you this. In the name of Muali."

Xhaitaan, already standing, took a step back from her. "What are you saying? Never have all the girls returned!" His voice was hushed, afraid, and he looked over his shoulder nervously. "Kisang will have us both killed for blasphemy!"

"Kisang will die ... very soon, now ..." Her voice was strange, harsh, and he recoiled from it. "Xhaitaan is King ... within two full moons Xhaitaan will be King of the amaTsimbaboue ..."

He knew instantly that she was prophesying; he feared for her – for them both. But he also knew that when the Spirits spoke through a medium they chose, they spoke truthfully. He waited for more, but nothing came; his goose bumps lowered, and slowly Tcana's eyes cleared. Then she was looking straight at him.

"Xita will come back. They will all come back, this time."

She turned and left the hut, the peasant skins she insisted on wearing swaying against her buttocks.

Xita came back from the Hill. With the others, every girl who had gone to the Hill, not one of them lost, she sang to Muali, the thrilling, haunting song of the new women consecrating themselves to their god and their people.

Xhaitaan and Tcana had not discussed it further during the two weeks of the ceremony. They had avoided each other's eyes, and waited, both knowing that the message was clear: if Xita and the others returned, Xhaitaan knew that the Muali his wife prayed to was more powerful than the one who claimed that Xita was too weak for the amaTsimbaboue.

The new women's feast, sumptuous and rich, seemed overblown to Xhaitaan. He found no pleasure in the dances or the food, and could think of nothing but his wife – chosen by Muali. Her Muali. The new Muali. The one that the High Priest would never accept.

Tcana knew what her husband was thinking and feeling. She shared his fear, but knew her road. She could only wonder that Muali had chosen her, Tcana, instead of speaking to the Oracle. Obviously, the Oracle was not a part of Muali's new formula. Her eyes strayed over the people of Tsimbaboue, gorging themselves on meat and beer. No huts were to be broken down this year, for the first time in memory. Everywhere there was movement, laughter, almost a delirium.

Except – except there, where Ncube sat, and as her eyes

rested on him he looked up, meeting her gaze, and she realised suddenly where her helpmeet lay.

Xhaitaan argued, as she had known he would. Sadly she watched him pace the floor of their hut, his hands gesturing, trying to understand, and when he had run out of steam he came to her arms and she held him until he slept. And then she drew herself away from him and left the Royal Compound as the first cocks began to crow.

Ncube's hut was quiet and still; Tcana peered through the window but could make nothing out. She settled on her haunches to wait, pulling around her the skin karosses which would hide her identity.

He came from outside; he had been walking - no, running - in the dim light Tcana could make out the salty droplets on his face and body.

"Tcana!" It was involuntary, before he remembered and saluted her as Royalty. She motioned him to be silent, and led him away from the hut.

"I need your help, Ncube."

He was surprised, unsure. "My help?"

She nodded. "I need your strength and your support, your wisdom and your understanding. Muali requires your strength." And then she told him, exactly as she had told her husband. But Ncube did not gasp in shock or fear. He held her gaze, thoughtful, and when she was finished he nodded.

"You will need more help than I can give, Rhaba."

Rhaba. A statement of honour to a woman of God, Muali's chosen one.

"Go carefully, Ncube. This thing cannot be shouted from the Hill, suddenly and without warning. Tell the people what I have told you - that Muali wants no more killings, no more weaklings struck down, as proven by his Sign - the return of the new women from the Hill, all of them. That he wants us to prosper, for our children to prosper. For can not a strong bull make strong calves on a weakling mother? This is Muali's message: that the weak live, and the strong protect them. But many of the strongest - " she glanced at the Hill - "will not listen. Go carefully."

When she left him, he touched his forehead in the Royal salute, and then, just before she turned away, he kissed his palm and offered it to her.

Muali's salute. The salute to a Rhaba.

The believers came slowly, and from the peasant stock only, since Ncube dared not yet speak to the higher ranking or the more powerful citizens of Tsimbaboue. Beginning with the families of those who had returned from the Hill, silently the Blackmouth's followers grew, worshipping still the Eagle with their bodies, the Snake with their hearts. For try as she might, Tcana knew she could not persuade them to accept a god without form. They needed a vision.

The fear of the Priests was uppermost in their minds, and they watched each other, afraid of traitors, of outsiders. Only when Ncube felt certain that each was ready for a new faith, did he cautiously introduce the vision that "a woman he knew" had seen – of Muali the Mamba, the black-mouthed serpent who killed faster than any other they knew of, and who now spoke to them of life.

The parents of those who in previous years had not returned from the Hill were also ripe for change, and those with daughters still too young to go. The anger inside them, in spite of outward appearances, was great; those who still had little girls were ready to believe that they were not meant to lose their children. The women converted most easily, as is often the way in religion, the men more slowly. And still, they were not told whom their new High Priestess was.

Tcana spoke to no-one else, except for Niswe, of her vision. Xhaitaan had begun to the think the whole thing had been forgotten; he was relieved that Tcana was taking it no further, and that he was not going to have to act, either for or against his wife. There had been a good harvest this year, better than in anyone's memory. The cattle had calved more than ever before, the goats were feeding healthy kids, the honey flowed and the bees were kind. Indeed, Muali was pleased with his people. And the amaTsimbaboue were pleased with Muali.

Which Muali, exactly, was another question, at least among

the three hundred strong followers the Blackmouth now had. Tcana, through Ncube, assured them that the harvest was the best because of the good response from the people, which in turn had pleased them and motivated more conversions.

Ncube had kept Chisa out of the group of elect. Uncertain of her loyalties - after all, the eagle's High Priest had ordered that she get the husband she had pursued - he had avoided her, but he realised that she was suspicious. She knew her husband too well to ignore the nightly visits he was making away from their hut. But she would bide her time. Chisa always discovered everything, in time.

The way she discovered it was not quite as she had imagined.

The wailing began in the early morning, almost before cockcrow. The high-pitched keening reached every ear, sending a chill down the spine and causing the scalp to prickle. And then the song began, the dry-rice voice calling the people to the massing-ground below the Hill.

An hour later, the High Priest stood above them, his calfskin mask in place, surrounded by ten of the Priests, their robes white against their leather bindings. Each held a staff capped with an image of their bird-god. The amaTsimbabouetcang, the Royalty, had grouped on the Royal platform, Tcana among them; the servants stood at the foot of the platform. Tcana's ears swam and hummed, and she felt her flesh melting and boiling inside her heated skin; yet still the bead at her throat burned hotter.

It was time. In the silence of tabu the High Priest raised his staff in the air, and the beaked mask surveyed the people, moving slowly from left to right. Breathless, they waited.

He broke the silence at last. "Muali has spoken, through his most revered Mouth; our Oracle brings Muali's message, and I speak it to you now." He paused for effect. "Among us, there are traitors." There was a restless shuffle, though none dared speak. "Indeed, there are many traitors. Traitors to the cause of Muali. Blasphemers! Witches! Evil spirits, who will clamber into bed with you at night, who will whisper in your ear foul lies, and try to tempt you with sweetness! Those who want to weaken the amaTsimbaboue, the proudest people to grind the dirt under their feet! They speak a new religion, a new god - an evil god!"

The crowd almost murmured; the shock was evident, and each turned to half-look at a neighbour, then swiftly away again.

"Muali has commanded that these people be found out. This treachery will not be allowed to pass us by! We are the People of God, and for God we will fight! Therefore, any one of you who knows of any one of these traitors is bound to report him. The penalty of ignoring this thing to save your friends, or even your family – is death."

Her fingers were weak, almost too weak, as they cast the golden powder into the fire. It spurted up immediately, creating a perfumed smoke, and she sat back on her skinny haunches, inhaling deeply. Her thoughts became broken, shredding as the drug took hold, and for a while she floated, letting her inner self explore the other world.

Slowly she came back, shaking, breathing raggedly. She stared into the embers of the fire, the flames low now, the smoke gone. Her face was wet with tears, her eyes rheumy, her chest tight. It was over, except for the waiting.

He did not let her wait long, and when he came, he struck quickly and deep. Her body was frail; the poison raced through it, and in fifteen minutes she was dead, her lungs paralysed by the neuro-toxin.

The Oracle had suffocated.

Already there were doubters. The High Priest held a strong sway over them; the fear he engendered was deep, and he had spoken strongly to the people. In the minority, the Believers had begun to tremble for their lives.

Ncube, at an order from Tcana which he (and perhaps she, too) had not understood, had brought eleven of the most trusted Believers to this place, hidden among the rocks. In silence they had sat, perfectly still, waiting – for what, they did not know.

They saw the brief flare of light reflected against the rocks – the Oracle's fire. And then, much later, stiff with the early chill and afraid that the dawn was coming, fearful of discovery, they saw the Mamba.

He wound through the grass and between the rocks, his head high, and without hesitating entered the Cave of the Mouth of

Muali. And still they waited, until he slid out again, soundless, purposeful, deliberate.

Awed, they sat on; suddenly, he stopped and seemed to turn to look at their hiding place. His head lifted even further off the darkened ground, standing out against the grey sky. Mesmerised, the twelve stared back, until at last he lowered his head and moved on to disappear into the bush.

The rumours spread quickly. The Oracle, before having had time to choose and train her replacement, was dead. It was unheard of; it was impossible! And, more ominous than even her death, it was said that a Blackmouth had killed her.

The Priests strove to deny the tales, but the Believers were gathering strength. The people began to demand that the Oracle sing for them, to prove she lived. The Mouth remained silent. They demanded a proper burial rite. There was no-one dead, the Priests said. The rumblings grew.

The Oracle, the High Priest eventually reluctantly admitted, had indeed died. But she was in contact with him by night, and he was praying. When he knew more, he would tell the amaTsimbaboue.

Bury her, they said. We want the proper burial. We want to see her body, to strew her with honey-combs as is the custom, to provide her with milk and meat for her after-life; bury her.

They did what they could, but the distorted, empurpled features told their own tale and the people, each throwing their tribute beside her body, saw and passed on.

The Mouth of Muali was dead, and a Blackmouth had killed her.

Mgane was disturbed. His people, for the first time, were divided. There were calls from those loyal to the Eagle for the death of the unknown High Priestess of the Mamba; they wanted blood for the untimely murder of their Oracle. Certainly, there were too many Believers to have them all put to death; the Oracle's passing, and the manner of her death, had converted many more, and now that they were out in the open their numbers were frighteningly obvious. Almost half of the amaTsimbaboue worshipped the Snake.

They gathered together, five hundred strong, and faced the old regime. Ncube was protected by a band of men; Chisa stood nearby with her family, understanding at last. He stared across at her. She had not been a bad wife, but if she chose to stay with her family – and the Eagle – so be it.

They looked at each other over the heads of the people, and even at this distance he felt her eyes piercing him. For a long moment she stared at him; her father glared, her mother spat. And then, slowly, head high, she walked away from them, making her careful way between the parting crowd. Tcana would not win her husband from her this way.

Surprised, he waited for her, and when she came to stand by him her family were aghast and disgusted. They turned their heads, laid fingers over their eyes and removed them again, signifying that they saw her no more, that she was no longer their daughter. From beside her husband she raised her chin defiantly at them, and then she too turned away. She smiled firmly at Ncube. Slowly, incredulously, he began to smile back.

Now only the High Priestess was still missing.

The Royalty and the Priesthood stood together. Chosen by the eagle, and under his protection, each knew that their strength must be in the power of the other, and in the loyalty of the people who would not accept the new religion. The High Priestess of the Blackmouth must be found.

Xhaitaan stood with them in the noon sun, looking desperately around for his wife. She was nowhere, and the cold fear in the pit of his stomach grew into a rock.

Niswe spread the calf-fat over Tcana's naked body, and then hung strings of snakeskin at her neck, her waist, her ankles. The skin apron clung to her hips and buttocks, and when she was ready Tcana slipped her right arm into the copper Mamba that Ncube had fashioned for her. It climbed her upper arm, from her elbow almost to her shoulder, and gleamed there in the firelight, the head flattened against her purple-black skin. A similar image adorned the heavy staff that she lifted from against the rock face. She looked upward, into the moonlit sky. "Now."

The walk back to the village took over half an hour, and all the way Tcana prayed to Muali, who had seen fit to relinquish the form of the bird and take that of the serpent – or who perhaps had never been the bird at all; who perhaps had come now to defeat the evil of the bird – and who had chosen her, Tcana, to head this new religion.

The chanting could be heard before the village was in sight; at its outskirts the Believers had gathered again after sunset, still watched by the Priests and Royal Family, and the remaining faithful of the eagle. Ncube led the song, the new Song of Muali which Chisa had, surprisingly, presented Ncube with to show her solidarity with the new religion, and with her husband:

> *Muali is great, the Great One.*
> *He chooses his form as he wishes,*
> *Swifter than lightning that lights up the sky.*
> *We have a new Mouth for Muali, chosen by Muali.*
> *She is Muali's Chosen One, our Rhaba, our Priestess.*
> *Great is Muali, and wise,*
> *And his Rhaba too is wise.*
> *We await our Rhaba;*
> *We await our Rhaba and with her, Muali.*
> *We await Muali.*

A distance away, the Kaffirs, the non-Believers, had gathered, muttering among themselves. At their head stood Kisang.

Kisang had waited for this opportunity too long to miss it when it came. Behind him now he had too many things to lose; the wrath of God, and the anger of the People of God. And the approval of the King, and of the High Priest. He wasted no time in assuming the head of those loyal to the old religion, in stirring up their fury and outrage. And now, he knew, he had his army. But first – first, the High Priestess.

Xhaitaan was still in the way of Kisang's ascension to the throne, it was true, but when he, Kisang, had proved himself, the people would want him, and not the nervous heap that Xhaitaan had become in this time of crisis. The strangeness of it bothered Kisang; his brother had always been courageous, always taken the initiative, never given way to fear ... It gave cause for wonder.

But not for long. As the High Priestess of the Blackmouth

appeared, Kisang knew without a doubt that Xhaitaan had relinquished all claim to the kingship of the amaTsimbaboue.

Tcana stepped into the moonlight off the brow of the Hill, and as the Believers turned to watch a hush fell over them. Silently they moved aside, opening a road for her to come into their midst, kissing their palms to her. This was the Chosen One, their spiritual leader, and that it was Tcana somehow came as no real surprise. After all, had not Muali chosen her from the beginning? Would she not have been their Oracle, had not Muali shown it was not yet time by allowing her to become Royalty? Thus she was twice blessed, and it was only natural for them to accept her immediately. She was their High Priestess and their Queen. Not an Oracle as in the old religion, but their Rhaba.

The non-Believers were stunned. This was their princess, and she had betrayed them and their god. They hissed, and began to stamp their feet. Kisang shivered briefly, remembering the impi of warriors who had stamped beneath his tree, the buffalo bleeding to death at their feet. Then he silenced them with a wave of his fat arm. Their time would come.

"She must die." The High Priest spoke with authority to the King's favourite son, who sat in audience with him. Around them, amid the images of the eagle that moved in the firelight, stood the Priests.

"No." Xhaitaan said it softly, but it grew in the room until he felt that it was heard in the village beyond.

"It is the law. She has committed treason against Muali and against her King. She must die."

"I am the King's proclaimed heir. I will soon be your King!"

It was true. Mgane, in the last few days, had deteriorated rapidly. When he had been told who the High Priestess of the Blackmouth was, he had stopped breathing, choking and trying to throw an invisible band from his chest. Indeed, Xhaitaan had thought he was dead, until he had begun to gasp, and his eyes had pulled back again into his skull. But his voice was little more than a whisper now, and he shook, and could not stand alone. His face was grey and drawn and the very fat seemed to be fleeing his body, as mice run from a burning hut.

"The only one who can order to be put to death a King's wife is the King himself." Xhaitaan glared in challenge at the High Priest. "My father is too sick to speak, and until he can, or until I replace him, you will leave Tcana alone." Not willing to wait for an answer he stood and strode to the door of the room, where he turned. "My father is the only one who might order you to kill Tcana. I will never do so, and nor may anyone else until after my death."

When he had gone the High Priest sat on for a moment before he spoke the word, almost to himself: "Kisang."

Tcana was protected day and night. Niswe slept with her, and Ncube outside the hut the Believers had hurriedly built for her. A guard of fifty was formed at night, and during the day she never had fewer than two hundred around her.

Kisang waited. He knew that the Priesthood were with him now; more than anything, they wanted Tcana dead, and unless they could persuade Mgane to order it before he died, Xhaitaan would protect her.

But Mgane was improving again. He could talk now, a little at a time, but he knew he was dying. He listened to the High Priest quietly, Xhaitaan at his side, Kisang at the foot of the bed, and when the tirade was over he looked at his heir. "Xhaitaan – it is the law."

Xhaitaan shook his head vigorously. "It is the law that only you can order it. You do not have to order this, Kai." It was the first time in many years that he had used the expression of child to father, and it touched the King now.

Kisang cut in contemptuously. "If you do not, your people will ever remember you as the King who failed them! The people demand justice. It is the law."

"What is it to you, whether she lives or dies?" Xhaitaan was becoming desperate. "Let her take her people, her Believers, and go beyond our land. Let them go, Lord. They cannot harm us if they leave, and we will then return to our ways."

Kisang grunted angrily. "They will form an army and come to take the House of God from us! Tcana must die! And I say that you are as guilty of treason as she, for you knew about it and did nothing!"

The accusation caused those listening to draw breath sharply. Mgane thought quickly. Kisang wanted blood, but the blood of the favourite son would not be shed to satisfy his lust! Yet the accusation of treason hung between them all, a strong one. Perhaps there was, after all, only one way to save Xhaitaan ...

"Tcana must die," Mgane whispered. "And those who remain Believers in this heresy must leave the City immediately."

Kisang armed his new-found forces with every weapon they could find in the peace-loving City of God. The ceremonial spears, and the hunting weapons, would have to do for the job at hand.

They surrounded the safe-hut of Tcana, and her people faced them, protecting their Rhaba. But Tcana came out; there would be no bloodshed in protection of herself.

"The King requires your presence, O Favoured One," sneered Kisang as she stood before him.

She dipped her dark head. Instantly, Niswe and Ncube protested. They did not understand, she reflected.

"I must go. Do you think Muali chose me, simply for this, to die? How thin is your faith in God!"

Rebuked, Ncube stood back. Niswe defiantly followed her, but Kisang thrust her roughly aside and she fell against her brother, weeping. The crowd parted as the small group, Kisang, four men, and their girl prisoner, moved towards Tsimbabouet-cang.

They placed her in one of the serving girls' huts. The Priest visited her, briefly, but only spat on the dung and mud floor and left again without speaking. She was called before Mgane at last, and meekly knelt at the dying man's side.

"Tcana," he gasped, labouring for breath. He tried to say more, but could not, and when she left him she could think only of the hurt his eyes spoke to her: You have betrayed me. You have betrayed me. You have betrayed me.

Dawn. At dawn, she would once again be led to the Hill. But this time, above the Oracle's cave, dressed again in white and hooded – was it really so long ago? – she would suffer the penalty of treason against Muali in full view of his people. The High Priest would bring his axe, the ceremonial one with the handle covered by a sheet of gold and copper, with the eagle at the head of the sharp iron blade, down across her neck and her head would tumble down the steep rock face to rest in the crevice below, among the skulls of others who were too weak or treacherous to uphold the religion of the Eagle. The amaTsimbaboue would be avenged.

She sat on in the darkness, alone with her God and dressed for her execution.

Chapter 26

Rhodesia

Mandhla was angry. The fools who had stolen food in Inganga had put him on the run, too. It had meant he'd had to come back to Bulawayo sooner than she. He castigated himself for not realising they were there. He'd been concentrating too much on the girl.

No matter. She was back, now. He went to see David in the township.

The flat felt empty without Kyle, and she buried herself, as usual, in her work. For supper she made a salad with the Chinese lettuce she'd bought from one of the street vendors who travelled around with vegetables in their bicycle baskets, and a new salad dressing she'd thought she'd try when shopping that morning. The lettuce was slightly bitter, but she thought it may have been the dressing, and carried on working. She was preparing for a new programme, this time on the intricacies of terrorism. Special Branch had promised her interviews with some of the captive terrs they were holding.

She must have been more tired than she'd thought. By nine o'clock the work was beginning to look hazy and she could hardly keep her eyes open. She wondered if she was getting 'flu; when she stood up she swayed slightly and felt dizzy. She turned off the light and headed for the bedroom, but the telephone rang and she went back to answer it.

"Hello?" Her voice sounded funny.

"Becky? What's wrong?"

For some reason she couldn't focus. She knew it was Peter, because he called her Becky ... she giggled into the telephone.

"Is that you, Peter?

"Becky, have you been drinking?"

"No, of course not." The words were slurred and she didn't know why. "Think I have 'flu or ... something. Don't feel well ..." She trailed off.

His voice was urgent. "Becky, are you there? Have you taken any medication tonight?"

"'Hmmm?" She tried to concentrate. "I don't ... I have to go ... sleepy. Call tomorrow ..." She put the receiver down but it dropped to the floor. "Damn." But she couldn't be bothered, and left it lying there. She found her way to the bedroom and fell onto the bed, hoping she'd be better in the morning. Then she fell deeply asleep.

Peter was on the radio immediately, and minutes later the two SB men who had been on duty outside were pounding up the stairs. The door was unlocked; they supposed later that she'd forgotten to check it when she'd felt ill.

When they got to the bedroom they thought for a moment they were too late. Then they heard her heavy breathing, and hauled her up, dragging her arms over their shoulders.

"Walk, Miss Rawlings! You have to walk!" they urged her, but her eyes only flickered open for a moment, unfocussed and dull, before they closed again. The men, with Rebecca between them, half-ran for the stairs, where they felt her trying to find her feet. Once or twice her legs moved as though she wanted to walk, but it was more a reflex than anything else. They got her into a car, placed the blue light on the roof and headed for the hospital.

Outside the Emergency entrance, orderlies met them. "Poison, or medication," the SB men said tersely, and handed her over.

She was still showing occasional signs of consciousness, and the sister on duty decided to try saline before the stomach pump. She was held in a sitting position on a stretcher-bed behind white curtains, supported by two nurses while the sister forced warm liquid into her mouth.

Miraculously, Peter arrived then – he had commandeered

a helicopter which happened to be at the base, and landed at the hospital's helipad, causing them to realise that their patient was more than simply a television presenter. He relieved the SB men of duty; they drove back to her flat and began checking for medicines. Failing that, they bagged the remains of the salad she'd obviously had for supper.

They wouldn't let him in, but a nurse approached him as he sat on a bench outside. "I need details. Are you a relative?"

"No." He gave her address and age. "Her family live in America. Her brother's in Malawi right now; we're trying to contact him."

The sister came out. "I think we'll have to pump her." But at that moment the nurse called her back and a few seconds later Peter heard retching. He stood up and began to pace, every muscle in his body tense. Finally the sister reappeared.

"That was some dosage she swallowed, Major. We'll test the vomit."

"Immediately, please. It's important we know."

"Well, whatever it was, it was already dissolved when she swallowed it. There are no remains of pills in her stomach. Odd things is, though ... there wasn't enough there to kill her. She began rousing quite well once we'd started."

He slammed his fist into his hand. The Mamba. He wondered whether the dosage had been meant to only frighten her – or him – or whether he had slipped up. After all, he wasn't medically trained. As far as Peter knew.

"Can I see her now?"

The sister smiled sympathetically. "I don't think she'd want you to see her as she is. We're cleaning her up; I'll let you know." She left him again to his pacing.

She was still very sleepy. She felt the cold night air as Peter and an orderly helped her into the helicopter, where she curled into a ball and fell asleep before the rotors were even at full power. She woke twice on the journey, briefly, confused and convinced she must be dreaming, and then again as Peter lifted her out of the chopper. He carried her into what she knew was a bedroom, and then someone, a stranger – no, two – were undressing her as she dozed, washing down her fouled body with a sponge and then covering her gently with blankets. Then she vaguely registered that Peter was there again, sitting beside her. She knew he kissed her once, and whispered something, but she didn't catch what it was, and then she fell deeply asleep again, feeling her hand lying in his.

Someone brought her food, shaking her into semi-consciousness. "Come on, Miss Rawlings, you've got to wake up now. It's breakfast time." She grunted and rolled over, trying to emerge from her insensate state. "Come on, you've got to eat," the voice insisted.

She felt ill. "Can't," she mumbled. "Sick."

"If you sit up you'll feel a whole lot better." There were two of them then, both men, smelling strangely of medicines and cleanliness. They pulled away the bedclothes and half-carried her to an adjoining bathroom, where they sat her on a chair and sponged her face. She began to rouse, but couldn't stand on her own. They brought her one of her own nightshirts – she briefly wondered where it had come from; she supposed Peter had taken it from her flat.

"Can you change yourself, or would you prefer us to help?"

"No! Thank you. I mean, I can manage, I think."

They understood her embarrassment. "It's all right," one of them said. "We're both medical doctors." She knew it was meant to reassure her, but they left her alone anyway, standing outside the bathroom door.

Wobbling, she took off the oversized hospital gown they had put her into and stared at herself in the mirror; there were black bruised circles under her eyes, and she was paler than she'd ever seen herself, her skin a casket white. She washed her face with water as hot as she could stand, and rubbed it hard with the towel to get the blood flowing again, then looked consideringly at the bath. She still smelt vaguely of vomit.

Outside, they heard her run the water and nodded at each other approvingly.

She looked around the bathroom. A man's, she decided. Nothing feminine here. She wondered where she was; it wasn't a hospital, yet there were doctors here ... then she saw her own toiletries case standing against the wall.

Whoever had packed it had thought of everything.

When she came out her mind was clearer and she felt refreshed. Her arms were too weak to tackle her hair, and it was still in plaits at either ear, but she had colour in her cheeks and she had dabbed perfume on her neck and body. The doctors were still there, playing cards on the bedside table, and the food tray was at the bottom of her bed. Just plain fruit salad, she noted with relief.

She climbed back into bed and they gave her the fruit. "I'm okay now," she assured them. "I'm sleepy but I'm okay. You can leave me."

They shook their heads. "Not yet Miss Rawlings. Sorry. Orders."

And then the singing began. It was fairly distant, but the volume was immense and she felt the deep sadness of the song. It sounded like hundreds of men's voices, all harmonising, and it made her want to cry.

"What is it?" she asked.

"The regimental song. The men are on parade. They sing it every morning. It's a funeral song, actually."

"It's beautiful." She focused suddenly. "I'm in Major Kennedy's home, aren't I? At the Selous Scouts base?"

"Yes. He'll be here shortly after they finish singing, and then we'll be able to leave you."

"Can you tell me what happened?"

They were embarrassed. "Sorry. Major's orders."

She didn't manage much of the fruit, but they assured her it didn't matter. They felt certain she would feel hungry for lunch, they said.

He came a few minutes later. He thanked them briefly, and they picked up their cards and went. Then he sat beside the bed, watching her.

"You look a whole lot better."

"I've bathed. What happened?"

He studied his hands, clasped between his knees. "You were poisoned. The Chinese lettuce you used for your salad was washed in a very, very strong solution made with sleeping tablets." He stopped.

"It's that wretched snake, isn't it?" she asked. "Don't you think it's high time I was told what's happening?"

He considered this, but she knew he'd decided. "His

war name is the Mamba. He's the best man the other side has, but he's fighting a personal vendetta. When he was abducted, my unit went after them. We got involved in a firefight with the terrs who took him and his friends; through unfortunate circumstances a girl was killed and then we had to pull out – attacked from the rear. My stick wasn't big enough and I couldn't sacrifice my men. He thinks we killed the girl and then deserted him, and he's somehow found out I was the commander of that unit. He's out to hit me wherever he thinks it'll hurt. He planted someone among my men and found out about you. That's all I can tell you."

"Is this your base?"

He looked her in the eye. "You're here for your safety, Becky, and nothing else. If you report anything you see or hear, even if it's something you may consider totally innocuous, it could harm my men. You might not comprehend the importance of something you say. Understand?"

"Yes. I have no eyes or ears while I am here. When do I go home?"

"When the doctors say you can ... And when we're sure you're safe."

They were interrupted by the arrival of coffee, served by a white man in uniform. He smiled at her and saluted Peter, then waited.

Peter laughed. "At ease, Reg. Miss Rawlings, may I present one of my best men. Reg Wright."

He shook her hand. "I've watched you on television, Miss Rawlings. So have most of the others here. The barracks are abuzz with your presence."

Peter smiled. "Miss Rawlings will do a tour of the barracks when she's ready. You can tell the men."

Reg Wright grinned and winked impishly at her. "They'll be waiting!" and he bowed out of the room.

She giggled; he looked at her. "Good to see you laugh again."

"You mean, at someone other than you." She dimpled. "Aren't I endangering your reputation by being here, Major Kennedy?"

"I'm more worried about yours. And it seems to me everyone including my enemies are now aware that you exist, and that I have a special relationship with you, so ..." He trailed off.

"My, we are serious this morning." She felt disadvantaged, cross-legged on the bed in her nightshirt while he stood there in full uniform, beret at an angle, the osprey rushing to the kill.

He stared out of the window in silence for a moment. "I want you to marry me."

It shocked her and she drew back, but he sat on the bed and held her shoulders, looking into her eyes. "Right now. Today."

She broke away and got off the bed, turning her back to him, her arms wrapped around herself. He didn't try to touch her or speak, and after a few minutes she turned back to him. Her eyes were grave and when she spoke, he was surprised at her words.

"Peter, do you understand what a covenant is?"

He nodded. "It's a vow."

"Yes. But it's a vow declared over blood, and it can't be broken until the death of one of the parties. I believe that marriage is a covenant, consummated with blood." She was watching him carefully, to be sure he understood. "Marriage is forever in God's eyes, Peter, because it is a covenant unto death."

She waited on him now. He nodded slowly. "I understand." He stood and strode around the room, and after a moment he stopped in front of her. "I do understand. And I do want you to marry me. Till death."

She lifted her fingers to his cheek and touched him softly. She nodded slowly, then leaned into him and kissed his mouth gently, her eyes locked on his. "Why today?"

"Because I've waited long enough."

"We haven't known each other long."

"I know what I want. Do you?"

She didn't hesitate. "Yes."

The chaplain at the barracks was delighted. So were the men. Somehow, by seven o'clock that evening, they had arranged the small army chapel to look like a cathedral, with flowers of all colours, shapes and sizes decking the walls and altar.

Kyle had caught the first 'plane back from Malawi and arrived in time to give her away. "It's very quick, Sharkie. Are you sure this is right?"

"Doesn't it feel right, to you?"

"Yes. Oddly enough, I suppose it does."

Over the telephone her father had actually cried. "I wish I could be there, honey."

"So do I, Daddy. But I promise we'll have a second ceremony back home, with Reverend Gregory, okay?"

"Okay. And then I get to give you away!" He paused. "I do bless you, Sharkie. I bless your marriage and I bless your husband. I trust your judgment."

When she hung up they were both crying.

She wore a white linen evening gown she'd bought in America and never used, and someone brought a length of silvery lace from Bulawayo into which she sewed a few flowers at the crown of the simple veil. Her hair, washed and shining, hung free except for the few thin plaits she wove into the body of it, threaded with tiny daisies. As she and Kyle arrived at the chapel one of the men thrust a bouquet of white orchids into her hand. Kuru Ndhlovu stood as best man – Mark couldn't be there – and as she came out on her husband's arm a full army salute with swords drawn awaited them.

Deliberately, she stood in front of the mirror with her back to him, watching his reflection as she reached up and removed the veil, then slid the linen dress down off her body; with a woman's intuitive cunning she had removed her underwear in the bathroom, and now she turned to face him, naked.

She heard him draw breath sharply, and he let his eyes travel over her. Vaguely, she realised that she wasn't shy of him, though she had expected to be. Perhaps it was the look in his eyes as he took in the strong, athletic body, tanned and straight, from the hollow at her throat to the perfection of shape at her ankles. Her hair hung to below her waist, and when he came to her that was what he touched first.

"This isn't much of a honeymoon night for you," he whispered.

She didn't answer, but tilted her mouth up to his and he kissed her. He felt her arms go round him and he slid his hands up under the curtain of hair, over her bare back, and the heat made him shiver. Her back muscles contracted as she arched against him and her mouth opened in a gasp; instantly his tongue found hers and she moaned. He moved a hand round under the hair until it found the soft rise at the edge of her right breast, and his fingertips brushed the scar.

"I was afraid, even then," he said. "I hardly knew you, but when they hit you I saw red."

She giggled into his shoulder. "And I thought you were mad at me."

She pulled his beret and its eagle from his head, and started on his shirt buttons. He stepped back to give her room, and her hair fell over her bare shoulders and breasts as she pushed the shirt from his body. Her eyes were misty, heavy; he lifted her and lay her on the bed, and she kissed his chest, touching his belly that constricted under her fingers. He slipped free of the rest of his clothing and suddenly they lay naked against each other. When he finally withdrew from her, exhausted, and fell asleep where he lay, she quietly got up and went through to the bathroom, where she wiped away the smear of covenant blood mingled with her husband's seed.

The barracks were no place for wives. Two days later she was moved into a flat they had found for her, completely away from the old one and surrounded by other military families – and, she knew, a strong guard. Someone had moved her things across, and Mangoi was sitting fatly on the bed, beneath the painting of the striking osprey.

The stone cobra was gone.

Chapter 27

Tsimbaboue

It was close to midnight when they allowed Niswe in to see her, and then only by direct orders from Xhaitaan.

She came dressed in skins, her head and face covered by a mourning veil of deep purple silk, her arms and neck chalky white with mourning clay. She carried a large leather bag - "At least let her die prepared, in our own rites to our God," she had begged. Xhaitaan did not care. His wife was to die, and he could barely see beyond the mists of pain, let alone think of rites.

Tcana was not surprised to see her. Together, they brought out the wet clay from the "rites" bag, and chalked Tcana's arms and neck. Silently, swiftly, they exchanged Tcana's robe for the skins, her hood for the veil and headdress.

As she pulled the hood over Niswe's face, Tcana hesitated. Niswe stared into her eyes and shook her head slowly, firmly.

"Do not falter, Rhaba. There is work for you."

The guards did not question the servant girl as she left the Royal Compound.

When the first grey light of morning touched the city, it found the followers of the eagle gathered at the foot of the Hill, awaiting the death of the woman who had betrayed them. The Believers were not present; they were preparing for their long march.

In the shadow of the walls of Tsimbabouetcang, hidden by the leaves of a shade tree, two figures waited and watched. The girl was dressed in skins, and wore a mourning headdress and purple veil. The man, tall and protective at her side, had shaved his head and cut deep grief slashes into his cheeks, rubbing ash into them.

The procession was led from the Royal Enclosure by the High Priest. Close behind him came four lesser Priests, then the ghostly white figure in the pointed hood, with not even slits for eyes. Following her were four more Priests.

They wound their way to the staircase, and disappeared between its walls. The amaTsimbaboue waited.

In the depths of the crowd stood Lila and Roro, both staring with lifeless eyes toward the Hill. This, then, was the final farewell to the daughter they would no longer be able to acknowledge had ever lived. Steeped in the tradition of their ancestors, unable to accept a prophet from their own family, they had rejected the new faith along with the child they had bred. Xalise was not present; they had left her at home rather than allow her to watch the death of her beloved sister.

Unknown to them, at that moment Xalise was packing her few belongings.

When they appeared again on the ledge above the Cavern, a restlessness came among the people below, but not a sound was made in the silence of tabu. The girl in the mourning veil shivered uncontrollably, her throat so tight and painful she could hardly breathe, struggling to keep silent herself, watching across the valley as the white shape knelt before the High Priest.

His voice rang across the still morning, a song of Sacrifice to the eagle, and slowly the sun appeared, pointing its shafts at the altar and the singing man. When the light moved down, towards the heap at his feet, he raised the axe which glinted gold in the orange glow of the sun. The singing hardly faltered as the light touched the white hood and the axe swung downward.

There was a terrible sigh from the amaTsimbaboue. The big blade was sharp, the aim sure. The hood, red suddenly, separated from the robe and tumbled to the crevice below.

They left then, carrying what possessions they had and driving before them their livestock, exiled from their city forever.

From a higher perch, Xhaitaan watched, the deep cuts in his cheeks echoing those in Ncube's. He studied the figure of the girl who walked beside Ncube, at the head of the procession – the way she carried her head, the grace of her shoulders – and suddenly he recognised the movements of the woman he loved, and the slashes in his flesh lost their sting as he breathed sharply. He knew.

He offered up a special prayer for Niswe, the first martyr of the Blackmouth.

Frustrated, Kisang and his followers also watched the Believers go. Kisang had his army at last, but they were impotent against the orders of the King. Not, he smirked, that that was going to be a problem for much longer. Mgane was dying.

Indeed, he died during the night. The Believers, camped a few hours' walk away, saw the fire light the sky to proclaim the death of the King, and were uneasy. Now Kisang would challenge Xhaitaan's right to the throne – and their own safe passage.

Kisang was swift in deciding how to win the people from Xhaitaan. The anger was still vivid in their hearts – the mamba Priestess's supposed death had appeased only a part of it – and they were uncertain of their loyalties. By custom, two days after the passing of the King the new Royal Leader must be proclaimed and enthroned. Kisang was not going to wait that long.

He led his army against the fleeing Believers an hour before dawn on the second night of their escape. Camped in the savannah plains to the South, the Believers were ready for him.

And so was Muali.

The fight was all the more terrible for the hastily constructed weapons each side fought with; the amaTsimbaboue had always been a peaceful people, and their only spears had been ceremonial ones, or those the young men took for their initiation rites in the Bush. The Believers used clubs, and branches cut from the trees around them, honed to fine points. Kisang's army had the few spears from the City, and more that the smiths had fashioned hurriedly for them, but it was not enough against the will of the Believers to live. Or against Muali.

Kisang stood several hundred feet away, to direct and encourage his men. There was no point, he reasoned, in engaging directly in the battle himself. What would his people do should he be injured? But he did not like what he saw. His army consisted of the majority of men who remained in Tsimbaboue – perhaps three hundred. The Believers' women and older children joined the fighting, and of them there were perhaps four hundred in total. In spite of their lesser weapons, things were going well for them. It made Kisang nervous. He realised suddenly how little experience he had in directing an army, how ill-equipped and unready his people were for battle. Almost involuntarily, he stepped forward to get a better view.

The sun was rising; the plain was bathed in an orange glow, lighting the dew drops that shone like precious stones on the grass and leaves. There was an almost unearthly stillness; the battle proceeded with hardly a sound, the people locked in a struggle that the eagle worshippers were becoming less enthusiastic for with each minute that passed, as the reality of slaughtering their neighbours and friends sank in.

Kisang felt suddenly that he was floating above the scene, not a part of it; and then he realised that he was not alone. Close to him, like a statue, was Tcana, the golden-copper serpent snaking up her arm. She stood motionless, watching him. Her eyes were level and unafraid, commanding, and the feeling in Kisang's gut reminded him suddenly of the buffalo, and of the impi.

She was dead! He had watched her die!

Something about her eyes ... he stared into them, mesmerised, unable to turn away. They glittered somehow, and in the morning sunlight the whites looked like silver rims. Her mouth was slightly open; the lips were darker than he remembered, almost black against the lighter colouring of her face and neck – that long, long, silvery neck ... Then she closed her eyes, breaking the spell, and turned to look over the fighting. He did likewise, but it was not the battle that greeted his sight.

The Mamba was perfectly still before him, not five feet away. Its head was at the level of his own, and the eyes stared into his, silver-rimmed. The great neck flattened; the mouth opened and he saw the black, black lips that gave the Blackmouth his name.

When Muali struck, in his fear Kisang hardly felt the pain.

They kept moving. They had buried their dead – surprisingly few – where they had fallen, piling rocks and branches onto the bodies. The Unbelievers' remains were left untouched, including Kisang's, but Ncube counted a total of one hundred and fifty-three slain Tsimbaboue men before he turned away.

En masse, the Mamba's people marched, carrying their belongings, driving their cattle and chickens, led by their Rhaba. And now, at the head of the procession, something else was carried ... something that had been taken out of its hiding place beneath the skin karosses, ventilated by an envelope in the folds. Something that cheered the Believers at the sight of it, giving them renewed strength and purpose.

They had taken it, she and Ncube, when the procession had left Tsimbabouetcang for the execution. With Niswe's blood staining the ground on the Hill, the Fire of Life had left the city of Tsimbaboue, the House of God.

Niswe was ever-present for Tcana. Her death had left a hollow place inside that twisted and rebelled and ached. So often she would turn, speech on her lips, expecting to find Niswe at her side, attending her; and then she remembered, and had to pray for extra strength. Now Xalise had replaced Niswe as the Rhaba's maid-servant.

Ncube was often her mouthpiece. The man who had converted so many of these followers with his words of persuasion now conveyed messages of encouragement from Muali. The ashes had caused his slashed cheeks to swell, the scars to stand out, and no-one when they looked at him would ever forget the sacrifice his sister had made.

Chisa marched behind her husband, attending him, feeding him, caring for him. Awed by the new religion and its power, she was a constant help to Ncube. She had realised, too, that with Tcana now a Rhaba, Ncube's respect had erased any lingering desire he had had for a union with his first love. Chisa, for the first time, was secure.

They did not ask where they were going. It was enough for them to have seen Kisang's strangled face. Muali was with them. Muali was with Tcana. And so, unquestioning, they followed her.

When they came at last to the rocky outcrops at the foot of the range of bald-headed mountains, Tcana stopped her people. They camped for three days while she went, alone, into the huge balancing rocks to pray.

Almost in a trance, no longer her own person, Tcana found herself a niche between the sun-heated granite boulders, beside a young baobab tree that seemed to be growing into the rocks themselves, forming a small cave between trunk and rock. There she stripped off the climbing snake from her arm, and rested the heavy staff against the wall of the cave. She sat on, waiting.

Three times the sun lowered itself behind the hills, and she could hear in the distance the Believers singing to Muali, led by Chisa, whose unexpected talent for music was now a godsend, since she invented songs on the spur of the moment, and could teach them easily to the Believers.

Tcana waited through the nights, naked and vulnerable, not knowing for what she waited, and on the third day she again greeted the rising of the sun with muttered words of praise to Muali, creator of –

She sat upright suddenly as the fragments fell into place. Muali did not simply augment life; Muali created life! Muali was the Creator of everything she could see stretched before her – and this morning he was revealing his total glory to her. In the voices of the hundreds of birds around her; in the tiny lizards that were climbing onto the rocks to pull the warmth from them as the sun heated them; in the rise and fall of the land that stretched in all directions below her; in the deep blue sky above her that hummed with Muali. Muali, whose mamba was simply another tool, and not Muali himself; Muali, who lived not in the forms of animals, but lived in the very Creation.

Slowly, she stood and gazed around her. The sun glowed on her skin and she felt its warmth on her bare shoulders, her breasts, her arms ... Muali's love. And here – here was where Muali had revealed his full power to her. Here was where they must stay.

So they settled here, at the far reaches of the Matopos hills, where the last of the emperor boulders piled like the toys of giants. They built their village with its back to the protection of the bald rocks, and round it were the stone walls such as had been Tsimbaboue's signature – but without the signs of the old Muali. No eagles guarded its entries; indeed, no statues at all – now and then someone spotted a mamba sliding in the distance, and that was enough guardianship for the people of Muali.

Tcana spent much of her time in the cavern, deeper into the hills. This was where the Life Fire now burnt brightly in the gloom of the rocks. Here she kept the garments of the Rhaba, the skins, the anointing fats, the staff, the serpentine armband hidden in a strong leather bag made from calf-skin. Here she prayed, almost ceaselessly, for Muali to shine his face on his people, to increase and prosper them. Here her handmaiden Xalise came to help as she prepared for her appearances to the people, to speak to them of Muali.

Sometimes she thought of Xhaitaan. And of Xita, whom Muali had led through the torment of the Hill. And of the Life Fire, that burnt now for the Believers. She would not think of the city of Tsimbaboue, or whether it had a new Life Fire. She would not think of whether it still worshipped, or indeed, still lived. Tcana knew that the People of the House of God and the People of God were separate.

The People of God: amaMuali. The men herded the cattle and bred them to increase their wealth; the women rallied to plant food for the future, encouraged always by Chisa and her songs. Others made fires and threw water onto the heated rock to crack away stone for their walls; those who could carve or work with clay made utensils for cooking, eating, drawing water that flowed from the hills. The children, and especially little Xalise, who would never have to go to the Hill, played and helped and played again.

And Chisa was with child.

The amaMuali were rebuilding their lives.

Ncube was crafting again. His long fingers flew over the wood, and under his touch bulls and oxen and figurines appeared. But no images of Muali; Tcana's armbands were all she would permit in imagery, and then only as a reminder of the delivery of the people who, instead of bowing to the eagle, now bowed to the sky above, and to the sun in whose warmth the mamba, one-time messenger of Muali, loved to stretch out.

Tcana saw him often. They shared these rocks. He came to lie upon them, to draw his warmth from them. At such times she would be perfectly still, almost afraid of disturbing him. And so they would remain for hours, the olive-black snake reaching his scales across the hot granite, the cinnamon-skinned girl squatting on her haunches, head low between her knees, watching and praying, toying with the misty bead at her throat with its crossed fish etching. And still, she waited.

And then one day, from her place atop the boulders, Tcana saw winding through the bush towards them the pale Traders from the north.

In Tsimbaboue, the House of God, the Life Fire was gone. Mgane was gone. Kisang was dead. Xhaitaan, his life-light gone, lost interest in everything around him and entered into another world, a shadowy world of the unreal. Slowly, the city and its people began to die.

Chapter 28

Rhodesia

"It isn't anything we can put a finger on. Unfounded suspicion. Maybe nothing." Tom Hearthwaite shrugged easily, but he looked worried. Peter knew that when a man's senses were honed the way those of this Special Branch man who stood before him were, unfounded suspicions should never be passed over.

"Have your men reported anything in particular? What gives you this feeling?"

"As I said – nothing, except coincidence and ... a feeling. He was seen staring at her a couple of days ago, but what man wouldn't ..." He paused, remembering she was now Peter's wife. "Sorry," he mumbled.

Peter was too focused to notice. "Go on."

"Yesterday he asked the caretaker at her new place for a job as a gardener, and one of the men thought he recognised him, so we checked back at the old flat. He took a job there shortly after she moved into the flat, and a week ago he simply left – the owners of the block said he'd not even come to ask for his pay. The old man who had worked there before him also just disappeared, and this one stepped into the breach. Claimed to be a friend of the previous gardener's and said the old man had had to go home in a hurry. You know what they're like, the story could be true. Unfortunately the old man hadn't given the flat owners any indication of where he came from or who he was, other than his name – Thomas. So we can't even check."

"Have you tried validating the man's papers?"

"He told the owner he had none. Of course, the man couldn't be bothered; his garden was being taken care of. Very well too, I might add."

It meant nothing. Mandhla Ndhlovu had gardened at the mission. Still ... Peter rubbed his chin thoughtfully and paced the small office.

"Also – " The SB man hesitated, then plunged on. "He was missing for a few days while Miss Rawlings was in Inganga." Peter looked at him in surprise and he shrugged. "I didn't totally withdraw my men."

Peter took the beret off his head and twirled it for a moment, then let it hang from his fingers. Absently his thumb ran over the metal eagle on the front. They daren't approach the man himself to ask for his credentials, lest he disappear again. There was nothing to substantiate Tom Hearthwaite's suspicion, but Peter, too, was beginning to get a feeling about it.

"Shall we pick him up?"

"No. Not yet. I want to send a man to take a look at him."

Kuru stood in the telephone booth, rattling the receiver and pretending to make a call. If the gardener didn't appear soon he'd have to move away and find another excuse to loiter.

He rounded the building just as Kuru was about to leave the tiny glass room. His walk was easy, casual – he was too confident of himself. Kuru remembered the familiar face amongst the men he'd passed while tracking the Mamba. It had been bearded, dirty. This one was clean-shaven and bright. But although the years had made a big difference, Kuru knew him now without the hair on his face.

It was his younger brother.

He couldn't see the back of the flats from where he stood, but he heard the motorbike start up. Rebecca drove slowly into the tarred road. Another of her rides. Kuru relaxed. Let the SB men follow her. For the moment, away from the Mamba, she was safe.

He headed for the SB offices in town.

Mandhla watched her go. He had seen the man in the 'phone booth, and thought he knew him, but couldn't be sure. At any event, he realised that he was running out of time. The woman's new home in the midst of other military families was much too hot for comfort.

He moved to the other side of the flats and headed for the motorbike he had hidden a block away. He wasn't worried about her destination – he knew it. Roughly, anyway. And once there, it wouldn't be difficult to find her. Not with the skills of David Khumalo combined with his own.

As always, she took the road that threaded through the Matopos. The sky was a clear deep blue, the colour of Sinoia's pool on a good day, and the warm air invigorated her. Winding past the dam, she tried to avoid thinking of Peter. She missed him too much.

She opened the throttle, leaning into the corners, feeling her hair lash behind her in its plaits, the hot freshness of the Matopos in her nostrils. She went into the now-familiar S-bends, seeing the glint of the water of the fish hatcheries, the breeding ponds. Then she turned into the tiny road she had found, which by now she knew so well.

But today she wanted to go further than she ever had before, deep into the hot grey boulders. The road became little more than a track, until she could no longer ride the big road bike. She left it on its stand, under the spread of an acacia, hanging the helmet loosely over the handlebars, and began to walk.

The beauty as she climbed soothed her, and the wildness of the new bush fed something inside her. She was sweating in the heat of the noonday sun, but she didn't notice as she jumped the rocks, using small trees and bushes for hand-holds, slipping and sliding down the coarse grain of the granite.

Surprisingly, there in the midst of the kopjies she found a huge baobab tree, old, older than ... she couldn't even guess. Crouched up against the rocks, it stood over forty feet tall, the misshapen trunk big enough to hide a Landrover behind, and at some time lightning had smacked into the bole and ripped its midriff open to expose the huge hollow centre. An enormous arm hung uselessly down to rest its fingers on the mound of grass and sand that moulded up to meet them.

Rebecca found herself climbing up onto the rocks, half-walking up the torn branch, till she could peer into the gaping cavern below. At the bottom was clean, white sand forming a firm floor, the twisted innards of the tree's roots and trunk forming deep walls.

She found footholds in the knotty walls that aided her climb downward to a few feet above the bottom, where the root system was a tangled mass around the edges. Then, letting her knee joints sag, she dropped lightly down to the sand. In the back of her mind a voice said, "No. You don't know whose spirit lives there."

True enough, she thought. Baobab trees were revered by the Africans and ascribed with medicinal and magical properties. They were homes for ancestors, storerooms for water or grain; they gave a fibre from the bark that would weave into blankets and mats and clothing, and the bark would grow again to cover the stripped area. They were landmarks for the lost, towering fatly on the horizon, and shelter from wild beasts. They were hosts for fertility rites and prayers, and meeting-places for the Courts of Elders. When the white pulp of the fruit was mixed with water it produced a refreshing drink, rich in calcium and vitamin C. If there was no water near, chewing on the water-saturated bark might save your life. The seeds inside the great pods could be sucked as sweets, or pounded and cooked into porridge; the ashes of the burnt bark gave salt to use in cooking. In the dry season the twisted, folded trees looked as though someone had struck them into the ground upside down, with the roots waving in the air; in the rains their foliage was thick and gave wonderfully cool shade from the hot sun ...

The tree had a peculiar effect on her; clean and sweet-smelling, yet she felt the presence of something unnatural. She sniffed deeply. There was no pungent smell of leopard or rock dassie, the big rock rabbits that inhabited the kopjies.

Protected from the heat of the sun by the thick wood all around her, she waited for her eyes to grow accustomed to the gloom.

Kuru waited, sipping lemonade. Peter was on his way.

The telephone jangled shrilly and Tom Hearthwaite reached for it. Kuru's eyes sharpened. It was the direct line. He watched Tom's face.

"Hearthwaite here ..." There was a silence and the thin, long face grew longer, the dark brows meeting above the base of his nose. "Dammit Greene, are you certain? You've checked his quarters? ... Yes, okay. Thanks. No, wait there." He crashed the receiver into its cradle and stared at Kuru. "Our man has disappeared. Greene went for a pee."

Kuru stood instantly, decisively. "Where will she have gone?"

Tom shrugged. "She's not easy to follow. Usually the crazy woman heads for the Matopos."

"Where?" he insisted.

He spread his hands helplessly. "It could be anywhere. But she often takes one particular route ... beyond the fisheries. There's a road, a small one. No sign posts, but it's at ninety degrees to a rock formation of the Virgin and Child."

Kuru nodded briefly. He knew it. "How far?"

"About five miles into the hills. There's a small path leading off to the left. It's not far off the track."

Kuru nodded and turned, striding for the door.

Mandhla stopped long enough to find David and withdraw their Rhoguns and knives from the cache at the edge of the Matopos. The Rhoguns had been lifted from one of the farms they had hit. Similar to the Uzi, it was shorter and lighter than the AK-47, and could be concealed in the backpacks they wore across their shoulders. Then they remounted the motorcycle and headed after Rebecca.

She wasn't where he had expected her to be. He cursed briefly; it meant time wasted looking for her. But on the dirt the tracks of her tires were easy to follow. He found the Honda easily enough at the end of the trail, the white eagle shining from the tank. He almost laughed.

"If you had studied your African folklore," he murmured, "you would know that the mamba swallowed the eagle."

They dismounted the cycle and looked around them, retrieving the weapons from the bag and dropping the canvas over the saddle. The ground was almost all rocks;

tracking would be difficult. Then David found a print at the bottom of a particularly easy slope, and they began to climb, the Rhoguns slung over their shoulders.

Peter swore vociferously at Tom, crashing his fist down onto the desk top. "What the hell do you mean?"

"He just took off when I told him where she usually goes."

Peter listened while Tom explained again the general location of her usual destination, and then he and Reg Wright pointed their Landrover towards the Matopos.

Once her eyes had adjusted, Rebecca could see around her quite well. One side of this natural cave was a wall of rock, where the tree had wrapped itself around the kopjie. There were old dassie droppings in one corner, and dimly she could make out ancient paintings on the rough granite. She ran her fingers over the cold rock face, trying to trace the faded figures.

Enraptured, she didn't watch where she put her feet, and the next step half dislodged a small rock jammed between the roots. She hastily pulled her toes away, but all that happened was that the rock fell slightly forward, revealing a small nook behind it. She bent lower and peered in, pushing the rock away completely.

Inside was a smallish leather bag, obviously very old and starting to come apart, although partly preserved by the air in the stopped-up hole. She began to open it, and then heard a sound above her.

She stiffened instantly. It had been the scuff of a foot on the rocks. It came again, and she heard heavy breathing. Hardly daring to breathe herself, she stood frozen against the wall of the cave.

Whoever it was had stopped, perhaps to look around him. It seemed an age before he moved again; she heard him jump lightly to another rock, and then the noises were gone. She waited a few minutes more, then pulled open the neck of the leather bag and reached inside it.

The first item was a circlet of beads made of wood and skin, worn smooth and bare, and now slightly cracked in places. But the central piece was an ovate bead about two inches long, of smoky dark blue glass, with the familiar ancient Christian symbol of a fish etched into it, and the Greek letters spelling ICTHUS – fish. The recognised anacronym for Jesus Christ, Son of God, Saviour. The thong was intact, and slowly Rebecca tied the necklet so that the bead rested in the hollow of her throat. How old was it? The thought awed her.

Her hand in the bag once more, she touched something cold and heavy, and drawing it out into the half-light she held it up against the small opening of the cave.

Her heart stopped beating for an instant, and when it started again it pounded in her ears and blocked her throat. It was an arm bracelet, winding its coils three times round before the head stood away, the mouth agape, the neck flat.

She dropped it, pulling her hand away as though it were hot. It clanged to the rocky wall and the sound echoed around her. She stared at it. The similarity, she knew positively, could not be coincidence. She remembered the prisoners at Inganga, and what Zulu and Alan had told her.

His sharp ears heard the faint clang behind them, and he turned instantly, David more slowly. They had lost her trail, and now Mandhla realised they must have passed her by. He began to climb back up the stone kopjie, casting for any signs of her presence.

Kuru left his Landrover beside the two motorcycles, and ran into the rocks, his trained eyes picking up on the trail much faster than his younger brother's had – and there were three sets of tracks for him to follow. His eyes moved constantly, scanning the bush around him, and he glided silently and swiftly from boulder to boulder, his FN strapped at his side, ready and waiting.

She reached out fearfully for the bangle and held it again to the light, fascinated. She felt the creature drawing her, as the stone one had, and slowly, very slowly, she slipped it onto her right arm. She could hear again the hiss of the black-mouthed snake as it had stood up to her, and see the silver lining of his eyes.

Her head was swimming. Trance-like, she stroked the thing, feeling every scale that had been lovingly shaped into the body rough against her fingertips. As if in a dream, she turned back to the hiding place and reached into it again. It went back further than she had thought, and on its floor lay the staff she somehow had known would be there.

She pulled it out reverently, and gazed in awe at the beaten copper that covered it, a thin sheet nailed with tiny tacks into the wood. It was headed again with the Mamba, winding its way up the copper and craning from the top, magnificent in its arrogance.

She breathed, and it was almost a sigh. The cave was moving around her, and she felt the same rush that had come when she had eaten the salad.

Vague visions swam before her, and then she was floating, flying high above a dark-skinned maiden beneath her dressed in skins. She spread her wings and soared, every tiny blade of grass in focus; she thrilled to the glory of the rushing air in her feathers, and climbed higher, and then dropped again, lower, to just above the girl's head. She saw the mamba then, standing up from its coils, the mouth open, open ... bewitched, she flew closer, and the eyes cast their spell and pulled her in, in ...

She moaned, and the sound was a cymbal-crash in her ears. She opened her eyes; she was lying on the floor of the cave and above was the narrow opening. Someone was there, squatting in the sunlight, staring in at her. The haze came together and the pieces fitted, like a scattered mosaic flying into position. The man was grinning at her, and she realised it was the gardener from the flats.

How strange, to find him here ...

Then, suddenly, something fell into place in her memory. The delivery boy, with the flame lilies and the snake. She sat up instantly, every warning bell in her system jangling.

His grin turned to a laugh. "I see the Madam knows me," he said in mock humility. He pushed aside the bush that guarded the entrance, and slid down onto the floor beside her. She shivered. His eyes in the darkness were silver-lined.

"What do you want?" Her throat had closed, and it came out as a croak.

He was arrogant again. "I want you. Or to be more

precise, I want your husband. After all, he has taken my woman and my brother, why should I not repay the kindness?" His voice deepened with emotion. "He left me and the other children to die. When he should have followed us, he delayed. When he finally found us, he killed one of our number. And then he deserted us. He left us to our fate. I think it is only fitting that he should find out what his carelessness has cost him."

His English was good, better than the average Ndebele. She was bewildered, and he saw it. It pleased him that in her fear she had the courage to be bewildered. His eyes travelled over her in the twilight, then stopped in shock. She was wearing the bracelet of the Rhaba, and in the other hand she held the staff.

He drew back from her, bitter, then abruptly dragged her to her feet, his fingers digging into her elbow. "Up," he commanded.

He shoved from below as she climbed up the baobab's walls. She scrambled into the light, screwing up her eyes. She hadn't realised it was so late. Already the sun was low in the sky. She looked around her, realising he would not be alone, and saw the companion. David stood against a rock further away, watching.

He followed her out of the cave, staying close, his hand gripping her arm as he propelled her forward. There he stopped and had a rapid conversation with the other terrorist. He pointed angrily to the bangle on her arm, and the staff she still clutched, and the other man seemed afeared by it, looking at her strangely. Her captor took the staff away and threw it at his friend, who caught it with his free hand, and then they began to move again, Mandhla still pushing her ahead of him.

He was heading down, across the rocks, and for a moment had to let go of her as she jumped to the next foothold. Immediately she touched down she moved sideways, trying to run, but he was onto her like a cat and her whole body jarred as he hauled her back. He twisted her arm up between her shoulder blades and whispered into the back of her neck.

"I can kill you slowly or I can kill you swiftly, or I may not kill you at all. I have not yet decided. Don't hurry me.

And above all, do not make my friend nervous. His finger may twitch on the trigger."

He shoved her and she fell onto the level of the grey stone, grazing the soft padding of her palms. She winced at the sting. He reached down, the Rhogun slung casually over his right arm, and twined his left hand in her plaits. He jerked her to her feet and forced her to look up at him.

"You wear the sign of our Rhaba," he said, "but your skin is the wrong colour. I don't know how you came to this cavern, but it is sacred to us, and what you wear is sacred. Be thankful; it has delayed your fate a while."

The other man said something to him in their own language and he stopped, thinking, staring in the direction she had left her 'bike. He made up his mind suddenly, and turned again towards the baobab. He pushed her again, half-dragging her with him, and she realised they were heading back to the tree cavern.

He thrust her up the broken branch, coming closely behind her, and she jumped once more onto the soft white sand below, where he joined her seconds later. He took off the light backpack he wore and dropped it onto the sandy floor.

David stood above them, but Mandhla waved him away. "Keep watch. They will follow soon." The figure disappeared from the opening and the Mamba pushed the girl before him to the ground, pulling her against the wooden wall. Hardly bothering to watch her, he opened his pack and shook out the few contents, picking up the water bottle that fell with the rest of the items.

Something rolled towards her and stopped at her feet; it was a dark blue cap of some sort and he watched her pick it up. Her skin crawled. It was a pilot's cap, and on the inner band some words had been penned: "Pilots are a girl's best friend. Ask John!"

She looked up at the man Peter had called the Mamba. "You killed him."

"Indeed. And what a stroke of luck to discover that he was a cousin of Major Kennedy." He drank deeply from the canister, then offered the water to her. She shook her head, repulsed and nauseated, thinking of Hilary, and of the survivors who must have thought they were the lucky ones, until the group of terrorists had appeared on the scene.

He looked at her musingly. "Miss Rawlings ... oh, I'm sorry, I forgot. Mrs. Kennedy ..." The sarcasm was tangible. "Mrs. Kennedy, you present me with a problem. For some reason my god and the god of my ancestors has chosen to protect you from me. However, you are also under the protection of the Eagle ... and I see you wear a bead with the symbol of the Christ. The three do not fit together, and I am confused."

"I am under the protection of neither eagle nor serpent, but of my God, in whose image I am made – Jesus Christ," she said defiantly. "Your god is false, as is the eagle. There is only one God, and he is a God of mercy and compassion, and of wrath against his enemies, of which you are one!"

"Ah. Definitely a Christian, then. In that case, you do not serve Muali."

"No, I do not." She suddenly realised the words worsened her situation.

"I was a Christian, once. But your God was not there to protect me when I needed it."

"I cannot answer for that. Perhaps you did not cry out to him in your hour of need."

"No. It was because I was meant for this task, and this alone. I will destroy Major Kennedy, and then we will destroy the white government of Ian Smith. This country will live freely!"

"I don't believe freedom is bought with bullets. I believe it's bought with love."

"Then," he spat, "I hope your faith is very strong in your God, because the time for your suffering has come." He entwined her plaits around his hand again, pulling her to her feet. "Take off your clothes."

She tried to shake her head but he held her fast. "No. I will not make this easy for you," she whispered.

He released her hair and his hand smashed into her temple, throwing her sideways. Her head hit hard wood and she felt everything swim away, but she did not lose consciousness. He had measured the blow perfectly. Dazed, she put her fingers to her head and they came away bloody.

She began to pray aloud the words of the Psalms she loved. *"Hear, O Lord, and answer me ..."*

"Your clothes," Mandhla broke in impatiently.

She stared at him defiantly, refusing with her eyes. *"Rescue me O Lord from evil men; protect me from men of violence who devise evil plans in their hearts and stir up war every day."*

He stepped forward and his fingers twined in the shoulder of her blouse; one wrench ripped it away, and then he twisted her around by her hair, slammed her into the wall of the tree, and unhooked her brassiere. He sucked on his teeth as the white breasts came free, crested with faint blue veins that traversed them to the ribs and then disappeared under the creamy skin. The pain had loosened her knee joints and she dropped onto the sand; he lifted her roughly and forced her to face him, her back to the tree.

Her words went on, but now she was looking him in the eye as she spoke, her voice wobbling. *"They make their tongues as sharp as a serpent's; the poison of vipers is on their lips."*

His eyes narrowed and she saw the anger building. "Shut up!"

She was thinking rapidly, and continued with the Psalm, as much to keep him distracted while she thought, as to build her own courage. *"Keep me, O Lord, from the hands of the wicked; protect me from men of violence who plan to trip my feet –"* She was cut off as his hand smashed across her cheek.

"I said shut up!" he hissed. She knew her prayers were worrying him; touching the spot where his knuckles had grazed her, she realised she felt no pain. There must come a moment, she thought, when his passions would be at a pitch and he would no longer be afraid of what she might do to him.

Her eyes cast around secretively under the lowered lids until she spotted a melon-sized rock lying against the trunk, almost hidden by the overhanging roots. She would have to lie near it; there was no chance he would allow his weapons in her range. She saw the greed in his eyes and hoped it was sufficient to stop him thinking of her strengths. She tried not to think of the second man and his rifle; at least she would strike one blow for herself.

Defiantly, her voice rose with the Psalm. *"Let the heads of those who surround me be covered with the trouble their lips have caused. Let burning coals fall upon them; may they be thrown into the fire, into miry pits, never to rise!"*

His hand smacked her temple and she crashed against the trunk again. Weeping, she almost shouted at him: *"Let slanderers not be established in the land; may disaster hunt down men of violence!"*

"Stop cursing me!" he shouted back. "Stop!" Suddenly he had an evil-tipped knife in his hand, and he ripped at the waistband of her jeans, infuriated by her words. He pulled her to her feet again and stood close to her; she smelt the rancid sweat on him and almost retched.

Her head ached and she felt dizzy and sick. Her head oozed stickiness into her hair, and still she prayed, her voice more of a moan now. *"O Lord, I call to you; come quickly to me – "*

He hit her again and her neck twisted backwards with the blow; she fell and he pulled her up yet again. She glanced surreptitiously toward the roots with their concealed weapon, and he laughed. She had underestimated him. Moving forward, he carelessly lifted the stone and threw it out of the hole above them; it bounced over the edge of the branch. She sobbed, hearing it click loudly against the bark, and stared at him, tears streaking her face. The look he wore froze her with fear and the breath caught in her throat.

He stepped forward, raising the knife, hatred spilling from him. "I have never disfigured a woman in my life," he said softly. "Perhaps it is time to begin."

She moved backward but met with wood, a wall that held her for him. The blade glittered in the dying sunlight that filtered from the opening, and she watched for a moment, then closed her eyes and prayed again, her voice no more than a whisper. *"The Lord is my strength and my shield, my heart trusts in him ..."*

She hardly felt the first cut. The steel was cool against her naked breast, and only when she opened her eyes did she see the thin slit above her nipple. The blood hesitated, then began to well into the cut as the knife made another groove crosswise. He did the same to the other, smiling grimly, watching her face. She forced her eyes away from the blood. The pain was beginning, and his face swam before her. She mustered her strength which seemed to be pouring out of her with the red liquid, and spat upward.

He had not expected it, and he flinched as it hit his cheek below the right eye. Angered, he wiped it away with the cloth of his shirt. "Your fear makes you bold. Perhaps too bold."

He had stopped playing with her; the lust in his eyes had transformed to hatred, and as he began to open his trousers she knew this rape would be as violent as he could make it.

Her head was singing, her whole body suddenly fatigued beyond measure. The stench of his body had her retching, and she no longer had the power to fight back. Just before she felt the blackness envelope her, the other man said something quietly into the tree, and vaguely she knew her persecutor was climbing out of the cave.

Her faint lasted only seconds, and then his stink was like smelling salts in her nostrils. She gagged and opened her eyes; his face was close to hers, smirking triumphantly.

"He is coming," he spat. "He is far still, but he will come. Be sure to cry out, so that he can find you. I'll be waiting."

And he was gone. The blackness returned, swam away, returned, and left. After the first sounds of him leaving, there was utter silence, and she knew the two terrorists had hidden themselves.

They knew, as she did, that Peter would come for her.

Oh God, please don't let him find me ...

She knew that she was dying; she felt it in her bones.

Kuru was one of the best trackers in Rhodesia. Following the trail of all three had not been difficult, but it had been of necessity slow. He moved like a leopard, silent and camouflaged; he had no backup until Peter came – as Kuru knew he would, with reinforcements – and could not let the Mamba know he was near.

Halfway up the kopjie with the crouching rock formation and the tree growing from its side, he knew suddenly he had found them, though he did not know where they were.

With intense concentration, his eyes scanned the rocks, the trees, every leaf, for a shape that did not quite fit, a shadow lying askew, a shape too solid to be bush, too broken to be rocks.

As his eyes suddenly met another pair across the bush, he realised they had seen each other at the same moment. An eternity passed, and then, very slowly, the eyes became part of a face that was rising as its body stood up.

"I see you, my brother," Mandhla said softly. His Rhogun dangled peaceably from loose fingers, its barrel tip dragging against the rock.

Kuru stood too, carefully, taking no chances. He knew the Mamba was not alone, from the trail. His cold eyes gazed back. "I have no brother. Come out of your hole, Mamba. With the girl."

His FN was pointed at Mandhla, who came slowly away from the bole of the enormous tree. From the corner of his eye Mandhla saw a tiny movement behind Kuru as David slowly raised his rifle. Kuru was concentrating so on the man before him that he had not seen the sentry.

Mandhla hesitated, then stepped forward, closer to his sibling. Closer to the FN. He stared into the barrel of the weapon and laughed easily.

"They have brainwashed you, brother," he said in Sindebele, using the term of endearment again. "Let me speak to you, and you'll see."

Kuru replied in English. "I see only a scorpion that stings its own. I see a snake who has run out of time."

David was ready, and suddenly Kuru saw his movement and turned slightly. Mandhla shouted suddenly and lunged forward, bringing up his Rhogun in a smooth movement; Kuru retaliated swiftly and Mandhla fell, his torso a bloody mass.

And then Kuru realised that his brother had fired not at him, but at his own comrade. At the instant Mandhla fell, so did David, thrown over the edge of the rocks by the force of the bullets spat from the Rhogun. He screamed briefly, and Kuru registered it with cold shock. Mandhla had killed his comrade to save his brother.

The younger man lay on his side, and the grey granite was staining redder all the time beneath him. His eyes were blacker than they had ever been, with the pain, and they pleaded with Kuru. He dropped swiftly to Mandhla's side, cradling the floppy head.

Mandhla's lips moved slightly, pulling into a half-smile.

"Is this how you repay me, brother?" he whispered, stumbling on the words.

Kuru trembled and pulled the bloody body against him. Dark organs spilled from the gaping stomach and Mandhla gasped. "I used them," he murmured, and almost laughed. "Those Russian officers ... they thought they had won ... that I believed them ..." This time he did laugh, a wheezing breath that brought pink bubbles to the corner of his mouth.

"Stay quiet, brother. I'll fetch help." Kuru felt his chest tighten and the pain at the base of his throat was too intense for more words.

Mandhla moved his head weakly. " ... ZIPRA ... they thought I ... no! They killed the ones I loved, and expected me to believe them ... I never ... I did not believe them. But I used them ... to repay Kennedy!"

"He did not desert you willingly." It was a sob, and Mandhla hardly caught the words. The black eyes began to dull, but they moved, and Kuru knew he understood but did not accept it. He tried again. "There was no blame to be placed. And especially not on the girl."

Mandhla nodded slightly. "His woman ..." He coughed abruptly and dark blood spewed from his mouth. He gasped for breath. "Pray for me, brother." His head fell suddenly and the breathing stopped. Kuru clutched the torn flesh to him, and his own uniform was darkened with his brother's blood.

There was a hand on his shoulder, warm and strong. He opened his eyes. Major Kennedy squatted beside him. Kuru turned to look into his face. Their eyes met, the anguished black pools and the gold-flecked blue ones that were crying with his friend.

The debt was repaid. A life for a life.

Already on the trail and closing fast, the rifle fire had drawn Peter and his men. There was nothing he could do now for Kuru. He stood slowly, and stared up at the tree towering above him, the gaping hole halfway up the trunk.

He began to climb.

THE END

The Author

Of British and Dutch extraction, JS Holloway was born and grew up in Central and Southern Africa. Her African history includes Northern and Southern Rhodesia (now Zambia and Zimbabwe), Malawi, Tanzania, Mozambique, the Congo, Swaziland, South Africa and Kenya. Afer leaving school she served in the Rhodesian Defence Forces (as one of only 12 female Rural IntAf Cadets in the country at that time). She has 25 years' broadcast experience in Rhodesia, South Africa and the UK, and her writing credits include scripting of hundreds of hours of TV, film, radio, and multimedia programming. In her own words:

One of my very earliest memories is of a safari; in the middle of the night a leopard snatched a woman from her tent—one of the guides' wives. I remember the screams and the chaos, and my mother telling me that the woman died. I have loved and loathed Africa, in myriad ways, ever since.

My mother read to me even before I was born, and another clear memory is from the ripe old age of three. A missionary priest in the Northern Rhodesian bush gave me a birthday gift—a picturebook version of *The Count of Monte Christo*, by Dumas. It became my most treasured possession; I thought it the most beautiful thing in the world, and there and then, barely out of toddlerhood, I knew that one day I wanted to "make books". I kept that book right through my life, through moving around all over Central and Southern Africa (11 schools, 37 homes!), until just a few years ago when we sold and gave away everything we had to go sailing.

I've fought in a bush war, camped beside hippos, hunted crocodile (well, just one!), had mad adventures on (and off) film and television sets, sat on boards for a script writing association, a governmental regulating committee, and Child Welfare; dragged up two children and a husband (who all turned out amazingly well in spite of me), done youth and women's and music and online ministries, sailed in the Indian Ocean islands and the east coast of Africa, ridden motorbikes across Southern Africa... and here I am now, half a century behind me, and just as crazy about books and writing as I always was, and pursuing what I love: writing, teaching, mentoring, developing new writers, giving workshops... and most of all, at last, I "make books"!

Feel free to email me at **jo.holloway@danceofeagles.com**—I love hearing from my readers.

About "Dance of Eagles"

This is the third edition of "Dance of Eagles", and contains some extra pieces of writing and a few small changes since the first version, as well as having a different cover. It was originally written when the author was just 24. At that time it was never intended for publication; it was more of a catharsis. It has since been refined a little but is essentially what was primarily put down on paper, when the memories of the Rhodesian War were still fresh in the author's mind. Its first appearance was as "Crest of Eagles", published by an American company in 2005, but was revised as "Dance of Eagles" in 2007 and published in the UK.

FOR MORE BOOKS BY THIS AUTHOR:

visit Sunpenny Publishing

www.sunpenny.com

SAMPLE CHAPTER

Raglands

by

J.S. Holloway

Chapter 1

In the black hollows of midnight, and the stark grey valleys thereafter, is a place our secret minds possess, a priest-hole filled with those darkling remembrances which we have otherwise blanked out of our day-conscious souls for fear they would paralyse us with their terrors. Yet instead of sensibly disposing of them forever, our atavistic nature hides them bosom-close, cherishing and nurturing them in cunning caves so abstruse that often we don't even suspect they still exist, lying quietly, patiently, in ambush. Like Sleepers.

- Asia Lysle, *Nostrum* magazine

Deep peace. The deep peace of a quiet pond, of a ploughed field, of a starlit night, of a leafy copse, of moss on stone, of moonlight on water, of snow on fen ... deep, deep peace.

In the jagged, fractured images that clustered in her core, somehow at some time she had created for herself a tiny splinter of untainted loveliness, an icon of purity, of utter serenity, green and glowing, as though her soul was forced to retain some tiny semblance of beauty amidst the other in order to survive. And now, as she stood on this unexpected ridge amidst the rolling landscape of Norfolk, the reality of it lay below her, the paradigm of perfection, as though an artist had discovered her fantasy fragment and recreated it exactly as she had envisaged it ... or as if she had dreamed it into existence from her own hunger.

This was it. Her oasis.

There was the willow-lined river describing a long, lazy S, complete with swans, ducklings, and arched stone bridges. On either side the village lined up and curtsied gracefully backward, spreading genteelly towards the manor house on the rise adjacent to her own vantage point, its chimneys just showing between the tall poplars that protected it. At the far end, a clutch of classic little workers' cottages with their slated roofs; in the centre the village green, surrounded by a grey stone Norman church, the pub, a few shops, and on the near side more houses, these much larger and in increasingly spacious gardens, and gravitating accordingly in splendour towards the manor. Behind the rows of housing on both sides lay agricultural lands, interspersed with small woods here and there that she was willing to bet were filled with white-tailed deer, squirrels, bluebirds and bunnies. Even the name was exquisite: Rosebrook.

Rosebrook. She let it roll over her tongue, like honeyed chocolate.

But she knew it would be too much to hope for that there'd be somewhere suitable to rent for the next six months.

It wasn't. Amazed, just over an hour later she stood in front of a dwelling that would have gladdened Anne Hathaway's heart. An artistic lady's-lace sign quietly proclaimed it Tea Rose Cottage. There was a FOR SALE sign, just beginning to rust, hanging slightly askew on the gate – but not, the murine little agent hurried to inform her, because there was anything wrong with the property; it was simply that the owners were holding out for more than the market would bear just at the moment. Considerably more, actually, she added sadly.

But would they be prepared to lease it short-term?

Oh indeed, the woman – Mildred – assured her, there would be no problem, except that they might want a *wee* bit more for it than was really quite polite ...

She swept aside Mildred's timid concerns. She had to have it, come what may, and truth was she could afford pretty much whatever fee they wanted. She didn't even need to look inside; she wanted the deal clinched as quickly as possible, before she could change her mind and run screaming for the hills and back to reality.

She had a mission to fulfill, and her every instinct told her that this was precisely the place to do it.

She had overlooked the fact that they would want references. Damn! She thought fast, and filled in an address on the form. Millie – sole occupier of the small estate agency in the next village along – made the phone call while she wandered along the wall of photographed properties for sale, for rent, for lease, pretending not to be listening fiercely to the conversation. Within minutes the phone was hung up and the little rodent face in its shades of grey was smiling at her, flushing unevenly with excitement.

"Oh my, so you're to be married! No wonder you want *Tea Rose Cottage* so much, it's just *perfect* for a honeymooning couple!"

Damn again! She must be slipping. Well, she'd handle it when the problem came up. Tomorrow is another day. She smiled brightly at the diminutive woman, and had the grace to blush. Thankfully, it was misunderstood by Melanie's romantic heart. *What a tangled web we weave ...*

And then the call to the owners of the cottage. She heard the mouse at her most persuasive, back turned, shoulders hunched, tail a-twitch. The rent they wanted was indeed outrageous, and even though she could afford it, on principle she managed (via the agent, brow sweating now), to beat the owners down just enough to palliate pride on both sides.

The legalities completed, cheque for the deposit and six months' rent in advance handed over, she hadn't even felt the slightest twinge of guilt when she signed with a flourish: *Katie Adams,* and by evening she was in possession of the keys and driving triumphantly back to London.

Packing never took her very long – she was habitually ready to leave at almost any given moment. Admittedly this was a little more complicated, since she'd actually be living somewhere else for some months at a stretch, but what fitted into the boot and passenger seat of the silver

Bugatti would be enough to go along with – the agent had assured her that the cottage was fully furnished and equipped. She could always return for more personal items if she needed them later on, once she had settled in.

Early the next afternoon she dropped the low roar of the Italian engine into neutral, then stopped it altogether, and was surrounded by the quiet that is peculiar to a country village. She stood proprietarily in front of the white five-bar and removed the sad *FOR SALE* sign, then swung the gate open and stepped onto the clean gravel of the driveway.

Parking the car at the front steps, she walked back to close the gate, revelling in the ataraxis that snuggled up to her like a puppy and licked her face. She felt its hopefulness, and dared to hope along with it; peace had not often been her bedfellow in the last few years.

As the door to the cottage swung open, the promise increased. The calm of the tasteful interior, ancient and modern mingling harmoniously, swept over her like a balm. She had a curious sense of the house itself welcoming her into its repose, softly eager for her, ready to offer her something not quite tangible but which she instinctively understood, and yearned for.

Someone had been in to clean and dust before her arrival, and she saw with pleasure the fresh flowers on the low coffee table, and a bowl of green apples on the light oak dining counter. A basket covered with a spotless white cloth held scones, still slightly warm, and the fridge in the roomy kitchen had been stocked with clotted cream, home made strawberry jam, milk, orange juice, and a richly aromatic casserole with a note advising her to "just pop into the oven to heat". There were six brown eggs, a double fold of bacon rashers obviously direct from the farm, two fat tomatoes, a chunk of Cheddar, a pat of butter, and on top of the fridge in a bread bin she found a home-baked round of crusty white bread. Tea and coffee stood by the kettle, with a sugar bowl filled and a Dutch sugar spoon ready beside it. Pretty country scenes decorated the mugs, and a yellow-and-gold floral tea set that looked suspiciously like Royal Albert stood on a tray nearby.

The kindness of the unseen provider touched her; when last had a stranger shown such concern for her wellbeing?

Hard to remember, now. She made a pot of tea and cut herself some of the bread, soft as cake on the inside. She wolfed down several slices, spread with the jam and accompanied by slabs of cheese, and considered again the thoughtfulness of the giver. Not what she had expected, after all the dire warnings she'd heard that country villagers didn't appreciate incomers, who were frozen out by all and sundry until they'd proved themselves – sometimes only years later.

Thirst slaked, hunger satiated, she looked again at the soft bulk of the Laura Ashley furniture that would normally have been anathema to her, yet was somehow so right in these surroundings, in her new persona. Afternoon sunshine pouring in through big French windows at one end buttered the fat couches and home-spun karakul rug. A stone fireplace with a sturdy mantelpiece graced the middle of an inner wall, chimney stretching up through the second floor to carry its warmth to the upper rooms. A comfortable wooden rocking chair padded with hand-embroidered cushions stood quietly in the inglenook, its arms waiting just for her.

At the front of the cottage a wide bay window held a ladies' writing desk from former times, larger than was normal, she realised with pleasure – she had expected to do most of her work at the farmhouse style kitchen table, but could now see herself sitting at the antique cherry-wood, washed in morning sunlight and looking out over the garden. Near the front door, with its stained glass panes set into the thick wood, a stone staircase with wooden inlaid steps trailed upward to the two bedrooms, bathroom and nursery that she knew from the agent's inventory lay above.

Almost reverentially, she lifted her laptop computer case onto the desk. Then she picked up the camera hold-all and liberal carpet-bag that went everywhere with her, and set her feet on the polished wood of the stairs.

Relaxing later in a vast, clawed bathtub that smacked of Louis XIV, unaccustomed scented bubbles floating round her shoulders and chin from a selection already set out for her, Katie Adams (fraud) realised she was just beginning to truly decompress, for the first time in many a year. A holiday feeling was stealing over her; and why not? She'd taken a six month sabbatical, informing all and sundry (to their surprised disgust) that she'd be out of the country and unavailable for further freelance work during that time. Utter secrecy was necessary if she was to complete the task before her. She could brook no interference, and no discovery.

She allowed herself a delicious shiver of anticipation, and sank deeper into the silky warm foam.

Meanwhile, the real Katie Adams – or the soon-to-be Katie Adams, to be more precise – was anything but relaxed. Surrounded by satin and lace and eager young tailoresses and assistants measuring her up, down and sideways, Katie was bothered and tired and could think of nothing better than being in a soothing bubble bath.

She sighed. Not much hope of that for hours, yet.

And where on the good Lord's earth was Asia *now*??

.

END OF SAMPLE CHAPTER

RAGLANDS will be available in late 2013 from all good online stores, or better still, support your local brick-and-mortar bookshop by ordering through them!

Sunpenny Publishing Group

ROSE & CROWN, BLUE JEANS, BOATHOOKS, SUNBERRY, CHRISTLIGHT, and EPTA Books

MORE BOOKS FROM the SUNPENNY GROUP
www.sunpenny.com

A Devil's Ransom, by Adele Jones
A Little Book of Pleasures, by William Wood
Blackbirds Baked in a Pie, by Eugene Barter
Blue Freedom, by Sandra Peut
Brandy Butter on Christmas Canal, by Shae O'Brien
Breaking the Circle, by Althea Barr
Bridge to Nowhere, by Stephanie Parker McKean
Don't Pass Me By, by Julie McGowan
Embracing Change, by Debbie Roome
Far Out: Sailing into a … , by Corinna Weyreter
Going Astray, by Christine Moore
If Horses Were Wishes, by Elizabeth Sellers
Just One More Summer, by Julie McGowan
My Sea is Wide, by Rowland Evans
Redemption on Red River, by Cheryl R. Cain
Someday, Maybe, by Jenny Piper
The Mountains Between, by Julie McGowan
The Skipper's Child, by Valerie Poore
The Shadow of a Parasol, by Beth Holland
Trouble Rides a Fast Horse, by Elizabeth Sellers
30 Days to Take-Off, by KC Lemmer
Uncharted Waters, by Sara DuBose
Watery Ways, by Valerie Poore